VISIONS

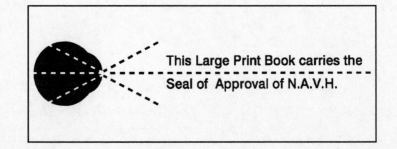

This Large Print Book carries the
Seal of Approval of N.A.V.H.

GALE
CENGAGE Learning®

LIBRARY OF CONGRESS CATALOGING-IN-PUBLICATION DATA

Armstrong, Kelley.
  Visions : a Cainsville novel / Kelley Armstrong. — Large print edition.
    pages cm. — (Wheeler Publishing large print hardcover)
    ISBN 978-1-4104-6771-3 (hardcover) — ISBN 1-4104-6771-6 (hardcover)
    1. Missing persons—Fiction. 2. Murder—Fiction. 3. Large type books.
  I. Title.
  PS3551.R4678V57 2014
  813'.54—dc23   2014026256

Published in 2014 by arrangement with Dutton, a member of Penguin Group (USA) LLC, a Penguin Random House Company

Printed in the United States of America
1 2 3 4 5 6 7 18 17 16 15 14

A CAINSVILLE NOVEL

VISIONS

KELLEY ARMSTRONG

WHEELER PUBLISHING
A part of Gale, Cengage Learning

GALE
CENGAGE Learning·

Farmington Hills, Mich • San Francisco • New York • Waterville, Maine
Meriden, Conn • Mason, Ohio • Chicago

FOR Jeff

CHAPTER ONE

The poppies were a bad sign. A death omen. It doesn't get much worse than that.

We hadn't planted them. When a gardener suggested it once, my mother had said, "They make opium from poppies," in whispered horror, as if her society friends might jump to the conclusion we were running an opium den in our basement. I'd wanted to laugh and tell her they used a different subspecies for drugs. I hadn't. Deep in my gut, I had not wanted poppies in our garden.

A silly superstition. Or so it seemed. But when I see omens and portents, they mean something.

It'd been three weeks since I'd left my family home, fleeing ahead of the media frenzy that erupted when I'd learned my real parents were notorious serial killers. While I worked on building a new life, I'd decided to come back to the empty house and grab a few things. I'd tossed my suitcases in the borrowed Buick and headed out back for a swim. I was walking toward the front of the house, raking my fingers through my wet hair, when I noticed a splash of red in the rock garden.

Poppies.

I reached down and rubbed a silky red petal. It felt real enough. I took out my phone, snapped a picture, and checked the result. Yep, I still saw poppies. Which meant they existed outside my head. Always a good sign.

Except for the part about poppies being a *bad* sign.

I shook it off, turned the corner, and —

There was someone sitting in my driver's seat.

I flashed to the poppies. A killer waiting to ambush me? Three weeks ago this would have been laughable. That was before I discovered the truth about my past.

Still, I couldn't imagine an assassin waiting, in plain view, in my car. Nor would anyone sneak onto the estate to steal a fifteen-year-old Buick when a half-dozen antique sports cars were garaged around back.

The most likely explanation these days? A reporter getting creative.

I continued forward, circling around the

car. I'd left the driver's window down. A woman sat behind the wheel. The roof cast her face into deep shadow and all I could see were sunglasses and blond hair. Ash-blond, like my own. It even looked like my current cut — a few inches long, tousled-curly.

"Hey," I said as I walked closer.

The woman didn't respond. I grabbed the handle, yanked open the door, and —

She fell out. Toppled, as I jumped back with a yelp, thinking even as I did that I was making a fool of myself, that someone was snapping a picture of this very juvenile prank —

She had no eyes.

The woman hung out of the car, wig falling off, sunglasses, too. Beneath the sunglasses were blood-crusted pits.

I staggered back, my own eyes shutting fast.

I was hallucinating. I'd seen this twice before, first on a dead man and then on a woman in the hospital. Both times, it was nothing more than a hallucination, an omen with some meaning I couldn't comprehend.

When I looked again, she'd be fine. I did, and —

Her eyes were still gone. Gouged out. Dried blood smeared down one cheek.

I'm not hallucinating. This time, I'm not hal-lucinating.

I bent to touch her neck. The skin was cold.

There's a dead woman in my car. A dead woman dressed to look like me.

I raced to the house, fumbling with the lock. The door opened. I swung in, hit the security code, then slammed and locked it. I reset the alarms, fished my gun and cell from my bag, and made a call.

I paced the hall waiting for the sound of a car in the drive. As I passed the front room, I caught a movement through the drawn sheers. I nudged one aside and peeked out to see a dark shape by the gardens. A big black dog — exactly like one I'd seen early this morning, fifty miles away in Cainsville.

The hounds will come to Cainsville, and when they do, you'll wish you'd made a very different choice today.

That's what Edgar Chandler said yesterday, before the police took him away, having arrested him for his involvement in two murders that had been pinned on my birth parents. Only a few people knew I'd rented an apartment in Cainsville, and he wasn't one of them. After the media had swarmed, I'd taken refuge in that sleepy little village

10

in the middle of nowhere.

A sleepy little village with disappearing gargoyles, vicious ravens, and, as of this morning, gigantic black hounds.

A sleepy little village where no one seemed to find it the least bit strange that I could read omens and see portents.

I rubbed my arms. I didn't want to see a connection between Chandler and Cainsville. I loved my new town. I loved the safety of it, the community of it, the way it had welcomed me and made me feel like I belonged.

I peeked out again. The dog was still there, and it was exactly as I remembered from this morning — a massive beast, over three feet tall, with shaggy black fur.

There was no way the dog could have followed me fifty miles. Yet what were the chances of seeing another just like it?

I took out my phone. As the camera clicked, the dog looked straight at me. Then it loped off across the lawn and disappeared through the trees.

A few minutes later, I caught the roar of a familiar engine and ran outside as a black Jag screeched to a stop. The door flew open. A man jumped out, ducking to avoid hitting his head.

Gabriel Walsh. Roughly thirty years old — I've never asked his age. At least six foot four — I've never measured him, either. A linebacker's build, with wavy black hair, strong features, dark shades, and a custom-tailored suit, despite the fact it was Memorial Day and he wasn't supposed to be working. He was, of course. Gabriel was always working.

When I first met my mother's former appeal lawyer, I'd mistaken him for hired muscle. A thug in an expensive suit. Three weeks later, I still thought the analogy wasn't a bad one.

He *did* have a reputation for ripping people apart, though usually only on witness stands. *Usually.*

Gabriel didn't even look at my car — or the corpse spilling out of it. His gaze shot straight to me, lips tightening as he bore down. Limped down, I should say. He'd been shot in the leg yesterday. And no, I didn't do it, as tempting as that could be sometimes.

"Where's your cane?" I called.

"I told you —"

"— to stay in the house. I only came out when I saw you drive up."

A grunt. A quick once-over. Then, "Are you all right?" His voice tinged with reluctance, as if he really hated to ask. *Ah, Gabriel.*

"I'm fine," I said. "And no, I didn't call the police."

"Good."

His shades swung toward the Buick. He started for it. If I'd been anyone else, he would have ordered me to stay back. Not because he wouldn't want to upset a client — such considerations aren't given space in Gabriel's busy brain. He'd insist because otherwise that client might get in his way or do something stupid, like leave fingerprints. As of yesterday, though, I wasn't just a client. He'd hired me as an investigative assistant, which damned well better mean I could be trusted near a potential crime scene.

I did hang back a few paces. Steeling myself for the sight. I didn't want to flinch in front of him.

He reached the driver's side. Stopped. Frowned. Lifted his shades. Lowered them. Looked at me.

"Did you . . . ?" He trailed off and shook his head. "Of course not."

I rounded the car to where he stood by the open driver's door. The body . . .

The body was gone.

CHAPTER TWO

"No," I whispered. "I saw . . ." I swallowed. "I saw someone in the car, and when I opened the door, the body fell out. I wasn't imagining it. I touched it."

"I'm sure you did. The question is . . ."

He looked around and I moved closer, leaning into the open doorway.

"There's no blood," I said. "But the only injury I could see was her eyes. And she was cold, really cold. She hadn't died recently."

He nodded. I didn't see any doubt in his expression, but my heart still pounded, my brain whirring to prove that I hadn't imagined it. No, that I hadn't *hallucinated* it.

"Poppies," I said. "There are poppies in the rock garden. I saw them right before I found the body."

I hurried around the garage with Gabriel limping after me.

There were no poppies in the rock garden.

"I took a picture to make sure I wasn't

imagining them," I said. "There were clearly —"

My photo showed the garden. With rocks. And ivy. And moss. And no poppies.

"They were *there*," I said. "I swear —"

"Am I questioning that?"

"No, but —"

"Then stop panicking."

"I'm not —"

"You are. You found a body, and you called me, and now it's gone, and you're panicking because you can't prove it was there. I don't doubt you saw something. We'll figure out what it was."

As I led Gabriel to the sitting room, his gaze flitted around, discreetly checking out the antiques, any one of which would pay the annual rent on my new apartment.

"Yes, this is what I walked away from," I said. "I know how you feel about that."

"I said nothing."

"But you're thinking something."

"Only that it's a very nice house."

Gabriel knows what it's like to be poor, having been raised by a drug-addicted pickpocket mother who'd disappeared when he was fifteen, leaving him to survive on his own. A street kid who put himself through law school. So no, he was not impressed by

15

the debutante who walked away from her Kenilworth mansion to work in a diner in Cainsville.

"Did you collect your things?" he asked.

"I did, including my laptop, so you can have your old one back. Don't worry, though, I'll pay rent for the full week."

I smiled, but he only nodded. I walked to the love seat. My dad's spot, where we used to sit together. As I sank into it, I began to relax.

Gabriel stopped beside my mother's chair, a spindly antique.

"That is not going to hold you," I said.

"Does it hold anyone?"

"Barely. Lovely to look at, but hellishly uncomfortable to sit on."

He surveyed the others. They all seemed made for people about six inches shorter than Gabriel.

I stood. "Take this."

"No, I —"

"Sit. Put your leg up. You're supposed to keep it elevated."

He grumbled but lowered himself onto the love seat and turned sideways to prop up his leg, proving it was hurting more than he'd let on.

I perched on my mother's chair. "So apparently I hallucinated a dead body."

16

"We don't know that for sure."

"Yeah, I think we do. Otherwise, someone left a corpse in my car while I went for a swim and then disposed of it while I was in the house waiting for you. Highly unlikely. The fact that she wore a wig to look like me only seems to seal the matter. It was an omen. A warning." I paused. "I prefer poppies."

A faint frown. "If it was indeed an apparition, would it not make more sense that you would see *yourself* dead in the car?"

"Maybe I see whatever my mind will accept."

When he didn't reply, I glanced over. He had his shades off as he stared at the wall, deep in thought. The first time I'd seen Gabriel without his sunglasses, I'd wished he'd put them back on. His eyes were an unnaturally pale blue. Empty eyes, I'd thought. I'd come to see that "empty" wasn't quite the right word. More like iced over. Still startling, though, that pale blue ringed with dark. I'd been with him many times when he'd removed his shades in front of strangers, and no one else seemed bothered by his eyes. I wondered what they saw. And, if it was different for me, why?

"So you spotted the poppies and then the body," he said after a moment. "That seems

17

an overload of omens."

He wasn't asking. Just working it out for himself. I swore he was more comfortable with my "ability" than I was. His great-aunt Rose was a psychic in Cainsville, and he'd grown up accepting things like the second sight.

"Would it not seem that the poppies were a portent *for* the body?" he said. "Meaning the body itself was real?"

"I don't think so. The eyes . . . Well, I told you about the eyes. What I didn't mention is that I've seen that before. Twice in the past few weeks." I explained and then said, "Both times it was a hallucination. Which seems to prove that this wasn't real, either, and that I shouldn't have called you —"

"No," he said. "That is *always* the first thing you should do under such circumstances." He said it as if his clients found corpses in cars all the time. "You came inside to call, and secured the house, correct?"

"Correct," I said.

"Did you hear any noise from outside?"

I started to shake my head. Then I remembered the hound and pulled out my cell phone, certain I'd see a photo of our empty front gardens. I didn't.

18

I passed him my phone. "What do you see?"

He looked at the screen. "A dog."

I exhaled in relief.

"Is that an omen?" he asked.

"I have no idea. But I saw that exact same dog in Cainsville this morning. I'm sure it was the same one. It's huge."

"And very distinctive." He tapped the phone, frowning. "In Cainsville, you say?" He rose. "We should speak to Rose."

Before we left, I reset the house alarm.

"You need one of those at your apartment," Gabriel said.

"I have a gun. And a cat."

He gave me a look.

"I cannot afford a security system, Gabriel. I suppose I could hock some things. I left most of my jewelry upstairs. I could go get it . . ."

"No, you'd be lucky to get a fraction of the value."

I'm sure Gabriel had enough experience with pawnshops to know, though most of what he would have hocked as a youth wouldn't have been his to begin with.

"You need a security system," he said. "One of Don's men installs excellent units at very reasonable prices." He meant Don

19

Gallagher, his primary client. Don headed the Satan's Saints. It was not a heavy metal band.

"Uh-huh. A biker who installs security systems? Does he keep a 'backup' copy of the code?"

"Petty larceny is hardly profitable enough for the Saints to bother with — if they involved themselves in criminal activity, which they do not. Any system I buy from them would be both secure and affordable."

Having survived that fall off the back of a truck without a scratch.

"I still can't afford —"

"I'll deduct it from your pay. Now, I seem to recall you saying once that your father had a garage full of cars?"

"Yes . . ."

"You should take one."

"I'm not —"

"Let's take a look."

He limped off, leaving me to follow.

CHAPTER THREE

Gabriel scanned the two rows of cars. His Jag might reach six figures, but he could have bought two of them for the price of any of these vintage sports models.

I stifled any twinge of guilt. Yes, Dad had inherited the Mills & Jones department store, but it'd been close to bankruptcy when he'd bought out the Mills family. He'd earned every penny to buy these vehicles, the same as Gabriel had for his.

"My dad loved fast cars," I said as I walked over.

"As does his daughter."

Gabriel's Jag had five hundred horses under the hood, but for him it was only a status symbol, a mobile business card that said, "I might be young, but I'm a fucking genius at what I do."

"Which is your favorite?" he asked.

I opened my mouth to say that I didn't have one, but he'd already noticed where my gaze slid. He walked behind the two-seater.

"A Maserati?" he said. "Not much trunk space."

"You don't buy a 1961 Maserati Spyder for trunk space."

"All right, then. Where are the keys?"

"I can't —"

"Does your mother use these cars?"

"No, but —"

"Does anyone else use them?"

"No, but —"

"You need a vehicle, Olivia. The fact that your mother continues upkeep on these suggests she considers them yours, for your use, the same as your laptop or your clothing. I suspect if you checked the will, your father left them to you. If you feel the need to check with her, do that."

"I don't. But a waitress with a Maserati? That's not who I want to be. Yes, I need a car, and once I'm working for you I'll rent or lease something. Right now —"

"Whose vehicle is that?"

He cut in as if I'd stopped talking a few sentences ago. For him, I probably had — or at least I'd stopped saying anything worth listening to. I followed his finger to a decade-old VW diesel Jetta tucked behind the Rolls.

"That belonged to our former housekeeper," I said. "She lived in and didn't have her own car, so Dad bought her the Jetta."

"No one drives it now?"

I shook my head. "She retired and our new housekeeper lives out."

"Then take that." When I opened my mouth to protest, he said, "Is it too ostentatious to drive in Cainsville?"

"No, but —"

"Do you expect you'd find any leased or used car with lower insurance or better gas mileage?"

"No, but —"

"Then it meets your standards and overrules your objections. We'll pick it up later."

He headed for the door. I looked at the VW. He was right. For now, this would be no worse than borrowing the Clarks' Buick.

As I came up behind him, Gabriel said, "Catch," and tossed his car keys over his shoulder. "Take the Jag. If you did indeed have a vision of yourself dead in that car, you shouldn't get behind the wheel. I'll follow you back to Cainsville and we'll speak to Rose."

"You don't have to —"

"I have business there."

When I still hesitated in the driveway, he waved at his car. "Take it. Go."

I handed him the Clarks' keys. "Thanks."

23

I wanted to say thanks for more than letting me drive his car. Thanks for dropping everything and coming out here. Thanks for not making me feel like I'd panicked over a false alarm. But Gabriel doesn't do well with gratitude. He prefers cash. So I settled for that simple "Thanks," which he brushed off with a wave as he limped to the death-mobile.

Cainsville, Illinois, was an hour's drive from Chicago, a perfectly reasonable commuting distance, which should have ensured the town became a bedroom community for the big city. While some residents did work in the city, it wasn't easy. No train. No bus. Not even a local taxi service. Commuters had to drive, which started with a slow twenty-minute trek along a country road that took you in the *opposite* direction to Chicago but led to the nearest highway exit — "near" being a relative term. Even those who wouldn't mind the commute would have trouble finding a house in Cainsville. Hemmed in by the highway, a river, and marshy ground, there was no room for expansion.

It was a small, insular community, still "fond of the old ways," as the elders liked to say. Yet every modern convenience —

including screamingly fast Internet service — was available to those who wanted it. A strange little town. And I adored it.

Driving back that afternoon, I took it all in, as if I'd been gone for weeks. The only road into town became Main Street, the commercial center of Cainsville . . . if you call a dozen shops and services a center. I would. Almost anything I could want was there, within a few minutes' walk of my apartment. Life doesn't get much more convenient than that.

Main Street looks as if it belongs in a small town preserved or restored for tourism. Except, without so much as a bed-and-breakfast, tourism wasn't the point for Cainsville. That's just how it looked — picture-perfect storefronts, mostly Renaissance Revival architecture. The street was as narrow as it must have been in the days of horses and buggies. In contrast, the sidewalks were wide and prettied up with overflowing flowerpots, freshly painted benches, and ornate iron trash bins.

This was a town for ambling, as those sidewalks suggested. No one was in a hurry. No one was much inclined to take their car, either, not unless they were leaving town or had the misfortune to live too far from the grocery store. There were a couple dozen people out and about, and if some of them didn't wave, it was only because they were too engrossed in conversation with a companion.

As I drove in, I looked for gargoyles. That had become a habit. I was too old for the annual May Day gargoyle hunt, where kids competed to see who'd found the most, but I still looked in hopes of spotting a new one, because in Cainsville not every gargoyle could be seen all the time.

I turned onto Rowan. My street. I pulled up across the road from my apartment building, and Gabriel parked behind me, in front of his aunt's tiny dollhouse Victorian. Rose's car was gone. Gabriel didn't suggest calling her cell to see when she'd be back. If he did, she'd rush home to help him.

Rose's relationship with her grandnephew isn't an easy one. Gabriel discourages emotional attachments the way most of us discourage door-to-door salesmen. They're inconvenient, intrusive, and liable to end up saddling you with something you never wanted in the first place, at a cost far higher than you wish to pay.

If Gabriel is attached to anyone, it's Rose. Yet when his mother left him, he didn't tell her. When Rose found out, he ran until she stopped looking for him. That's hard to understand, but there was something in Gabriel's psyche, perhaps arising from his family's con-artist past, that said you don't take anything from those you care about. You took only from marks, and marks were always strangers. If Rose had learned that Seanna had abandoned him, she'd have looked after him, and he couldn't accept that. Or maybe he just couldn't believe she'd actually want to.

Gabriel stayed at my place for an hour, prowling the apartment, checking the windows, and engaging in stare-downs with the cat. Then he declared Rose wasn't returning anytime soon and stumped off to speak to my landlord, Grace, about the security system before heading back to Chicago.

The next morning, I had the seven-to-three diner shift. My fellow weekday server, Susie, has a second job and we work around her schedule. Which means I have a mix of day and evening shifts that my body hasn't quite adjusted to yet.

I don't love my job. Oh hell, let's be honest — I barely like it. But as impressive as a master's degree from Yale might sound, it doesn't qualify you for shit, especially when you have no work experience and you majored in Victorian literature.

If there was one thing I did like about my job, it was the people. The owner — an ex-con named Larry — was a dream boss. The regulars were mostly seniors — I swear half the town collects social security — and they'd embraced me like a runaway come home. Even finding out who my birth parents were hadn't changed that.

This was my first shift back after Edgar Chandler's arrest. Everyone had heard what happened and they were all so pleased, so very pleased. Which seems a little odd, but in Cainsville "a little odd" was the norm.

"Such an exciting adventure," Ida Clark said when I brought her lunch. Ida and her husband, Walter, are probably in their seventies. It was their car I'd borrowed.

"A terribly exciting adventure, don't you think?" she said to Walter, who nodded and said yes, terribly exciting.

"Liv was *shot* at," said a voice from across the diner. "She watched a man die and had to hide in the basement while being stalked by a killer. I don't think 'exciting' is the word you're looking for."

That was Patrick. The diner's resident novelist. Also the only person under forty who'd dare speak to the town elders that way.

Ida glared at him. "It *is* exciting. She

proved her parents are innocent."

"For two out of eight murders," I said.

"Still, that's grounds for an appeal. But what exactly happened to that poor young couple? The newspapers weren't very forthcoming. Did —"

"Good God, leave her alone," Patrick said. "You're monopolizing the only server, and some of us require coffee."

He raised his empty mug, and I seized the excuse to hurry off.

As I filled Patrick's mug, he murmured, "Don't tell them anything. I'm sure it's a messy business, and we don't want to tax their old hearts."

There was no way Ida could have overheard, but she aimed a deadly scowl his way. He only smiled and lifted his mug in salute.

After the lunch rush passed, I brought fresh hot water for the Clarks. Several others had joined them, most notably Veronica, one of the elders I knew best, though I can't say I knew any of them *well,* despite hours of chitchat. Mostly, they just wanted to talk about me, and if I swung the conversation their way, they'd deflect. "We're old and boring, dear," they'd say. "Tell us about yourself."

With Veronica, it was more of a two-way

conversation, but only because she'd talk about the town and its traditions. An amateur historian. And, like all the elders, a professional busybody, though I say that in the nicest way. They don't pry — they're just endlessly curious.

Veronica had brought in a sheaf of papers. I only caught a glimpse of a dark-haired woman's photo. When I filled their teacups, she said, "You're in the city quite often, aren't you, Olivia?"

"Oh, we shouldn't bother her with this," Ida said.

"With what?" I asked.

"Posting notices for Ciara Conway," Veronica said. "I'm sure the police are doing all they can, but every little bit extra helps."

"Olivia hasn't been around since Friday," Ida reminded her. "With everything that was happening, I doubt she's even heard one of our young women has gone missing."

There were very few "young women" in Cainsville, and I'd met none named Ciara. When I said as much, Ida explained: "Her mother grew up here." Meaning Ciara had likely come to visit her maternal grandparents, which in the eyes of the elders made her a local. That was Cainsville. Gabriel had never lived here, either, and they considered him one of their own.

"When did she disappear?" I asked.

"Saturday."

I glanced at the papers. "So you're . . . posting flyers? That's certainly how it used to be done, but these days —"

"There are other methods," Ida said. "We know. But the old ways are still useful."

Veronica pushed the stack toward me. She said something else, but I was too busy staring at the photo on the flyer.

Ciara Conway was the dead woman I'd seen in the car.

"Liv?" Walter said.

"S-sorry." I wrenched my gaze from the photo. "Sure, I'll take some to the city. I'll be there tomorrow, doing work for Gabriel. Just leave me a stack."

I retreated as fast as I could. I took another table's order, but after I'd finished, I stared at the words on my pad as if I'd written them in a foreign language.

"Olivia?" Ida said. "Are you all right, dear?"

I nodded. As I headed for the kitchen, Larry watched me, his wide face drawn with concern.

"Liv's been investigating the deaths of young people," Patrick said to the elders.

"You don't go shoving pictures of missing girls in her face."

I said no, I was fine, but Larry took the order pad from my hand and told me to go home and take it easy. The lunch rush was over. He'd handle the rest of my shift.

Any other time, I'd have protested. But I kept seeing that smiling girl on the photo as an eyeless corpse.

"I'll walk you home," Patrick said. "You look a little woozy."

"We were just heading that way," Ida began. "We can —"

"Got it." Patrick smiled at Ida. "Rest your old bones."

BLACK SHUCK

If looks could kill, the one Ida aimed Patrick's way would have drawn and quartered him. Which was far worse than the usual ones that only wished him a swift and relatively painless death.

Olivia's long strides consumed the sidewalk, leaving him jogging to catch up. He wondered what was really bothering her. While he was certain her basement ordeal *had* been traumatic, resilience was in her blood. She should be over it by now.

When Olivia noticed he'd fallen behind, she slowed her pace. Together they passed through the tiny park and on to the walkway that led to her Rowan Street apartment.

"How's Gabriel?" he said.

He hadn't meant to ask. He would prefer not to, or if he did, he would like it to be a show of fake concern. He'd lived a very long time without taking any interest in his *epil.* Gabriel was different. Or perhaps Patrick

was simply getting old. Soft.

"I heard he was injured in that business at the Evans house," he continued.

"Shot in the leg." The briefest pause. "He won't use his cane. He's going to make it worse."

Patrick had to bite back a laugh at the way she said it. First she acknowledged he'd been shot, almost casually. Then she complained about the cane. Worried about Gabriel and loath to admit it.

After a few more steps, she asked, "What do you know about dogs? Symbolically, I mean. Folklore, occultism, whatever. From your writing research."

"Any specific type of canine?"

"Big black ones."

He tried not to react. Fortunately, she was still walking with her gaze straight ahead.

"Mmm, it depends on the culture," he said. "If you're looking at the British Isles —"

"Probably."

"Black Shuck."

Before he could explain, she nodded. "*The Hound of the Baskervilles.* I did my thesis on Conan Doyle. He based his book on the legend of the Black Shuck."

"You didn't need to ask me, then."

She shrugged and looked uncomfortable.

"It didn't . . . It didn't seem . . ."

It didn't seem to fit. Because the Black Shuck was a portent of death, and she could interpret those instinctively. That was how her old blood manifested. If she'd seen a death omen, she wouldn't have needed to consult him.

"Is there anything else in the lore?" she asked. "Besides the Black Shuck?"

"No," he lied.

Patrick left Olivia at her building door. Grace was on the porch, and he knew better than to pass her. Before they parted, he tried to get Olivia to tell him why she was asking about the black dog. She wouldn't.

Had she seen a Cŵn? That seemed most likely. She'd spotted one in Chicago and realized it was no ordinary pet — and no ordinary omen.

If she had truly seen a Cŵn, that meant . . . well, it meant trouble. For her. For Gabriel. For all of them.

CHAPTER FOUR

My landlord, Grace, sat in her usual place — a folding chair on the front stoop. She looked like one of the town's many gargoyles, a wizened imp scowling at the world, daring it to cause trouble.

I said a quick hello as I reached for the doorknob.

"Scone?" she said.

"What?"

"You were at work, weren't you? Where's my scone?"

No, not an imp. A troll. A gray-haired lump of a snaggletoothed beast, guarding her gate, one gnarled hand raised for the toll.

"I forgot," I said. "I'm sorry. I'll grab you two tomorrow. With coffee."

Her beady eyes narrowed. "What's wrong, girl?"

"Nothing."

"If you're apologizing and offering me

extras, something's wrong."

"I'm just . . . off today."

I opened the door and stepped through.

"Well, get some rest and eat something. You're too pale. You look like you've seen a ghost."

Maybe I have, I thought as the door closed behind me.

When I swung into my apartment, TC was perched on the back of the sofa. I dropped my bag with a clunk and he only snarled a yawn, his yellow eyes narrowing as if I'd disturbed his rest. Then he hopped down and wound around my ankles, completely oblivious to the fact that I was racing to my bedroom.

"I'm changing it to DC," I muttered. "*Damn* Cat."

TC wasn't a name, as I was quick to point out to anyone who asked. It was an acronym for "The Cat." I refused to name him because I was not yet resigned to the possibility I might actually be stuck with him.

TC was a black cat, which should have given me all the ammunition I needed to get rid of him. Except in some parts of the world, including Cainsville, they're considered good luck. And it wasn't as if I'd "let" the beast into my home in the first place.

He was a stray who'd zoomed in after a mouse and refused to leave.

The suitcases I'd brought from home sat in the corner, still packed. I tugged one onto its side, took out each piece, and stacked it. Then I lifted TC — protesting — off the second bag, pulled out my dresses and wrapped shoes, and made absolutely sure I hadn't stuffed any other clothing in there. Then I looked at the piles surrounding me, searching for something specific, something I wasn't seeing.

When I found that corpse in my car, I'd paid little attention to what she was wearing — not surprisingly, perhaps. Seeing those missing person posters brought it back, though. I'd noticed the corpse had been wearing a green shirt. I'd packed a green shirt. Now it was gone.

As I twisted, my gaze caught on the row of shoes. Four pairs. Trainers, heels, pumps, and boots. There was one missing. My Jimmy Choo green lace-up sandals. Completely impractical, but I loved them, and I was absolutely certain I'd packed them.

I took out my cell phone. Then I set it down. Picked it up. Set it down. Finally I gave in and hit speed dial.

The phone went straight to voice mail and I remembered why I wasn't starting my new job with Gabriel today — because he had business at the courthouse.

"Sorry," I said when his voice mail beeped. "It's nothing important. Talk to you later."

I'd just hung up when I had a call from Howard, my mother's lawyer. He was checking in on me, which would have been very sweet if it hadn't been a duty call on behalf of my mother. That might also have been sweet — of her — if she were the one actually calling. Still, I know better than to read too much into it. My mother doesn't handle stress well. Hell, my mother doesn't handle life well. Having the world find out her daughter's birth parents were serial killers? Then having that daughter insist on investigating their crimes? That kind of stress could drive my mother to a heart attack . . . or so she seemed to think.

When our early calls had proven difficult, she'd turned them over to Howard. Once she's ready to speak to me again, she'll be ready to come home. For now, she's hiding — in every way.

I told Howard to let her know I'd been to the house for my things and I'd borrowed the Jetta. If she wanted to talk about any of that, she could call. She didn't.

Next I researched the case of Ciara Conway,

what little "case" there was. As Veronica said, Ciara had been reported missing Saturday. As for when she'd actually disappeared, that was harder to say. Until a month ago, she'd been a twenty-two-year-old Northwestern student, living with her long-term boyfriend. Then she'd left him.

Neither her parents nor her ex could provide a list of friends she might have couch-surfed with, and I got the impression Ciara hadn't actually "left" her boyfriend. I'd worked in shelters long enough to recognize the clues. Ciara had a problem — drugs or alcohol. Her parents and boyfriend had finally resorted to tough love. He kicked her out and told her to clean up. Her parents wouldn't take her in. She found places to stay, while her loved ones made daily check-in calls, until last Wednesday, when she'd stopped answering. By Friday, her phone was out of service, the battery dead. Now her parents and boyfriend were racked with guilt, frantic with fear, and the police weren't much help because they'd seen this scenario a hundred times and knew it was just a matter of time before Ciara came off her bender, borrowed a phone, and called for money.

She wouldn't. Ciara Conway was dead. And the only people who knew that were me and her killer.

I was still searching when Gabriel called back. Street noise in the background meant he was hurrying — or hobbling — somewhere.

"I'm sorry I called," I said. "I forgot you had a trial today."

"No trial. I'm simply at the courthouse speaking to a few people about your mother's new appeal, which we'll discuss later. What is it?"

"Nothing urgent. Go ahead and do whatever —"

"I'm not doing anything right now except obtaining dinner."

I told him about Ciara Conway, and my missing shirt and shoes.

"I didn't see my shoes on her," I said. "Hell, I could be mistaken about the shirt. And maybe the dead body only resembled Ciara —"

"Olivia."

I inhaled. "Stop backpedaling, I know. The body was Ciara Conway's and she was wearing my shirt, which I know I'd packed. Still, I can't see how anyone could dress her, stage her in that car, and take her away again."

"How long were you in the pool?"

"Maybe an hour."

"And twenty minutes in the house afterward, waiting for me. The yard is private, with both a fence and greenery blocking the road and the neighbors. It's risky but not impossible. Without a body, there is little we can do, but I want to speak to Chandler."

"Chandler?"

"If you found a dead body dressed to look like you, that isn't a portent. It's a threat. Edgar Chandler made a very clear one against you Sunday. Ergo, I'd like to speak to him. In the meantime, you need to talk to Pamela about omens."

CHAPTER FIVE

All my life, I've had superstitious ditties stuck in my head, popping up on cue. I'd thought I'd picked them up from a nanny or other caregiver. Then I met Pamela Larsen, heard her voice, and knew exactly who'd planted those rhymes. Speaking to her about it had been at the top of my to-do list. Yet while I'd visited Sunday night to tell her we'd proven she and my father hadn't killed Jan Gunderson and Peter Evans, it definitely hadn't been the time to say, "Oh, and by the way, I can read omens."

Gabriel picked me up at six. He wanted to accompany me and drive me to my parents' afterward, to make damned sure I took that VW. On the way, I told him I wanted to make another prison visit. One that had proved impossible when I'd attempted it myself. Visiting my biological father, Todd Larsen.

I struggled with seeing Todd. My newly

risen memories of him were mingled with ones of my adoptive dad, the one I grew up with, perfect memories of a perfect father, and that made it all sorts of complicated. I'd resolved a few days ago to see him. Telling Gabriel was the first step toward making that happen.

Seeing Pamela had been much easier. I'd needed Gabriel's help the first time, but since then I could visit when I liked, and we had no problem getting in today. When I arrived, she was watching the visiting room door, and as soon as I walked through, her face lit up and she rose, arms going out. We couldn't hug — that wasn't allowed — but she still reached out as if we could.

I grew up not knowing I was adopted, with people always telling me how much I looked like my parents. I had Lena Taylor's ash-blond hair, slender build, and green eyes, and Arthur Jones's height and features. They hadn't adopted me until I was almost three, and by then they'd have known I could pass for theirs. Yet after meeting Pamela Larsen, I realized any resemblance between me and my adoptive parents was purely superficial. Though Pamela is dark-haired and dark-eyed, our facial structure is the same. She's an inch or so shorter than my five-eight and about forty pounds heavier, but there's little doubt we're mother and daughter.

As I walked over to her, I smiled, which made her light up all the more. Even the sight of Gabriel didn't elicit the usual glower. As soon as we sat, though, her gaze went to him.

"If you're here to convince me to hire you again —"

"I am not. I'm accompanying Olivia."

Her lips pressed together. "I don't appreciate you using my daughter to get to me. I haven't decided who'll represent me. When I do, I'll let you know. I'm interviewing other lawyers now."

"Excellent."

Her lips compressed again.

I cut in. "As entertaining as it is to watch you two outstare each other, that's not what I'm here for. Gabriel *is* your best chance for an appeal, but ultimately it's your choice."

"Has he asked you to pay for my defense?" she said.

"I would not," Gabriel said. "While I have made initial inquiries on your behalf, testing the waters for the appeal, we can discuss those later. For now, Olivia has unrelated questions."

"I . . ." I took a deep breath. "There's no

way to say this without sounding like I'm nuts, so I'm just going to go for it. I can see omens. See them, read them, interpret them."

I explained what had been happening. I didn't get far before her eyes widened. She turned to Gabriel. "I'd like you to leave." She paused and, though it seemed painful, added, "Please."

He glanced at me. I nodded. When he was gone, I finished my explanation. Then she sat there, saying nothing.

"You know what I'm talking about, don't you?" I said.

"No, I don't think I do, Olivia."

I leaned forward, my voice softening. "I know this isn't easy to talk about, but I have to understand. It's . . ." I tried for a smile. "It's freaking me out a little, and I could really use some help."

It took a lot to admit that. I'd proven my birth parents innocent of two murders, and I wanted to seize on that and declare them innocent of all. But I couldn't. I didn't dare, because if I did, I don't think I could handle finding out I was wrong.

For twenty years, I'd had a father I adored and a mother I loved. Then I'd discovered the Larsens, and all those lost memories flooded back. I'd had another father I'd adored, in Todd. And a mother who'd loved me with a fierce and deep maternal passion that Lena Taylor could never quite manage.

I kept my distance now, as a cushion. Protecting my sanity and, yes, my heart — though I squirmed at the notion. I'm not an emotional person. But I am someone who loves deeply and completely. Someone who can be hurt just as deeply and completely.

I was taking a chance by letting her see how much I needed her answers. A chance by letting her see how much I needed *her.*

When I said the words, I saw something inside her reach out — then shut down, as hard and as fast as Gabriel could, that wall dropping behind his eyes.

"I'm sorry, baby." She reached out as if she could take my hand. "I don't know what you're talking about."

I jerked back as if she'd slapped me. "You're the one who taught me all those superstitions. I hear your voice in my head, saying them."

Her lips worked as if preparing a lie, but after a moment she said, "Yes, that was me." She leaned across the table, her manacled hands resting on it. "I was young, Olivia. As young as you are now, and not nearly as educated or as worldly. My mother had filled my head with those superstitions, and

47

I thought they were fun. Silly and fun and harmless. So I passed them along to you."

"What about the fact that the omens I see really *do* predict future events?"

She shifted, as if uncomfortable. "The thing with superstitions is that it's very easy to find justification. If you search hard enough —"

"I know. Find a lucky penny and win two bucks on a scratch card. Voilà, it worked."

This was exactly what I'd been telling myself all my life. Omens were like horoscopes — if you want to believe, you can find "proof." I had expected this very argument from Gabriel, always logical and rational. I had not expected it from Pamela, and it was made so much worse by the fact that I could tell she was lying to me. Lying after I'd opened myself up to her.

"I know that's why people believe in superstitions and petty magics," I continued. "If I see a death omen, though, someone dies. But I'm the *only* one who sees it. I notice eight crows on a wire and everyone else sees six."

Her head jerked up. "You've spoken to someone about this?"

"No," I lied. "I've only asked what they see."

She leaned even farther across the table.

"Do you know why I'm in here, Olivia? Because I was a foolish girl playing at being a good witch, with amulets and brews to protect my family from colds and misfortune. Then someone tipped off the police, claiming we were responsible for these ritualistic murders, and my silly Wiccan baubles damned us more than DNA ever could. Whatever you think you're experiencing, you must tell no one. For your own sake."

I met her gaze. "What *am* I experiencing?"

She pulled back. "I have no idea. You've been under a lot of stress, and —"

"I'm sorry I bothered you with this," I said, rising stiffly.

She put her hand on mine as the guard cleared her throat in warning. "Don't be angry, Olivia," she said. "I know that look. Your grandma used to call it 'getting your dander up.' You'd do it every time —"

"Don't."

"I'm just saying —"

"I came to talk about this. If you won't help, I'll go."

I could hear the hurt in my voice and I could feel it in the way I hesitated, waiting for her to change her mind. A few seconds passed, seemingly endless, and I realized I had to follow through, had to leave. Then her mouth opened and my heart jumped in relief.

"I'd like to speak to Gabriel," she said.

Another three seconds of silence before I found my voice, as steady as I could manage. "You want to speak to — ?"

"He knows, doesn't he? You've told him about these omens."

My disappointment burned away in a flare of anger. "Whether I —"

"He knows. I can tell." She leaned over the table. "I've been trying to stay out of this, Olivia, but I need to ask. What exactly is the nature of your relationship with him?"

"I hired him to help me investigate your case."

"And otherwise?" she asked.

"Otherwise what?"

"There's something going on between you two, and I'm going to be blunt, because I need to ask. Are you sleeping with him?"

"No."

"Is there any romantic — ?"

"No. Gabriel has never made anything even resembling a pass at me. Whatever you think of his ethics, he knows the grounds for disbarment. Hell, he probably has a laminated list in his wallet."

"So it's a simple client–lawyer relationship?" She waved at the door with its small glass pane, blacked out by the wall of Gabriel's back. "He's right there. He's been there since he left, and he only left because you wanted him to go. He jumped to do your bidding. Now he's hovering there, waiting for any sign that you need him."

"Gabriel doesn't jump. Or hover."

"Nor does he give up his evening to accompany a mere client on a visit to her imprisoned mother. Is he on the clock now, Olivia?"

"You're right — I'm not just a client. We worked side by side on your case. I wouldn't presume to call him a friend, but he offered to come with me and I'm happy for the company." I looked at her. "Is that what you want to talk to him about? Our relationship? Because if it is —"

She shook her head. "I want to talk about the case. My case."

I nodded brusquely and left.

CHAPTER SIX

As I waited for Gabriel, I fought against disappointment and hurt. Pamela was the only person who could help me understand what I was going through. And she'd refused. Not only refused, but acted as if I was an overimaginative child.

I thought I felt my cell phone vibrate in my back pocket. Which was impossible, because I'd left it in the car to avoid turning it in at security. Still, the sensation startled me enough that I turned and . . .

I saw the hound. The big black dog from yesterday, crossing a hall junction ten feet away. It was on a leash, being led by a woman. It turned and fixed its red-brown eyes on mine. I blinked, and when I opened my eyes, I was looking at a black Lab in a harness. I blinked again, to be sure, but it was definitely a Labrador retriever, probably being brought in for prisoner therapy.

I watched the dog and its handler go. Then

I paced outside the visitors' room until the door opened. As Gabriel stepped out, I motioned that I'd be another minute. He nodded, and I slipped back into the room as they were taking Pamela away. The guard warned that my time was up.

"I know. Just one last thing I need to tell her."

Pamela gave me a wary look and tried to cover it with a smile. "What is it, baby?"

"I've been seeing a dog. I saw it twice yesterday. The same dog, fifty miles apart. About this big" — I lifted my hand above my waist — "with black fur. I think it's some kind of hound."

As I spoke, Pamela's eyes widened, her face filling with horror and dread. Before I could say a word, that expression vanished, replaced with feigned confusion and concern.

"That's odd," she said, her voice strangled.

"You don't know anything about it?" I asked.

"No, I don't."

I met her gaze. "Don't do this, Pamela. Please. Something's going on and I need —"

"You need to forget it," she said. "You've been through a lot, baby, and the best thing you can do right now is look after yourself."

"That's what I'm trying —"

"No, you're not. Go home. Turn off the phone. Take a hot bath. Relax and try to forget all this. That's the best thing you can do. The *only* thing you can do."

She let the guard lead her away and never looked back.

On the drive to my parents' place, I told Gabriel what Pamela had said. As I spoke, his hands tightened on the wheel.

"She knows something," I said.

"That goes without saying. She admitted to teaching you about omens, and there is no doubt you can read them. Therefore a connection exists."

We drove in silence for a few minutes.

"I practically begged," I said, my voice barely above a whisper. "No. Forget 'practically.' I did beg. I told her I needed it. And she turned me down. *Flat.* Made me feel . . ." I settled my hands in my lap. "I'm going to stop seeing her."

He glanced over.

"Until she agrees to talk about the omens," I said. "If she contacts you asking to speak with me, will you tell her that?"

"I will. It is, quite possibly, the one thing that will force her hand. As for getting help elsewhere, you still need to talk to Rose about the hound and the body."

"I know."

"I tried to visit Chandler yesterday. He won't see me. Not surprising, I suppose, given that we put him in there. That will change. He'll eventually decide he can manipulate me to his advantage. In the meantime, I'll visit Anderson."

"His bodyguard." I paused. "Former bodyguard, who may not be any happier with you, considering you blew off half his foot."

"I'm going to offer to defend him."

I glanced over. "Seriously?"

"He will be more forthcoming with his lawyer, and he might be able to tell me whom Chandler would hire to put that body in your car. As for his foot . . ." He shrugged. "It was business. He was acting on his employer's behalf; I was acting on my client's. I'm sure he'll see reason."

"Good luck with it."

"Luck has nothing to do with that. He will hire me, and I will find out everything he knows about Edgar Chandler's associates."

My dad kept the labeled keys for his car collection in a garage safe. I was grabbing the set for the Jetta when Gabriel reached past me and took the ones for the Maserati.

I sighed. "I almost hope that means you're taking the car hostage pending payment of your bill. Otherwise, I believe we've already had this conversation, and —"

"And you're taking the Jetta. For now. I accept that decision, even if I think it's foolish. This" — he dangled the keys — "is temporary. We're going for a ride."

"We are?"

"I have a long night ahead of me. I'd like a coffee, and I suspect the Maserati will get me one faster than the Jetta."

I could have pointed out that the short walk to the house would get him one even faster. As might his own car, waiting in the drive. But I looked at the keys, considering. He dangled them again, as if to say, "You want this — I know you do."

"When's the last time you took it out?" he asked.

My smile evaporated. "Not since my dad —"

Gabriel cut in before I could go there. "Then you should take it for a spin. Cars like that shouldn't be left in storage. It causes mechanical issues. With brakes and tires and engines and such."

My smile returned. "You have no idea what you're talking about, do you?"

"Not a word."

This wasn't about getting a coffee. It was about getting me out of my post-Pamela funk. So I took the keys and waved him to the passenger seat.

CHAPTER SEVEN

I put the top down and whipped along my
favorite roads, ones where the danger — of
cops or traffic or, most important, kids —
was minimal and I could put the hammer
down and go. People used to joke that I'd
inherited my father's love for fast cars.
Some of my earliest memories were of being out with him in this very car, me in my
booster seat, straining against the harness
like a dog with its nose out the window, feeling the rush of wind, closing my eyes and
imagining I was flying.

It was a rush like no other. Okay, when I
was seventeen I discovered a rush I liked
just as well, but that's altogether different.
Or maybe not so different — the adrenaline
rush, the descent into the absolutely physical, where nothing else mattered except
what I felt. And what I felt was glorious.
That evening, it knocked every vestige of
hurt from my brain, and when I grinned

over at Gabriel, he granted me a rare smile in return.

After about twenty minutes of roaring around, I slowed and said, "There's a place up here where we can grab you a coffee."

"Does it have your mochas?"

"Nope. Straight-up coffee, which is fine —"

"Go someplace else, then. Get your mocha. We have time."

Another grin for him before I veered around the corner and sped off again.

After we got our coffees, Gabriel suggested we walk for a bit to stretch our legs. Stretch *his* legs, I'm guessing — my dad was six-two, and I remember him complaining about the Spyder's lack of legroom.

"Can I ask what Pamela talked to you about?" I said as we set out. "She said some things that made me worry it might not be a business chat."

"It was. She hired me back."

I stopped short. "Really?"

"Moreover, she will complete payment of her past-due bill first thing tomorrow, along with a sizable retainer."

I gaped at him. Pamela had money — a healthy inheritance — with nothing to spend it on. Yet she hadn't paid her initial bill. She claimed Gabriel screwed her over, but I suspect after their falling-out over the failed appeal she'd known withholding payment was the best revenge. That was why Gabriel came to me in the first place, hoping to recoup his losses. She'd been slowly paying him back as he'd helped me. Now, minutes after claiming she was still lawyer-shopping, she'd not only hired him but repaid him?

"You know your mother and I don't get along," he said.

"To put it mildly."

"But I do feel the need to give her some credit here, and say that I think this is her way of apologizing for lying about the omens. That does not excuse the lie but proves she isn't actively trying to thwart you, Olivia. Pamela and I have our differences, but I don't question her attachment to you. If she won't speak of the omens, she has a reason. I agree, however, that despite her olive branch here, you are correct to refrain from visiting until she agrees to discuss it. But it *is* an olive branch. She knows you want me on this case."

"But she also knows she'd be an idiot not to hire you back. She was just toying with you."

"Yes, she would have eventually rehired

me. Then we'd have spent a week dickering, as I insisted on repayment and a retainer. The fact she offered both willingly indicates it is an apology to you."

"Okay."

"It also means I can put you to work on her case. It will be part of your job with me. A *large* part once the police investigation slows and I begin the appeal in earnest. At that point, you may find it difficult to continue at the diner —"

I shot him a look.

"I said, 'at that point.' " He slowed at the corner, hand going against my back as if to stop me from running into nonexistent traffic. "I even qualified it with 'may.' "

I shook my head. He wanted me to quit the diner, namely so I'd be at his beck and call for research. I refused so I wouldn't be beholden to him for my entire income.

As we walked, we discussed our next move on the Larsens' case.

My birth parents had been convicted of killing four young couples in what was presumed to be some kind of ritual. The murders themselves had been swift strangulations. No sex. No torture. No sign that the victims even had time to realize what was going on. It was only after their deaths that those "ritualistic elements" took shape.

Five things had been done to the corpses. A symbol had been carved into each thigh and another painted with woad on the stomachs. For the women, a twig of mistletoe pierced the symbol on their stomachs. They all had a stone in their mouths and a section of skin removed from their backs.

As we'd discovered, the last victims — Jan Gunderson and Peter Evans — definitely hadn't been killed by the Larsens. Peter had learned that his father was involved in MKULTRA — mind control experiments for the CIA — in the fifties and sixties. Now, MKULTRA was a matter of public record, and while Will Evans would have hated for Peter to find out, it wasn't exactly a state secret. What *was* a secret was the fact that Evans had continued the work with his old mentor, Edgar Chandler. Chandler had left the CIA but was still working on creating a mind control drug for his pharmaceutical firm, by means that I suspect were less than legal and certainly less than ethical.

According to Chandler, Peter had threatened to expose their experiments, and his father killed him. Then Peter's girlfriend, Jan, showed up and Evans killed her, too. Being an expert in serial killers and having full knowledge of the recent crimes from a police friend, Evans had staged the bodies to match my parents' other alleged victims.

Is that what really happened? I'm not sure. There's a reason I did my master's thesis on Sir Arthur Conan Doyle. I'm drawn to his greatest creation because I understand how Sherlock Holmes thinks — logic over emotion. But there's a place for intuition there, too — not surprising given Conan Doyle's own interest in the supernatural. I'd spent enough time with both Will Evans and Edgar Chandler to know that Evans was, basically, a good man. Chandler was not.

When Gabriel and I started investigating, Chandler had taken control of the situation. In the twenty years since Peter Evans's murder, he'd actually found a way to do what the CIA could not — formulate some kind of drug that controlled the actions of others. He'd used it to kill two potential witnesses. Except Jan's senile father and Peter's drugged-out old friend weren't really witnesses at all. Murdering them had just been an excuse to test his product. Then he used it to kill Evans himself, robbing Evans of the opportunity to tell his side of the story.

I suspect Evans had made the mistake of calling Chandler when Peter found out. I suspect Chandler was responsible for Peter's and Jan's deaths. Will Evans may have played a role, but I would like to believe he did not murder his own son. Maybe, then, I'm a little bit sentimental after all. Whatever the exact answer, there is no doubt that one of them — Chandler or Evans — murdered the two, and my parents did not. Chandler had provided enough evidence for that.

Our investigation would slow while the police investigated Chandler's claims. As a defense lawyer, Gabriel acted as if he had nothing but disdain for the police, but as a shrewd investigator himself he did respect their abilities and the tools they had at their disposal. He'd let the police investigate, assimilate what they learned into our research, and then jump back in.

As Gabriel mentioned talking to the police, I thought of something else he needed to speak to them about. Just before Will Evans died, he'd shown me old photos of Gabriel's mother. Dead on a coroner's table. Gabriel was supposed to go to the station and identify the pictures. Confirm Seanna was dead — that she had been dead since she'd left him, since he'd presumed she abandoned him. I thought of asking if he'd done that and, if not, reminding him of my offer to go along. I didn't. Couldn't. The night was going well, and that was sure to ruin it. So we continued talking about the case.

Though we'd wait for details from the police investigation, we wouldn't stop work entirely. We'd solved Peter's and Jan's murders by focusing on them. Now I'd do the same with the other six victims, researching them as people, not numbers in a serial killer's tally.

Did I expect to find my parents innocent of all crimes? No. But did I hope I would? Of course. So I would investigate to set my mind at ease, and whatever I found, Gabriel could use in his appeal.

When Gabriel's phone buzzed, he took it out and glanced in annoyance at the screen before pocketing it. Three more steps and he yanked it out again, hammered in a quick text, and hit Send hard enough to launch the message into space.

"Client being a pain?" I said. "As a new employee, I can pry now without seeming like I'm prying."

"It simply wasn't the person I'm waiting to hear from. I'm having . . ." He stuffed the phone back into his pocket. "I'm trying to resolve a matter, and the other party won't return my calls." He adjusted his suit coat. "I'll deal with it in the morning."

We crossed the road. A calico cat leapt

onto a newspaper box and began washing its ears.

"Storm's coming." I looked up into the clear evening sky, so cloudless I could see the faint twinkle of distant stars through the dusk. "Or not."

"Hmm."

"Either way, we'd better head back to the car."

I started in that direction. Gabriel took a few steps beside me, then glanced back at the cat, still cleaning its ears. He took out his phone again and punched in another text, and we carried on in silence.

CHAPTER EIGHT

Wednesday morning, I drove my newly acquired VW into Chicago for my first day working with Gabriel. His office is a greystone near Garfield Park. A beautiful old building in a respectable but not exactly prestigious neighborhood. I'd expected something flashier — the Jag version of a lawyer's office. He could afford that. So why the greystone? It meant something. With Gabriel, everything means something.

The problem with old Chicago neighborhoods is a distinct lack of parking. Gabriel gets the spot in the narrow lane between his building and the next. I was supposed to park on the street, but I got a call from Gabriel five minutes before I arrived. Apparently, the media had staked out his office hoping for a sound bite on my birth parents' case. I parked a few blocks away, and he picked me up.

There was indeed a news van in front of

his building. Gabriel roared past and veered into the parking spot sharply enough to knock me against the door. He paused before pulling up, and glanced off to the left, down the road, as if he'd spotted something.

"There's something I need to do first," he said.

"Okay, let me out here. I'm sure Lydia —"

"You should come with me. We need to talk."

I sighed as the Jag roared back onto the road.

I twisted to face him. "Are you trying to give me whiplash my first day — ?"

I caught sight of a familiar figure walking down the sidewalk.

"James?" I said.

Gabriel rammed the car into drive, and it lurched forward.

"Gabriel? Hold on. That's —"

"Reporters. Yes, I see them."

"No, it's James."

He frowned as if he had no idea what I was talking about, and it didn't matter that he still had his shades on and I couldn't see his eyes — I knew that's what he'd spotted a moment ago. James.

"Gabriel, stop the car."

He looked over at me. "Give me ten minutes, Olivia."

"What is going on?"

"Ten minutes. Please."

When I heard that "please," my stomach dropped. I opened the door. The pavement whizzed past.

"Olivia."

I reached for my seat belt. He hit the brakes.

"I can explain," he said.

"Explain what, Gabriel?" I could barely get the words out, my heart pounded so hard. "What have you done?"

I didn't wait for an answer. I got out of the car as James jogged toward us. Thirty years old. Blond hair. Trim, fit, and handsome. Dressed in a suit as expensive as Gabriel's.

James Morgan. My ex-fiancé. We were supposed to get married this weekend, actually. I'd realized that yesterday, when my phone sent me a to-do list for the rehearsal party.

Gabriel pulled to the curb and was out of his car before James caught up.

"Liv . . ." James said.

Gabriel stepped up beside me. "If you've come to speak to me, you should have made an appointment." He turned to me. "Would you excuse us, Olivia?"

"Speak to you?" I said. "Why would he — ?"

"A business matter," Gabriel said. "It will only take a moment."

"What possible *business* — ?"

"I hired him," James said. "To look after you."

I stared at James. "What?"

"I can explain later," Gabriel said. "I've been trying to contact Mr. Morgan to discuss the matter —"

"What *matter*?"

James turned to me. "After we talked the last time, I spoke to him, hoping to contact you. He convinced me not to."

"What?"

Gabriel's face stayed expressionless. "If you failed to provide him with your new contact information, I could presume you didn't wish to speak to him. I merely reiterated that —"

James stepped toward him. "You told me she needed time to herself and I should respect that, but in the meantime, since I was obviously concerned, you would act as go-between."

"I did *not* say —" Gabriel began.

"You agreed to persuade her to speak to me while monitoring the situation."

I gaped at Gabriel. "You told him — ?"

"No, he misunderstood the nature —"

"There's no goddamned misunderstanding, Walsh," James said. "You promised to persuade Liv to speak to me. And you promised to look out for her. For a fee."

I stared at Gabriel, and as I did, I knew James was telling the truth. Of course he was. James always did . . . and Gabriel did not. Yet I still stared, looking for something — anything — in Gabriel's face to tell me this wasn't true.

"It wasn't quite like that," Gabriel said finally.

"Not *quite* like that?" I said. "What part's wrong? The one where you took money to act as a romantic go-between and did nothing? Oh, no, wait — you did do something. When I flirted with Ricky Gallagher, you did your damnedest to stop it."

"Who's Ricky?" James asked.

"Or was it the part where you came crawling back after I fired your ass? When you acted like you really wanted to work together again, while all you were really thinking about was the money James was paying you?"

"Olivia, you know that isn't —"

"At Evans's house, you said you would have left me in that basement."

As I spoke the words, I could smell the place — the slightly musty stink overlaid with lemon laundry detergent and blood. Gabriel's blood. He'd been badly injured, and we'd escaped to the basement, only to discover he wouldn't fit out the window. He'd told me to leave him. When I refused, he said if the situation was reversed, he'd leave me, and I'd told him it didn't matter. I would stay. I *had* stayed.

I continued. "But you wouldn't have abandoned me to my fate, would you? Because you were being *paid* to protect me."

"That's not —"

"The whole goddamned time, you were being *paid* to protect me!" My voice rang out along the street, and James moved forward, his hand going to my arm, but I stepped away and looked at Gabriel. "That's why you stayed the other night. Why you were so goddamned insistent that I get a security system, and I thought, I actually thought . . ."

I couldn't finish. I wouldn't humiliate myself like that.

"Olivia." Gabriel lowered his voice. "I can explain this. Give me five minutes. Please."

"This is why you offered me the job, wasn't it? Here I thought I'd accomplished the impossible. I'd impressed Gabriel Walsh.

But that wasn't it at all. You offered me that job so you could keep pulling in a paycheck from James, because you hadn't finished your task. You hadn't earned the bonus for getting us back together."

"No, Olivia. *No.* That is not —"

"Is he lying?" I said. "Look me in the eye and tell me you did not agree to protect me."

"Yes, I did, but that is *not* why —"

"Don't." I turned to James. That's when I saw the reporting crew. Thirty feet away. Taping us.

Gabriel noticed them. "Let's go talk —"

"I don't have anything to say."

I started walking away. Gabriel continued trying — give him five minutes, let him explain. He wouldn't raise his voice, though, not with a camera crew right there, and as soon as I was out of earshot, he went silent.

"Come this way," whispered a voice at my ear.

I looked over, and it took a moment to focus and realize James was beside me. *Oh God, James . . .*

"This way," he said again, hand on my elbow.

The camera crew was bearing down now. They hadn't dared approach with Gabriel there, but this was James Morgan, perfectly civilized, perfectly polite, perfectly unlikely to right-hook them if they got in his face.

"Mr. Morgan?" one called. "Ms. Jones?"

"Not now, please." James put his arm around me and steered me across the road, calling to them, "This is a private matter. Thank you."

The crew followed, the reporter calling questions. Shoes clomped on the pavement.

"Ms. Jones isn't giving interviews," I heard Gabriel say. "If you would like to speak about the developments in Pamela Larsen's case, I can spare a minute."

I didn't look back.

CHAPTER NINE

If my car had been closer, I think I'd have climbed in and driven away with a distracted "I'll call you later" for James. Fortunately, by the time we reached the VW, I'd recovered enough not to do anything so rude.

James suggested we go for coffee, and he insisted on driving. I was too shell-shocked to argue — with the coffee or handing over my keys. He drove me to a fancy shop tucked into a nearby pocket of gentrification. It was the kind of place I'd normally love — quiet and intimate. Today, though, I wished he'd just pulled into the nearest Starbucks.

I felt exposed here. A half-dozen people turned to watch me walk in. They knew who I was, from my picture in the papers. In the three weeks since the news broke, I'd been into the city almost daily. I'd probably been recognized every time, but after the first week I hadn't given a shit. Why? Because

Gabriel had been at my side, and his don't-give-a-fuck-what-you-think-of-me attitude had rubbed off.

With James, it felt completely different.

I'd been in the paper before this debacle. When you come from money, you attend events that get coverage. The only noteworthy thing I'd ever done, though, was getting engaged to James Morgan. CEO of Chicago's fastest-growing tech firm. Son of a former Illinois senator. Fixture on the city's most-eligible-bachelor lists. Now here he was telling me he hadn't abandoned me. He'd only done what I asked and given me space.

"I know . . ." He exhaled and rubbed his thumb on his chin, a nervous gesture I knew well. ". . . what I did was wrong. Stupid. Hell, the only reason you're sitting here right now is because you're waiting for an explanation. Waiting for me to tell you how I can justify paying a guy to protect you."

True, though I had an idea what that explanation would be.

He rubbed his chin harder, thumb pressing in. "This is embarrassing as hell, Liv. If I didn't need to explain . . ."

"You do."

His thumbnail absently nicked his lip, and he straightened abruptly. "He talked me into it. Which sounds like a lame excuse, but I wouldn't say it if it wasn't true, because it's damn humiliating. I walked into Walsh's office knowing exactly what I wanted — to talk to you, apologize to you, be the man I hadn't been when you needed me most. I walked in with a clear purpose . . . and an hour later I walked out having hired Gabriel Walsh to do that job for me. He made it seem . . ." James shoved back, chair legs squeaking. "Damn it, Liv. I feel like I was conned. I know that's ridiculous. He's an attorney, not a two-bit hustler."

Actually, Gabriel was both. An attorney from a long line of hustlers. Earlier, when James said that Gabriel "convinced" him not to talk to me, I'd had a good idea how this had played out. Gabriel had seen the opportunity for profit and pounced. He'd made his case, and James had fallen for it, like so many before him. Like me.

James continued explaining. I didn't need it, but like a sinner at confession, he had to spill all the details of his mistake. Yes, it *had* been a mistake. Clearly, I did not appreciate my former fiancé hiring someone to take care of me and win me back, but James knew he'd been wrong, and I knew he'd been manipulated by a master. Could I forgive him for that? Yes. I could.

There was more, too, a mistake I didn't need to forgive him for, because apparently it never happened. Last week, I'd seen a gossip-page piece on a reunion between James and his former girlfriend, getting back together. Now, over coffee, he explained that the encounter had been arranged by his mother, in collaboration with his all-too-willing ex. It had indeed only been an encounter — a few minutes at an event where he'd spoken to Eva, unaware the photo had been snapped, and then he'd left the event, alone. After the article came out, James had contacted Gabriel in a panic and been assured the matter would be set straight. Gabriel had never said a word to me.

"I was an idiot to trust him," James said. "I knew his reputation. Hell, I spoke to one of my firm's lawyers and I got an earful — about the cases he's represented, the criminals he's set free, the allegations against him. Assault, blackmail, intimidation . . . There's even a rumor he has a sealed juvenile record."

He did. For pickpocketing. Which was, I'm sure, only one of many juvenile offenses. As for the rest? I'd seen him deck a reporter. I'd seen him arrange for drugs to be given to a reluctant witness. I'd helped him move a body to delay its discovery. I suspected that any rumors short of murder were true. And I hadn't cared.

For James, though, I acted as if this was all a huge revelation to me.

He continued, "But when I dug deep enough, all the information I received said that Walsh could, in his way, be trusted. Hire him and he'd do what he was paid for. Apparently not."

Except he had. He protected me, staying by my side throughout our investigation. As for playing matchmaker? The thought of Gabriel saying, "Hey, maybe you should call your ex. He seems like a nice guy," was ludicrous. I suppose he figured warning me off Ricky Gallagher was enough.

"So . . ." James said. "I screwed up, and I know you're upset —"

"Not with you."

"Then . . ."

He laid his closed fist on the table and opened it. In his palm was a ring. My engagement ring.

My heart seized, and I stared as if he were holding out a vial of poison.

My God, how could I even think that?

I'd planned to marry this man. To spend my life with him. And now it was like he belonged in some half-remembered dream. I had loved him. I still felt something that could be love. He was the same guy he'd been when I'd taken that ring a year ago. James had not changed. But I had.

"Liv?"

I looked up and saw his panic, his confusion. If any part of me wasn't already consumed with self-loathing, that look devoured it in a single chomp.

"I . . . need time," I said. "So much has happened, and I'm still confused and . . ." I swallowed. "I know that's what I said last week, but after that article on you and Eva, I was sure it was over. Absolutely sure. That's not your fault. It's not my fault. But I need . . ."

"Forty-eight hours before I ask you to recommit?" James tried for a smile.

"I —"

He closed his hand over the ring. "No, you're right. I'm moving too fast. I'll walk you back to your car, and when you're ready — to talk, to have dinner, anything — just call."

KING OF PENTACLES

Thursday morning, Rose watched the girl head off to work at the diner. She looked fine, perfectly groomed in that casual, understated way that made it seem as if she rolled out of bed with her hair brushed and makeup on. *Poised,* that was the best word to describe Olivia Taylor-Jones, the girl Rose preferred to call Eden, at least in the privacy of her own mind. Today, though, that poise was a facade, one she couldn't quite pull off, her head bowed, gait lagging, as if she'd really rather go back to bed and huddle under the sheets.

Yesterday, Rose had been at the door, seeing a client off, when Eden returned home mere hours after leaving for her first day of work with Gabriel. Eden had gone into her apartment and pulled the blind on her bedroom window, though it was still morning. That's when Rose knew the cards were right.

During her client reading, the damned King of Pentacles had kept coming up. That was Gabriel's card — lord of self-discipline, power, and security. Except it had been reversed, which emphasized the negative aspects of those traits. Authoritative, manipulative, and controlling. When Eden came home early, Rose knew what the card meant. Gabriel had screwed up. Again.

It was almost noon on Thursday when he finally phoned, ostensibly to check in on her. It was tempting to tell him she was fine and then say, "Well, I have to go now." See what he'd do. Teach him a lesson. Only she knew what he'd do — sign off and continue dwelling on the problem alone.

Rose had learned long ago that there was no "teaching" Gabriel anything. Part of that was stubbornness, but part of it was skittishness, too. Perhaps "skittish" wasn't the right word. It implied nervousness, like a colt snatching food from your hand before dancing off. Gabriel was more like a stray cat. He always had been, even before Seanna left.

When Seanna became pregnant, she'd refused Rose's help and ran from Cainsville. Rose didn't find her until Gabriel was a toddler. She'd been allowed to take him on weekends, leaving Seanna to her men.

Once, during that first year, Rose hadn't taken him back to Chicago. When Seanna came around — two days later — Rose informed her that she was keeping the boy until her niece got her act together. Seanna snatched Gabriel, and it had been two years before Rose saw him again. Rose herself *was* quite capable of learning lessons, and she'd learned that one, restricting her efforts to what she could do for Gabriel on their weekends together.

As for socializing him, it had been too late. By the time they first met, Gabriel was already that stray cat, cautiously allowing only the most modest degree of attention, ready to run if he got even the slightest hint that he wasn't wanted. That's what having a mother like Seanna did to a child. There was no undoing it. All Rose could do was understand and work around his limitations.

"What happened with Olivia?" she asked finally.

A pause. "You've spoken to her?"

"No, but I've seen her, and it's obvious she's upset about something. It's also obvious she didn't work a full shift for you yesterday, which suggests the problem originated there."

A long pause, requiring a prodding "Gabriel?" Then he told her what had happened, and as he did, she sank into the chair and sighed silently.

For such a brilliant man, he really *did* seem incapable of learning. He'd betrayed Eden's trust once, and she'd soundly smacked him down for it. He'd worked his way back from that, winning her trust again . . . only to commit nearly the same offense, multiplied by ten.

"You know, if you really didn't want to see her again, I'm sure a simple 'get lost' would have sufficed. Olivia doesn't strike me as a young woman who lingers where she's not wanted."

"I was not trying to get rid of her."

"Are you sure? Because you're doing an excellent job of it, though your technique seems overcomplicated."

"Working together on a dangerous case meant I'd naturally watch out for her. So there was no harm —"

"— in taking payment for it. Just as there was no harm in taking money from a reporter for setting up that interview a couple of weeks ago. As for the fact that she didn't *want* the interview, clearly she wasn't the best judge of that, and you were only acting in her best interests."

A faint noise that was probably meant to be a snort but sounded more like a growl.

"Did you really think you'd get away with it, Gabriel?"

"I miscalculated the timetable."

Rose closed her eyes and shook her head. She didn't have any problem with him taking money from James Morgan. Walshes had been taking advantage of gullibility and stupidity ever since they conned their fellow cavemen out of their spears. Highwaymen, pirates, swindlers, and card sharks . . . their family history was both colorful and dark. Rose might have the second sight, but it wasn't reliable enough to provide her with a steady income. For that, she needed a Walsh's true powers — the ability to lie, con, and cheat anyone out of anything.

"I should have told her," he said.

"Yes, you should have."

Silence, long enough for Rose to wonder if he'd hung up. Then, "I was trying to give the money back."

"What?"

"I called Morgan on Sunday to say that I was ending our agreement and returning his retainer. I wanted to wire it to him, but he wouldn't provide banking information. That's what I was waiting on, before I told Olivia."

When it came to money, Gabriel had . . . issues. Deep-rooted issues. Yet he'd planned to give back income he'd already earned? Rose sat there, stunned, before finding her voice.

"And you told Olivia this?" she asked.

"Of course not. He hadn't taken it back."

"But you told her you ended the agreement and you were *trying* to return his money?"

"No."

"Why not?"

"Because I have no proof."

Rose argued the point, but Gabriel wouldn't budge. He had delayed telling Eden until he had proof, and, having no proof, he would not mention it. Nor would he further discuss the matter with Rose, let alone accept advice on how to mend the rift. He would not even admit he wished to mend it.

"I have an appointment," he said when she pushed too hard. "I should go."

"All right," she said, stifling a sigh. "But if you need anything . . ."

"I do."

The response was so unexpected, she hesitated.

Gabriel continued, "Or I should say, Olivia needs something. A security system. There was a threat."

"What kind?"

"I'm not at liberty to explain. I can simply say that I take the threat seriously, and I was getting a system installed for her. I would like that done as soon as possible. Perhaps you could suggest you see the need for it."

"Tell her I saw danger in the cards?"

"Precisely. Tell her that you can get one installed without involving me in the matter."

"But *shouldn't* you be involved in the matter? If I tell her that you asked me to make sure she got this system, when you are no longer being *paid* to protect her —"

"No."

"It would show her that —"

"No. Leave me out of it. Please. I'd only like you to suggest she requires it and provide the appropriate contact information. I'm sorry to ask —"

"You never need to be sorry, Gabriel."

"Well, I am. But it's for Olivia, not me. I know you're fond of her."

She was. The question, though, was what *Gabriel* felt for Eden. Rose didn't need the sight to know her nephew had lost more than a mere client.

Damn it, Gabriel. You knew better, and yet you went ahead and messed this up anyway. Why?

She knew why. Partly because he couldn't help himself when it came to money, but partly, too, because it kept Eden firmly on the other side of the barrier. A Walsh never conned the people he cared about. Ergo, by conning Eden, Gabriel said, "I don't care," which would be perfectly fine . . . if it were true.

"Rose?"

"Yes."

"If you could do this for her . . ."

"I will," she said. *But not for her.*

CHAPTER TEN

It'd been a quiet two days. Too quiet. There were moments when I almost wished I'd spot a giant black dog or stumble over a bed of poppies, just to give my brain something else to obsess over. Then I'd realize what I was asking for and feel even worse, as if I'd wished for someone's death to distract me.

I hated letting Gabriel's betrayal bother me so much. I wanted to slough it off and bounce back. I had the last time. But now I hadn't just lost my lawyer. I'd lost a job I'd wanted. I'd lost a person I could confide in. And yes, damn it, I'd lost a friend, which was only made worse by knowing he hadn't been a friend at all, only a paid companion.

Maybe the friendship part bothered me more than it ought, but I . . . well, don't make friends easily. Or I make them too easily. My calendar used to overflow with lunches and coffees and get-togethers, my in-box brimming with messages from high school friends, college friends, friends I met through my volunteerism. Then my world went to hell, and I found myself alone. Sure, when I retrieved messages, there were friends checking up on me. How was I doing? Did I need anything? When I sent back reassuring notes, they went quiet. Not abandoning me, but presuming I had it under control. I was Olivia Taylor-Jones — I always had everything under control. As for the thought that I might need a shoulder to sob on? Olivia Taylor-Jones didn't sob. So they went their own way, presuming I'd be in touch when I was ready for lunches and coffees again. And that stung, just a little, but it wasn't their fault.

If there's a ten-point scale of friendship, I don't think I've had anyone rate above a six since high school. There are dozens of fours and fives, but that's where they stay and that's how I like it. So when things had gone so horribly wrong, there'd been no one there to say, "Call me, damn it. We're going for a drink, whether you like it or not." Even James had backed off after we'd argued.

Into that void came Gabriel. The furthest thing from a potential friend I could imagine. And yet, in the last month, closer to me than any actual friend had been in years.

He was the guy who came running when I called. Who stuck by me no matter how bad — or dangerous — things got. The guy who might not say, "We're going for a drink, damn it," but took me driving instead and bought me mochas to raise my spirits. Like a puppy starving for attention, I'd eagerly lapped it up.

James had been played by Gabriel, but it was nothing compared with the way I'd been played. And despite it all, I missed him. Missed him and hated myself for it.

After Wednesday morning, Gabriel had sent several "call me" texts. By evening, they'd escalated to complete messages, asking to talk, telling me he wanted to explain the situation, could we meet and discuss it? There were moments when I thought he sincerely wanted to do that. Then came a text on Friday — *need to talk re: Pamela's case* — and I understood exactly why he was so eager to smooth things over.

I called him back at lunch.

Before he could speak, I said, "You're worried that I'm going to convince Pamela to fire you. I wouldn't do that. I want her to have the best legal representation possible, and that's still you."

Silence, broken only by the hiss of a less-than-perfect connection. Then he said slowly, "I appreciate your support. And in return . . ."

"In return?"

"What would you like in return?"

Anger sizzled through me. "I'm not bargaining, Gabriel. I'm saying I won't jeopardize her defense out of spite. This is a clean break."

"Break?" he said.

"Yes. As we agreed, I'll pay your bill in full as soon as my trust fund comes due, and I won't interfere with you and Pamela, so there is no need to call again trying to mend this —"

"Is that what you want?"

"What?"

"In return for supporting me as Pamela's lawyer, you want me to promise not to contact you?"

"Did I say I'm not bargaining here, Gabriel?" I snapped. "You have got the case, and you'll get your bill paid. There are no strings attached. No expectations. I'm telling you so you don't need to call, pretending you want to smooth this over, because you're worried about losing Pamela's case. You won't."

"Meaning that if I attempt further contact, you *will* rescind your support?"

"Are you even listen— ?" I clipped the

word off so hard I nipped my tongue and cursed. "Fine. If that helps you understand it, let's go with that. It's a bargain. Or a threat. Whichever you prefer. Your bill will be paid, and I will not interfere with Pamela's case, if you don't contact me again. Now, I'm going to hang up —"

"Wait," he said. "I understand you wish to end our working relationship, but if you're serious about giving Pamela the best defense possible, I cannot agree to no contact. You were a critical part of the investigation that prompted her new appeal, and as such —"

"You'll need to speak to me."

"In a purely professional capacity. Related only to that case. While it will be months before an appeal is heard, I will need to talk to you. Soon. We can meet at the diner if that's simplest."

"The phone works perfectly well."

Silence. Then, "This would be easier in person, Olivia."

"At some point, yes, I'm sure that will be necessary. For now, though, the phone will do. Better yet, e-mail me any questions, and I'll get back to you by the end of the day."

Pause. "All right, then. In the meantime, Rose needs to speak to you."

"I really don't have time for —"

"She's had . . . I don't know exactly. A vision. A reading. Something that bothered her, and she'd like to speak to you about it."

I'm sure she would. And I'm sure it would go something like, "I've had a vision of great calamity befalling you if you don't pay my nephew's bill."

Gabriel continued before I could cut in. "I would like you to speak to her, Olivia. About her vision and about what happened earlier this week. The hound, the poppies, and Ciara Conway."

"What did you tell her?"

"Nothing, of course. You are — or were — my client, which means I certainly would not discuss the fact that you found a dead body. However, I'd like you to tell her. I think it would help."

"I haven't seen anything since Monday. Not even an omen."

"I'd still like you to speak to Rose, Olivia. She has important —"

"I should go. E-mail me those questions."

"One last thing . . ."

I exhaled through my teeth, breath hissing into a "Yes?"

"About Todd. Your father. I would like —" He cleared his throat. "In recognition of the fact that I may have overstepped my bounds accepting payment from James —"

"May?" The word came out between a snarl and a squeak.

"I would like to continue facilitating your reunion with Todd. As you know, that's not proving as easily done as it should be. Lydia is investigating, and I would like her to continue doing so. Without charge."

I hesitated. Damn it. He was right that I'd hit roadblocks trying to see Todd myself, but I really didn't like the idea of being indebted to Gabriel.

"Hold off," I said. "For now. I'll . . . give it some thought. We can talk later."

I hung up before he could argue. When I got home that evening, I called James and agreed to dinner the next night.

I know people often think being rich means a life of leisure. It can, if your goal is to do as little as possible, but most who have enough cash to quit working don't. My father definitely didn't, and I learned from his example. I like to be very busy — it's the only thing that truly clears my mind. So for the past couple of days, I'd come home from work and, well, worked.

What I wanted to do was dive back into the Larsen case. I'd meant what I said about wanting them to have the best possible chance at a solid appeal, and my personal issues wouldn't interfere with that. I'd be fine with investigating and turning over my work to Gabriel for free.

The problem was that he had the case files. I had only a partial copy. I'd spent a couple of hours compiling notes on the other victims — then researching them online — but I felt as if I was investigating with a patch over one eye, my field of vision and depth perception shot to hell. Was that really because I didn't have the full file? Or because I didn't have my detecting partner? I won't lie. I missed him. I've said that. Won't say it again.

Before they were caught, my parents had been known as the Valentine Killer. It meant that they'd killed couples . . . in Chicago, where Valentine's Day will forever be tainted by the memory of a bloody mob massacre. No one used that name anymore. From the time of their arrest, they'd become "the Larsens."

Their first alleged victims were Amanda Mays and her fiancé, Ken Perkins. Next came a married couple, Marty and Lisa Tyson. Then Stacey Pasolini and Eddie Hilton. Finally, Jan and Peter — the two we'd proven they hadn't killed.

Jan and Peter had fit the pattern, though. Twentysomething couple, Chicagoans, white, middle-class. Beyond that, the profile varied. Dating, married, engaged. Blond, brunette. College educated and not. Employed and not. All that suggested the victims hadn't been selected with any great care.

I compiled everything I could find on the six remaining victims. Minimal analysis for now. Then I moved to Ciara Conway. I read every scrap of Internet "news" on her disappearance — from snippets in the papers to blog posts to Facebook updates. I use the term "news" loosely, because there really wasn't anything, save wild conjecture. The obvious investigative path here would be to speak to Ciara's family and friends, but I couldn't listen to them hoping and praying she'd return when I knew she wouldn't. So I sat on my ass and surfed.

I dug up enough details to fill in a better picture of her life. It had been a good one, by any standards. She grew up in the suburb of Oak Park. Affluent but not outrageously so. They'd lived in the same house since she was born. Dad was an architect; mom was a biologist. Her older brother was studying for his PhD in medical research. Ciara herself was no slouch, winning an athletic scholarship to Northwestern, where she'd been studying neurobiology. There her grades had fluctuated, suggesting that's when the addiction issues kicked in.

I was still doing online searching when my cell rang. A Chicago number. It wasn't one I recognized, but my brain was preoccupied and I answered on autopilot.

"It's Lydia." A pause. "Gabriel's secretary."

As I struggled for a polite response, she continued, "I'm sorry for using my home number. I wasn't sure you'd answer otherwise. This isn't about Gabriel."

"Okay . . ."

"Richard Gallagher would like you to call him."

"Rich . . . ? Oh. Ricky."

I relaxed. Lydia seemed to do the same, laughing softly.

"Yes, Ricky. I'm not sure he likes being introduced that way, so I don't take the chance. I understand you met him last week."

"I did."

"Apparently you made an impression. He's called twice for your number. While I'm very good at telling clients no, that boy could charm the habit off a nun. I finally agreed to pass along a message to call him. Do you have his number?"

"I do."

"Can I tell him you'll call? He's coming into the office Monday, and as much as I am determined not to give out your number, he's even harder to resist in person."

I chuckled. "I can imagine. Yes, I'll call him."

"Thank you." A pause, then, "How are you, Olivia?"

I stiffened. "Fine."

"I don't know what happened between you and Gabriel, but . . ." She exhaled. "No, I'll mind my own business and only say that I'm glad he'll still be representing Pamela. He really is her best possible chance."

"I know."

"Have a good weekend, and if you ever need anything and would prefer not to contact Gabriel, you can call me at the office or here, at my personal number."

"Thank you."

It wasn't until I hung up that I realized what I'd done. Promised to call Ricky Gallagher. Shit.

The bigger *shit* was that I wanted to call him. Which was a problem when I was supposed to be attempting a reconciliation with my ex.

Ricky was Don Gallagher's son. Yes, Don "leader of the Satan's Saints" Gallagher. Ricky was taking his MBA part-time at the

University of Chicago. Which sounds as if he's trying to break out of the family business. He's not. He just figures an MBA might help him run it.

A biker MBA student. The "biker" part should have had me running. Except I liked Ricky, and it wasn't because he was charming and, yes, very easy on the eyes. There'd been something between us, that click that says, "This is someone I want to know better."

When Gabriel had noticed that spark, he'd stomped on it. Clearly a case of a good girl looking for a little bad in her life and exercising very poor judgment. At the time, part of me had wondered if he'd had a more personal reason. Now I knew he'd done it for James.

I had to call Ricky, meaning I had to tell him personally that I didn't want to go out with him. In other words, I had to lie.

SOFT SELL

Ricky finished proofing his term paper for management strategy. As he added his name to the first page, he paused before typing *Richard*. No one called him that. Outside of school, no one even called him Rick.

He had gone through a stage in high school where he'd insisted on Rick. It was the same stage where he'd cut his hair short, worn preppy clothes, garaged his bike, and bought a used car. When you grew up in a gang, *that* was teenaged rebellion. It lasted less than a school term before he realized that he was only rebelling for the sake of rebelling. He *liked* being Ricky Gallagher, with everything that entailed.

Someone rapped on the clubhouse office door.

"Come in."

It was Wallace, his father's sergeant at arms. Wallace did not go by Wally. A new recruit tried calling him that once. The result had required plastic surgery.

Wallace looked around for Don. Not long ago, that look would have been followed by, "Boss in?" But now it was just a visual check before he turned to Ricky.

"Got a lead on Tucker," Wallace said. "Bastard's holed up across the border in Wisconsin. Gonna go pay him a visit. You wanna ride along?"

"Sure. Give me five. Just finishing a term paper."

Wallace's gaze flicked to the laptop screen. No sign of derision crossed his face. This, too, meant Ricky was making headway. He'd grown up like the favorite nephew in a huge clan of uncles. Growing *out* of that role proved difficult. Going to college hadn't helped. His father fully approved, but to the gang it was a sign that maybe their boy was a little too intellectual, too mainstream . . . too soft. Dropping out wouldn't earn their respect, though. No more than insisting on being called Rick. He would earn his place, and he would do it as Ricky Gallagher, MBA.

After Wallace left, Ricky's cell phone rang. Call display showed a number he didn't recognize. He hesitated before answering.

"It's Olivia," a contralto voice said. "Olivia Jones. Lydia said you were trying to get in touch with me."

"I was."

The tightness in her voice told him this wasn't a call she'd wanted to make. She might have flirted with him at the clubhouse, but after that business at Desiree Barbosa's apartment, she'd clearly decided he was not someone she cared to know better. Damn Gabriel.

He made small talk for a few minutes, but her voice stayed tight, wary, and finally there was nothing more he could do but take his shot, on the very slim chance he was mistaken.

"Are you free for dinner tonight?"

"No, I'm sorry. I —"

"Tomorrow night? The night after that?"

A sudden laugh, as if in spite of herself.

"Yep, I am persistent," he said. "And flexible. Name the time. Name the place. French cuisine next Saturday night or a hot dog stand for lunch tomorrow."

"I can't."

"Sure you can. Where are you right now? I'll bring a picnic."

She laughed again. A good sign.

"See? It's easier to say yes." He shifted the phone to his other hand. "Go out with me, Olivia. Just once. I'm sorry about what happened with Desiree. If I'd had any idea that

Gabriel didn't warn you what he planned
—"

"That's not it."

"No?"

"I'm having dinner tonight with my, um, former fiancé."

"James Morgan?"

"Uh, yes."

She seemed surprised he knew her ex's name. He didn't tell her that he'd come home after their first meeting and looked up everything he could find on Olivia Taylor-Jones. Prep work. Like being interested in a business and learning everything you could before initiating a takeover. Which was an analogy no woman would appreciate, and he'd never make it. But he wanted to get to know her better, and when Ricky went after something, he used every tool at his disposal. He'd learned that from Gabriel, a lesson taught by example from the moment Gabriel decided he wanted to be the Saints' lawyer.

As for James Morgan, he hadn't needed to research the man. Ricky was an MBA student who took his studies seriously. He knew exactly who Morgan was, and while he was damned sure he wouldn't want to compete with him corporately, he suspected he had a decent shot here.

"So you're having dinner with James tonight. Have lunch with me tomorrow."

"I can't. Dinner with James means —"

"You're testing the waters for a reunion. Great. But as long as he's still your *former* fiancé, you're free to see me. Comparison shop."

A sputtered laugh.

"One date, Olivia."

"I really can't. I'm sorry."

He smiled in spite of the refusal. The honest regret in her voice told him he wasn't out of the running yet. She just needed a softer sell.

"A drink, then," he said. "Not a date."

"I don't think —"

"I'll settle for coffee."

"You *really* don't give up."

"Nope. I just downgrade the offer until I get buy-in. Have coffee with me. Absolutely no strings attached. I won't even angle for a date." When she hesitated, he smiled. "Coffee it is, then. Sunday afternoon —"

"I'm working." A pause. "Can we make it Monday or Tuesday? Anytime before three?"

"Tuesday's my heavy school day, so let's go for Monday."

CHAPTER ELEVEN

When I returned to my apartment after my Saturday shift, TC wasn't there. Usually, he was in the towel-lined cardboard box I'd assigned him as a bed. The only time he hadn't been was when I'd found him hiding under my bed, and I suspected someone had broken in.

I searched the apartment, which took about three minutes. Then I searched again. I even pulled out the can of cat treats. Yes, I'd bought him treats. Give it another month and I'd be collecting his shed whiskers and claws like a proud momma preserving her baby's first haircut and lost teeth.

I shook the treats. I called his name — well, his acronym. Then I conducted a calm and measured search of the apartment. Oh hell, who am I kidding? I tore about, checking every cat-sized space frantically, certain he'd suffered some horrible ailment that prevented him from answering my calls, even for fake-tuna treats.

There were a very limited number of places he could hide in those few hundred square feet, and I checked them all three times. I even looked in the fridge and stove. Hey, I'd been distracted lately; he could have hopped in while I wasn't paying attention.

Once I was sure he wasn't in the apartment, I hurried out to the front stoop, where Grace was on troll duty.

"Have you seen my cat?" I asked.

"You mean that stray that you insist isn't actually yours but you keep feeding —"

"He's not in my apartment."

"Did you leave the window open?"

"No." I'd kept my windows locked since I'd discovered Ciara Conway's body.

"Well, I haven't been in there, and I'm the only one with a key." She peered up at me. "Didn't I see you carting trash down to the bin this morning?"

"Right." I'd taken two bags because I'd forgotten last week.

"Then he snuck out while you were doing that."

"Maybe. If you see him —"

"Don't ask me to put him in your room. Still got the claw marks from the last time I touched the damned beast. Stray cats are like two-timing men. He got tired of you and took off. He doesn't find anyone new? He'll come slinking back. By then, if you're smart, you'll have decided you're better without him."

I headed down the steps, scouring the yard for signs of TC. Behind me, Grace snorted and muttered. I checked my watch. I was meeting James in ninety minutes, but . . .

I crossed the street to Rose's house. When she answered the door, she looked down at me like I was a five-year-old caught ringing the bell, about to dash away. I tried not to quail under that stare. Rose may be in her late fifties, but she's a brown belt in karate, a few inches taller than me, and as sturdy as an oak.

"Miss Olivia."

"Hey, um, Gabriel said you wanted to speak to me."

"I did. But you keep sneaking out your back door."

"I didn't sneak —"

Her look stopped the excuse in my throat.

"Okay," I said. "I snuck. Gabriel and I have . . . parted ways, and I figured you were checking to be sure he's getting his due. I wasn't in the mood for that conversation. I *will* pay his bill."

"I know you will. What I wanted to discuss has nothing to do with Gabriel. Come in, and I'll make tea."

"I can't. I have a . . . an engagement."

"A date with James Morgan." When I looked surprised, she said, "I have the sight, remember?"

"Or Gabriel told you James hired him to get me back."

"Either way, a date with James seems —"

"I'd rather not discuss it."

"Because I'll tell you it's a terrible idea? That you *know* it's a terrible idea and that you're only doing it because you feel guilty?"

"Um, no. I —"

"The cards tell me that if you pursue this reconciliation, you will regret it."

"Uh-huh." I shook my head. "If you want to help me, use your cards to find my damned cat."

I expected her to shoot back some variation on what Grace had said, that I hadn't wanted TC in the first place. But she frowned. "He's gone?"

"He is. If you see him, please let me know. Otherwise, if you still want to talk, let's make an appointment."

"Tomorrow morning," she said. "Nine A.M."

"Okay."

"Meaning you have absolutely no desire to reconcile with James Morgan."

"What?"

"You're going out with him tonight. You just agreed to meet me first thing tomorrow, meaning you do not intend to spend the night —"

"Goodbye, Rose," I said. "If I can't make it by nine, I'll call."

Rose was right — I had no intention of spending the night with James. I'll admit to a tiny temptation to reconsider, just to prove her wrong. It wasn't that I didn't want to sleep with him. I like sex. Hell, I *really* like sex. After three weeks, James probably expected me to suggest room service for dinner. Except he'd see that as reconciliation, which meant I couldn't. Not yet.

I didn't make any long-term decisions during that dinner date, but the awkwardness dissipated. While the old feelings didn't reignite, I could sense them there, waiting to kindle as we talked. When I said I had to head home right after dinner, he didn't argue, just walked me to my car and kissed me good night. It was a nice kiss. A long one, enough for me to feel *that* particular spark, but I didn't pursue it. We promised to talk later, and parted.

It was past midnight by the time I got home. My building was silent, which was nothing new. I'd been there almost a month, and I hadn't caught more than glimpses of my neighbors. Grace had sworn my apartment was the only vacancy, but by this point I suspected half the building was empty.

I stumbled into my apartment, bolted the door, and shed my shoes and dress as I walked. I collapsed into bed in my bra and panties.

As exhausted as I was, I didn't fall right to sleep. I'd had an espresso to keep me awake on the hour's drive home. So I hit the mattress and fell into twilight sleep, surfing between consciousness and slumber until I lost track of time and place. When I woke touching hair, I thought I was still with James, that I'd spent the night after all. I pushed my fingers into his hair and touched —

Cold skin. Ice-cold skin.

I jerked awake, flailing, the hair entwined in my fingers, and I scrambled away, the hair falling free. It hit my bare leg, and I stifled a yelp as I looked down to see —

My hair. Lying on the bed.

There was a confused, nightmare moment where my hands flew to my head . . . which was, of course, covered in hair. I leaned forward, my hands on the bed, eyes shut while I heaved breath. As the oxygen overload hit, I truly woke up, and I sat there, eyes still closed, shuddering, trying to throw off the nightmare. Finally, I straightened, opened my eyes, and —

I saw hair. Not mine this time. Dark, short hair, almost hidden under the tangled sheets. There was clearly no one else in bed with me. The dark hair peeked out, covering a lump barely bigger than —

The cat.

I yanked away the sheet, certain I'd see my poor cat. Someone had killed him and put him here, in bed —

Something rolled from the covers.

I saw skin and a nose and a mouth and —

Black pits where eyes should be.

The neck. Cut clean through. Ragged, bloodless skin and —

The head of Ciara Conway. In my bed.

As I backed away, I touched hair again. I let out a shriek before stuffing my fist in my mouth. A blond wig lay where I'd flung it. I looked at the head and then at the wig, and I tumbled out of bed, kicking free of the twisted covers, hitting the floor hard and then sprinting out the bedroom door.

Phone. I need my —

I spotted my purse on the floor. I grabbed

it and yanked the clasp, contents spilling out, clinking and clicking over the hardwood floor. I snatched up my phone and hit the speed-dial number without realizing whom I'd called until I saw the name flash on the screen. *Gabriel.* I hit the End button. Then I stared at the phone.

Who should I call?

Seriously? You're asking who to call when there's a severed head in your bed?

I hit 9. Then 1. Then I stopped.

I needed to take a photo. Ciara Conway's head was in my bed, and this time I was getting proof.

My fingers shook and my gorge rose, but I went back to the bed, took the picture, and then I e-mailed it to myself and —

My phone vibrated. The sudden movement made me let go. As the phone hit the floor, I saw Gabriel's name pop up on the screen. Shit. I grabbed for it and —

Something hit the side of my skull. Pain exploded. Everything went dark.

CHAPTER TWELVE

My eyes fluttered open, then closed again, the effort too much, the light too painful. My hand clenched something soft and cool. Sheets. A pillow under my head. I was lying in bed. I opened my eyes. Blue. I saw pale robin's-egg blue. Then eyes; light irises ringed dark, gorgeous eyes framed with inky lashes and . . .

"Olivia."

The deep timbre was almost a rumble. I knew that voice. I knew those eyes. My brain sputtered, neurons firing, pain threatening to snuff out thought. Then . . .

Gabriel.

I was in bed. Looking up at Gabriel. My head pounding like I'd downed a fifth of tequila.

I shot up so fast my head and stomach lurched, and I retched. My hands flew to my mouth, my eyes clenched shut. I smelled plastic and felt something cool bump my cheek and opened my eyes to see my bed-room garbage pail shoved under my chin.

I shook my head and backed up as my stomach settled. As I swallowed, I looked around. I *was* in bed. Gabriel *was* there. But he was standing beside me, fully dressed, and —

And I was *not* fully dressed. I grabbed the sheet to cover up, then froze as I saw the bedding. A memory flashed, and my brain finally clicked on, reminding me of what I'd seen —

I scrambled up, knocking into Gabriel as I flew out of bed. I whirled and stood there, breath coming fast, stomach clenching as my gaze swept over the twisted sheets.

"Olivia?"

"There's . . . there's a . . ."

I looked around. No wig. No head. I grabbed the sheets and pulled them straight. Nothing. I ran to the other side of the bed. Nothing on the floor.

"Phone," I said. "I took a picture. I need —"

I stopped, staring at Gabriel, my brain still sputtering as it jammed puzzle pieces into place.

"I . . . I didn't mean to call you," I said.

It was, quite possibly, the stupidest thing

to be worrying about. But that's what came out.

"I hit speed dial, and I wasn't . . . I wasn't thinking. I'm sorry. I . . ." I blinked and it was like moving through a room stuffed with cotton, everything soft and blurry and unfocused and thick.

"Sit down," he said.

"I . . . There was a . . ." I spun around. "My phone. I took a picture this time. I need —"

"Olivia? Sit."

When I didn't move, he propelled me down onto the edge of the bed. Pain shot through my skull. I winced. My fingers rose to touch the side of my head, but Gabriel caught them.

"Yes, you've got a goose egg, possibly a concussion." He crouched in front of me. "Do you know what day it is?"

"Sat — No, Sunday. June third."

"And your name?"

"Well, that one's tougher, since I apparently have two. I'll go with Olivia Taylor-Jones for today."

He lifted two fingers. "How many — ?"

I swatted his hand away. "I'm fine." I paused. "You didn't need to come out."

"After you called me at one thirty in the morning, hung up, and wouldn't answer when I phoned back?"

That wasn't really an excuse for driving an hour to check on me. I could have been drunk-calling. Or dialed wrong and then couldn't face talking to him. If he *had* been convinced it was urgent, his aunt lived across the road and could have checked on me.

"I was already out," he said, reading my thoughts.

He looked as if he'd just gotten out of bed. His shirt was misbuttoned. His hair looked finger-combed, already falling forward in a cowlick, his cheeks dark enough that I was sure he hadn't shaved since Friday. Like hell he'd been "out." Not looking like that. Unless the bed had been "out" . . . as in "not his own."

"You should have just called Rose," I said.

"She doesn't keep a phone in her room." He straightened. "I'm here now, Olivia, so let's not argue about why. Tell me what happened."

"What hap— ? Oh God." I jumped up too fast, and my stomach lurched. I doubled over, one hand to my head, the other to my mouth. He took me by the shoulders and tried to get me to sit down, but I shook my head. Even that movement made my stomach wobble.

"Olivia? Sit. You've taken a serious blow to the head. Tell me what happened so I can get you to the hospital."

"No, I don't need — I'm just — It's all muddled, and I'm having trouble —"

"— focusing. Which is why you need a doctor."

"My phone. Did he take — Or she — I didn't see —"

Gabriel had my phone. I didn't notice where it had come from. I really *was* having trouble staying focused, my brain sharpening only to slide off into jumbled thoughts.

When I looked up, Gabriel was flipping through the photos on my phone, and I considered snatching it back. Not that there was anything private on it, but you don't go through someone else's phone any more than you'd hunt through her purse for breath mints. Yet my head hurt too much to work up any righteous indignation. Besides, he wouldn't have any interest in uncovering anything personal. He'd go straight to what he wanted: the photos.

"They've been erased," he said.

"What? No. There are the ones I took of the hound and —"

"They've all been erased." He continued tapping the screen, gaze fixed on it.

"Wait. I e-mailed it to myself —"

"Yes, I see." He stopped. Froze, actually, staring down at the tiny screen. I'd say he paled, but with his fair skin it wasn't easy to tell.

"That's Ciara Conway's . . ." he began.

"Head. In my bed. Which I discovered when I was half asleep and —" I took a deep breath. "It was her head. With a blond wig. I don't think that's in the photo. I threw it off over . . ." I pointed. "Over there. It's gone. Along with the head."

My foggy brain slid away and —

And I was still dressed in only my bra and panties.

Well, at least it's a nice *set of bra and panties.*

Yep, these were the thoughts going through my brain as I looked at a photo of a decapitated head on my bed.

I blinked hard and squeezed the bridge of my nose.

"You need to see someone," he said. "You might have —"

"— a wee bit of shock at waking to find a head beside me. Not a concussion or brain damage." *I hope.* "Where was I? Right. I sent the photo, and then I got hit. I didn't see my attacker. I presume he — or she — was in here the whole time. Am I supposed to do something? I mean, obviously, yes. I should have been on the phone to the police, not my ex-lawyer . . ."

"There's no evidence. The police would have presumed you had a nightmare and fell out of bed."

"Until I showed them the photos."

"Even then . . ." He didn't say more, but I knew what he meant. Even with this photo of a weirdly bloodless, almost waxen, eyeless head, lying on my sheets, they'd have thought someone had played an elaborate prank on me. Or worse, that I was playing one on them. I *was* Eden Larsen, child of serial killers.

"So now what?" I said.

"Now you get that security system. This is obviously a very serious threat —"

"I mean what do I do about Ciara Conway?"

A flicker of annoyance, as if I'd interrupted him with something meaningless, like "Umm, I'm not wearing pants." We didn't have proof that Ciara Conway was dead, and it wasn't like he gave a damn about her. The important thing was . . .

What *was* the important thing? Making sure I was safe? Why? Because he sure as hell didn't give a damn about that, either, not unless someone was paying him to, and —

My hand shot to my head, and I winced as fresh pain stabbed through it.

Gabriel moved closer, bending down. "Olivia . . ."

"Okay. So someone killed Ciara Conway and is leaving body parts, dressed like me, as a warning. Locking my doors isn't going to solve the problem."

"Which is why you need a security system."

Not what I meant. But what did I mean? *I have to get to the bottom of this, and I need your help.*

Fresh pain stabbed through my head, bringing a wave of nausea.

If Gabriel wants to help me find a security system, wonderful. Let that be the extent of his involvement. He'll be happy with that. He's sure as hell not going to suggest —

"We should look into this," he said.

I ran to the bathroom and heaved into the toilet. One would think my reaction was all the answer he needed, but when I finished puking, he was standing there, calmly holding a towel. He handed it to me and then waited to make sure I was done vomiting before saying, "If you won't see a doctor tonight, you need to do so tomorrow."

I shook my head and washed up.

"I've been investigating Ciara Conway," he said.

"Okay." I tossed the dirty towel in the hamper and brushed past him. "Give me what you have, and I'll add it to what I know. I'll get the security system installed. In the meantime, if you don't mind, I'm going to put on some clothing."

"Thank you."

I glowered at him. "If it offended you, you could have just asked."

"You were distraught, and I didn't want —"

I walked into my bedroom and slapped the door shut, cutting him off.

CHAPTER THIRTEEN

When I came out, dressed, Gabriel picked up the conversation as if I'd never left. "It seems clear that this is related to Pamela's case."

"Really? Or just clear enough that you could tack it onto her bill?"

Ice seeped into his eyes. "I am not looking for payment, Olivia."

"Sure you are. A job means billing. Double-billing if you're lucky."

And there it was. Out on the table. His chance to defend himself.

Silence. That's what I got. Sixty seconds of stone-cold silence.

"Go," I said, turning away. "I appreciate you coming out here and —"

"I'm not leaving. You were attacked tonight, in case you've forgotten, and those locks on your door didn't keep out a killer. Or me."

I wasn't sure which was worse. At least

the killer had left.

"I'll sleep on your sofa bed."

"*Hell,* no," I said.

"Don't be dramatic, Olivia. I've done it before."

He stood there, strumming with impatience. I glanced at the sofa, and I remembered looking out from my bedroom a week ago, seeing him there after Will Evans accused him of murdering his mother. I'd watched him sleeping, and I'd thought how young he looked, how vulnerable, and how, God help me, I trusted him. *I'd trusted him.*

"I don't care if you've done it before," I said. "You are never doing it again."

Something flickered across his face, too fast to leave any impression before his eyes iced over. "All right. Then you'll spend the remainder of the night at Rose's."

"I'm not —"

"Anderson is dead."

"What?"

"Michael Anderson, Chandler's bodyguard."

"I know who you mean," I said. "What happened?"

"He was in the hospital, under guard, and when they delivered his dinner, he was dead. He apparently overdosed on morphine, but somehow I don't think he's bright enough to have jiggered the dispensing system."

"Definitely not. Murder, then."

"Except, according to the guard, no one went in his room. I spent the evening at the hospital looking into it. I got home too late to notify you."

"I thought you said you were *out* when I called. That's why you came over."

He waved off the distinction. "The point is that, between his death and the attack on you, it's clear you shouldn't be alone tonight. Moreover, you need someone to wake you every hour in case you have a concussion. Either you go to Rose's or I stay here."

"I'll go to Rose's."

I went back into my room and grabbed my phone. When I came out, he was gathering the spilled contents of my purse and stuffing them back in.

"Ready?" Gabriel asked, straightening.

I nodded.

"It still works," he said when I checked the lock on leaving. "I picked it. It's a cheap dead bolt that only keeps out casual thieves. We'll find you something better tomorrow and arrange for that security system."

I nodded again. We headed out. In the stairwell, he said, "I could use your help investigating Ms. Conway and any links to

Pamela's case."

"You think there *are* links? Because of the . . . postmortem mutilation?"

He glanced over sharply, and I knew he hadn't considered that. As I said it, though, he did, those busy wheels churning.

"The mutilations have nothing in common," he said. "But yes, I'll give it more thought. In the meantime, there is a connection of some sort. There must be. Someone is warning you, and that someone has tracked you to Cainsville. I cannot imagine that is unrelated to your parents' case. I cannot imagine you've made *murderous* enemies otherwise."

He emphasized *murderous* as if clarifying that he'd certainly believed me capable of making enemies, just not to that degree. I could have taken offense at that, but in Gabriel's world, if you aren't making the occasional enemy, you aren't trying hard enough.

"Back to the point. I could use your help," he said. "I would pay you, of course."

"I can't —"

"It would be research based. There would be no need for you to come into the office. Interaction would be minimal."

"I'm not arguing about the work, Gabriel. I'm already investigating. I'll turn over anything you can use."

We reached the ground floor.

"I'll need to contact you, then," he said. "I realize we have an agreement —"

"You're helping investigate a threat against me. I don't expect you to pass messages through a third party. Call, e-mail, text, whatever."

He nodded and held the door for me.

Gabriel had a key to Rose's house. He opened the door as he rang the bell in warning, then ushered me in and called, "It's Gabriel," up the stairs. He went to speak to Rose, leaving me in the front hall. I heard a whispered conversation, but it was brief and I didn't catch what he said. Then he came down and escorted me up, past a closed door that I presumed led to Rose's room, to an open door at the end. Inside was a spare bedroom.

"What did you tell her?" I asked.

"Only that you'd taken a blow to the head and shouldn't be left alone. I would like to explain more, if you're all right with that."

"I am."

"How much can I tell her?"

"Everything."

He nodded. "Thank you."

"And thank you," I said. "For tonight."

He murmured something and backed out of the room.

My pounding head made it impossible to fall into anything resembling actual sleep. I should have taken a painkiller, but if Gabriel had caught me, he'd have insisted on that middle-of-the-night emergency room visit. So now I was lying in bed, picking up snatches of Rose and Gabriel talking downstairs. After a while, it was as if a door had been opened, and I could hear them clearly.

"— so *when* are you going to tell her?" Rose was saying.

"I don't intend to."

"Because you can't prove it? That's a ridiculous excuse and you know it. Tell her and —"

"No. This is better."

"Better? How is this *better,* Gabriel?"

"I should go."

"You're not driving back to Chicago tonight."

"I need —"

"It's four A.M. You'll take the other spare room."

"I have to work —"

"It's Sunday."

"I've been busy with Pamela Larsen's case and falling behind on paperwork."

Rose sighed. "Fine. Go. I'll speak to Olivia in the morning."

"But not about —"

"Of course not."

"She needs to see a doctor. She'll argue —"

"I will look after Olivia for you, Gabriel."

"That's not —"

"Yes. I know. Now go."

CHAPTER FOURTEEN

After I finally did fall asleep, Rose came in every hour to ask the date and my name and how many fingers she was holding up. I played along without complaint. This wasn't how she'd planned to spend her Saturday night, so I was grateful . . . until 7 A.M., when I recited a dozen Sherlock Holmes quotes, back-to-back, and she declared I was clearly not suffering from a concussion and we could both get some sleep. Which would have been lovely, if my phone hadn't buzzed an hour later.

Gabriel.

"Where's your cat?" he said in greeting.

"Wha— ?"

"TC. Your cat." He bit the words off, impatient. "I just realized I didn't see him at the apartment last night. Where is he?"

"Gone. The accommodations were not to his liking, apparently."

"When?"

I rubbed my face as I sat up. "Yesterday after my shift. He must have slipped out while I was taking the trash —"

"Did you see him leave?"

"No. I'm just presuming . . ." I realized where this was going. "You think someone took him?"

I must have sounded alarmed, because his voice smoothed out. "No, that'd be too much trouble. It seems unlikely, though, to be a coincidence that he vanished hours before this happened. I suspect someone was testing the door and let him out. I'm sure he's fine. However, that would mean the intruder was at your apartment earlier that day. I'll question Grace about that. Nothing escapes her notice, and she's usually forthcoming with me."

After talking to Gabriel, I tried to sneak home, but Rose caught me. We had breakfast. We talked. There wasn't much to discuss. Yes, poppies were a death omen. Yes, the most common hound folklore was the Black Shuck. Yes, finding a dead girl in my car — and her head in my bed — was terrible . . . and clearly an omen of the "you need a security system now" variety. She promised to read the cards and see what came up.

In the meantime, I had to see the doctor. Rose had set up the appointment. Dr. Webster made house calls, even on Sundays. She checked me out and decided I might have suffered a mild concussion but nothing requiring more than rest and painkillers.

After Dr. Webster left, I covered every inch of my apartment, looking for clues. There wasn't so much as a stray hair from the wig. All I had were the photos, blurry from my hands trembling.

I made notes from my memories of the night before. Then I looked up Ciara Conway on the Internet again and found nothing new. She was still missing, and would remain so until her killer decided to part with her corpse, which he or she seemed in no hurry to do.

That was the hardest part of all this to wrap my head around. Her killer was storing her body, toting it about, using it to scare me, as if it was a plastic tarantula. There was something truly chilling about that. What complete lack of respect for life would allow someone to cart a body around like a prop, would allow someone to say, "You know, I can't sneak the *whole* body into her apartment, so let's just chop off the head"? And what did it have to do with me?

Someone had murdered a young woman,

one who resembled me in a very superficial "height, weight, body shape" way, and had a family connection to the tiny town where I now lived. As much as I wanted to believe my assailant had just . . . oh, I don't know, found Ciara dead from an overdose and decided to use her body, the chances of that were infinitesimal. She'd been selected. Killed to warn me not to dig deeper into my parents' crimes or deeper into Chandler's crimes or . . . Oh, hell, I didn't even know what the warning meant. I supposed I'd find out, whether I wanted to or not.

The next morning, I was in a coffee shop, sitting across from a guy getting nonstop stares from the businesswomen, as much for his biker-patch leather jacket as for his rugged good looks. The first time we'd met, I thought Ricky reminded me of a blond young Marlon Brando without the angst. I'd even speculated there'd be a cleft chin when he shaved his stubble. There was. There was also a dimple, showing up when I walked in and he fixed me with a grin that made me stutter-step . . . and nearly bolt back out the door.

Lydia had said that Ricky was even harder to resist in person. She was right. Fortunately, that grin, as dazzling as it was, said only, *I'm glad to see you.*

"Hey." He stood as I walked over. No hug. No squeeze on the arm. Just standing, as if that's what you should do when a woman walked to your table, though you didn't go so far as to pull out her chair, suggesting she couldn't handle it herself. I swear every woman around us sighed a little.

I just smiled and said, "Hey," back.

"What can I get you?" he asked.

"I can —"

"My invitation. My treat. And if you feel guilty about that, you can get it next time." Another flash of a grin. "Which means there has to be a next time. See? I have it all worked out."

"A mocha, please."

He was back in a minute, setting it down and swinging into his chair with, "So you have to work at three, right?"

"I do."

"Plenty of time, but I'll watch the clock to be sure. What are you up to these days?"

I told him, and he earned the distinction of being the first person who didn't react like I was punishing myself by working in the diner. He understood. His life might seem radically different from mine, but it wasn't really. We'd both been raised in a

134

successful family business, where it was expected that if you wanted a job, that's where you'd work, and if you wanted to just focus on your studies, that was fine, too. We were also both only children raised by a devoted father — as healthy a father–child relationship as you could ask for, whether Daddy owned a landmark department store or ran a notorious biker gang. Ricky's mother wasn't in the picture. He didn't go into detail, but it seemed she was a doctor in Philadelphia. He saw her now and then, and they had a good relationship, but she was more like a distant aunt.

The only thing that kept it from being a perfect coffee break was Ricky's phone, which kept buzzing. He hit Ignore every time, but it was almost nonstop, and he finally apologized.

"I'd turn the damned thing off, but my dad needs to be able to get hold of me at any time. Club rules. If he calls, I have to take it. Otherwise, it's just birthday wishes."

"Birthday? You mean it's your . . . ? Shit. I'm sorry. I would never have suggested today —"

"Um, pretty sure I suggested it. I don't have plans until tonight, and then it's just take-Ricky-to-dinner-and-embarrass-the-hell-out-of-him."

"Do they make the servers sing 'Happy Birthday'?"

"Probably. Most of the guys have known me since I was in diapers. To some of them I still am."

"And how old *are* you?"

A pause.

"Ah, so you aren't telling?"

"No, just . . . I'm probably not as old as you think I am." When I didn't reply right away, he said, "Uh-huh. That's what I thought."

"Sorry, I'm . . . just surprised. It doesn't matter, of course."

"Because you aren't planning to go out with me. But if you were considering it, that would be fine, because two years is not a big age gap. And yes, I know how old you are."

"So you just turned twenty-three?"

"That's not two years."

"Well, I'll be twenty-five this fall, so if you're twenty-two today, that means you're actually two and a half years younger —"

"You stop counting half years at three. That's the rule."

"Is it?"

"It is. It'd be fine if I was two years *older* than you, right?" He knew the answer to that, considering I'd been engaged to a thirty-year-old. "In fact, one could argue that this would be all the more reason to go out with me, while you decide whether you want to recommit to James. What better way to explore your options than to date a guy who has nothing in common with your former fiancé."

"James has an MBA."

"And I don't yet. See? Totally different. So I *would* suggest we go out if I hadn't already promised not to bring it up. Now I'll drop the subject by asking you the topic of your master's thesis. Also? It's one."

"I wasn't checking —"

"Yes, you were. Subtly. I promised not to push for a date, and when I veered off track, you checked your watch, seeing if it was late enough to bolt, should I continue. I promise no more pushing, prodding, or even hinting. We have thirty minutes. I've already set the alarm on my phone."

At 1:30, Ricky and I were walking into the parking lot behind the coffee shop. His motorcycle was right up front, squeezed into a spot too small for a car. I was parked at the far side.

Beside the lot was a playground. Empty swings twisted forlornly in the brisk wind. Brightly colored ride-on animals rocked, riderless. There was an air of desolation here, of abandonment. Kids in this neighborhood had better things to do than ride smiling purple hippos. I thought of the park in Cainsville, clearly beloved for generations, and I felt a pang of sympathy for this one, and for the kids here. Silly, I know, but I thought, *I'm glad I live in a place where kids still want to ride purple hippos.*

We were saying our goodbyes when Ricky trailed off midsentence, staring at something over my shoulder. I turned and saw . . .

The hound stood in the park, watching us. Ricky was staring, but not in the way one might look at a big dog on the loose, with concern or trepidation. He looked as I imagine I must have when I saw it the second time — in confusion and disbelief, certain my eyes were playing tricks on me.

"Wow, that's a big dog," I managed finally.

"Dog . . ." His voice was oddly hollow, distant, and uncertain. "Yeah. That's . . . a dog?" His voice rose as if in question. A hard blink, followed by a short laugh. "Obviously." He rubbed his thumbs over his eyes and pinched the bridge of his nose. "Clearly I've had too much caffeine."

"It is a very *big* dog." Standing there. Staring. At Ricky.

"An unaccompanied and unrestrained big

dog. I should walk you to your car."

"It's right over there. I'll be —"

"No. I'll walk you to your car."

His voice had taken on a tone I'd heard in the clubhouse with one of the girls and, later, with Gabriel. A reminder that while he was charming and easygoing, he was still a gang leader's son. He followed it with a softer "This way?" and I nodded.

As we crossed the lot, he kept his gaze on the beast, and I could say that was just common sense — don't turn your back on a threat — but Ricky still looked confused, as if trying to figure out what the hell he was seeing. I wanted to ask: *Exactly how big is it? Does it have reddish-brown eyes?* What really made my stomach twist, though, was the way the beast stared at him.

"So, Wednesday?"

Ricky's voice startled me, and I looked around to realize we were at my car already. I glanced back over my shoulder.

"It's gone." His tone was light, jaunty even. "So, Wednesday, do you want to come here again or someplace else?"

"Wednesday? I —"

"Or Thursday. Maybe a walk this time. It's supposed to be perfect weather."

"You really are persistent."

"Damned straight. But I haven't heard a

no. Wednesday, then? Same time? Coffee or a walk?"

I paused beside the Jetta. "I can't. I'm sending the wrong message —"

"The message that you enjoy my company? That you had a hurricane blast through your life a month ago and you're still sorting through the pieces and you could use the occasional coffee break with a normal — well, relatively normal — guy? The rules don't change unless you change them, Olivia. The only message you're sending says I don't bore you to tears."

"Okay. Wednesday. I'll figure out where and text you. Is that okay?"

"Texting me anytime, for any reason, is absolutely okay." He opened my car door and I climbed in.

CHAPTER FIFTEEN

Ten minutes into my shift, I got a call from Rose. She left a message asking me to phone back, which I would have, on my break, if her damned nephew hadn't called three times after that.

After the first time, I'd left my phone in the back — and on vibrate — but it didn't help.

"Liv . . ." Larry said, bringing my phone out.

"I know. I'm sorry. It's just —"

"Gabriel. I saw. Don't apologize. He's your lawyer. Take the call in back, and I'll cover for you."

When Gabriel answered, I said, "Have I ever told you about Margie? The server I replaced, in part because she kept getting calls during her shift?"

"I didn't realize you were at work, as I'm no longer in possession of your schedule."

"And my voice mail wasn't working?"

"I wasn't about to trust that you wouldn't simply delete the message unheard."

"Texting?"

"The buttons do not accommodate larger-than-average fingers." Which meant, apparently, that I'd hallucinated all the times we'd communicated by text message. He continued, "I was unable to arrange for a security system installation today. It will be done tomorrow. In the meantime, you will stay with Rose."

"I will?"

"I'll tell her you'll be by after your shift. As will I. We need to discuss a matter relating to both your mother and Ciara Conway. Nothing urgent, but I have a busy week."

"I don't get off until eleven."

"I realize that. I'll meet you at Rose's. I presume you'll want to gather an overnight bag from your apartment, and I'll ask you to wait until I arrive to do so."

"Okay."

Silence. Then, "I'm serious about this, Olivia. I don't want you going to your apartment alone at night —"

"Didn't I say okay?"

"Too quickly, suggesting you're humoring me and have no intention of actually doing as I asked."

"Mmm, if that was your idea of *asking,*

I'd hate to see how you give orders. I inconvenienced you and Rose last night because I didn't get that security system. Insisting on staying in my apartment tonight without one would be careless and immature."

"All right. I'll see you at eleven."

"Gabriel's running late," Rose said as she let me inside. "He had a call from a client."

"I'll phone him," I said. "We don't need to do this —"

"He'll be here in fifteen minutes. It'd be a bigger inconvenience if he has to turn back."

True. A light was on in Rose's parlor, so I headed in there.

"What's wrong?" she said as I took a seat.

"Nothing."

"Do you remember what I said about the key to being a good psychic?"

"Being willing to make guesses and be proven wrong? Yes, you're wrong this time. Sorry."

"I meant observation and interpretation." She sat down across from me. "You have never walked into this room and not taken advantage of the opportunity to poke about. Something happened today."

I hesitated, then said, "I saw the hound again."

"Where?"

"In Chicago. The thing is, I wasn't alone, and the person I was with saw it, too. But . . . something about it bothered him, more than it should have, and I'm worried. For him."

"Was it James?"

"No. Ricky Gallagher. He's —"

"Don's son. Does Gabriel know you're seeing him?"

"I'm not. It was just coffee."

"I see. While I've never met the Gallaghers, I do follow them in the news, since they are my nephew's primary clients. I've seen photos of young Mr. Gallagher."

"I'm trying to reconcile with James."

"By going to coffee with an attractive young man? I would offer to do a reading to see where that will lead, but I don't need the cards for that."

I glowered at her. "Can I talk about the hound? Or are you testing out a career move? Advice to the lovelorn?"

"That wouldn't help you at all. Love doesn't enter into this choice. Lust versus duty. The perfect conundrum for a student of Victorian literature, though, one would hope, less of a struggle for a modern young woman. May I suggest that James Morgan is a wonderful catch . . . for someone else, and that if you persist —"

"So Ricky and I saw this hound."

She sighed but waved for me to continue.

"It seemed to . . . confuse him," I said.

Now she leaned forward. "As if he recognized it?"

"No. And yes. It was like . . . Hell, I don't even know how to explain it. Like when you catch a scent and it's familiar but you can't place it. When I see an omen, I know it means something. What do other people sense? They must trigger something, or there wouldn't be superstitions about them. Ricky *did* sense something about the hound, which paid no attention to me. It was staring at *him.*"

"And the other times?"

"It looked at me. My concern is that it *is* a fetch. A harbinger of death."

"Ricky's death."

"Right. You see it: you die. For me, it's a warning, because I can read omens. But if Ricky saw it . . ." I exhaled. "I texted him, tonight, pretending I just wanted to say I enjoyed our coffee, but I let out a huge sigh of relief when he texted back. Which feels crazy."

For ten seconds, Rose didn't respond.

"So . . ." I finally prodded.

"I'm deciding how to tell you this without

giving you ammunition to think you really are imagining things, which is what you'd prefer."

"I don't want —"

"I've told you the sight runs in the Walsh family. When I started having prophetic dreams, my relatives all told me how lucky I was, how they wished it was them. They were lying. They were thanking the gods it *wasn't* them. People think it would be wonderful to see into the future. Just as, I'm sure, they think it would be wonderful to see warnings and signs. But it's not. For every ounce it makes your life easier, it makes it a pound harder. You have a gift you cannot share without being locked in a mental institution. Which is one reason I'd urge you to mend fences with Gabriel. He accepts what you can do, and you will need someone like that in your life. Besides me."

"I —"

"My sales pitch for my nephew ends there. Back to the point. While this is clearly no ordinary beast, others can see it. So it exists and seems supernatural in nature. But is it a fetch? Patrick's correct — that's the most common meaning of a large black dog. And yet . . ."

"What else is there?"

"You keep calling it a hound. But it

doesn't resemble a typical American hound dog, and that term's not used in traditional folklore. It's called a Black Shuck in eastern England, *barghest* or *gytrash* in northern England, *moddey dhoo* in Manx, Church Grim throughout England . . . but never hound."

"Conan Doyle."

"Ah. *Hound of the Baskervilles.* Of course." She nodded, but I sat there, thinking, until I finally said, "I thought of it as a hound before Patrick said Black Shuck. But I also thought of *The Hound of the Baskervilles* before he said Black Shuck. 'There stood a foul thing, a great, black beast, shaped like a hound, yet larger than any hound that ever mortal eye has rested upon.' So . . . I don't know. I guess I was thinking Baskervilles."

"Either way, I'm not convinced it's a fetch," Rose said. "I think you're correct that others can sometimes sense the supernatural. Seeing it affected Ricky Gallagher, and he wasn't sure why. I'll look into folklore on black dogs and hounds. In the meantime, I believe I heard Gabriel drive up. If you'll let him in, I'll make tea."

Rose brought tea and then left us alone. We talked about Pamela first. Gabriel had officially launched an appeal. Chandler still wouldn't speak to him. There were no leads in Anderson's murder, probably because the police didn't consider it a murder at all. For them it was simple: a man loses half his foot, is facing life in prison, and ODs on morphine.

Next up on the agenda? Ciara Conway. Gabriel couldn't do more than quietly investigate, much as I had been doing. If he wanted to ask the police about it in an official capacity, he needed an excuse . . . like having his office check into it on behalf of the elders of Cainsville.

"I could use your help obtaining theirs," he said. "The town elders aren't blind to my . . . unconventional business practices."

"They'll suspect you aren't offering out of the goodness of your heart."

"I can ask for compensation, but that reduces the chance they'll agree."

"I'll speak to them," I said. "But how do I explain *my* interest?"

"By working for me."

I stiffened.

"It's a way to gain work experience while helping your new town. I'm going to formalize your job offer. I know we'd planned to discuss that on your first shift. I'll get it in writing for you now. Hours, pay, and such. I need a day or two to put something together."

"I don't want —"

"I would like to make the offer, which you may then refuse." He stood. "Tell Rose I said goodbye. I'll see myself out."

I followed him out to the hall.

"Gabriel?" I said as he opened the front door.

He turned, a stray slip of moonlight illuminating a sliver of his face, blue eyes glowing almost preternaturally in the darkness. "Yes?"

I opened my mouth to say thank you, then stopped.

"Good night," I said finally.

A dip of his head, the moonlight evaporating, his expression lost in the darkness. "Good night, Olivia."

He backed out and pulled the door shut behind him.

CHAPTER SIXTEEN

At lunch, I called Ricky to discuss where to meet tomorrow. It took my entire break. What can I say? He's a good conversationalist.

When my phone rang early that afternoon, I saw who was calling and . . . and I hesitated. Then I felt bad about hesitating and called James back.

"I'll make it quick," he said. "I had lunch with the deputy mayor, and he asked me to join his table at a fund-raiser tonight. It's a plus one, of course, which means I'm in the market for a guest and really hoping you'll say yes, because if my mother finds out I have tickets, you know who I'll have to take. I'd rather have you on my arm."

"So that's why I'm invited? Ornamental value?"

"Of course. Why else?"

I laughed.

"Come with me, Liv. It's not a public

statement. I'll deflect any questions about our relationship. It'll be as painless as possible, and I'll take you for ice cream afterward."

"Scooter's?"

"Technically, that's frozen custard. But yes, Scooter's. So you'll come?"

"For the custard."

In the past month, I'd learned a lot about myself. I might even have matured, though I'm not sure I'd go that far. What I had not done, though, was develop any greater appreciation for charity dinners.

It was worse now, with everyone knowing who I really was. I got cold shoulders. I got sidelong looks. I got stares. I saw matrons in evening gowns whip out their phones, and they may have just been messaging a friend, but I suspect some were tweeting *OMG, I can't believe who's here!* complete with photos.

But I'd come for James, so I pushed all that aside, and I chatted and I smiled and I laughed. I flirted and I charmed. I even danced.

I was slow dancing with James as he was whispering in my ear. I listened to his voice and smiled at his sardonic commentary, and I felt the familiar warmth of him, inhaled the familiar smell of him, and I remembered why I'd wanted to spend the rest of my life with this man. I was happy.

The feel of his body against mine reminded me of something else I'd missed in the last month and made me wonder why the hell I hadn't dragged him to the nearest hotel last week. And then . . .

I sensed something. James led me off the floor afterward, but I didn't hear a word he said because I was busy listening and looking and inhaling, trying to find what had caught my attention.

I've always been particularly receptive to sensory input. Step into a busy room like this and my brain used to reel, looking for signs in every sight, sound, and smell. Now I know what's happening, and that initial blast fades quickly once my brain realizes no omens need to be interpreted.

Except now something did need interpretation, and I couldn't figure out what it was. It was only a prickle that said, "Pay attention."

"Liv?"

I snapped out of it and forced a smile. "Hmm?"

"I lost you for a moment there."

"Just . . ." I made a face. "The usual."

"All a little too much?" James said, because whatever had happened, he was still the guy who'd known me best.

"We can go outside," he said. "It's a nice night for a walk, and I won't argue with the chance to escape."

"That sounds —"

There. A smell. Wafting . . .

I inhaled. Nothing.

Damn it.

I forced my focus back to James. "I would love a walk. Just give me five minutes in the ladies' room."

He pecked my cheek and said he'd be over by the bar, talking to a city councilor who'd been trying to get his attention. Everyone wanted James's attention. And I had it, even now, as I walked away — feeling his gaze on me, looking back to see his smile, making me feel as it always had, that mix of surprise and wonder at my good luck.

As I walked toward the back hall, I cleared my mind and followed my gut. Sounds easy. Not for me. I prefer to lead with my brain — with mindfulness, intention, and purpose. Now I followed my gut down one corridor and then another until . . .

I caught the distant baying of hounds. I heard hounds, and I smelled horses, and I froze in my tracks as my gut and my brain and my heart screamed, "Get the hell out of here! Now!"

I stood there, fighting the urge to run, just run, before I saw . . .

Saw what?

Saw *it*. That's all I knew, that the hounds and horses meant *it* was coming and I had to flee as fast as my legs would take me or —

"Olivia?"

I looked up. A man stood at the hall junction. He was maybe sixty. Fit and trim and handsome in a way that had me taking a second look, even though he was more than twice my age. My gaze went to his face, and it stayed there, as if transfixed.

I knew him. That's what it was. I recognized him. He was . . .

I had no idea who he was. Just a good-looking older guy in a tux, smiling at me and holding two champagne glasses. But he'd said my name, and something about his face was so familiar . . .

An associate or acquaintance of my dad? That was my guess. He had that look — an older man smiling at me fondly, as if I was the daughter of a friend.

"It's good to see you again," he said as I walked over. "I was beginning to wonder if you'd come."

Someone who knew James, then. I smiled. "James talked me into it. Did you enjoy the dinner? The cheesecake was amazing. I stole most of his."

A smile. Indulgent and a little patronizing, as if to say, *Small talk? I thought you were better than that.*

"I mean, I wasn't sure if you'd follow me." He lifted the champagne glasses. "But I came prepared."

I felt as if I was standing on a boat, the floor bobbing beneath me, the very walls shimmering, not quite solid. Yet my brain clung to logic.

"Have we met?" I asked. "I'm sorry if I don't recognize —"

"You wouldn't. You were very young. I knew your parents, and I'm so pleased to see how well you've grown. They must be very proud."

"My father passed last year, but my mother is well, thank you."

His eyes glittered as he shook his head. Then he held out the champagne. "Let's enjoy this while we speak. It's quite good."

I stared at the flute, amber liquid popping within.

Don't touch it. Don't drink it. Dear God, whatever you do, do not drink that.

I shook my head. "Thank you, but no. I —"

"Why not?"

I started at his rudeness. "I've had enough, and —"

"That's not it at all." His dark eyes bore into mine. "You sense something."

I opened my mouth with a quick denial, but the words wouldn't come.

He's not some family friend cornering you in a back hall. You know that. So stop pretending. Look at him. What do you see?

I see a man. I hear hounds. I smell horses. I feel —

I feel terror and wonder, and I want to run and I don't want to run. I want to stay here and I want to drink the champagne and I want to say . . .

I want to say what?

"Something is telling you not to take what I offer. Taste the foods. Sip the wine. Never leave. Follow me forever. Is that it, Olivia?"

"I don't know what —"

"You're raw and untrained. It's all there, but your young mind doesn't quite know what to make of it. It misfires. It misidentifies. Your lore is correct, yet you are not applying it where it ought to be applied." He lifted a glass. "It's safe to accept my food and my drink. Just don't ask me for salt." A soft laugh, as if sharing a private joke.

Again I opened my mouth to protest. But what good would that do? I knew this

156

wasn't just a man.

Not a man? *Not human?* What the hell else could he be?

"I don't understand," I said finally.

He gave me a sympathetic look. "I know. But you're a smart girl, and you'll figure it out as soon as you admit there's something to be figured out. About me. About Cainsville."

"What about Cainsville?"

"What about it indeed. Just an ordinary little town. So very ordinary."

"If you have something to tell me —"

"That's more like it. But I can't. Not my place. I'm just" — he pursed his lips, as if choosing his words — "making contact. I have what you want, Olivia. I could get metaphysical and say that I have what your soul wants, what your heart and mind want, what you need to be happy and complete in your very uncommon life. And I do. But for now, I'll settle for saying that I have the answers you want. Particularly the ones you want most."

"Which are those?"

"You know, just as you know, deep down, that when I say I knew your parents, I'm not talking about Arthur Jones and Lena Taylor."

He reached into his pocket and tossed

something to me. I caught it. A tooth. No, more like a tusk. A couple of inches long, carved with strange markings and capped with copper.

"A boar's tusk," he explained. "Or the tip of one. Keep it with you. For protection."

"From what? The hounds?" I said before I could stop myself.

He smiled that indulgent you-are-such-a-child smile. "You don't need protection from the hounds, Olivia. They mean you no harm. Nor do I. Others, however . . ." He stepped toward me and lowered his voice. "Beware and be wary, *bychan.*"

Then he set the champagne flutes on the floor and started to walk away.

"Who are you?" I called after him.

He glanced back. "Who? Is that really your question?"

"*What* are you?"

I met his gaze, and I heard the hounds baying, and I heard horses snorting and hooves pounding, and I smelled sweat and musk and wet earth.

"Cŵn Annwn," I said, whispering the unfamiliar words as if they'd been pulled from me. I expected him to frown, to ask, "What?" But he only chuckled, and then he walked away.

CHAPTER SEVENTEEN

After the man left, I wandered back toward the party, dazed, as if I'd taken another blow to the head, the world fuzzy and off-kilter, the ground unsteady.

"Liv?"

I saw James hurrying toward me and snapped out of it.

"Hey," I said. "Sorry. Restroom break took a little longer than I thought."

He laughed. "It happens. I was starting —" He glanced at my hand. "What's that?"

I lifted the boar's tusk. "I found it on the floor. At first I thought it was a pendant, but . . ."

"It looks like a tusk."

I tried not to seem relieved. I hadn't dared identify it, half expecting James wouldn't see what I did.

"Weird, huh?" I said. "Definitely not a pendant. Maybe some kind of good luck charm." I put my arm through his and slid the tusk into my bag.

"I was starting to wonder if I'd missed a signal and was supposed to meet you here." He grinned my way. "I know you like back halls."

"I do."

His hand slid down to my rear. I tensed. I didn't mean to, but I was still off balance and struggling to find my way back. He pulled his hand away fast.

"Sorry," I said. "Just . . . distracted."

I tried to remember the dance, what it had felt like, my body against his. Then I pushed my mind back to the last charity event we'd attended, when we'd slipped into a back corridor and had sex against the wall, delicious sex. I felt the first licks of heat, but it wasn't enough. Yet I didn't want to say no, either. I could feel that slow ache. I just couldn't shake thoughts of the man I'd just met.

"Let's do something this weekend," I said. "I mean, if you're not busy —"

"I'm not." His arm tightened around me as he moved closer while we walked.

"I'm done working at three on Friday and I'm off Saturday. I can try to wrangle Sunday, too. We could go away. If you want."

He grinned. "I do."

"Good."

"And right now, I think it's late enough to say our goodbyes and spend some quality time eating frozen custard. If you still want."

I smiled. "I do."

It takes a special talent to enjoy frozen custard mere minutes after being confronted by an otherworldly being who hands you a boar's tusk. I have that talent. It's called acting. I'd been a dedicated member of every school troupe from elementary through college. I'm a natural, which may be what comes from growing up feeling as if I was playing a role in someone else's drama. For James's sake, I had to eat custard and smile and laugh, because that's what he expected and he hadn't done anything to deserve less. So I enjoyed our post-date treat and then zoomed home, punched in the code to my new security system, and took out my phone to . . .

To what?

Call Gabriel. That was the first thing I thought of. I had to call Gabriel and tell him . . .

It wasn't a question of "tell him what?" I *could* tell him about this. He'd listen. He'd believe. He'd strategize. The question was, *Why him?* I'd reflex-dialed Gabriel Saturday night, but that had at least been for professional advice — how to handle finding a part of a corpse in my bed. This was personal.

At work the next day, the Clarks came by midmorning, as they usually did, for tea and scones. I waited until my break. Then I spoke to them about Ciara Conway. I wanted to talk about her. I could move through my days, act like nothing was wrong, but I was keenly aware that a young woman was dead and her family didn't know it. If there was anything I could do to ease my conscience, I would do it.

"I feel like I should do something," I said after we talked. "I'm not exactly a detective, but Gabriel taught me how to do some basic legwork. Maybe I can prod the police into conducting a better investigation."

"You did very well with your mother's case," Ida said. "You may have found your calling: Olivia Jones, private eye." She looked at her husband. "We don't have one of those in Cainsville, do we?"

"I don't believe we do."

"And we sorely need one," Patrick said from across the diner, his gaze not rising from his laptop screen. "To chase down overdue parking tickets and find lost puppies. Speaking of which . . ." He glanced at me. "Did I hear that your cat has disappeared?"

I nodded. "I've hated to mention it, with Ms. Conway missing."

Ida frowned. "The black stray?"

"Yes. I was taking out trash that morning. He must have slipped out. But if you do spot him, I'd like to know he's okay."

"Of course."

Ida looked around at several of the other elders, dotting tables throughout the diner, as if knowing they'd be listening in. They all glanced over and said no, they hadn't seen TC, but they'd keep an eye out.

"I'll speak to Grace," Ida said. "She might know more than she's saying."

"Good luck with that," Patrick called over, still typing.

"Well," I said. "If I can't find my own cat, I suspect I'm not exactly ready to be a PI. Nor am I ready to investigate Ms. Conway's disappearance. But I'd like to try."

"With Gabriel's help, of course," Walter said.

"Er . . . yes, Gabriel has offered to provide —"

"You'll be working with him, won't you?" Ida pressed. "I haven't seen him around. I hope that doesn't mean anything. We were so happy to see you two together."

"We were never . . . together," I said. "It's a business partnership —"

"Yes, yes. I mean working together. You still are, aren't you?"

"Liv?" Patrick raised his mug. "Break's over, isn't it?"

While he was giving me a way out of this conversation, I could tell this was important to the elders. They might tease about me becoming a PI, but they knew I needed Gabriel for this.

"Yes," I said. "I'll be working with Gabriel."

Ida smiled. "Excellent. Then we'll provide you with anything we can."

As I walked up behind Patrick, he lifted his empty coffee cup as if he recognized the sound of my steps.

I retrieved the pot. "I'm officially still on lunch," I said as I filled his mug.

"Which means you'll get a much better tip today. In fact, I think I'll double it."

"Awesome. What's double of nothing?"

He smiled. "My favor is much more valuable than any monetary reward."

"Good, because I need to draw on that favor." I sat down across from him. "You know some Welsh, right?"

"I do." He closed his laptop. "Let's step outside."

"This will only take a second. One word. Maybe two — I can't tell with Welsh. It sounds like *coon anoon.*"

Patrick went still, and the hairs on my neck rose. I turned to see a half-dozen pairs of old eyes fixed on me. They all glanced away quickly, as if I'd imagined it, but was I imagining, too, that the noise level had dropped to nothing? As if no one wanted to miss what I said next? Which would be a little creepy, if that wasn't par for the course in Cainsville. For a bunch of folks past retirement age, they all have very good hearing — or top-notch hearing aids.

"You know the word?" I asked Patrick.

"Say it again?"

I did. He frowned, his eyes going to the side as if accessing memories. That frown didn't go away, which told me he wasn't finding what he was looking for.

"It sounds vaguely familiar, but no."

"You know Welsh, Patrick?" said a voice beside us.

I looked over to see Ida looming as much as a woman barely over five feet tall can loom.

"Liv said you know Welsh?" she said.

"I'm a man of many talents."

"But you don't know what Cŵn Annwn means?" I said.

"I do not."

I had one hand in my pocket, gripping the boar's tusk. I'd considered showing it to him, but as I thought that, I could feel the weight of his gaze on me.

Not here. Not here.

He wasn't communicating a telepathic message or anything so New Agey. It was his body language communicating the message that he wasn't comfortable talking in front of the old folks.

Sometimes in Cainsville, I felt like the new girl at school, with the popular clique calling dibs on my friendship. That's great, but I was really more intrigued by the weird guy in the corner. While the weird guy is quite willing to mock the clique, he knows his boundaries, too, and poaching the new girl too openly is beyond those limits. I'd talk to Patrick later.

CHAPTER EIGHTEEN

I'd taken Ricky up on his offer of a walk instead of coffee. We met at Burnham Park and walked along the lakefront. We were talking about his classes when my phone rang. I hit Ignore. Gabriel called again, then broke down and texted, telling me to check my e-mail. I apologized to Ricky before I did, but two calls and a text could mean it was urgent news about Pamela.

I read Gabriel's e-mail, cursed, and shoved the phone into my pocket.

"Pamela?"

"No, a job offer."

After I told him about it, he said, "Knowing Gabriel and his wallet, he's offering you about the same as you'd make waiting tables, right?"

"Not exactly. Triple my hourly rate at the diner."

"Shit. That's not bad. And this is a job you actually want." He lifted a hand against my protest. "I saw you work with him, Liv, and I've heard you talk about it. The only problem? Gabriel. You guys are on the outs. No, he didn't tell me. Your name came up, though, and I've known Gabriel long enough to tell something was wrong."

"I'd rather not explain, because he's your lawyer, too. I'll only say that what happened wasn't a reflection on his legal ability."

"Obviously, or you'd have kicked his ass off Pamela's case." A group of joggers veered around us, Ricky having made no move to get out of their way. "You feel as if, by accepting his offer, he wins. But if you *don't* take it, you lose."

"No, I —"

"Yes, if you don't take it, you lose. You want this job. But it means going back to someone who hurt you."

"He didn't —"

"Can you look at it another way? Who's the one taking the real chance here? The professional and financial risk? Gabriel. A guy who does not take risks. Not personal. Not professional. Certainly not financial."

"Exactly. So what's his endgame?"

Ricky paused at the water's edge, hands shoved into his pockets as he looked out over the lake. "Ah, that's the problem. You don't trust the offer is genuine."

"He just made a generous job offer, for a research and investigative position . . . to a debutante waitress with a degree in Victorian lit. He's up to something."

"Gabriel's always up to something. But if you're looking for an ulterior motive here, I don't see it. Again, flip it around. He's busy. He's turning down clients, well-paying clients. Now that he has Pamela's case, it'll only get worse. One thing they teach you in business school? As soon as you can afford it, delegate, as much as possible. Gabriel should have done that years ago, but he has very particular needs. You know what happened in Desiree's apartment. Did you ever threaten to tell anyone?"

"Of course not."

"Exactly. One more reason you are that very rare person Gabriel could hire to fix his staffing problem. There's no endgame, Olivia. I'd stake my bike on it."

I chuckled. "You might not want to do that. I've never ridden one, but I'm a fast learner and I bet it's got more horsepower than my Jetta."

"Probably. But my offer for a ride is still open."

"Uh-huh. I know all about that deal. And as attractive as it is . . ."

He laughed, then sobered. "All joking

aside, yeah, the rule is: only girlfriends and wives on the back of the bike. But I'm not going to be a dick about it. If you want a ride — on the bike, nothing else — ask. Just promise never to tell anyone. Back to the wager, though, I totally would bet my bike, because I know, while it's never a sure thing to bet against Gabriel's capacity for duplicity, in this case I think he's on the level." He turned toward me. "I'm not saying to forgive him. Just don't let your personal issues stop you from getting what you want professionally, or he's done double the damage. It's not an indentured servant contract. You lose nothing by giving it a shot. Think about it, okay?"

"I will."

CHAPTER NINETEEN

On my way home, I called Rose and asked to speak to her. She was free at seven, and at 6:55 I was walking through her door.

"Okay," I said as I pulled off my shoes. "I have a question that requires all your fortune-telling skills."

"Excellent." She ushered me into the parlor. "What is it?"

"Exactly how big an idiot am I if I agree to work for Gabriel?"

"I can tell you that without even checking the cards."

"Let me guess. It will be the best decision I could possibly make, and I'll never regret it."

"Oh, no, I'm sure you'll regret it. Many times. As I'm sure it's not the best decision you'll ever make. It will, however, rank near the top. He will make mistakes. So will you. There will be times when we'd best hope there are no firearms at hand. Ultimately, though, it is the first step on a life course that will make you happier and more satisfied than any other."

"Uh-huh. I'd rather go with the cards."

"Are you serious?" she said, sliding into her chair.

I slumped into mine and sighed. "As tempting as it is to ask for otherworldly reassurance, this is one mistake I need to make myself. I called him before I came over. I start work tomorrow. I may leave my gun at home. Just in case." I straightened. "That's settled. Now let's head straight to the real reason I'm here. You don't know Welsh, do you?"

"Welsh?"

"Yeah, it's a long shot, I know."

"Not so long. Walshes originally came from Wales —"

"— before moving to Ireland, where they got their name because it means Welshman. Well, the translation is 'foreigner,' but literally it means Welshman."

"Very good."

"About this question, though. I have a feeling it falls under the same very broad heading as omens, second sight, and fae."

"Really?" She shifted, interest piqued. "What is it?"

"Cŵn Annwn. Don't ask me to spell it.

From what I've learned of Welsh, you can probably count on it having no more than one vowel."

"I suspect you're right. I don't recognize the word, but I'll take a stab at the spelling and do some research." She waved at the floor-to-ceiling wall of old books behind her. "If it's in there, I'll find it. You're sure it's Welsh?"

"No, but it's a solid guess."

"Where did you hear it?"

I told her the whole story of my meeting with the man at the charity dinner. When I finished, she sat there, speechless.

"I'd drank half a glass of champagne," I said. "And taken no drugs that I'm aware of. Plus, he gave me this." I laid the boar's tusk on the table. "Which seems to prove I didn't temporarily fall down the rabbit hole, as much as it seemed like it."

"I don't doubt you, Olivia. I'm just . . . I've heard of such things. Meetings . . ." She trailed off. "You say you smelled horses?"

I nodded. "I smelled forest, too, and I heard pounding hooves and baying hounds. I asked him if that" — I pointed at the tusk — "would protect me from the hounds. He said I didn't need protection from them. He knew what I was talking about."

"Horses. Hounds. Cŵn Annwn." She fell quiet, thinking.

"There was something about salt, too. I wouldn't take the drink from him, and he said I was misapplying my folklore. That I only had to be worried if he offered me salt."

"That's a common motif in fae lore. Eat their food or drink their wine and you'll never be able to leave."

"That's it," I said. "He said taking a drink from him wouldn't trap me."

"Horses. Hounds. Forest. Salt." She inhaled sharply. "The Hunt."

She leapt up so fast she startled me. Moments later she had a book in her hand, flipping through it as she came back to her chair. She set it in front of me.

I looked down at an old painting of wild-haired hunters on wild-eyed steeds, accompanied by fearsome black hounds. And boars. And ravens.

The hair on my neck prickled.

The heading on the facing page? *Cŵn Annwn.* Literally, the hounds of the Otherworld. Better known as the Wild Hunt. They escorted the dead to the afterlife. According to the lore, if you heard the howling of the hounds, you would die.

"Um, not liking that part," I said, pointing.

"It's true, though. You will die. Someday. I can guarantee it."

I gave her a look.

"Well, you heard the hounds baying last night, and you're still alive, aren't you? Did it sound soft or loud?"

"Soft."

"They were close, then. That's the lore — the louder they are, the farther they are." She pulled out her chair and sat. "There are stories of the Wild Hunt from all across the British Isles and onto the Continent. Their appearance, their purpose, even their intentions — good, evil, indifferent — it all changes, depending on who you ask." She closed the book. "I'll compile what I can. I doubt we'll determine their true purpose, but it can't hurt."

"Their true . . . ? You actually think I saw . . . ?"

"My great-grandmother told me she saw them once, around here. She was a teenager, sneaking off to meet a boy, and she heard the hounds. She ran, but it was too late. They rode right past her, men on flaming black steeds, wearing cloaks with hoods that hid their faces save for glowing red eyes. One of the riders slowed and called out in a terrible voice, telling her to stay out of the woods on the eve of St. Martin. She ran home and immediately gave all her prized possessions to family and friends, as she prepared for her death. She lived to ninety-seven."

"Well, that part's comforting. I'm not so sure about the flaming steeds."

"I have a better account of her story written down here somewhere. I'd tell it to my babysitting charges when they wanted spooky tales. Seanna used to beg me for it. When Gabriel was born, everyone presumed she'd named him after the archangel. I knew better. There's another name for the Wild Hunt: Gabriel's Hounds."

"Kinda thinking she'd have been better off naming him after the angel."

"Oh, I don't know. Archangel or hound from hell . . . with Gabriel, it depends on the day."

"Not sure I see the angelic part."

She took the last cookie from the plate. "He offered you the job of your dreams, didn't he?"

"I don't think angels are supposed to grant wishes."

"They should. It would make them much more interesting." She polished off the cookie and wiped away the crumbs. "Now, to bed with you. Put this aside for now."

I took my keys from my pocket.

"Uh-uh," she said. "Upstairs."

"I have a security system now."

"Which will not help you against other-worldly beings. You'll stay here until I've consulted the cards tomorrow and taken a better look at that tusk. I believe I mentioned my house is warded." She looked at me. "You thought I was joking? I was not. You're safe here. Now off to bed. Gabriel expects you in the morning, and he'll be more hell-hound than angel if you're late."

CHAPTER TWENTY

As it turned out, I didn't need to get an early start the next morning. Gabriel called saying he had an urgent meeting and wouldn't be in the office until ten thirty.

I decided to head into the city early and pick up a coffee for James. I garnered a few looks in the coffee shop, but I ignored them, as I'd been ignoring the whispers and glances for weeks.

I also ignored the first text message from Ricky — a simple *You around?* check-in. Then he sent a second one: *Call me. ASAP. Kinda important.* As I waited for the elevator, I managed to shift the coffees to one hand and speed-dial with the other. Yes, Ricky was on speed dial already, but only because not many people were anymore and, well, yes, we did talk a few times a day.

"What's up?" I said when he answered. I could hear the sound of a lecturer in the background. "You're in class? How about I call back —"

"Hold on."

A whispered "Excuse me," then his footsteps tapping quickly down stairs, the lecturer's voice growing louder. The whoosh of a door. The lecturer's voice faded. Ricky's footfalls continued, taking him past a loud group of students in the hall.

"Have you seen the *Post* this morning?" he asked when it was quiet again.

"These days, I don't see the *Post* any morning I can avoid it." The *Trib* and the *Sun-Times* had begun losing interest in my story weeks ago. The *Post* had not.

"Yeah, I don't blame you. But you might want to grab a copy."

I swore. The elevator dinged.

"Where are you?" Ricky asked.

"James's office. Taking him coffee before —"

"Don't get on the elevator," he cut in.

"Um, too late," I said as the doors closed. "What's up?"

He said he was going to e-mail me something. It came through almost immediately, as the packed elevator made the slow climb to James's floor at the top. I opened the e-mail, checked the attachment, and . . .

My chest seized. "Shit."

"Yeah. I'm sorry. If I'd caught anyone taking that . . ." Ricky trailed off, threat unfinished. "I'm sorry."

I lowered my voice. "You're not the idiot who chose a favorite coffee haunt."

"I don't think that would have mattered. Eventually someone was going to . . . I'd say 'catch us,' but that implies we were sneaking around. Actually, it's better that it was your usual spot. Clearly we weren't hiding. That should help."

He sounded about as convinced as I felt. "I'll talk to my dad and explain it," he said.

"I'll handle James."

"Okay. Call me later?" he said.

"I will."

A pause. Then, "Will you?"

"Of course."

When I hung up, we were nearly at James's floor. Two other riders were staring at me. One looked away and whispered to her companion when I glanced over. I knew what she was talking about. A picture in the *Post.* With a caption, explaining that Pamela and Todd Larsen's daughter — former debutante and fiancée of James Morgan — had been spotted having coffee with the son of biker club Satan's Saints president Don Gallagher.

There was nothing incriminating in the photo. I was leaning back, casual and at ease, laughing. Ricky leaned forward, talking, his forearms on the table. It did not look like a romantic assignation. But it did look . . . intimate.

I quickly texted James to tell him I was coming and there was something we needed to talk about. The answer came back as I stepped off the elevator. *All right.* With those two words, I knew he'd seen the picture. I slowed, in case he was about to text back not to come to his office.

He didn't.

So I began the long walk. Down the corridor. Through the lounge — an open area where executives could hang out, chat, hold informal meetings. The minute I stepped into that open area, with executives and support staff milling about, I felt like I'd embarked on the walk of shame, that morning-after scurry from a one-night stand, ripped panty hose in your purse, makeup smeared, hair an unholy mess, cocktail dress and heels at 8 A.M. It didn't matter if I was perfectly dressed and groomed. It didn't matter if I'd only been "caught" having coffee with an attractive guy. It didn't matter if I wasn't engaged to James again, wasn't even in a committed relationship again. I still felt shame.

Because I wanted more than coffee with Ricky.

I made it to the desk of James's admin assistant, Karen. We'd always gotten along great. Today, I had only to look at her expression to know not to ask about her kids.

James opened his door as if he'd been waiting there. He ushered me in and told Karen to hold his calls.

"You've seen the *Post*," I said as he closed the door behind us.

"My mother sent it to me."

He walked behind his desk. Which left me to sit in front of it, like an errant employee. That rankled, but the lingering shame kept my annoyance from crystallizing into anger.

"I'm sorry," I said, still standing. "I just found out about it on the elevator or I wouldn't have shown up like this. I was coming by to say hi." I pointed at the coffee cups I'd set on his desk.

"Did he warn you?"

The way he said "he" rankled, too, harder now, anger sparking, but I pushed it down.

"It was just coffee," I said. "If it was anything else, I'd never have gone where I could be recognized." I finally took my seat. "These days, anywhere I go, I could be recognized. But I'm trying to forget that

I'm news. Trying to live my life as if I'm not. That's all I can do, James, or I lock myself away and hide. I can't do that."

"No one's asking you to."

"This kind of thing is going to happen. Next time it will be me and Gabriel."

"He's the lawyer representing your birth mother."

"Yes, but what if I have dinner with him? Or drinks? I can't restrict my social pool to women and guys over sixty. Hell, if the woman's cute, they'll probably make insinuations there, too. That's what the *Post* does. They're the ones who posted the shot of you and Eva."

"Eva is not a member of the Hells Angels."

"It's Satan's Saints, actually. A small, regional . . ." I caught his look. "It was just coffee."

"With a biker. When I'm preparing to run for senator. Do you have any idea how that looks?"

I hesitated. My gaze rose to his. "This is . . . This is about your *political* chances?"

"Granted, I'm not thrilled that you're having coffee with another man. But I know you aren't sleeping with him. You have better taste than that."

"Better *taste*?"

James continued. "The point is that you

183

need to be more circumspect."

"Okay, next time we'll have a beer in a dive bar twenty miles outside town. We'll wear disguises. That will make for a much less incriminating photo."

"Liv . . ."

Faint warning in his voice now, the tone that said I was being dramatic. Being childish. I'd always accepted the reprimand in that tone because I was keenly aware of our age difference. I'd led a sheltered life. I'd felt young. I no longer felt young.

I looked at him. "So me having coffee with a biker is a political issue, but me having serial killers for parents isn't?"

"You've proven they were innocent —"

"Of two murders. Out of eight. What happens if the courts decide that's not enough? Are you going to set the wedding for the week after the appeal, to be sure?"

His shoulders dropped. "Of course not, Liv. Yes, there were concerns when the news came out. They weren't my concerns, as you'll recall. I still wanted to get married once things cooled down. You've done nothing wrong. I can see beyond your background."

"*See beyond it?* How very big of you. Is that a campaign strategy? A man who believes in people. Believes in second chances."

I braced for the chiding tone again, but he shook his head.

"All right, maybe I am jealous of this biker. I read the comments online. Most have nothing to do with me or us. They're about you and him — how attractive he is, what a striking couple you make . . ."

"We're not a —"

"I know. I've blown this out of proportion. He's a client of Walsh's, and I presume you were discussing your issues with keeping Walsh on Pamela's case. But I'm going to ask you to stop meeting him."

I stared at him.

"Let's have dinner tonight," he said. "Are you working?"

I shook my head.

"Great. Dinner it is, then. We'll talk more then. For now, the only thing I want is for you to agree not to see him again."

I cleared my throat. "This isn't working."

"What?"

"This reconciliation. I wanted it to work. I really did. But it's not."

"Don't start that, Liv," he said. "Come to dinner and —"

"I can't. I'm stringing you along, waiting for it all to come rushing back, and it's not.

It's just not. I'm sorry."

I walked out.

CHAPTER TWENTY-ONE

Lydia was waiting for me at Gabriel's office, on her feet as soon as I came in, offering to take the linen blazer I'd worn. She's tall — about an inch above my five-eight — with the kind of wiry body and quick moves that suggest a lifetime of aerobics . . . or at least hard-core yoga.

Lydia has to be in her sixties. Her *late* sixties — past retirement age. Today she wore a stunning quartz Armani pantsuit that perfectly complemented her dark skin, with a price tag that suggested she worked more for excitement than income these days.

"I'm glad you're here, Olivia," she said. "That's what you go by, I presume?"

I must have flinched, because she shook her head, laughing softly. "I'm sorry. I guess that can be a loaded question for you. I meant do you go by Olivia, Liv . . . ? I've only ever heard Gabriel call you by your full name. I wasn't sure if that was your preference."

"Olivia's fine, but it's usually Liv. It's a name of many diminutives. The only one I hate is Olive."

She smiled. "That makes it easier. I'm always having to discreetly correct clients who call Gabriel Gabe."

"Ah, I heard he doesn't like that. So is he back?"

"Not yet. He's running late. He asked me to give you the grand tour."

I noticed a newspaper on Lydia's desk.

"There was something about me in the *Post* today," I said.

"The photo of you and Ricky? Yes, I know. Gabriel had me set up a Google alert so I can monitor news mentioning you. With his clientele, he needs to be on top of any whisper of trouble."

"Did he . . . see that?"

"Gabriel reads the *Tribune.* I buy the *Post* for him to browse if he has a trial being covered. With Pamela's appeal, I've been doing that, but he doesn't always have time to read it. I saw no reason to buy it for him today."

"Thanks. I know he wouldn't want his employee dating a client. It really was just coffee. Ricky and I aren't . . . involved."

"No?" Her brows lifted. "That's a waste."

I laughed, and she began the grand tour.

The office wasn't large, and I'd seen most of it before. There was the reception area, Gabriel's office, and the room where he met clients. He didn't bring them into his office, though there was no reason not to. His office was gorgeous, a Victorian library with gleaming wood and floor-to-ceiling bookcases. The meeting room, on the other hand, was modern and sterile. Completely devoid of personality. So, was Gabriel's personality expressed in his private office, off-limits to common clients? Hell if I knew.

As Gabriel had warned, there wasn't an office for me. For now he'd put me in his, at a table in the corner, with a chair wheeled in from the meeting room. Not what I expected. Nor what I particularly wanted.

After the tour, Lydia and I talked about Todd. She wanted to know if I'd like her to start trying to get me in to see him again. I said yes. The longer I waited, the more I wanted that visit, and if I was working for Gabriel, I could accept this as an employee benefit rather than a personal favor.

"It's not as easy as it should be, is it?" I said. "I know it can't be easy to walk into a maximum security prison and chat with a notorious serial killer, but . . ."

"You're his daughter. It should not be difficult at all. I couldn't even get an answer on *why* it was. The prison system can be a pain to work with, but this is odd. I kept hearing that a visit wasn't currently possible, and no one I speak to knows why. Unfortunately, they don't seem all that interested in finding out why, either."

"Could he be refusing to see me?"

"If so, they'd tell me. That's common enough."

"Could he be refusing but have asked them not to tell me?"

She shook her head. "No one there is going to do Todd Larsen any favors. It's a puzzle I haven't quite figured out, but I will."

"Thank you."

My first task was to read through Pamela's file, which Gabriel had updated after Chandler's arrest. The police were still investigating Chandler's case and not required to share what they'd learned yet.

"There isn't much new there," said a voice, echoing my thoughts as I read.

I looked up to see Gabriel filling the doorway, his shadow stretching nearly to the meeting room table. He looked exhausted. There were no bags under his eyes. No stubble on his face. His shirt and pants were as perfectly pressed. But there was a dullness to his eyes, stress lines around his mouth, a shaving nick on his jaw.

He looked around. "Why are you in here?"

"Bigger table for spreading papers. I'm profiling Chandler and the other six victims, as we'd discussed. I'll tidy up when I'm done, and if you need the room, just kick me out."

A faint tightening of his lips told me my excuse didn't cut it. He'd set me up in his office and I should damn well be where he put me.

He walked away. I took that as a dismissal until he called, "Olivia?" with an edge of irritation, and I realized he'd meant for me to follow him.

In his office, he told me what he'd learned about Ciara's disappearance. He'd spoken to the detective in charge. They'd confirmed my suspicions that she'd been a drug user. Addicted to meth for almost a year, according to her parents, which only made the police more certain she was alive, just lying low.

I'd compiled a list of people we could speak to — friends and teachers mostly. He promised we'd start those interviews next week. It wasn't as if Ciara was going anywhere, unfortunately.

My first day of work was exactly what I expected. While our conversation felt stiff and awkward and distant, I'd expected this, too. What I hadn't expected was how it would feel working under Gabriel. Under the guy who'd betrayed me. Twice.

I was collecting files before leaving for the day when Gabriel stopped me.

"Did I give you too much?" he asked.

"No. This is fine."

His pale eyes bored into mine, trying to read me. I resisted the urge to look away.

"It's been a long day," I said.

"Because it's almost seven. You could have left sooner."

"I didn't mean that. Just . . . If I look tired, it's not the work. I was up late talking to Rose." I forced a half smile. "Blame her."

He kept studying me. "It will get easier."

I don't want it to get easier. I don't want this to get comfortable, me working for you. I want things the way they were.

"It's fine," I said. "I'll see you Tuesday."

After that, I dragged my ass home. I was almost there when I got the icing on my day's cake. A text from Ricky. *Not calling, huh?* Quickly followed by *Understand things might have changed. Not trying to give you grief.*

I cursed and resisted the urge to text back while driving. I pulled into the parking lot behind my building and sent: *Give me 5.*

I hadn't wanted to call Ricky too soon, because that seemed disrespectful to James: "Hey, I just dumped my ex. So how about dinner?" Then I got distracted by my disappointing day with Gabriel. But I should have sent a quick note that all was fine.

I walked into my apartment. The first thing I did was look for TC. Every damned time, I looked.

Then I called Ricky.

"I'm sorry," I said when he answered.

"Nothing to be sorry for. We're okay to talk, then?"

"Yes. It's . . . sorted. With James. We're fine."

As I said that, I realized it could be interpreted as "James and I are fine," not "You and I are fine." I didn't clarify. I wasn't ready to tell Ricky about the breakup. He couldn't exactly say, "Great news!" and I didn't need more awkward today.

"You around?" he said. "I was hoping to catch you before you left the city."

I paused, considering lying and driving back to the city. I could feel the tug of his voice, like someone trying to pull me out of deep water, and I wanted to grab hold, but

I couldn't manage it.

"No, I'm home," I said. "What's your schedule like tomorrow?"

"All clear past eleven."

"How about here, then? In Cainsville. That might be better for now. The town doesn't even have a newspaper."

He chuckled. "Bonus. What time do you get off work?"

"Three."

"I'll swing by and meet you at the diner."

CHAPTER TWENTY-TWO

I hung up with Ricky and sat on the couch, staring at my blank wall. All my walls were blank. And mauve. I'd wanted to paint them, to get rid of a lingering smell, but I hadn't gotten around to it. Now that just seemed like one more failure. I'd broken it off with a great guy. I was unsatisfied with my dream job. Lost my cat. Hadn't painted my walls. Also, I had forgotten to pick up a coffee to get me through my evening of research work. The last was a problem fixed by a ten-foot trek to the coffeemaker, but I was in a funk, and it seemed insurmountable.

My cell dinged with a text from Gabriel.
Skip the client files.
I'd barely finished reading that when a second came in.
Pamela priority. Then Ciara.
Ten seconds later.
Take time off if you need it. Will discuss

Tuesday.

I slumped lower into the couch. Gabriel had apparently decided I *was* put off by the amount of work. I could call back and say, "It's not the work. It's you. I quit." The perfect revenge. Toy with him until he dangled an offer I couldn't refuse and then, just when he thought he'd snagged me and his schedule would ease, I'd quit. *Mwa-ha-ha. Take that, you scoundrel.*

Yeah.

There wasn't even a moment's pleasure in the thought. I didn't want revenge. I didn't want . . .

I didn't want to hurt Gabriel.

There it was. Plain and simple, and stupid as hell. He'd hurt me. Shouldn't I want some payback? Maybe not the immature scenario I'd just imagined, but at the very least I shouldn't *mind* hurting him, if that's what came of it.

Ninety minutes had passed since I'd left the office, and he was still trying to figure out why I hadn't been my usual upbeat self. Still trying to make it right. I could say he really didn't want to lose his new employee, and I'm sure it was partly that, but it was also . . .

I looked at those texts and I didn't see Gabriel, hard-assed lawyer. I saw a boy

196

whose mother had left when he was fifteen, who must have left so many times before that he never once considered the possibility she was dead, just presumed she'd abandoned him and went about his life as if that sort of thing happened. As if that's what you should expect from people. They'd get tired of you. They'd decide you were more trouble than you were worth. And they'd leave.

I picked up the phone and texted back. *That's fine. Send more if you have it. See you Tuesday.*

I sent the message, hauled my ass off the sofa, and changed for a run.

Normally I ran down Main Street. Tonight, I wasn't feeling sociable, so I headed into the residential neighborhoods as I struggled to slough off my mood. Then, as I turned a corner, I glimpsed a streak of black fur tearing behind a hedge, and I stopped.

"TC?" I called.

Silly, of course. He wasn't the only black animal in Cainsville. But when I paused, my legs twitched, as if urging me to keep going. I checked around the hedge. No sign of any furred critters. I scanned the yard but still saw nothing. So I resumed my jog.

I'd gone halfway down the quiet street

when a shape darted across the intersection ahead. There was no doubt it was a black cat, roughly the same size as TC.

I whistled. The cat scampered along the next street and vanished out of sight.

"TC?" I called as I hurried after him.

Seriously? Take a hint, girl. Dude's running the other way. You've never chased a guy before. Don't start now.

I just wanted to make sure he was okay. That he hadn't been . . .

What? Abducted from my apartment? Kidnapped and dumped here, a mile away, and somehow couldn't find his way home? It was a *mile*. Real pets cross continents for their people.

When I reached the corner, there was no sign of TC, but I jogged along looking left and right. At the next corner, I stopped on the curb and closed my eyes. I felt a twinge and opened my eyes just as a black cat dashed into a yard.

Let me get close enough to make sure it's him. That's all I need.

When I neared the house, I slowed. The shuttered windows made the house look as if it was asleep. No, as if it was drowsing, waiting . . .

I shook off the feeling. Still, the house was worth staring at. Victorian literature was my area of specialty, but I'd always taken an interest in architecture, too, and this house combined the two perfectly. It was a Queen Anne, which often conjures up images of the most over-the-top, wedding-cake Victorians, but this one had the hallmarks while showing dignified restraint. Less of a flouncy can-can dancer than a well-born lady who knows how to rock a fancy dress and killer pair of heels.

It had an asymmetrical front, with a rounded porch extending along the left side. There was no Queen Anne tower, but the front window and the one above it were large, three-sided bays, forming a half tower. The details were Free Classic style, meaning they lacked the ornate gingerbread, instead favoring columns and simpler molding.

I continued forward. The street was lined with oaks and elms and maples, not one of which was under a hundred years old. An evening breeze made the leaves dance, and brought the faint perfume of magnolia blossoms.

I reached the house. The yard was emerald green and perfectly trimmed, as were the rose bushes and hydrangeas. The gardens were otherwise empty, though. Weeded, as if someone had meant to plant but lost track of time and missed the season.

A wrought-iron fence surrounded the house. On every post was a chimera head, like the ones in the park. I touched a minotaur.

This fence wasn't something you could hire the local builder to install, even a hundred years ago. Gorgeous, expensive custom work. I walked down to the next chimera. That's when I glanced up at the house and noticed the frieze under the cornices. Gargoyles.

"Mrrowwww."

The plaintive cry made me jump. It was TC, beyond a doubt. The call came from the side of the house, but I could see nothing there. Then it sounded again.

I bent outside the fence and called him. I whistled. I chirped. I clucked. I made every "here, kitty kitty" noise I could think of, and as I did, his cries grew louder and more urgent.

He's hurt. He's trapped.

He couldn't be. I'd just seen him.

I pushed through the latched gate and up onto the porch. I rang the bell. I used the knocker. Brass, with a cuckoo's head — a good marriage omen. I called a hello. TC yowled louder.

No one was home. That's why the shutters were closed. The owners were gone for a while, the house battened down tight.

I cast one last look at the leaded-glass sidelights to be sure a light wouldn't suddenly flick on, then I went back down the porch steps and around the side of the house. I immediately saw where the noise had come from: an open basement window. I hurried over. The window was a side-slider, open maybe six inches. Below, all was dark, but I could hear TC meowing.

My flashlight app is far from perfect, but when I reached my phone through the window, it dimly lit a typical old-house basement, with a dirt floor and bare walls. And a cat. My cat. Yowling for me to rescue him.

"What?" I said. "Ten minutes ago you run away from me, then you jump through a window to hide, find yourself trapped, and decide maybe I'm not so bad after all? I should leave you down there."

He yowled louder.

"Yeah, yeah," I muttered.

I looked around. One shutter near the front of the house had come unfastened and tapped in the breeze. I walked over, opened it, and stood on tiptoes to peer into the house.

The room was as empty as the basement.

The owners hadn't just left for a while. No one lived here. I stepped back for a better look. The house was in excellent shape for its age. Well tended, too. How could a place like this sit empty without even a For Sale sign on the lawn?

Not my concern, really. What mattered was that it was empty and my damned cat was trapped in the basement.

I went around to the back door. While I had no issue with breaking into an empty house for good cause, I sure as hell wasn't doing it from the front.

The backyard was at least a half acre — classic Victorian garden, with grass replaced by cobblestone walks and flowerbeds. There was an empty fishpond, too, with a fountain. Moss and ivy covered fantastical statuary — fairies and green men, mermaids and fauns. Cleaned up and filled in, it would be a showpiece. Right now, it had a desolate, almost haunting air, and I paused there, feeling the tug of it, inviting me to wander in the twilight. Lovely thought, if my damned cat wasn't still yowling.

I went through a walled patio and tried the back door. Unlocked. Not surprising. I was the only person in town with a security system, or so Grace had muttered when I explained to her how it worked.

I eased open the door.

CHAPTER TWENTY-THREE

The house was so silent even my breathing seemed to echo through the empty rooms. TC had stopped yowling, as if knowing rescue was imminent. I stepped slowly into the kitchen as my eyes adjusted to the near dark.

No appliances. Bare counters covered in a layer of dust. Leaded-glass doors on the cupboards showed they were equally bare.

The basement door was right there, in the kitchen. I took out my gun before opening it. Yes, I carried a gun jogging. Gabriel had bought me a holster and insisted on it after I found Ciara in my car. I was happy for it now. I didn't care if the house was obviously empty — I wasn't venturing unarmed into the pitch-black basement of an abandoned house chasing my missing cat. That screams slasher flick.

I called TC from the top of the stairs. He responded with a cry, but it was muffled, as if there was a door between us. I took it slow going down the stairs, ignoring his increasingly frantic yowls.

"I'm coming, I'm coming," I called. "Remind me again why I wanted you back? Damn cat."

The basement opened into a large room with several closed doors. It was as still as the main floor. I cast my mock flashlight around and saw more of what I'd spotted through the window. Dirt floor. Bare walls.

TC scratched at one of the closed doors. When I opened it, he darted out. I bent to pet him. As soon as I touched his side, I stopped. I could feel his ribs. His fur was matted and bedraggled.

Had he been trapped — ?

No, I'd seen him outside. He must have just had a hard time on the streets.

A hard time on the streets of Cainsville? This wasn't Englewood. He hadn't been in this condition when he first adopted me. Thin, yes. Fleas, yes. But basically fine.

I pushed the door open farther and hit the light switch. Nothing happened. The power was off. I could see a puddle under the window, as if rain had come in. It hadn't rained since Saturday night. There were mice, too, or what remained of them. Food and water.

"You were trapped down here," I said. "That wasn't you I saw."

Yet it had been, in a way. An omen that had led me to him. When I bent, he rubbed against me and lifted onto his hind legs. I gingerly picked him up, expecting him to leap down — we didn't have a cuddly-kitty relationship. He settled into my arms and purred.

"That happy to see me, huh?" I said. "Something tells me you won't take off for a jaunt anytime soon." I settled him in my arms. "Let's get you home. I think I've got a can of tuna in the cupboard."

He purred louder. I carried him up the stairs, talking to him, reaching out to push open the door, and —

My hand hit the solid door. Okay, apparently I'd shut it when I came down. That was an old habit from living at home, where my mother would get so flustered over an open basement door, you'd think hordes of bats and spiders were preparing to launch an assault.

I reached for the handle. It turned easily. I pushed. Nothing happened. I pushed harder. Still nothing.

The door was sticking. Old houses. Swollen wood. Whatever. I put TC down, twisted the handle, and rammed my shoulder against it. Pain shot through my shoulder. The door didn't budge. I shone the light in the crack between the door and the frame, then turned the handle and watched the bolt disengage. I ran the light up and down, but there was no sign of anything else holding it closed.

"No need to panic," I told the cat, who was placidly cleaning his ears. "There's no one here, so we haven't been locked in the basement. We're just stuck. Temporarily."

He meowed and trotted back down the stairs.

"Good idea," I said. "Search for an alternate exit."

I had just reached the bottom of the steps when my phone rang. Gabriel.

"What's up?" I said as casually as I could for someone trapped in the basement of an abandoned house.

"I need information from the Meade file. You took it, correct?"

"Right. You asked me to have a look —"

"Yes, I know. But I need witness contact information from it. Are you at home?"

I looked around. "Not exactly."

"It's rather urgent. A new development in the case, and I have to check with the witness before the prosecution does. If you aren't close by, I'll need to go out to your apartment."

"I have a security system now and updated locks."

"Then I'll take the code. You can change it after."

That didn't cover the updated locks, which he presumably could still pick. Hell, I was sure he could disarm the alarm, too — he was just pretending otherwise to make me feel secure.

"I'm close to home," I said as I walked across the basement, looking for doors or large windows. "Just give me —"

The cat yowled.

"Is that TC?" Gabriel said.

"It is. I found him."

A louder yowl as the cat called my attention to something. I hurried toward him. It was a dead mouse. Lovely. He kept yowling even when I patted his head.

"He doesn't sound very happy, Olivia," Gabriel said.

"I know. He wants to get home."

A pause as the cat kept it up.

"Are you sure?" His voice lowered. "I know you miss him, but if he doesn't want to go back with you —"

"Oh, for God's sake. I never wanted a cat in the first place. Do you really think I'd be dragging him home now? Scratching and yowling?"

The cat stopped.

"Thank you," I whispered. Then to Gabriel, "Can I call you back?"

"How far are you from home?"

"About a mile."

"All right. While you walk, tell me what you found in —"

"Actually, now's not a good time," I said, staring up at another window I'd never fit through. "I'll call you back."

TC meowed. Loudly. It echoed through the empty basement.

"Where are you, Olivia?"

"Can I call — ?"

TC began scratching at a different closed door. While yowling.

"Olivia. Where — ?"

"On my way home. Soon." I checked the room where TC had been scratching. One window. No bigger than the rest. I closed the door again. "I've just . . . I've had a setback. Can I just call you — ?"

"You're not outside, are you?"

I sighed. "No, okay? I'm . . . I found TC in the basement of an abandoned house. Well, I'm not sure you'd call it abandoned — it's just not being lived in. I'm having trouble getting out of the basement."

"Trouble?"

The cat sat on the bottom step, looking up at me, silent now.

"I went downstairs, and I must have closed the door, but it won't open. It doesn't seem to be locked, but I can't get it —"

"You're chatting with me about work when someone has locked you in a basement?"

"*You* were chatting about work. I was looking for an exit. And no one has me locked —"

"The door mysteriously closes behind you and won't reopen?"

"I might have closed it, like I said. There's no one here. The place is so quiet I'd hear a mouse scampering."

A ding sounded at the other end of the line. Then the familiar whoosh of a closing elevator door.

"Where are you?" I asked carefully.

"Coming to get you."

"No, no, no. Go back up to your condo. I'm fine."

"You're locked in the basement of an empty house, not even a week after being knocked out by someone who left a severed head in your bed. Also after repeatedly seeing a fetch —"

"It wasn't a fetch. Rose thinks . . . Never

mind. The point is —"

"The point is that you are trapped in a basement." His footsteps echoed. Parking garage.

"And you are an hour away."

"If I drove the speed limit. Which I do not."

I sighed. "I'm fine, Gabriel. If I really can't get out, my phone obviously works. I can call the police."

"After breaking into an empty house?"

"It was unlocked. Look, if I need to, I can call Rose."

"She's in the city tonight on a date."

"Date?" I tried to picture it and failed. "Okay, then I'll call someone at the diner — if and when I'm absolutely sure that I can't get out. My cell phone battery is half full. The house is silent. I'm not going to die down here."

"What's the address?" His car's engine roared to life.

"Gabriel? Really. Don't do this. I made a stupid mistake —"

"I'll call you for the address when I'm in Cainsville. If you hear anything, phone the police. Don't worry about trespassing charges. I can fix that."

He hung up. TC rubbed against me, purring.

"Oh, now you're happy. You yowled on purpose, didn't you?" I was kidding, of course, but when he glanced up, I swear he looked very pleased with himself.

"We don't need rescuing," I said as I tramped up the stairs. "He knows that. He's making a big deal out of it so I'll owe him. Then he can get away with even more shit, because I'll remember the times he came running to help me, and I'll feel guilty." I glanced at TC, leaping up the stairs alongside me. "You do realize that, don't you?"

He purred.

I'd get this damn door open if I dislocated my shoulder doing it. I twisted the handle, went to ram it with my shoulder . . . and fell through as it opened. I tripped over the top step and landed on my hip on the kitchen floor, my cell phone skidding across the linoleum. TC trotted over to it, bent, and nosed it my way.

"Thank you," I muttered as I sat up and grabbed it back. "You are truly helpful. You're lucky my gun didn't fall out and shoot you. Accidents happen, you know. Tragic kitty accidents."

He only sniffed.

I speed-dialed Gabriel. It went to voice mail. Not surprising — it was much harder to rescue someone if she called and told you she didn't need rescue. I told him exactly that and texted the same message, abbreviated. There could be no question now — I was fine and I'd notified him, so I owed him nothing.

"Okay, TC," I said, pushing myself up. "Time to go home."

He darted across the kitchen and into the next room.

"Um, wrong door?" I called.

As I followed the cat, I noticed the elaborate frieze in the front parlor. I looked at one section. Seven magpies. Six leaned over, beak to their neighbor's head, as if whispering to him. The seventh stood there, oblivious.

Seven for a secret, not to be told.

The old rhyme played in my head.

One for sorrow,
Two for mirth,
Three for a wedding,
Four for birth,
Five for silver,
Six for gold;
Seven for a secret,
Not to be told;
Eight for heaven,
Nine for hell,
And ten is for the devil's own self.

I craned my neck to scan the entire frieze. They were all magpies, in their groups, from one to ten. The first magpie with its wing over its head, weeping. Then two with their heads thrown back, laughing. I quickly snapped pictures. Then I backed up to the dining room. The frieze here was crows, illustrating a similar rhyme.

One for bad news,
Two for mirth.
Three is a wedding,
Four is a birth.
Five is for riches,
Six is a thief.
Seven, a journey,
Eight is for grief.
Nine is a secret,
Ten is for sorrow.
Eleven is for love,
Twelve is the hope of joy for tomorrow.

TC meowed from the next room. Right. This wasn't an open house. Time to get my damn cat and go.

"Come on," I whispered. "We need to leave out the back —"

He darted in the opposite direction.

"Hey!"

I rounded the corner into the front hall . . .
only to see him leaping up the stairs.

CHAPTER TWENTY-FOUR

"No! The exit is here!"

I jabbed my finger toward the front door. The problem with animals? Rational explanation doesn't work. Nor does a firm "Get back here now!" At least not with cats, which is why I'm really more of a dog person.

I sighed and ran up the stairs. They ended in a hallway with doors on either side and one at the end. All except the one at the end were open just enough for a cat to slip through.

"TC?"

I couldn't pick up so much as the padding of little paws.

"Look," I said. "I'm very good at reading signs, and if you're telling me you wanted out of that basement but don't want to go home with me, that's fine. Just let me put you outside, okay?"

"Mrrow."

His call came from farther down the hall. Then a scratch at the door — which seemed to be the one that was closed.

"Really? Damn it, you *are* a pain in the ass."

I turned the handle and —

Locked. There was an old-fashioned keyhole, empty, and when I shone my light, I could see the latch was engaged.

TC meowed again — from my left, through one of the partly open doors.

"Thank God," I muttered as I pushed open the door. "Now come —"

He leapt onto a windowsill. I sighed and walked in. It was brighter up here. No closed shutters on these windows, just drawn shades.

Partway to the window, I stopped and stared at the floor. The blocks of parquet formed a pattern in the middle of the room. A symbol.

It was about three feet across, with intricately cut pieces of various shades, painstakingly laid out to form a triskelion. Each "arm" was a stylized bird's head, done in an old Celtic style, like in the Book of Kells. When I got the angle right, I could tell what kind of birds they were, even with the stylized design. The beaks, ear tufts, and facial disks gave it away. Owls. I was taking out my cell to snap another picture when TC yowled.

He was still on the window ledge, now scratching at the blind.

I sighed. "That's not an exit."

When he ignored me, I tugged the blind open a few inches.

"See? Not an exit."

Rising moonlight shone through. If I wanted a picture, I *could* use more light. I fully opened the blind to reveal a stained-glass window. Odd for a second story. It wasn't even all that decorative — panels of leaded glass with a deformed circle of yellow glass in the middle. I turned back to the floor mosaic, and when I did, I had to take a second look. The yellow circle of stained glass cast a light that illuminated the head of one owl.

There were two more windows along the side wall. A lot for a small corner room. I pulled up their blinds. One window had a circle of red, the other blue. The moonlight shone through and lit up the other two heads. I stood, marveling at it . . . until fourth-grade science kicked in and I realized the moon shouldn't be able to hit three windows at just the right angle to illuminate all three heads at the same time. Even if there was a moment when it could, what was the chance that moment happened to be right now?

I drew closer and took more pictures. There was a symbol of some kind in the middle of the triskelion, but it was impossible to make out from this angle. I stepped into the circle and —

I was walking through a field. There was no moment of transition. No moment of internal shock, either. It felt as if I'd been walking through a field all along. Walking and humming. Except my voice was high, like a child's. Long grass swished as I cut through it, and the tops tickled my dangling hand. I looked down to see a small and slender girlish hand.

When a butterfly flitted past, I watched it go. A white butterfly. Good luck. I smiled and kept walking. I could smell water ahead, the slightly swampy, pungent smell. That's what guided me. With each step, I heard a clink and a rattle, and I reached into my pocket, felt stones there, and pulled out three. Two black, one white. More black than white. I smiled and took out two more. Two black now, three white. More white than black. I smiled again, equally pleased.

Black, white. Dark, light. Good and bad, bad and good. It depended on how you looked at it, and the interpretation was ever changing. I was a creature of the dark and the light. The night and the day. The owl and the raven. I could choose light or I could choose dark, and it was not a choice of good or evil, but only a choice of one or the other, left or right, in or out, up or down.

I could hear the water now, rushing over rapids. Soon I spotted a small river. On the other side, gnarled trees choked out the sunlight. I smelled the forest, damp and dark and decaying. I looked from the sun-dappled meadow to the dark forest, and I felt no glimmer of preference. Two sides to life, both equally alive, equally rich, equally intriguing.

I was done in the meadow for today. I'd cut through vines and climb the twisted trees and see what new wonders lay within the forest. All I had to do was cross the stream.

I pushed through the waist-high grass until I saw the water ahead, rushing and crashing over the rocks. Then I stopped.

There was a woman on the riverbank. The ugliest woman I'd ever seen. She looked like a corpse — dressed in tatters, washing her hands in the stream, tangled dark hair writhing over bone-thin arms, skin like jerky, twisted and tough and shrunken. Her face was horrible, with a long nose, blackened, jagged teeth, and sunken eyes — one black and one gray.

"Y mae mor salw â Gwrach y Rhibyn," I whispered.

She lifted her head, recognizing her name. *Gwrach y Rhibyn.* Those sunken eyes looked straight at me. Then she began to wail, so loud my hands flew to my ears.

"Fy mhlentyn, fy mhlentyn bach," she shrieked. *"Fy mhlentyn, fy mhlentyn bach."*

My child. My little child.

Death is near. I have seen Gwrach y Rhibyn, and she warns me.

I staggered backward . . . into the bedroom, where I stood in the triskelion circle.

"Well, that wasn't just a little bit weird," I muttered.

TC chirped.

"Yeah, I know. These days, weird is my life. I should get that on a T-shirt."

I struggled to focus. It was surprisingly easy. I had just emerged from a dream state after stepping into a magically lit symbol ingrained in the floor of an old, abandoned house. I should be running for the door. Or huddled on the floor, rocking. But somehow it was like seeing red-eyed hounds and strange men who gave me boar's tusks. I could mentally lift the vision wholesale and stick it into the already overflowing "crazy shit I'll deal with later" box in my brain. At least I wasn't still trying to find rational explanations. That was progress. Or the sign of a complete mental breakdown.

I turned to TC. "Now can we go?"

He scampered out.

In the hall, I spotted him at the end, nudging that one closed door. "You have the worst sense of direction, don't you? That's locked —"

TC pushed it half open with his paw.

"No!" I said, lunging after him. "Not in —"

He dashed through. I didn't spend a second wondering how the heck a locked door got opened, because for once the rational explanation was the one that made sense. It was also the one that had me taking out my gun.

That door had been locked. Absolutely, undeniably locked. If it wasn't now, that meant I wasn't the only person here.

I suppose the intruder expected me to tear through after TC, having lured him in with some ripe-smelling tidbit. But while I was fond of my cat, it was a "break into an abandoned house for him" kind of affection, not "run into a death trap for him."

Gun raised, I kicked open the door and peered in. Steep steps rose into darkness.

The attic.

"TC?" I called.

A bump sounded above, as if he'd jumped onto something. Then a loud thump, and I had to stop myself from running up after him.

"TC?" I called. "Are you okay?"

Another thump, lighter. Then an odd *bump-bump-bump* over the floorboards. I pointed my gun with one hand while lifting my flashlight-phone with the other. TC appeared, dragging something behind him. At the top of the stairs, he stopped and meowed.

"Come down here," I said.

He answered with a "No, you come here" yowl. When I didn't move, he nudged his trophy to the edge of the steps. I could make out a rough covering, like fur. He grabbed the fur and pulled the thing closer to the edge.

"Is that a rat?" I said.

It was too big for a mouse. Hell, it looked big enough to be a raccoon — a young one, at least. I stepped forward then stopped, as I remembered why I was staying at the base of the stairs.

"Come down," I said. "*Now.* I'm not chasing —"

He disappeared. I fought a groan. I should

leave. I really should. But if someone was up there, TC might get hurt. I was about to call him again when the bundle at the top of the stairs moved. He was pushing it toward the edge. Determined to bring his prize with him.

"I don't want —"

Too late. He gave the thing a shove and down it came, bump-bumping over the steps as it rolled, while he trotted behind it. When his trophy was halfway down, I started to realize what it was, but I just stood there, light shining on the thing, watching it roll, telling myself I was wrong, had to be wrong, until it came to rest at my feet, and I was looking down at the head of Ciara Conway.

CHAPTER TWENTY-FIVE

I scooped up TC and got the hell out of that house, not stopping until I was on the front sidewalk. Then I called Gabriel. It went to voice mail.

"Goddamn you," I muttered, then said, "Gabriel? I need you to call me now. This isn't a joke. *Call me.*"

I hung up and dialed 911. No more screwing around. I didn't care if Ciara's head vanished before the police got here. My conscience could no longer rest knowing that she was dead and I was carrying on as if nothing had happened. If Gabriel would have advised otherwise, well, then he should answer his damned phone.

My call went to the state police. I asked if I should report a problem to the local PD instead and they said yes. Did I want them to connect me? Just then my phone beeped with an incoming call from Gabriel. I asked the dispatcher for the number instead.

Records would show that I'd placed this call. Better to speak to my lawyer now.

"I'm in town," Gabriel said before I could speak. "I need the address. If you don't know it —"

"Did you get my messages?" I said. "Any of them?"

"Messages?"

He waited patiently until I finished cursing him out and then said, "Is something wrong, Olivia?"

"My damned cat just found Ciara Conway's head. In the house where he was trapped."

"Do you have an address?" he said, less casually now.

I gave it to him. "It's over —"

"I know where it is. I'm less than a mile away."

"I'll be waiting out —"

"Stay on the line, Olivia. Tell me what happened."

I did. His car careered around the corner as I was getting to the part about calling 911. He'd climbed out and was closing the car door when TC zoomed past me.

"Watch out!" I said before he slammed the door on the cat.

TC jumped into the Jag and perched on the front seat.

"You might not want him in there," I said. "He has claws."

Gabriel closed the door. "At least we'll know where he is."

"Just don't bill me for the damage."

He took a flashlight from the trunk, then walked over. "As I was saying, yes, you were correct to call 911. It establishes a timeline, as does my call. I will handle contacting the local police, but I want to take a look inside first. Verify that the head is still there and keep it within sight. You can wait in the car with the cat if you like."

"It's not the head that sent me flying out of that house. It's remembering what happened the last time. I got out before I was knocked out."

"Good. Did you hear anyone inside?"

I said no, then explained about the attic door.

"That is odd," he said as I led him into the yard. "But the basement door did something similar, and I don't believe it 'just stuck.' Let's see what we have."

The head was still at the bottom of the attic steps. The head. That's how I thought of it now. Disconnected from any formerly living human being, because otherwise my gut started shouting, "It's her *head*. Ciara

Conway's head. Severed from her body. Carted around. Tossed into a bed. Dragged by a cat. Pushed down the stairs. The poor girl's head." The horror and the indignity of that was too much. So it became "the head."

Gabriel seemed to have no such issues. He crouched and examined it from all angles.

"It appears to have been preserved," he said. "Most likely embalmed. That would explain the lack of rot and of scent, though TC still picked it up. A substandard job, then. Is it in the same condition as the last time you found it?"

I nodded.

He straightened, frowning down at the head as if it perplexed him. "You said you presume TC came in through the open basement window?"

"Yes. He'd been down there a while. Fortunately, he had water and found food."

"Meaning he could have been down there since he disappeared. Right before you found that head in your bed. Which he then found in the same house where he'd been trapped."

"And that makes no sense, which means the head must have been planted while I was rescuing him. I was trapped in the basement just long enough for that to happen."

"Possible, but that presumes the killer was either following you on your jog and took advantage — having the head conveniently nearby — or he was already in the house. I suspect TC didn't jump through that window. He was brought and left here. That could mean there is no one in this house tonight. TC was being kept here, as was the head."

"Which he smelled through two stories? Despite it being embalmed? And that doesn't explain stuck and unlocking doors."

"I know. It's not a puzzle we'll solve tonight. For now, we need to call the police. First, though, I want to take a look in the attic. Do you want to come or guard the evidence?"

"I'll go. You can guard."

"That wasn't one of the options."

"I know," I said as I brushed past him.

Gabriel didn't try to stop me, but he didn't hang back at the foot of the stairs, either. He came up until he could see what I was doing, while keeping one eye on the "evidence" below.

"Don't touch anything," he said. "Try not to leave too many footprints."

"I've been shedding hair lately. Is that a problem?"

"I will explain the footprints and any additional forensic evidence by saying you came up after the cat. I'm merely asking you to keep that evidence to a minimum."

"I was joking about the hair."

"I wasn't. Quickly now. We've established a timeline, and the longer it takes to phone . . ."

Unlike the basement, this space wasn't empty. It wasn't exactly jam-packed, either, just dotted with covered furniture and storage chests. From the dust, none of it had belonged to the previous owners. Not unless they'd moved out fifty years ago. As I walked, I remembered what Gabriel had said about footprints, and I stopped dead, cursing under my breath.

"What's wrong?" Gabriel's head crested the steps.

"You mentioned footprints. If someone's up here, that would be a sure sign of it." I backed up a few steps and waved my light around.

Gabriel gave me 1.3 seconds before saying, "Anything?"

I took another five before answering. "Not even my own, because someone has swept a path. I can see a few of TC's prints, but he seems to have stuck mostly to the cleared part. Meaning at the end of this path, presumably, is where the head was. Or where the killer is lying in wait." I raised my voice. "Did you hear that? I know where you are!"

"And now he knows where you are," Gabriel muttered.

"Like he wouldn't have the moment we started talking. Also, it could be a she."

"Olivia . . ."

"I'm moving. Following this handy path to my doom. Did I mention I had a vision down there? I think it was some kind of banshee. Which is —"

"I know what a banshee is, and I hope you're joking, and that you would not venture up here after hearing a death knell."

I said nothing.

"Olivia . . . ?"

"Hold on." A few more steps. "I think I see where . . ."

I trailed off as I shone the flashlight at the path's end. It was a table. Covered in a sheet. With something under that sheet.

The rest of Ciara Conway.

CHAPTER TWENTY-SIX

As Gabriel phoned it in, I moved around the table, illuminating every surface with the flashlight beam. The swath swept around the table left enough room for the killer to maneuver without leaving footprints. I couldn't smell the body or the embalming fluid; the stink of bleach was too strong. He — or she — had washed everything down. Laid Ciara out here, covered her, cleaned up, and left.

When Gabriel finished his call, he came up for a look himself. He surveyed the area and then scanned the floor with the flashlight, until he was reassured I hadn't messed up anything. We left the sheet in place.

"We should wait downstairs," he said.

We went down to the second-floor hallway. As we waited, I told him about the banshee. I was showing him the owl triskelion when a voice called, "Hello!" from the back door.

The police had arrived.

Gabriel handled things from there. I'd met the chief before. Eddie Burton. A quiet man in his forties, with a wife and two teenagers who'd come along to the diner with him for dinner once a week. Sending the chief wasn't unusual. He was pretty much the entire force. There was a local college boy taking police sciences who worked during the summer months, and two of the elders — Veronica and Roger — who volunteered. That was it.

Burton gave absolutely no sign that he considered me in any way connected to this crime. That surprised me. I'd just found a dead body mutilated postmortem . . . and my parents were supposedly serial killers who'd mutilated their victims postmortem. Even I wondered if there was some connection. Yet when Gabriel explained what had happened, Burton accepted his account.

I supposed it was pretty damned unlikely that I'd call the cops if I'd killed Ciara. Paw prints in the attic confirmed my story, as did those in the basement, along with the dead mice and my cat's condition.

While Burton seemed to know what he was doing, I expected they'd need to call in the state police for this. I was wrong. As far as Burton was concerned, this was just a dump site. The city would handle the murder investigation, picking up from the missing persons' case, and they'd want to process the scene. Escorting them in seemed the extent of Burton's duties. That and the paperwork.

"Gonna be a lot of paperwork," he said with a sigh. Then he flushed. "No disrespect to Ms. Conway. Horrible way for a girl to go. Horrible for anyone, of course, but a nice girl like that . . ." He shook his head. "I hope they catch whoever did this."

He said it with all due gravity, but with the distinct air of one who'd play no role in that "catching."

"Won't they at least consider the possibility she was killed here?" I asked.

"Doesn't seem like it. Looks like some kind of sicko serial —" He stopped, his pale face flushing again. "Sorry, Miss Jones."

"I meant, couldn't she have been killed within Cainsville, if not necessarily in this house?"

He looked as if I'd suggested aliens had murdered Ciara Conway. "We don't get that sort of thing here."

"I'm sure Cainsville has a very low murder rate —"

"It has *no* murder rate," he said. "Never

been a homicide. Accidents, sure, but that's it."

I glanced at Gabriel, expecting a faint eye roll that said he'd dispute this — in private — later. But he nodded and said, "Chief Burton's right. Which is not to say that I share his opinion that this murder absolutely could not have taken place within the town limits, but it seems unlikely. However, given the hiding place for the body, the killer may have a connection to Cainsville, as Ms. Conway did."

"Hopefully an equally distant one," Burton said. A rap sounded at the door. "That'd be Doc Webster. If you two would like to get on home, you can just let her in on your way out."

"Thank you," I said. "And thank you for making this easy."

Another frown, as if he was trying to figure out why he *wouldn't* have made it easy, and I was reminded yet again why I loved this town.

"Next time you come by the diner, coffee and pie are on me," I said.

His frown deepened. "That wouldn't be right, Miss Jones, but thank you for offering."

Gabriel had gone ahead to let Dr. Webster in. I stopped partway to the door and turned back to Burton.

"I'd like to apologize to the owners for breaking in," I said. "Are they local?"

"She was. Died a few years back." He hastened to add, "Cancer. She was seventy. Had a husband, but I'm not sure if he's around anymore. Alive, I mean. The house was hers, and he moved back to the city after she died. He never really got used to Cainsville. Left as soon as he could." A note of wonder in his voice, as if he couldn't imagine such a thing.

"So it's owned by her children?"

"Never had any. They married late in life. Nephew owns it, I think. Maybe great-nephew. He's never lived here, and there's some reason it can't be sold. Contested will, maybe? It's complicated. Damned shame, too, place like this. Should have a family living in it. You leave a house like this empty and . . ." He waved toward the attic, as if to say harboring corpses was the fate that befell abandoned homes. "Damned shame."

It was.

TC hadn't scratched up Gabriel's car, which was a relief because I had not failed to note that he'd never actually replied when I said I wouldn't be on the hook for damages. I took him back to my apartment

and he happily trotted inside. TC, that is —
not Gabriel, although he did come in,
without comment or request, rather like the
cat, presuming he'd be welcome and making himself at home.

Gabriel watched TC settle into his
cardboard-box bed. "He certainly seems
happy to be home, which suggests he didn't
leave willingly."

I got the lone can of tuna down from a
cupboard. "Or he did, and he regrets it
now."

I opened the can. TC sprang up and flew
onto the counter, purring urgently as I
dumped the tuna onto a plate.

"I don't know what happened," I said.
"And I'm not sure I ever will. Too many
unknowns, which seems to be the story of
my life these days."

I pointed Gabriel in the direction of the
files I'd brought home. While he fetched the
pages he needed, I looked around the tiny
kitchen.

"Can I make you a coffee? Tea? I've got a
few Dr Peppers in the fridge. After tonight,
they'd probably go down a lot better with a
couple ounces of rum or whiskey, but I
haven't gotten around to alcohol stocking.
Sorry."

Gabriel waved off the apology. "Soda's

fine. I don't usually drink."

"I suspected that," I said as I got out the pop. "No matter how bad a day we have, you've never said, 'God, I could use a drink right now.' I know I have. Silently. Many times."

"Then say so. I'm not a recovering alcoholic, Olivia. Nor do I have any issue with others imbibing. I do have a drink sometimes, socially, but otherwise . . . it's not for me."

Because of his mother. I was sure of that. Whatever mistakes she'd made, he was determined not to repeat them or share her weaknesses. Which is probably why I'd known never to say, "God, I could use a drink," in front of him.

"Rose has a liquor cabinet," he said, rising. "Put those back and we'll go over there, get you something."

I shook my head. "I was kidding. I don't need —"

"I saw her light on. We should speak to her anyway, about your vision."

I sighed. "I'm not running to her every time something strange happens to me."

"Why not? She enjoys the challenge. This isn't like running to a fortune-teller every time you have a decision to make. You are experiencing events with a clear preternatural origin. You can't simply ignore them."

He looked impatient, a little annoyed, as if I was refusing to visit the dentist for a sore tooth.

When he checked his watch, I said, "Go on home. I'll be fine."

"That wasn't what I meant."

"You were reminding me that I'm being unreasonably stubborn, while you're here, helping me, out of the goodness of your heart."

A flicker in his eyes. My darts rarely pierce Gabriel, but every now and then they manage.

"You got my messages to turn back," I said. "You didn't come out here to help me. You came because I'm not sure I made the right choice agreeing to work for you, and you wanted to seal my employment, through obligation if necessary."

"That's ridiculous." The words were said with the right degree of scorn and affront, but if you hang around Gabriel long enough, you learn to detect the tonal shifts that give lie to his words.

"I would like you to speak to Rose," he said. "It's not yet ten. Come along."

I considered letting him go out the door first then locking it behind him, but that was petty. Besides, he could pick the lock.

"At least call her first," I said. "She did have a date. Just because she's home doesn't mean she's alone."

He gave me a perplexed look.

"Call," I said.

He did.

Rose didn't have company. And she wasn't particularly happy about it.

"Waste of my night," she grumbled when I asked her how it went. "We're still on the appetizers, and he asks if I know how to bake banana bread. Can you believe that?"

"First dates are awkward," I said as we walked into the front room. "He was probably struggling to make conversation."

She snorted. "Conversation, my ass. I can tell you why he was asking. Because his late wife baked banana bread and he misses it. For date number two, he'd invite me to his place, where I'd find all the ingredients and her old recipe. Widowers. They aren't looking for companionship; they're looking for a new housekeeper. This is why I should stick to women." When I looked surprised, she shrugged. "I'm flexible."

"Widens the dating pool," I said as I sat.

"It does. I'm updating my profile tonight. Widowers — and widows — need not apply."

"You found him through an online service?"

She scowled at me. "Ask me in that tone again when you're no longer a skinny twenty-five-year-old, and we'll see if your attitude changes, missy."

"I wasn't judging. I'm just not sure that's safe."

A grunt from beside me elicited a glare from Rose.

"Don't start, Gabriel," she said. "I'm well aware of your views on the subject."

"Because I've defended two clients accused of crimes committed against women they found through an online dating service. Neither was guilty, of course —"

"Of course," I said.

"But the fact remains that it does not seem a safe way to find a relationship. With either gender."

She turned to me. "So you've stumbled into trouble again. Shouldn't the omens warn you against that?"

"I don't know. Shouldn't the cards warn you against bad dates?"

She grumbled under her breath. "All right. Explain."

CHAPTER TWENTY-SEVEN

Rose handled the discovery of Ciara's body as matter-of-factly as her nephew had. To them, the point was what it meant for me — why the corpse was being used to threaten me, and whether tonight's events were a continuation of that threat or mere happenstance.

I showed her the photos of the dining room and parlor friezes.

"Where is this?" she asked, her voice tight.

"Beechwood Street. It's a Victorian with leaded windows —"

"The Carew house," she said. "I wasn't sure which empty house you meant. There are probably a half-dozen in Cainsville at any time, owned by the town. They aren't an easy sell to newcomers between the commuting issues and the approval committee."

"Approval committee?" I said.

"For new purchasers."

"Is that legal?"

"It's been challenged a few times," Gabriel said. "But race, religion, sexual orientation, and socioeconomic status play no role in the process, so it isn't discriminatory. It's all about whether you're suitable."

"Which is a very nebulous determination," Rose said. "As off-putting as it sounds, the average prospective home owner does pass, and those who don't? Do you really want to live in a town that doesn't want you? They move on. All that, however, means that sometimes houses don't sell, and the homeowners won't be happy if it's because of local politics. So if a house is on the market more than six months, the town buys it. Then they keep it for someone from Cainsville. Usually a young couple who grew up here."

"Chief Burton thought there was a legal issue holding up the sale."

"There was. Years ago. But the town owns it now."

So I could buy it? The words were almost on my lips before I realized how horrible they sounded. Ciara Conway's body had been found there only an hour ago. And my first thought was, "Really? It's for sale?" Yet there was something about the house, a pull I couldn't shake.

Rose continued, "The reason I recognize

the house is these." She pointed at the photos I'd taken of the friezes. "I remember going there as a very young girl. My mother would take me for readings."

"The owner was a psychic?"

"Not . . . exactly." Rose's gaze rose to meet my eyes. "She could read omens."

I opened my mouth to say, "What?," but nothing came out and I sat there, goose bumps rising on my arms.

"You knew someone who could read omens?" That was Gabriel, a chill creeping into his gaze. "I think Olivia could have used this information sooner."

"There wasn't any information to give her. I vaguely recalled a woman in Cainsville with the same gift. I've been going through my old diaries, trying to remember details. I also wanted to speak to the elders, see if someone remembered her. When I had more, I planned to tell Olivia."

"That's fine," I said, ignoring the look on Gabriel's face that said otherwise. "This woman who lived there — she could do what I do?"

"I believe so. From what I recall, my mother would go to her for guidance. The woman would ask questions, interpreting omens that my mother had seen, and suggest a course of action. A variation on what

I do. She died before I came into my own power. Otherwise, I'm sure I would have had more dealings with her."

"Then she's not the woman who lived there last."

"Oh, no. The one I knew was at least ninety, and I wasn't even school age yet. As I recall, her husband built the house for her, which explains the friezes. I vaguely remember a grandson and his wife who lived there when I was growing up. At some point it was bought by the last owner."

Gabriel cleared his throat. "The point is that this house was owned by someone with the same ability as Olivia. That is worth looking into, as someone using that house is threatening Olivia. Show Rose the triskelion."

I did, and I told her about the vision.

"Bean nighe," she said as she rose. "The washerwoman."

"So not a banshee?"

Rose took a book from her shelf, flipped through it, and laid it open for me at a folklore encyclopedia entry on *bean sidhe.*

"Banshees," she said. "*Bean sidhe* is the Irish Gaelic spelling of the word. It's been anglicized as banshee."

"And a *bean nighe* is a form of *bean sidhe,"* I said as I read. "It's an old woman who washes the clothing of the dead. Which isn't quite what I saw — No, here it is. *Gwrach y Rhibyn.* Is that how it's spelled? That's worse than *bean sidhe.* It's the word from the vision, though, and the description matches. Ugly old woman washing in a stream while wailing death warnings. A Welsh cross between the *bean nighe* and the traditional *bean sidhe.* It's not a fetch, though. She's warning me of death in general. I'm guessing it was an omen telling me Ciara's body was upstairs. As for why I saw it when I stepped onto the triskelion . . ."

"I'm presuming it has something to do with the original owner," Rose said. "It seems to be some sort of conduit, possibly activated by those three lights. I'll look into it. Now, tea?"

"Olivia was hoping for —" Gabriel began.

"I'm fine. I should get back home."

"Not tonight, after what happened," Rose said. "You'll go back with Gabriel and pack an overnight bag while I make tea."

I argued. It didn't help. So I shut up and got my bag.

Gabriel left at midnight. I stood in the front room window as the taillights of his Jag vanished into the darkness. When I turned,

Rose was there, watching me.

"He should have left when I got my bag," I said. "He really didn't need another late night like this. He's tired. Overworked."

"You'll be helping with that."

"With his workload, yes. But I'm the reason he'll be getting home at one this morning when he has a court appearance at nine."

"He'll be fine. I don't think he sleeps more than five hours under the best of circumstances. What you're seeing isn't exhaustion. It's strain. The situation with you is part of it. Gabriel isn't accustomed to personal drama. It's untidy and it confuses him."

"Uh-huh." I turned back to the window.

"I'm serious, Olivia. He *is* accustomed to clients being angry with him. Furious, even. It's part of the process — they're fighting for their freedom and they never think their lawyer is doing enough. Gabriel knows he will be vindicated at trial, when they see him perform miracles. If they do remain angry — and I'm sure some do — he doesn't care. It's a business relationship. Yours is more than business. Your opinion of him — and your continuing relationship with him — matters. My nephew is not accustomed to that, and he's struggling with it."

Be patient with him. That's what she meant. Except that, with Gabriel, excuses felt dangerous. Cut him slack and he'd haul in as much rope as he could, then think you a fool for letting him.

I thought of another reason he might be exhausted, another source of stress. One I was much more comfortable with, because it had nothing to do with me.

I turned from the window. "Has he identified the photos of his mother yet?"

"Photos of his mother?"

"At the police station."

As a crease furrowed between her eyes, I realized he'd never told her.

"Sorry," I said quickly. "I thought — You should ask him about it."

I started for the stairs, mumbling about my morning shift. She stepped into my path.

"Olivia. What are you talking about?"

"I shouldn't —"

"Yes, you should. And you will. What is this about Gabriel's mother?"

I hesitated, but I could tell by her expression it would be cruel to walk away without explaining. So I told her.

"It might not have even been a photo of Seanna," I said as I finished. "Will Evans was clearly trying to separate me from Gabriel and —"

She walked to her desk and opened a drawer.

I continued. "Gabriel might have already established it wasn't Seanna, which is why he never mentioned it to you, and —"

She handed me a small photo album, opened to photos of Gabriel. He couldn't have been more than thirteen. He had his wavy black hair, pale blue eyes, and strong features — too intense for a gangly, acne-pocked adolescent. What I recognized most, though, was his expression. Wary, as if he was ready to bolt at the slightest provocation. But there was challenge there, too, a hardness already. As if he was hoping for provocation. An excuse to run. To escape.

The photo Rose wanted me to see, though, was in the top corner.

"Seanna," I whispered.

"Is that who you saw?"

I nodded. Rose lowered herself into a chair.

"Dead," she whispered. "All this time, she was dead." Grief crossed her face, but she blinked it back. "This would explain some of the strain."

"Maybe a lot of it."

She shook her head. "It's not as if this

means he'll now realize his mother was a good woman who didn't abandon him. How much do you know about the situation?"

I told her.

"I suppose you're wondering how I let it happen," she said.

"No, Evans told me Gabriel didn't let on Seanna had disappeared, and when you found out, he ran. He kept going until he was over eighteen. Too old for anyone to put him in foster care. Presumably you wouldn't have gotten custody. That's what Evans said."

"I wouldn't. I have a criminal record." She glanced over, as if gauging my reaction. When I gave none, she continued, "I was also living with a woman at the time. I'd have given her up in a heartbeat for Gabriel, but the fact remains that I would not have been deemed a suitable parent. As for Seanna, I knew she wasn't making an honest living, but for a Walsh, I'd have been more shocked if she was. There'd been drugs in her youth, but she told me she gave that up when Gabriel was born, and she hid the signs from me. I only knew she was not a good mother. She neglected him. Yet even there, I couldn't prove anything. There was no obvious physical abuse or anything like that. She was just a lousy parent, and there are plenty of those."

She fussed with the blinds before continuing. "Gabriel certainly wouldn't give me more ammunition. He was as stubborn as a child as he is now. If I interfered, Seanna would refuse me access to him. So I told myself that being a good aunt was enough, that taking him when I could was enough. After she disappeared, I learned the rest, from the police. The addictions — to drugs, to alcohol, to men. And the disappearances. By the time she left, she'd been taking off for weeks at a time. Even now, Gabriel won't confirm that. He doesn't talk about it. Refuses. Push, and I'll stop hearing from him for a while."

"So about this . . . confirming her death. I shouldn't push?"

"No, he has to do it, which means he'll *need* a push. You might be the only person who can get away with it."

CHAPTER TWENTY-EIGHT

I expected my diner shift to be stressful, given that I'd found the body of a former resident the night before. The elders did speak to me about it, expressing their horror and grief in whispers, along with sympathy that I'd had to go through that. The others didn't mention it. I supposed that wasn't so shocking. Chief Burton had said Ciara's body would be transferred to the city for the autopsy. That meant the news wouldn't hit the Chicago papers until tomorrow. Apparently, the elders weren't breaking the news until the city did.

Gabriel presumed the CPD would want more than the statement I gave Burton, but he was their contact, and he was in court all day, so I heard nothing.

When three o'clock came, I was in the back with Susie for our shift change. The idea is to update the evening server for a smooth hand-off, but there's usually nothing to say, so Susie tells me about her day. One of her kids had won the school spelling bee — they still have spelling bees? — and I was listening to her story of the victory when the diner doorbell jingled. There wasn't any need to cut her short for that — it's a "seat yourself" kind of place.

When the bell dinged, the diner had been buzzing with the tea-hour crowd. Now it went silent. Heavy footsteps crossed the floor.

"Can we help you?" I heard Ida ask.

"Is Liv around?"

I recognized the voice but stood there for a second, trying to figure out why Ricky was here.

Because I'd invited him.

Shit. I'd totally forgotten. Normally we texted a few times a day, but he'd had a full schedule. Susie was still talking, and I didn't want to interrupt. The elders would make him feel welcome.

"How do you know Olivia?" It was Walter . . . and his tone was *not* welcoming.

"Don't you read the papers?" Patrick cut in. "There was a nice photo of them in the *Post* yesterday. Rick Gallagher, isn't it?"

"Yes . . ." Ricky said warily as I mentally willed Susie to hurry up with her story.

"He's one of Gabriel's clients," Patrick

253

said. "A Satan's Saints biker. See the patch on his jacket? That says he's a certified motorcycle gang member. Excuse the old folks, Rick. We don't get many bikers in Cainsville."

Patrick's tone was breezy, but he had to know he was being offensive.

"Is Olivia here?" Ricky asked again.

"In the back," Patrick said. "Have a seat. So where'd you park your bike?"

Susie was close enough to being done that I was able to blurt a quick "That's so great. Tell her I said congrats," before racing out.

Ricky stood with his hands in his jacket pockets, responding to Patrick's needling with clipped answers. If he was nicer, he'd look like a fool. If he got pissy, he'd seem to be overreacting. So he stayed neutral, but I could tell by the set of his jaw it was a struggle.

"Hey," I called as I walked in. "When did you get here?"

Ricky relaxed. "Just arrived," he said as he strolled over. "Ready to go?"

"I am."

As I turned toward the door, I caught Ida's disapproving frown. I stifled the urge to stiffen. Really? *This* was where they passed judgment?

I ignored her and the looks from the others, and let Ricky hold the door for me as we left.

"Not having coffee there, I take it?" he said.

"I am so sorry," I said. "If I had any idea they'd do that —"

"It's fine. I'm used to it. They aren't as much concerned *about* me as they're concerned *for* you, and I can't argue with that. Good to live in a place where people give a shit. I just hope I didn't cause you any trouble."

"Never," I said emphatically.

He smiled. "Good. So where to?"

We walked and talked. I showed him the park and the gargoyles, because he seemed genuinely interested. Then I told him what had happened to me last night, because it was going to be in the papers. I skipped the part about the triskelion and the vision, of course. And the part about finding Ciara's head in my bed earlier.

One thing we didn't talk about? My breakup. What if I said, "I ended it with James," and he said, "That's nice," and we continued on as we were?

When he suggested we grab dinner, I said I had to get home — work to do for Gabriel. He escorted me to my apartment.

Grace was on the front stoop. She did a double take when I walked up with Ricky. Really, it wasn't as if he *looked* like a biker. Sure, the leather-jacket-in-June could be a giveaway, but he'd slung it over his arm as soon as we'd set out.

Ricky said goodbye at the sidewalk. As I climbed the steps, Grace said, "Who's that?"

"A friend," I said, and walked inside.

As the door closed behind me, I stopped.

A friend . . . Did I want more than that? Hell, yes. Was I really questioning whether *Ricky* wanted more? No. He'd been clear about that from the start.

The truth, God help me, was that Rose was right. To a point, that is. She'd said my Ricky-versus-James conflict was lust versus duty. That oversimplified it, but there was an element of truth there. I felt a duty to James. Incredible guilt, too. More than that, I felt shame. I had loved him. I had wanted to spend my life with him. How does that evaporate in a month? What does that say about me? Nothing I want to say, that's for sure. So I'd kept trying to find that spark again, certain it was there.

I used to say — though never aloud — that I'd started dating James when I discovered he wasn't nearly as boring as I'd expected. But given where I came from, that bar was set pretty low. Society guys weren't to my taste. Even the rebels were boringly predictable in their rebellion. I don't think I really understood how constrained my world was until I left it. I met Rose and Patrick and Grace, and others who intrigued me because they were so far from my norm. And then there was Gabriel and, yes, Ricky, and compared with them — God, how I hate to say this — the light that had drawn me to James had faded into a barely notice-able glow. They were complex and fascinat-ing and original and real. So vibrantly real. And there was the guilt, because James was a good man. A good, solid man I'd loved. Who now bored me to tears.

Then there was Ricky. Lust? My dreams called me a liar if I denied that. I wanted him. Wanted him bad. But not just as a lover. I wanted to be with him. To get to know him. I couldn't remember the last time anyone had made me feel the way Ricky did. Like I was just as fascinating and complex and real as he was.

So why had I said no to dinner? Because I was an idiot. I was feeling skittish and unsettled and spooked by everything that was happening in my life. There was only one person who made me feel like my feet were firmly on the ground. And I'd let him walk away.

I hurried out the door.

Halfway to Main Street, I heard the roar of Ricky's bike and broke into a jog. I reached the corner just as he was zooming past. He saw me and cut a U-turn, revving back to where I waited on the corner.

"I —" I began.

He motioned for me to wait while he pulled off his helmet. My heart tripped, willing him to hurry and get the damned thing off before I lost my nerve.

"Yes to dinner," I said. "And a ride. Yes. I want to."

He gave a slow, sexy grin that made my insides heat. Then he caught himself. "You sure? We can grab your car if you want. If you're fine with the bike, like I said before, there are no strings —"

"I'm okay with strings."

He still hesitated.

"I broke it off with James yesterday," I said. "He wanted me to stop seeing you. I wouldn't do that."

He leaned over and put his hand to the back of my neck, and I knew what was coming, but when he kissed me, I still started in surprise. It was like spending the day baking at the side of a pool then finally jumping in, that initial burst of exhilarating shock, followed by a slow, exquisite chill sliding through my body, making me wonder why the hell I'd waited so long to take the plunge.

It was no quick kiss, either. It was long and deep and oh-so-delicious. It took a car passing for both of us to realize we were making out on Main Street.

After a moment's pause to catch our breath, Ricky handed me his helmet. "Wear this. It'll be loose, but it's better than nothing."

"What about you?"

"By law, I don't have to wear one. It's a personal choice. I'll stick to back roads. Less traffic means a whole lot less chance I'll need it."

"You wear it, then. I'll be —"

He eased the helmet over my head. "There. Now hop on."

I looked down, realizing I was still in my work uniform — a blouse and skirt. I motioned to it. "Should I go back and change?"

His eyes sparked with mischief. "You can, but I sure as hell won't complain if you don't. I'll keep the speed down so you won't get cold."

"Don't," I said. "Speed is good."

"All right, then. Let me get over to the curb so you can climb on without flashing."

I didn't understand what he meant until I had to hike my skirt up to get my leg over the seat. Then I had to keep it hiked up to wrap my legs around him, which explained his look when I'd asked about keeping the skirt on.

He reached back to grip my bare knee. "You need to hang on."

"Right." I felt down either side of the seat. "Where?"

He took both my hands and wrapped them around his waist.

"Oh," I said.

"Yep. Now scoot forward and get a good grip."

Getting that grip meant scooting all the way forward, against him, legs wrapped around him. When I fidgeted, he glanced back.

"Changing your mind?" he asked.

"No, just . . ." I closed any remaining gap between us and leaned against his back, my hands on his thighs. "This okay?"

He chuckled and looked back. "You need to ask?" he said, then revved the engine and pushed off.

Patrick stood outside the diner and watched the motorcycle speed off.

"Are you going to say anything?" Ida demanded as she marched up beside him.

"It's a very nice bike."

She scowled.

"It is," he said. "I've often thought it would be fun to drive a motorcycle, and if I did, that's what I'd want. An understated Harley. Lots of power but not too flashy. I might even join a gang. I don't think his would take me, though."

"There was a Cŵn Annwn in Cainsville, Patrick."

"Mmm, technically no," he said. "The boy is no more *cŵn* than Gabriel is *bòcan*. Less so, even. *Disgynyddion* not *epil*. Grandchild, I'd wager. He has the blood. Nothing more."

"He is still Cŵn Annwn," she said. "He does not belong here. We should have —"

"— killed a *boinne-fala* boy who obviously

261

has no clue what he is and no idea of the trespass he's committing?" Patrick turned to her. "Kill him and insult his people? Cast the first spear in a war we don't dare start?"

"The *bòcan* has a point."

It was Veronica, coming out of the diner to join them. She took a place beside Walter, who said nothing in his consort's defense, which suggested, more than any words, that he didn't agree with Ida. He just knew better than to say so.

"The boy doesn't know what he is," Veronica said. "No more than Gabriel or Olivia know what they are. He committed no intentional offense. We could complain, but if the Cŵn Annwn don't realize that one of their *disgynyddion* is acquainted with Olivia, I don't think it behooves us to tell them."

"It certainly does not," Walter said.

"Do you honestly think they don't know?" Ida turned on them. "They've hired him to seduce her. He is a criminal, after all."

"A biker, not a gigolo," Patrick said. "That's clever, don't you think? Cŵn Annwn running a motorcycle gang? It's so hard to ride a horse down the highway these days."

Ida glowered at him. "You aren't taking this seriously."

"If I wasn't, I'd be back inside, finishing

my chapter, not here, pointing out the idiocy of your theory. The Gallagher boy is a client of Gabriel's. That's how he knows Olivia, not because he was set on her by some shady stranger offering him money to fuck her."

"There's no need to be vulgar," Ida snapped.

"Yes, there is. *Boinne-fala* nature is vulgar. The boy meets Olivia. She's an attractive young woman; he's an attractive young man. Both are unattached. Both are in their sexual prime. Do you really think money needs to change hands for that" — he waved in the direction of the long-vanished bike — "to happen?"

"It's not just *boinne-fala* nature," Veronica cut in before Ida could snap something back. "It's *their* nature. From their old blood. I'm sure it's no coincidence that Gabriel represents the Gallaghers. He met them; they recognized a connection. Cŵn Annwn and Tylwyth Teg may not trust one another, but we understand one another. Gabriel meets the Gallaghers. Gabriel meets Olivia. Olivia meets Rick Gallagher and that" — she gestured down the road — "is what happens. Just as it did for her parents."

"*Cachu*," Ida spat.

Patrick looked over in mock shock at the

curse. He did not, however, disagree with the sentiment.

A few other elders had joined them, silently listening, as they usually did. One — Minnie — finally spoke, her whispery voice tentative. "What if he isn't merely Cŵn Annwn? What if he's —"

"He isn't," Ida cut in. "He's a boy. A random *disgynyddion.* Nothing more."

"But if he's with her, isn't it possible —"

"No." Ida turned a look on Minnie, and her anger rippled her glamor, light seeping out before she reined it in. "He is not."

She turned her hard look on the others, daring them to disagree. None did, though Patrick knew they were all thinking the same thing. Wondering the same thing. Not daring to say Arawn's name but wondering, fearing, nonetheless.

"It's a fling," Ida said. "Patrick is right. Their nature taking control. Nothing more."

Walter rubbed his chin and said nothing.

Ida turned to Patrick. "Where's Gabriel in all this?"

"Left standing on the sidelines, it appears," Patrick said. "There seems to have been some tension between them lately."

"What?"

"It's nothing too serious, considering they were together last night. My guess is he'd done something to upset her."

"Really?" Ida's gaze bored into his. "I don't know where he'd get that from."

"About what happened last night . . ." Patrick said.

"We're handling it."

"I hope so, because it's a problem, one that suggests the Gallagher boy might not be the only Cŵn Annwn trespassing in Cainsville."

Ida said nothing. They all went silent. Last night was, quite possibly, the first time in decades that Patrick wished he'd been part of the inner circle, just to see their reactions to the news. One of their special children found murdered. In Cainsville, no less. While he doubted the girl had actually been killed here, the fact remained that someone had murdered Ciara Conway and put her body in the Carew house. It was a message. About Olivia. One they did not wish to receive.

"We'll solve that," Ida said. "You handle this." She waved in the direction Olivia had gone. "Whatever is wrong between her and Gabriel, fix it. Now."

CHAPTER TWENTY-NINE

When Ricky passed the town limits and hit the gas, I found the rush I'd been looking for all my life. My earliest memories of life with Pamela and Todd Larsen? Me on a swing, Todd pushing me. Me in his arms as he swung me. Faster, higher, the air whooshing past like hits of pure oxygen. My first taste of a drug I'd never forget. No merry-go-rounds for me. I wanted roller coasters. I wanted go-carts and snow sleds. Faster. Higher. I remember my dad taking me out in the Spyder, and even before I was old enough to drive, he'd hand me the keys on a lonely stretch of road just like this, letting me take the wheel and go. Just go.

The wind whipping over my bare arms and legs was the most delicious burn imaginable, something I'd never gotten in a convertible, even with the top down. I could feel the motorcycle, too, in a way I never felt a car, no matter how perfectly the engine roared and rumbled. This rumble went right through me, vibrating against my bare thighs and, yes, everyplace else that vibration feels so damned good, making me really glad I hadn't put on a pair of jeans.

Leaning against Ricky's back, my legs wrapped around his hips, the burn of the wind and the rumble of the bike . . . It was a rush — an erotic blood rush, head rush, oh-my-God-this-is-amazing rush. I won't say it was better than sex, but I've had some that didn't live up to this.

It's not surprising, then, that as we rode, me leaning against him, legs wrapped around him, my fingers slid higher and crept inward, until my hands were wrapped around his inner thighs. When I realized that, I pulled back to a more appropriate hold. He slowed for a turn and stopped the bike, took my hands and put them where they'd been, twisting to look at me and mouthing, "Okay?"

I nudged open the visor. "I don't want to distract you."

"I don't get distracted. I get focused."

I rubbed the insides of his thighs and his lips parted, lust shimmering in his dark eyes. He pulled off my helmet and kissed me. It wasn't an easy angle, and the awkward, hungry kiss felt like teasing.

"You want to get off?" he whispered.

"Eventually."

He laughed, abrupt with surprise and ragged with desire. "Hell, yeah. The bike, I meant. Do you want me to stop?"

"Not yet."

I kissed him, our lips half meeting, tongues brushing, teeth clicking as we struggled for that elusive connection, the frustration of not finding it only raising the heat.

"I want more," I said.

He chuckled. "That's the idea."

"The bike, I mean. Faster." My fingers moved to his crotch, rock-hard under his jeans. "Yes?"

"Shit, yes," he said, his voice hoarse.

I pulled my hand away. "I shouldn't while you're driving . . ."

"You should." He put my hand back where it had been. "You absolutely should."

He kissed me again, and I started to think that getting off — the bike and otherwise — right away wasn't such a bad plan. When he went to put my helmet back on, I stopped him.

"I'd like to leave it off," I said.

He hesitated.

"Please." I moved against him. "I want to feel it."

"You really want to feel it?" He leaned

back and whispered a suggestion in my ear.

I pulled my leg up, turning sideways on the bike. Then I slid off my panties. I was going to stuff them into my pocket, but he took them and put them in the saddlebag. He took something from the bag as well — a condom. He lifted it, a question and a clear signal of where he figured this was heading. I nodded, and he pushed it down into his pocket.

I swung my leg back over the bike, hiked up my skirt, wrapped my legs around him, and put my hands back where they'd been. He pushed off.

If the earlier ride had been better than a few sexual encounters I'd had, the one I got now beat most of them. It was incredible, hair blowing, wind wailing past my ears, skirt hiked up around my hips, sitting bare-assed on the seat, the bike buzzing and rumbling under me, my hands on Ricky's crotch, rubbing him.

He wasn't lying when he said distraction only made him more focused. It was as if the bike itself responded, sailing over hills and around curves with a perfection of speed and motion that was beyond exhilarating. Beyond exciting. I leaned against his back and felt him under my fingers and the bike rumbling under me and . . . I came.

On the back of a bike. A completely unexpected, amazing orgasm that kept going until, the next thing I knew, Ricky was veering off onto a dirt trail into a patch of woods, hitting the brakes before the bike was even safely hidden by the trees, and then he was pulling me off the bike with a hoarse "Yes?" and the second I said yes in return, I swear he had the condom on and was inside me, before we even hit the ground.

I was still orgasming from the bike when the fresh waves hit, so intense I didn't care where we were, didn't even know if I was horizontal yet, only cared that it kept going. And it did, just long enough to leave me lying on the grass, panting, eyes rolling in ecstasy, with Ricky poised over me, whispering, "Shit, holy shit," until we both caught our breath and he laughed, a little awkwardly, as if embarrassed. "That was, uh, not quite as finessed as I'd hoped. Sorry. I got carried away."

"Oh, I like carried away. I was already there, if you couldn't tell."

"Yeah, that was . . . Holy shit." His cheeks colored. "I'll stop saying that. I sound like a sixteen-year-old after his first time."

"Don't," I said, grabbing the front of his T-shirt and pulling him down for a kiss.

"I'm just saying —"

"You're apologizing. I'm pretty sure if anyone should apologize, it's the person who had her hands where they should never be on someone operating a motor vehicle."

"Oh, I wasn't complaining. I just — I thought I had it under control, and then —"

"Stop. I said yes. You used a condom. If you keep apologizing, I'm going to presume that means you don't ever want to do that again, and I'm really hoping that's not the case because . . ." My tongue slipped between my teeth. "Hell and damn, that was good."

He smiled, but I could tell he was still worrying he'd messed up, been too eager, disappointed me.

Since we'd first met, Ricky had pursued me with the confidence of a man twice his age. Now that he'd succeeded, the doubts and vulnerability peeked through, and I knew they'd vanish again when he got his footing, but it was fascinating to see, more contradictions adding to his endless tangle of them.

He kissed me then, one hand behind my head, cushioning it from the ground, the other under my ass. When a car passed, he broke the kiss only long enough to make sure the long grass hid us. Then another noise stopped him: my grumbling stomach.

"It's reminding me that I promised you dinner," he said. "And I should damn well deliver before I try for more."

"I'm not so sure about that."

"Dinner? Or more sex?"

I laughed. "I mean that after lying on the grass, I'm not in any condition to be taken to a restaurant."

"Would you settle for pizza? Delivered?"

I slid from under him and sat up. "Delivered where?"

"Here, of course."

We were in the middle of nowhere, on an empty road surrounded, I was sure, by more empty roads.

"If you could manage that —" I began.

"— you'd spend the night with me? Yes, you have work in the morning. I'll get you back in time. But if I can manage to get pizza delivered here, will you let me find us a place for the night? I know that's not what you had in mind."

"I —"

He cut me off with a quick kiss. "I aim to impress, and I need a bed to do it. Besides, you don't believe I can get a pizza delivered out here, so . . ."

"Go on and try."

"We have a deal?"

"We do."

He had to walk to his bike to get decent cell service. Then he used his phone to look up a place. He called one. I heard a male voice answer. Ricky said he had the wrong number, hung up, and called another place. He got a woman this time and shifted into full charm mode, chatting away. After about two exchanges, I knew he had her. It was too damned easy for him. So I decided to make it tougher.

I started unbuttoning my blouse. He caught the movement and looked over. He could have looked away. He didn't. As I stripteased, his eyes never left me. Nor did he falter for one goddamned second in his other conquest, even as the growing bulge in his jeans told me my performance was not unappreciated. Less than two minutes later, he hung up.

"Pizza's on its way, isn't it?" I said.

"Yep. Twenty minutes. Which gives you plenty of time to finish." He took a step forward. "Unless you want help."

"Not yet," I said.

"You'll tell me when?"

"You'll wait until I do?"

He grinned, his look sending heat through

me. "That might require ropes. Strong ropes."

"Another time," I said. "For now, you'll wait. Right there. Until I'm ready."

"Yes, ma'am," he said, and eased back to watch the show.

I think Ricky was right: strong ropes would be required to hold him back when he wanted something. Possibly chains. I teased until it was clear he was about two seconds from breaking. Then I said the word and got very enthusiastic, very satisfying sex, with a few minutes to spare before pizza arrived and we ate, half dressed, on the grass.

At the motor inn, he did indeed show me exactly how attentive he could be. I was soundly asleep ten minutes after, the clock having not yet even struck nine.

Chapter Thirty

Two days ago, I'd compared my trek through James's office to a walk of shame, stumbling back after an unexpected all-nighter, everyone who sees you knowing what you were up to. Now I was doing exactly that. Getting dropped off at the diner at seven in the morning, still wearing my uniform from the night before, still with the guy I'd left with the afternoon before. And I didn't give a shit.

Ricky had offered to leave sooner so he could drop me behind my apartment and I could walk to work. I didn't see the point. Anyone spotting his bike in Cainsville would know exactly what had happened. I'd spot-cleaned and ironed my uniform at the motel, and I'd showered and put on lipstick and mascara from my purse. Good enough.

There was one thing I'd forgotten — to turn my phone back on and check for messages. Being with Ricky was like going on a vacation, and I sure as hell hadn't wanted to be reminded of my "back home life" with voice mail and texts. When I did turn it on, I had three missed calls, three voice mails, and four texts. Six were from Gabriel. I ignored them and checked the others.

One voice mail was from Rose. She'd found some interesting information, let her know when I could come by. One missed call and one voice mail were from James. I hadn't heard from him since I'd walked out of his office, and *now* he phones. Damn it. He'd left a simple "I'd like to talk. Call me." I sent him a text saying I was at work. Did I promise to call later? I did not.

The last non-Gabriel message cheered me up. A text from Ricky sent right after he'd dropped me off. A simple *Have a good day at work. Talk later.*

Then it was on to Gabriel. Two missed calls. One voice mail. Three texts. All with the same message: "Where the hell are you, damn it?" Not in those exact words. Gabriel would never be so crude. But the messages became increasingly curt, his patience fraying.

I sent a text before I started setting tables. *Got your messages. Early night. Missed calls. Sorry! Give me 5.* While Ricky and I didn't plan to hide our relationship from Gabriel and Ricky's father, neither of us was exactly anxious to deal with those conversations.

I called exactly five minutes after sending the text, holding the phone between my cheek and shoulder as I kept setting tables.

"You need to be more conscientious about checking your messages, Olivia," Gabriel said in greeting.

"I know. I'm sorry."

A pause, as if he'd expected me to argue that it was a Saturday. After a moment, he said, "I was calling for a reason."

"I figured that. Again, I'm sorry. It won't happen again."

Another pause. Then, "Ciara Conway's body has gone missing."

I stopped, fork in hand. "What?"

"Her body disappeared at some point during transfer or handoff. I haven't yet been able to obtain details. I only found out last night."

"Her body?" I said carefully. "So they still have —"

"No, her head was taken, too. The entire corpse."

"Does that happen? Is it just misplaced? Someone was getting their kicks scaring me with it, but I can't imagine they'd steal it back to continue the fun."

"I don't know, but I wanted you to hear

about it as soon as possible, given the circumstances. You're at the diner, correct?"

"I am," I said as I resumed setting the tables. "I was supposed to be off, but I switched a shift."

"All right. The detective handling the Conway case would like you to come into the station and answer questions. Normally, I would insist it be done at your home, to avoid inconvenience, but I suspect you wouldn't want that, so I've agreed to bring you to the station later. I presume you're free tonight?"

"Uh . . ." I'd agreed to meet up with Ricky later for drinks. "What time?"

"Meet me at the office at five, and I'll drive us over to the station. We'll have dinner afterward. We have a few matters to discuss."

When I hesitated, he said, "Olivia?" a little sharply, as if my agreement was merely a formality and any delay in giving it kept him from more pressing matters.

"That's fine," I said. "I'll see you at five."

As it turned out, I didn't need to feel bad about canceling with Ricky. He bailed first, with a text message saying he had urgent "club stuff" to deal with. A few days ago, I'd have thought nothing of him changing plans, but let's face it, sleeping together changes things. Of course, I worried this was an "Oh, shit" morning-after brush-off. I said it was fine and I'd just had something come up, too . . . which then got him worried.

A flurry of texts followed. Ricky made it clear that he wanted to see me after our separate engagements and would like to spend the night with me. At a hotel if that's what I was comfortable with, but he'd prefer his place or mine. Just tell him what I wanted. I did, in detail, which led to a break-time flurry of a whole other kind of texts. The upshot was that when I headed to the city, I'd bring an overnight bag.

"The detective who'll be interviewing you is Ruben Fuentes," Gabriel said as he drove us to the station. "You may notice that he doesn't like me, but that is no reflection on his handling of this case, so don't be alarmed."

"I think I'd be more alarmed if he did like you."

Gabriel slanted a look my way.

"What?" I said. "Are there cops who do?"

"The degree of antagonism varies, but that's a given, under the professional circumstances. A detective's job is to find the

279

killer. A defense attorney's job is to prove his incompetence in doing so. Fortunately, with many, that's not difficult. The law enforcement profession seems to attract an inordinate number of idiots."

"I'm sure they love to hear you say that. Just like I'm sure you *do* say it. In front of them."

"Not often." He cut off a car to make a right turn. "My goal is to keep my clients out of jail. Not to make friends."

"Then don't take offense when I point that out."

"I don't. I merely take offense at the glee with which you point it out. Back to the subject at hand. Fuentes is competent. I've never personally embarrassed him. He dislikes me because, when he was in Vice, I had his partner investigated for bribery."

"Was he actually accepting bribes?"

"Irrelevant," he said. "He was investigated and moved to a different department to avoid the temptation that Vice offers. Fuentes has not forgiven me. However, I trust he will deal with you fairly, and if he does not, I'll handle it. Given his antagonism, you may wish to cool our interplay."

"Pretend you're a necessary evil?"

"I wouldn't go that far."

"Oh, I can manage that performance.

Minimal acting required."

He glanced over to see if I was joking. I gave him an enigmatic smile and changed the subject.

CHAPTER THIRTY-ONE

Gabriel has a habit of steering me, with a hand at my back, as we walk. In the beginning, that guiding hand rarely even brushed the folds of my shirt. Gabriel doesn't do physical contact. But as we got to know each other, it became an actual tap on the arm or his hand lightly on my back. It sounds very intimate and personal. It wasn't. More like a sheepdog herding a wayward lamb.

Now, as he guided me through the station door, I jumped at his touch. A couple of departing officers noticed. Gabriel did not — he was too intent on his destination. As we walked, I kept about a foot farther away than usual. Again, he was distracted, not realizing I wasn't in my normal place until he reached to steer me toward the front desk . . . and discovered I wasn't within reach. His lips tightened in annoyance, and he caught my gaze. I dropped it as soon as our eyes met.

A middle-aged detective who'd been watching the exchange came forward.

"Gabriel," he said.

Professionally, I'm guessing police officers don't call lawyers by their first name, any more than lawyers would use an officer's. They stick to the proper titles, unless they're friends. Gabriel was not, I was certain, friends with any law enforcement officer, and this man's tone was pure condescension, as if Gabriel did not deserve the respect of *Mr. Walsh.*

"Detective Fuentes," Gabriel said. "This is Ms. Taylor-Jones."

"Olivia, please."

I kept my gaze lowered. After we shook hands, I cast a nervous look at two young officers who'd been watching and whispering as we came in. They weren't the only ones, but they were being the most obvious about it. *That's her. The Larsen girl.*

Gabriel moved closer. Protective. I don't think he realized he was doing it, and when I inched away, he shot me a puzzled look. Fuentes noticed, though — that as well as my general discomfort at being watched and assessed. He gave a sharp look at the whispering young officers, then said, "This way, please," and led me down the hall.

While we walked, I stayed close to Fuentes. Gabriel shot me a look behind the detective's back. I returned it, resisting the urge to mouth, "It was your idea, dumbass." Apparently, when he said to downplay our relationship, he meant verbally — don't joke with him, whisper with him, act too familiar with him. But it was the body language that counted most, and mine said, "This guy might be my lawyer, but he makes me nervous."

As Fuentes led us into an office, I cast a furtive glance at Gabriel. "Does Mr. Walsh need to be here? I'm sure he has better things to do, and it's only an interview. I'm not a suspect. I mean, obviously, I guess I am, but this isn't that kind of interview, right?"

"As your legal representation, it is best that I'm present for all questioning," Gabriel said.

"You can dismiss him," Fuentes told me. Then he added grudgingly, "But he's right. He should stay." A sympathetic smile my way. "I'll keep this as brief as I can."

I nodded and took a seat.

The interview proceeded without incident. I'd established my role, and I played it well — the poor lost girl, overwhelmed by the twists her life had taken, still shaken by the discovery of Ciara's body, nervous about this interview, even more nervous about having to associate with Gabriel Walsh, Necessary Evil. Basically, I did a dead-on impersonation of a helpless blond kitten.

Fuentes responded the way any decent person might, keeping the interview simple and nonconfrontational. We seemed to be nearing the end when another detective rapped on the interview room door then stuck her head in.

"Sorry to interrupt," she said. "It's about the Conway case."

"So is this," Fuentes said, nodding toward me.

"It'll just be a minute. We have a bit of a . . . situation."

Fuentes apologized to me. He walked to the door and stepped partway out, keeping it open, as if being chivalrous, not leaving me alone with the big bad wolf. Of course, that open door meant I could eavesdrop, which I did.

"The family won't make an ID based on the photos," the other detective said. "They want a DNA comparison."

"With what? We don't have a body."

"The techs took samples at the scene."

"Do we have an exemplar? I didn't think there was one in the missing persons file."

"There isn't," she said. "The parents want to be tested for comparison."

"They want us to do three DNA tests and a familial comparison, when we have perfectly good photographs to make an ID? Did you tell them this isn't *CSI*? Those tests take time and money, and they'll delay the investigation."

"I know, but someone put the idea in their head that photos aren't good enough. Now they're adamant. They won't believe it's her without a body or a DNA test."

"Keep listening," Gabriel murmured as he rose. "I'm going to use the restroom."

He brushed past the officers, who were still talking. It seemed Ciara's parents were here, and the other detective wanted Fuentes to try talking them out of their *CSI*-inspired madness. Fuentes stepped farther into the hall, letting the door close, as if deeming it safe now that Gabriel was gone.

As soon as the door clicked shut, I glanced at the Conway file. In the movies, this would be where I peeked at that file and saw the status of their investigation. Had Gabriel known Fuentes would close that door if he left, meaning he trusted me to take advantage of the situation? But if Fuentes walked in and caught me out of my chair, reading the file . . .

I reached out and eased the folder my way, my gaze fixed on the door, watching that handle —

The knob turned. I yanked my hands back. Gabriel walked in. Fuentes moved into the opening again, still talking to the other detective.

Gabriel leaned over to me. "Could you please go ask Detective Fuentes if he'd like us to come back later?"

I nodded.

"There's no reason to doubt that body was Ciara Conway, is there?" I said to Gabriel when we were in the parking lot.

"No," he said. "Despite the mutilations, the photos should be enough. If I was defending her killer, I would call the identification into question to plant doubt. But I suspect the parents are simply in denial."

"Someone *advised* them to have it done. Planted the idea."

"Likely a family member who has watched too much television. The wave of interest in forensic and crime scene analysis has been the bane of prosecutors for years now."

"And a boon for defense attorneys."

A faint smile. He opened the driver's door and climbed in. I followed.

As the car backed up, I said, "I didn't get

a look at the file."

"Hmm?" He checked his mirrors.

"I know you went to the restroom so Fuentes would leave and I'd read the file. I couldn't. I'm sorry."

A twitch of his lips. "Now who's been watching too many crime shows? The risk of being caught is too great, and you wouldn't have had time to read the file. You need a permanent copy." As he talked, he flipped through his phone. Then he passed it over. "Like this."

I enlarged the photo on his phone to see a page from the file.

"How the hell — ?" I stopped. "That's what you were doing in the restroom? You'd scooped the pages and were taking pictures of them? Shit. I didn't see a thing."

"That would be the point. I'll print those, and we'll have a look at them later."

SPECIAL INTEREST GROUP

James Morgan checked his cell phone as he walked through the underground parking lot. Looking for something from Olivia. A call, a text, an e-mail . . . It was past seven and Saturday. She'd said she was free today. Yet she hadn't rung him back.

He'd just finished drinks with Neil, his father's former campaign manager. Neil was still harping about the damned photo in the *Post.*

"Reconcile or dump her," Neil said. "I can massage it either way, but this waffling makes you look indecisive."

He could solve the problem by telling Neil that Olivia had dumped him. But she'd done that before, and he wasn't yet ready to accept it as her final word on the matter. He'd been fielding calls from his real estate broker, asking what he wanted to do with the house he'd bought. A *house,* damn it. For them. The best goddamned house he could find, and she'd loved it. She'd loved him. Now she just walked away? There must be more to it. And he had a good idea where that blame could be laid: on the shoulders of one Gabriel Walsh.

"Mr. Morgan?"

He glanced up sharply. When he saw the young man approaching him — mid-twenties, suit and tie, reedy and pale — James had to smooth the annoyance from his reaction. One problem with working in technology was that not everyone in the field had baseline social skills. To them, staking out James Morgan's car was a perfectly fine way to apply for a job.

A few months ago, he'd have brushed the kid off, politely but firmly, warning him this was not the way to make friends in the world that existed outside his basement. Now, though, even if he didn't plan to run for senator for years, he had to start paying more attention to how he reacted to strangers. Especially strangers who probably had a blog, Twitter, Facebook, and serious hacker skills.

"Yes," James said, plastering on a smile. "How can I help you?"

"The question is, how can I help you?" The young man held out a card. "Tristan Crouch. The Belarus Group." He paused.

"Have you heard of us?"

A salesman? God, that was even worse.

"No," James said, struggling to keep the curt edge from his voice. "I'm sorry, but I was just about to head home —"

"I heard you're scheduled to attend a dinner party with the POTUS in a few months. You could ask him about us. I'm sure he recalls us fondly. We were instrumental in his own senatorial campaign."

James stopped.

Tristan smiled. "Yes, I know, I'm too young to have done more than man the phones for that, but I'm using 'we' in the imperial sense. The group has sent me to make the first contact and to relay a few suggestions. They're interested in what they see. They just have . . . concerns."

James should politely excuse himself now. Tell Tristan that he appreciated his group's interest and he'd love to have drinks next week, giving him time to do his research on them. But there was something in the young man's tone and in his gaze that brushed aside James's doubts, and as Tristan spoke, James began to recall hearing of this Belarus Group. He should listen.

"The most immediate concern is your change of marital status." Tristan smiled. "Or should I say the lack of a change."

James tried not to wince. Damn Olivia. Why did she have to make everything so complicated?

"We like Ms. Taylor-Jones," Tristan said. "We believe she complements you perfectly. Attractive, but not unduly so. Ambitious, but again not unduly so. She's bright and witty and charming. From a solid local family. And now she comes with a very intriguing backstory, and we are impressed that you appear to see past that. Most men in your position would not."

"There's no question of that. I love her."

Tristan's smile held a touch of condescension, unsettling in one so young. "That always helps. We feel that your choice to support her through this tragic revelation will further endear you to voters. However, it would be better if you were more actively supporting her. We saw the photo in the *Post*."

Now James did wince. "I —"

"A biker." Tristan's lips twisted in distaste.

"And an MBA student who is clearly trying to get out of the family business. As for his association with Olivia, it is purely professional. They share a lawyer."

"Which brings me to issue number two. How well do you know Mr. Walsh?"

"His reputation —"

"We deal in fact, Mr. Morgan. Not gossip." Tristan opened his briefcase and handed James two folders. "That is the information we have collected on both Mr. Walsh and Mr. Gallagher. Neither is someone we wish to see associating with our candidate's future wife."

"I —"

"Our concern extends beyond their reputations for criminal and unsavory activities." The young man's voice dropped to a soothing murmur. "We fear for Ms. Jones's safety, as we believe you should."

"What?"

"We can see how she would find these two men appealing. They are both attractive and single, both powerful and successful in their own way, much like you. There is also the added appeal of . . ." Tristan seemed to search for a word. "Edge, perhaps. Excitement. Danger. These men have it in spades. While you . . ."

James heard the words hanging between them. *While you do not.*

You are James Morgan. You've made every most eligible bachelor list in the city for three years running. Women flirt with you everyplace you go. They buy you drinks. They give you their numbers. They pass you hotel room keys. And who is Olivia Taylor-Jones? The daughter of convicted serial killers. Yet she dumps you for a biker. A twenty-two-year-old biker.

He heard the words as if someone whispered them in his ear, and he felt the outrage of them.

If you want her, she should be yours.

He looked up sharply. He could have sworn he actually *did* hear those words, but Tristan only stood there, waiting and watching him.

She should be yours. You deserve her. They do not.

"I'll leave those files with you, Mr. Morgan," Tristan said. "And I'll leave you with two thoughts. One, we would be very pleased if you reunited with your fiancée. Two, if you do not, and there is no one there to protect her . . ." His eyes bored into James's. "She is dealing with dangerous men who will hurt her. You need to understand that."

James nodded.

"Tell me you understand that."

James felt his lips moving, as if someone was pulling them for him. "Yes, I understand that. I'll look after her. I'll fix this."

Tristan smiled. "Excellent. We'll be in touch soon."

He walked past James, heading for the

exit. James glanced down at his hands — at the files and the business card. On the card he saw only a name. No contact information.

He turned. "Do you have . . . ?"

He was alone in the parking garage.

CHAPTER THIRTY-TWO

Gabriel had to stop by the office. He left the car idling as he ran in. While he was gone, my cell phone rang. It was James.

"We need to talk," he said when I answered.

"This isn't a good time," I said. "I'm —"

"Côte d'Azur."

"What?"

"Côte d'Azur. The French Riviera. Next weekend. The two of us. To get this damned mess sorted out."

I almost said that I wasn't free next weekend. But that implied I'd go otherwise. The door opened and Gabriel slid back into the car.

I motioned I was on the phone and started opening my door to take the call outside, but he put the car in drive, with a flash of his watch, as if to say we had somewhere to be.

"Liv?" James prompted.

"There's nothing to sort out," I said. "I'm sorry. It didn't work. We tried —"

"Tried? Two dates, Olivia. I got two dates and a damned coffee before you were off running around with —" He sucked back the rest and his tone smoothed. "We haven't tried, and we can't, not here in Chicago, with everything that's going on. You're confused —"

"I'm not confused, James. I'm —" I looked over at Gabriel and lowered my voice again. "It's my fault, okay? Blame me. But I've made up my mind. We —"

"What do you want from me, Liv? Clearly you're waiting for the right response and I'm not giving it. I've tried staying away. I've tried *not* staying away. I want this, Olivia. I want you."

"And to hell with what I want?"

"I don't think you know what you want."

I bit my tongue. Hard. When I could manage it, I said, "I do know, James. And I'm sorry if it doesn't fit your plans, but that's my decision. Goodbye."

I hung up and exhaled.

"You made the right choice," Gabriel said.

I glanced over, to make sure he was actually talking about my phone conversation. Of course he was. It wouldn't occur to Ga-

297

briel not to eavesdrop — or to pretend he hadn't.

I made a noise in my throat, one that most people would interpret as "I don't want to talk about it."

He ignored it. "I understand it may be difficult to give up the financial and social stability that a marriage to James Morgan would offer. Yet while you may not be living in the style to which you are accustomed, you seem comfortable enough to manage until you receive your trust fund."

"You think I was marrying James for 'financial and social stability'?"

He frowned, as if to say, *Why else?*

I shook my head. "I was marrying him because I loved him, Gabriel."

He gave a derisive snort.

"Excuse me?" I said.

A look over his shades. "You can't really expect me to believe you'd tie yourself to a man like Morgan for some silly romantic notion. You're better than that."

"I think that's meant to be a compliment, but given the choice between lowering your opinion of me and letting myself be painted as a gold digger —"

"Gold digging would be marrying a rich seventy-year-old in hopes he'll die while you can still enjoy his money. You chose a suitable match — in age, social standing, wealth, and looks. A man who would provide a satisfactory and easy life for you. Traditionally, that is the way for a woman to secure her future."

"Sure. In the nineteenth century."

"And that doesn't apply today? In your social circles?"

He had a point, but I wouldn't concede it. "It wasn't like that with me. I have my trust fund, as you've pointed out. I had a family business that I could have joined. I have a graduate degree. Your low opinion of James is based on the fact you were able to fleece him, and to you that makes him a fool. James Morgan is a good and decent man."

"Which is why it wouldn't have worked."

"Ouch."

"That's not an insult, Olivia. James Morgan is completely decent and completely mediocre, and he'd have made you completely miserable. At least if you were marrying him for stability, you'd get something out of it. But love?" His expression conveyed his opinion of the concept. "I'm glad to see you're done with him. Don't backslide again."

"Backslide? Weren't you the one taking money to help me get back with him?"

His hands tightened on the wheel. There

was a moment of silence when I wished I hadn't said anything. Yes, he'd insulted me, but in his world there was nothing wrong with doing whatever it took to find a stable life.

"I didn't take money for that," he said finally, adjusting his grip on the wheel. "Morgan insisted on making it part of the deal, so I agreed, but I didn't accept payment for a service I didn't provide. I wasn't planning to accept . . ." He trailed off.

"To accept what?"

He shook his head, gaze forward. "Nothing."

"Okay, let's . . . I'd like to move past that. Put it behind us."

He exhaled. "So would I."

"That doesn't mean I'm okay with it," I said. "Or that I don't think you'll do it again."

"I won't." We were stopped at a light. He took off his shades and met my gaze. "I know I made a mistake. I knew I was making a mistake at the time. Even if I didn't see the harm in it, you felt betrayed. I understand that. It will not happen again."

It would. Not that he was lying. He meant it. But a time would come when he'd betray my trust again and he'd tell himself it was necessary or that I wouldn't be upset or that it didn't count. I had to deal with the possibility. I didn't need to forgive him if it happened again, but I couldn't tell myself it wouldn't. Either way I'd get hurt, but at least if I had my eyes open, it might dull the sting.

I nodded, and it must not have looked convincing enough, because he kept his gaze on me and said, "I mean it, Olivia."

"I know you do. Thank you."

He nodded, put on his sunglasses, and roared through as the light turned green.

I felt more centered after my talk with Gabriel. It was like sweeping away the last of the cobwebs, the stage clear to start again. It helped that he was in a rare truly good mood. We went to dinner at my favorite steak house — he'd made a reservation.

As we ate, Gabriel regaled me with the story of a past case, one he knew would amuse me. Compared with other diners deep in conversation, his gestures were restrained, his affect muted, his tone even, but for Gabriel he was positively animated. Possibly even a little drunk, having finished almost an entire glass of wine. His blue eyes glowed with a warmth I'd never seen, even at his most engaged, and I wanted to lean back and bask in it. But every time I relaxed, a little voice reminded me I needed to discuss something with him while he was in a good mood.

When we moved on to dessert, I worked up the nerve. I took a bite of my cheesecake, then said, as casually as I could manage, "Earlier, being at the station, it reminded me of something."

He sipped his coffee, brows arching, waiting for me to continue.

"Have you identified those photos yet?"

As soon as I said the words, I regretted them. He froze, coffee mug at his lips. He'd been having a good night, something he probably hadn't had in a very long time, something he deserved, and with six words I'd completely fucked it up.

"I'm so sorry," I said. "This isn't the time. I just — So, about the Meade case —"

"I haven't had a chance to see the photos," he said, lowering his mug. "I need to, obviously, and I will."

"I'll go with you," I said. "Whenever you're ready."

At that, he met my gaze and he smiled. It wasn't more than a wry twist of the lips, but it reached his eyes, warming them, as if I'd just volunteered to do a year's worth of research free of charge. Even when the look vanished, the smile lingered as he nodded.

"It's simply a matter of finding time." He leaned back in his seat. "I should make time, I suppose. It's not going to magically manufacture itself. Let me know when you're ready and we'll go."

"Whenever you are."

"What's your shift tomorrow? Yes, I know, it's Sunday, but if you're free . . ."

He'd decided to do this thing, and if we didn't arrange a time, he'd find an excuse to postpone.

"I have tomorrow off," I said. "I can meet you anytime."

"I'll pick you up."

"No, that's fine. I —"

"You're doing this for me. I'll pick you up. I might even let you drive."

He smiled then, a real smile, and I couldn't do anything but agree . . . to a time late enough for me to get my ass home from Ricky's.

CHAPTER THIRTY-THREE

I drove Gabriel back to his office. I'm sure there was no way in hell a few ounces of wine could legally intoxicate a guy over two hundred pounds, but it was definitely more than he was used to. Besides, I was happy for any excuse to get into the driver's seat. I took the long way and told myself I was just making sure he was sober, windows down, fresh air rushing in. He wasn't in any hurry, either, and we sat outside his office talking for almost an hour before I remembered he really needed his sleep. For once, he seemed relaxed enough to actually get it. So I said goodbye, grabbed the key Ricky had left behind my tire, and headed for his place.

Ricky's apartment was in a graduate housing complex on East Hyde Park. He lived with his dad, but he wanted a place for when he had classes. Technically, being a part-time student, I suspect he shouldn't have gotten into graduate housing at all, but I wasn't surprised that he'd managed it. Between Ricky's charm and persuasion and Gabriel's lock picking and sleight of hand, if I took enough lessons, I could become a first-rate private eye. Or a master criminal.

The building was quiet. Not a lot of students around in June. The floor layout was an odd C shape, with the elevator depositing me on the far side. I had to round a corner, then another —

I stopped. Ricky's apartment was two doors down. I could see the number. But someone was trying the doorknob. My hand went to my purse, sliding inside to where my gun rested. Even as I reacted, I chastised myself. Going for my gun because a drunk student had the wrong apartment? But my gut told me it wasn't a drunk student, and when I caught a glimpse of his profile, I jerked back around the corner, heart pounding.

It was the guy from the motel a month ago. The guy whose attack made me flee to Cainsville. A random motel clerk obsessed with my parents. And now he was here? Breaking into Ricky's apartment? How did that make sense?

I peeked around the corner and realized it wasn't the same man. He had a similar build — tall and wiry — but this guy was younger, had lighter hair, and bore only a passing resemblance to my attacker. Yet I couldn't seem to shake the association. I moved my gun into my jacket pocket before I rounded the corner.

"Can I help you?" I said.

He was taking something long and silver from his pocket. A lock pick? When I spoke, he jumped and turned, dropping the object back into his coat.

I double-checked the number on the door, confirming it was Ricky's.

"Are you looking for someone?" I said.

He paused. "Rick Gallagher," he said finally. "Is this his place?"

"Is he expecting you?" I asked.

"Olivia Taylor-Jones," he said, snapping his fingers. "I knew I recognized you. So you're coming to see Rick?"

"How do you know him?"

"Are you expecting him back soon?"

I sized him up. A reporter? From a school paper or blog? I'd been worried about that when the picture hit the *Post*. Ricky hadn't. While he didn't advertise who he was, he didn't hide it, either. Professors and students who knew his background presumed he was trying to "break the cycle." He didn't disillusion them.

"You should leave now," I said.

A brief smile. "Should I?"

I met his gaze. "Yes."

"When do you expect Rick back?"

"Do you want to leave a name and number? I'll tell him you dropped by."

He held my gaze, easing closer as my fingers tightened around the gun in my pocket. "Why don't I come inside and wait with you."

I sputtered a laugh. That seemed to surprise him. Had he really expected me to agree? He stood there, eyes locked on mine, as if he could . . . I don't know, hypnotize me? When I just smiled and shook my head, he looked honestly baffled.

"I think you should let me come inside with you," he said.

"I think you should haul ass back to the elevator before I call the police."

He blinked, finally breaking eye contact. One last look at me with that perplexed frown. Then he walked past, so close his jacket brushed me. I stood my ground.

"Shall I tell him who called?" I said.

He kept going. I waited until the elevator dinged, then I hurried to the stairwell. I zoomed down the flights and made it to the first floor just as he was walking through the front door.

I could see him outside, but the reflection

of the lights against the glass made him seem to disappear as he walked. Not vanish or fade, but blend into his surroundings.

He passed a parked light gray car, and his jeans and jacket seemed to lighten to match, leaving a gray blur. Obviously a trick of the darkness and the reflection of light. As soon as he was far enough away, I opened the door to see better, but once I did, I lost track of him completely.

He must have darted between parked cars. I went out and looked around. No sign of him.

I spent another few minutes looking. I wanted to see where he would go, what he drove, maybe get a license number. But I'd waited too long before stepping outside, and now he was gone. After one last look, I retreated inside.

CHAPTER THIRTY-FOUR

Ricky's apartment was what I'd expect for student housing — a place the size of mine, with a bedroom, bath, and all-purpose living and dining area. About as tidy as mine, too, which meant not spotless but not noticeably messy. Casual and lived in. I got comfortable on the bed while I did some work for Gabriel.

When the door opened a few minutes later, boot steps told me it was Ricky. He rounded the corner into the bedroom. I started to close the laptop.

"Don't let me disturb you," he said. "I'm just enjoying the view."

He stood at the foot of the bed, a little bleary-eyed after a long day but waking up now, brown eyes glittering as they traveled over me, facedown on his bed, dressed only in my panties. As he admired me, I twisted to look over my shoulder and did the same back. He'd shucked his jacket at the door and wore a dark T-shirt, tight across his biceps, the edge of one tattoo peeking from under a sleeve. His blond hair was mussed from the helmet, raked back with his fingers, falling forward now as he watched me. His jeans were faded, fraying at the seams, sculpted to his thighs and everything else. I rose and his gaze never left me, sliding down then back up to my face, lingering at points in between. Then he lifted his hand, stopping me.

"Don't you have work to do?" he said, gesturing at the laptop.

"Yes," I said. "But not with this." I closed the computer and shot a pointed look at his bulging crotch.

A rough chuckle. "As tempting as that is, I'm going to have to insist you go back to work. You tested my distractibility. Now I get to test yours."

"Oh?"

"Um-hmm."

He walked over, opened the laptop, set it up, and waited for me to flip onto my stomach. Once I did, he retreated. A moment later, the bedsprings creaked. Hands slid over my calves, up to my thighs, squeezing gently before tugging down my panties. The hands again, pushing me up a little, parting my knees, and then . . . a warm mouth, hot tongue, and . . .

"Oh," I said.

"Um-hmm."

I sighed, quietly closed the laptop, and let myself be fully distracted.

An hour later, we were stretched out on the bed, naked, talking, drinking beer, and eating leftover nachos he'd brought home. He did most of the eating. I was still stuffed from dinner. He asked where we'd gone. When I told him, he whistled.

"Very nice. Gabriel footed the bill, I hope."

"He did, though he can expense it. Also, he's picking me up at my apartment at ten tomorrow, so I can't sleep in as late as I'd hoped. I suspect he'll want me to do some work after that."

"I'll be home studying. Got a midterm next week. Seems tomorrow's going to be a write-off for us, then. I'm expected to hang at the clubhouse a few nights a week, and I've been remiss. If I don't, my dad will know something's up." He took a last slug of beer and crushed the can. "Once we've gone public — with my dad and Gabriel — I'm going to need to ask you to join me now and then, if you can. Not your scene, I know . . ."

"That's fine."

"I'll make it easy. But if the guys know I'm seeing you, they'll wonder why you're not there with me. Whether you think you're too good for them or I'm embarrassed by them." He made a face as he popped open another beer. "Politics. Motorcycle gang or country club, there's always politics."

"Do you usually date girls from there?" I said. "I know one seemed a little territorial."

He sputtered a mouthful of beer. "Lily? She's eighteen."

"You're twenty-two. It's not cradle-robbing."

"With Lily, it would be. She's a very young eighteen. I don't date girls who hang out at the clubhouse. Ever. Did you actually see them?"

"I'm not judging."

He laughed. "Judge away. That is not my dating pool. I mostly go out with girls from school. Not a lot of that, though. I'm too busy, and it's too complicated. Either way, no one expects me to bring casual dates to the clubhouse."

"If you need me, I'm there."

"Okay. I, um, wouldn't make plans for next Saturday then. If you want me to keep my mouth shut a little longer, I will, but I'd rather come clean with my dad."

"Just warn me, and I'll talk to Gabriel. We can both get the this-is-a-bad-idea speech at once."

"I know." He took a long drink of his beer, then said, "But it's not going to change anything, right?"

"Not for me."

"Good." He put the beer aside and pulled me over.

When I told Ricky about his late-night visitor, he didn't seem too concerned. He doubted it had anything to do with the club. There were territorial issues, of course. I'd gotten a crash course on that from Ricky a while back. In Chicago, there were Illinois natives the Outlaws and the Hell's Lovers as well as chapters of other gangs, like the Hells Angels and Wheels of Soul. They were all much bigger than Satan's Saints, and the Saints basically stayed out of their way, having no interest in expanding their territory. As for "territory" in their less-than-legal activities, Ricky said it didn't overlap much with others'. His father had carved out their own niche.

Most likely, Ricky figured, it was exactly what I'd suspected — a third-rate reporter hoping for a story. If the guy came around again, he'd take care of it.

It was probably a good thing I'd be spending Sunday night at my apartment. TC was not impressed with my gallivanting. Can't blame him, really. Get trapped in a basement, finally make it home . . . and your damn owner only pops in on breaks to give you food and water before vanishing again.

I got back an hour before Gabriel was due to arrive. I had a call from Howard, which I returned. Just a check-in for my mother — I'd gotten busy and forgotten yesterday. TC spent the next half hour following me and jumping onto the nearest tall object to give me the stink-eye. When a rap came at the door, he planted himself in front of it, as if forbidding me to answer. I moved past him. He stalked back into the living room.

I opened the door to find Gabriel standing there, a coffee in hand. He passed it to me. "Yes, I'm early, but I need to get a photograph of Seanna from Rose. I'll give you this while it's still warm."

"Thank you." When he started to go, I stepped into the hall after him. "Gabriel?"
"Hmm?"
He turned. His shades were on, but I didn't need to see his eyes to know he was still in a good mood. The mocha suggested

it. His stance and expression, relaxed and at ease, confirmed it. I hated to screw that up. I really did. But I had to warn him.

"She knows. Rose, I mean. If you planned to grab a photo and not mention why . . . She already knows."

"Ah."

"I'm sorry," I said, setting my drink down. "I asked her if you'd been to the station, and . . ."

"She didn't know what you were talking about. You had no reason to think I wouldn't have told her. I intended to. I just hadn't gotten to it. I'll apologize, then, for putting you in that position."

His face was still relaxed, no sign of concern. When I glanced up, he lifted his shades onto his forehead, and there was nothing more to see in his eyes. Calm and centered.

"Okay," I said. "I just wanted to warn you."

"I'd need to explain when I asked for photos of Seanna anyway. It's not as if I'd want a few for decorating my apartment." A quirk of his lips, no bitterness in his eyes. "This saves me from having that conversation, and since it saves you from having to listen to it, we'll go over together."

SILENCE

Gabriel looked better than Rose had seen him in weeks. Happier than she'd seen him in . . . Well, that was harder. Even as a child, "happy" was never a word she'd use to describe Gabriel. Not angry or sad, either. His emotional continuum seemed to range from content to unsettled. Today, he was closer to happy than she'd have thought possible.

The reason for his mood was obvious. Eden had forgiven him. Oh, Rose was sure there was more to it than that — work must be going well, his schedule easing, his leg healing, life moving back on track. But the reconciliation was significant. The cards had foretold it, in their damnably decisive way. There were, as always, two choices, two paths. Gabriel would win Eden back and ease further out of isolation. Or he would not, and he'd shut down again.

There was no middle ground. There never

was. This path, this outcome. That path, that outcome. And little she could do to set anyone's feet on the right one. Like being bound and gagged, watching people you cared about heading to their doom.

But Gabriel was on the correct path now, and she saw that as soon as he came in, barely a word for her, still midconversation with Eden. He'd won her back, and he was happy. Which suggested, she supposed, that he didn't know she'd gotten in only an hour ago, and whose bed she'd come from.

Rose was not about to enlighten him. It was none of his business. When he found out, he'd make it his business. He'd interfere. She didn't need the cards to tell her that. It wouldn't be sexual jealousy. That was still firmly on the other side of the wall, a nonissue for as long as he could keep it a nonissue. For now, it would be jealousy of Eden's time. Of her attention. Sparked by deeper feelings, but that wall would not be breached anytime soon.

Rose wasn't going to interfere. In any of it. Let Gabriel find out about Ricky Gallagher in his own time. Let Eden enjoy her fling, which she obviously was, given her own cheerful mood. As for the cards, they were staying silent on this, which she presumed meant it wasn't worth divining. A minor complication with no major impact either way.

Rose gave Gabriel the photos, and he tucked them into his pocket without a glance. Not intentionally ignoring them but paying them no mind because he was listening to Eden as she pointed out some interesting artifact in the room. When she finished, Gabriel turned to Rose and said, "You have something you wanted to tell Olivia?"

"Right," Eden said. "You left a message about the boar's tusk. Sorry I didn't get a chance to pop over."

Rose told them what she'd dug up. Wild boars had been native to the British Isles before being hunted to extermination centuries ago. Those hunts found their way into the folklore. Even King Arthur had his boar hunt quest.

They were also linked to the Wild Hunt. In some stories, that was what the riders chased through the ancient forests: a giant ghostly boar. Other times, in pictures, the beasts almost seemed to run with them, alongside the steeds and hounds.

In Celtic lore, the boar's tusk could be a symbol of fertility or protection. Given what the mysterious man had said when he gave it to Eden, Rose was going with protection.

That was the sense she'd gotten when she handled the thing as well. She'd also found Celtic and Druidic references to horn amulets, used as protection against the evil eye. This seemed a variation on that.

All that she could have guessed without her books — or even the second sight. The real question was what the engraved symbols meant. She'd managed to identify a few as Celtic, and they supported the protection theory. There were also a sun and a moon, the symbols linked, with writing below. No matter how hard she dug, though, she found nothing that would help her decipher the writing.

When she held the tusk, she felt unsettled. The urge to put it away, hide it away, was almost overwhelming. The thing didn't feel evil. It just felt . . . as if it didn't belong here, in her house, in her hand. In Cainsville.

That's what she felt most of all. That it didn't belong in Cainsville. This was no ordinary town. She'd always known that. As for exactly what its peculiarities hid, she'd been raised not to question, and she didn't. Her soul rested quietest that way. Eden's soul would, too. As would Gabriel's. So she told them about the tusk and the folklore and the symbols she'd deciphered, and as

for the rest — her feelings about it and
Cainsville and their connection — she said
nothing at all.

CHAPTER THIRTY-FIVE

The police station wasn't the same one we'd been to yesterday. This one was in an area of the city I didn't recognize. An area I'd never have had any reason to visit. While some of the historically "bad" areas of Chicago had been redeveloped, this one had been left alone. Left well alone.

Was this where Gabriel grew up? I supposed so. It was where Seanna's body had been found, in one of these buildings, probably still empty fifteen years later.

The detective who retrieved us at the front desk was young, new to his shield, given this task because of it. He didn't even seem to notice me. He was too busy sizing up Gabriel.

"You have quite the reputation, Mr. Walsh," he said as we walked through the station. He managed a smile that I'm sure he intended to be confident, but it wavered at the edges. "I expected you to be older."

Gabriel grunted, taking in his surroundings.

"I don't know what all this is about," the detective said. "But it better not be some kind of trick. They told me to watch for tricks."

Gabriel turned his gaze on the young man then, cold blue eyes swinging his way and pinning him, squirming, under that empty stare.

The detective began, "I'm just saying —"

"Nothing new. Nothing interesting. I make you nervous. You're talking to hide it, which only reveals it all the more. A word of advice, detective? If you're given the chance to take the witness stand, avoid it. You're not ready."

"There's no trick," I cut in before the detective could reply. "As Mr. Walsh explained, I was shown photographs by William Evans before he died. They were reportedly from a cold case your department has on file. We'd like to confirm that by seeing the originals."

"You could have asked us to compare them with the ones found at the scene."

"Yes, but given it's my parents' freedom at stake, I'd like to check all avenues myself."

"Parents . . ." He stared at me. Recognition clicked. "Miss . . ."

"Taylor-Jones," Gabriel said. "I mentioned she was accompanying me, did I not?"

"Um, right. I just didn't make the connection."

"Now you have. The photographs, please?"

The young man led us into the bullpen, and I realized he intended for us to identify the photos there — in front of the other detectives. Now, as he saw the detectives at their desks, Gabriel faltered. Just a split-second hesitation before he found his resolve again, his expression never losing that impassivity.

"Can we do this in private?" I asked.

"No," Gabriel began. "This is —"

"May I do it in private?" I met the young detective's gaze with an anxious look. "Please?"

"R-right. Of course. Let me grab the folder."

As he hurried off, Gabriel dipped his chin, saying nothing but acknowledging what I'd done, telling me it was appreciated.

The detective retrieved the folder and led us into another hall. As we walked, he babbled about how he'd be in contact with the detectives in the Evans case, make sure they got my statement regarding the identification and the file if it was a match.

When we reached an open interrogation room, the detective led us inside. He set the folder on the table and motioned for us to sit. I did. Gabriel didn't. He stood behind me and squeezed my shoulder, as if I was the one needing reassurance, and I shifted back, resting against his hand.

The detective kept up a steady stream of chatter as he prepared to open the folder. Telling me how the photos might be disturbing, but if I'd seen them already then he guessed I didn't really need to be warned, blah, blah, blah. Part of me wanted to tell him to shut up. Just shut up. I might have, too, if I hadn't suspected the prattle actually let Gabriel relax as the detective focused on me.

I couldn't see Gabriel's face as the folder opened. I suspect he was happier that way, no one to witness his reaction. I could feel him there, though, his thumb rubbing my back the only sign of his agitation.

"Are these the photos you saw at the scene?" the detective asked.

"They are," I said.

"And I believe I can identify the victim," Gabriel said.

I glanced back. Gabriel's face was blank,

324

his eyes equally blank, fixed on the photographs.

"Her name was Seanna Walsh," he said. "She was my mother."

Things went awkwardly after that. Detective What's-his-name — yes, I should really pay more attention — decided Gabriel was launching some scheme. By claiming a long-dead addict was his mother? That wasn't just ridiculous — it was unbelievably offensive. I gave the detective hell. By the end of it, I think he had decided I wasn't nearly as nice as I'd seemed. In fact, given the choice, he'd probably rather have dealt with Gabriel, who took the accusation in stride, calming me down when I lit into the detective.

Gabriel handed over the photographs he'd brought. One was of both him and Seanna. He provided his mother's vital statistics and the name of the detective who'd handled her missing persons report. He did this all with perfect calm, perfect civility, perfect professionalism. By the end, the detective apologized. Gabriel graciously accepted it. I was still pissed.

We were halfway down the hall when the detective came jogging after us.

"Mr. Walsh," he said.

Gabriel turned.

"The remains —" He stopped himself and flushed. "Your mother, I mean. Her body is buried at Homewood. That's —"

"I know what it is."

"Arrangements can be made to move her. To bury her properly, in a marked grave."

Gabriel's perfect calm cracked then, not enough for the detective to notice, just a hairline fracture. I could see the panic in his eyes, as he struggled to give the gracious response, to say yes, that would be fine, thank you very much. But he couldn't. He could not act like he gave a damn where his mother's body lay, like he'd pay a cent to move her. He just froze.

"We'll be in touch," I said.

Gabriel nodded stiffly, put his hand to my back, and led me out.

As we walked to the car, I kept sneaking glances at Gabriel. I thought I was being discreet about it. He had his shades on, gaze forward, as if lost in thought. As we turned into the lot, though, he said, "You can stop fretting, Olivia. I'm not going to collapse."

"I know. I'm just —"

"Fretting."

"Concerned."

"I'm fine. I've had plenty of time to

prepare for it." A few more steps. "This afternoon we could work on the Conway investigation, now that her death is official." He paused, then added, "If you're free," as if just remembering he should check.

"I am. Nothing planned until my diner shift tomorrow."

He checked his watch. "I should get you lunch first."

"Can I buy this time?"

"You can."

"I should probably drive, too."

He bent to open the car door and looked over the top of his shades. "Did I say I was fine?"

"Just to be sure. I'm only thinking of you."

He shook his head and waved me over to the driver's side.

We passed the Mills & Jones department store. As we idled at a light, I looked over at the store, taking up half a city block of real estate, a Chicago landmark. I used to be there a few times a week, meeting my dad or hanging out with him. Since his death, I could count on one hand the number of times I'd walked through those massive front doors. I just can't do it anymore.

I felt guilty about that sometimes. Guilty, too, about not taking a hand in the busi-

327

ness. I had a seat on the board. Or I did. By now, for all I knew, they'd voted to kick my ass off. Would I care? I don't know.

"Olivia?" Gabriel's quiet voice.

"Hmm?"

He waved at the light, green now. I pulled through.

CHAPTER THIRTY-SIX

Under normal circumstances, Gabriel orders an average-sized meal and eats it all, never picking anything out, never leaving anything. But there's no hint of voraciousness. He approaches food the way he seems to approach everything in life: with dispassionate intent.

Usually, he just glances at the menu, and I can never tell if that's decisiveness or a complete lack of interest in the options. Today, he considered. And he ate as if he actually tasted the food.

What was it like to find out that your mother hadn't abandoned you after all? That she'd been dead for half your life? As Rose said, this didn't change anything about the kind of parent Seanna Walsh had been. Gabriel had probably spent his childhood waiting for the day when she would leave for good. When it came, he carried on. At fifteen. Not only surviving, but putting himself through law school. That's an act of will I cannot even begin to fathom.

After walking out of the worst neighborhoods of Chicago and into a life with six-figure sports cars and four-figure suits, did he ever worry that Seanna would find out what he'd made of himself and show up on his doorstep with her hand out?

I'm sure he had. I'm sure, too, that he'd feared what would happen if he refused. That she'd go to the papers, tell them about his past, what he came from. The rumors were already there, and he did nothing to stop them. A defense attorney from the wrong side of town, with a juvenile record, and questionable sources of income? It only meant that he understood some of his clients in a way no Ivy League suit ever could. What Gabriel would fear was a different sort of public reaction to his past. Not condemnation or scorn. Pity.

Now she was gone. Forever. Was he relieved? Yes, I think he was.

As we walked to the parking lot after lunch, Gabriel glanced behind us twice.

"Is someone there?" I asked.

"Perhaps . . ." A slow scan of the busy road. "A reporter most likely." He handed me the car keys. "If we're approached, keep going. I'll deal with it."

When we reached the lot, Gabriel turned sharply, and I saw James striding our way.

"I'd like to speak to Olivia," James said as he approached.

"I'm sure you would," Gabriel said, sliding between us. "However, that is normally accomplished by a phone call, not waylaying her in a parking lot."

"I was dining downtown and spotted her —"

Gabriel motioned to James's hand. "You're still holding your keys, and you're short of breath."

James dropped his keys into his pocket and stepped sideways to address me. "An associate saw you in the restaurant and called me. He was concerned about your choice of dining companion."

"And you came running to her rescue?" Gabriel said. "How noble."

"No, I came to speak to her, because I seem to be having some difficulty accomplishing that." Another sidestep, Gabriel having eased over to block him again. "If you won't return my calls, I have no way of communicating with you, Liv. I don't know where you work. I don't know your new address."

"Perhaps, given your penchant for waylaying her, you can understand why she wouldn't be eager to share that information."

James glowered at Gabriel. He had to look up to do it, and I could tell he didn't like that.

"This is a private conversation," James said. "Could you leave, please, Mr. Walsh?"

"Absolutely not."

James pulled out his wallet. "How much?" he asked.

"How much what?"

"How much will it cost to make you walk away? I know there's a price."

James's lips curved, pleased with his jab. Gabriel only tilted his head.

"How much do you have?" he asked.

James pulled out a wad of bills. "Will five hundred do it?"

"I believe so."

Gabriel pocketed the money and walked away. I smiled and shook my head.

"You're okay with that?" James said as Gabriel left. "Your lawyer just took money to leave you alone with me."

"You offered it," I said. "It's not as if he turned me over to a potential mugger. Now, what — ?"

Gabriel returned and stepped between me and James again.

"Second thoughts?" James said. "I'll take

my money back."

"Certainly not. I did as you asked. I walked away."

I had to laugh.

James scowled at me. "You find this amusing?"

"Yes, I do. However, at the risk of losing further amusement, I'm going to end this group hug. James, please don't track me down."

"It's over," Gabriel said. "Leave her alone. That is the message she's trying to convey. If you need it in writing, I can arrange that. In the form of a restraining order."

"Excuse me?" James said.

"He's not serious," I said.

"Yes, actually, I am," Gabriel said. "At present, the situation does not qualify, but I am serving notice, Mr. Morgan. If you waylay Olivia again, there will be consequences."

"Is that a threat?"

"No, it's a warning."

"All right," I said. "Let's not blow this out of proportion."

"I don't think I am." Gabriel lifted his shades. "Am I, Mr. Morgan?"

Before James could answer, Gabriel laid his hand on my shoulder, steering me toward the car.

"You're going to allow him to do that?" James said. "Speak for you? Threaten me? Shuttle you off?" He strode toward us. "I'm not letting you walk away with this thug —"

"If you lay a hand on her —"

"Go to hell, Walsh." James started past him. When Gabriel blocked him again, James snarled, "You're not going to stop me —"

"Actually, I will."

"James, *please.* Just turn around and walk away. Gabriel? Can we go? I don't want to do this."

Gabriel waved for me to continue toward the car. As we turned, James lunged. His fingers closed on my arm, and I was pulling away when I saw a blur of motion. His hand jerked free. At a bone-cracking thump, I spun to see Gabriel with his fist wrapped in James's shirtfront, James slammed up against an SUV and gasping in pain and shock.

"Are you psychotic?" James struggled to get free, but Gabriel kept his hold. "Liv, tell your pit bull —"

"I warned you not to touch her," Gabriel said, his tone conversational.

"She is my fiancée," James spat.

"*Ex*-fiancée, a concept you appear to have difficulty comprehending, which is at the root of this problem. However, if you are suggesting that even as her fiancé you would have the right to touch her, you are mistaken on a very important point of law. You do not. You will not. Is that clear?"

"Is that a threat?"

"No. This is a threat." Gabriel leaned down. "If Olivia wishes to speak to you, she will contact you. If *you* contact *her,* I will take action."

"What? Beat me up and throw me in the river?"

"McNeil."

"The McNeil? Where the fuck is — ?" James stopped. He froze. Then, slowly, he lifted his gaze to Gabriel's.

"Good," Gabriel said. "We understand each other. If you bother Olivia again, I will have a little chat with the SEC. Tell them about your arrangement with Mr. McNeil."

James said, "I don't know what you're talking about," about ten seconds too late. He tried to yank his shirt from Gabriel's grasp. "That isn't a game you want to play, Walsh."

"No?" Gabriel's lips curved in what could have been mistaken for a smile. "Try me and see how much I want to play it. And how good I am at it."

Gabriel released him. James recovered,

shame and fury blazing in his eyes. Fury at me, too, for standing there, watching him be humiliated. Even now, his glower said, "Aren't you going to say anything?"

I turned and headed to the car. It wasn't until we were in it that I said to Gabriel, "He isn't usually like that."

"Because he usually gets what he wants."

"No, he's just upset —"

"Because he's not getting what he wants, and it isn't an experience he's accustomed to." Gabriel glanced back, making sure James was gone. "Are you aware of his reputation in the corporate world, Olivia?"

"If you're referring to what I presume is an SEC violation, I honestly have no idea what that's about. I don't even know a Mc-Neil."

"Of course not. Because he keeps you out of that. I have a reputation for being ruthless in my professional life. Correct?"

I nodded.

"So does James Morgan. Which is how he has reached his level of success. But he handles himself differently in public. He comes from a political family. He has political aspirations. Ruthlessness would make him seem cold. Calculating. Unpleasant. So he's mastered the art of the dual personality." Gabriel eased back in his seat. "I suspect it's not entirely an act. He's found a way to be tough professionally, while remaining warm and amiable personally. Except when he doesn't get what he wants. Am I correct that he initially pursued you? Actively and doggedly pursued you?"

"It wasn't *aggressive* —"

"Of course not. But if my sources are correct, it was a determined pursuit and courtship. He was an aspiring politician, and he knew the role that traditional marriage plays in such aspirations. He needed a young wife, from a good family, attractive, intelligent, and well educated, a suitable match in all regards."

"You make it sound like he was choosing a horse."

A pause. "You're insulted," he said, as if he couldn't quite fathom why. "I'm not saying he chose you merely because you fulfilled a list of requirements. He was already involved with someone who did that. Marriage to you promised more personal satisfaction, so he dropped her, pursued and won you. Then this happened. He set about getting you back, confident that he would not only win *you* but win your gratitude for taking you back under the circumstances."

I snorted.

"Therein lies the problem. A man like

James Morgan is not accustomed to being thwarted and will not take it lightly." He glanced over. "You think I overreacted, don't you?"

"I think you intentionally overreacted. Like killing a fly with a baseball bat, just to make sure it never bothers you again."

His lips curved. "An apt analogy." The smile faded. "However, not entirely accurate. His behavior concerns me, Olivia. He refuses to accept that he's lost you, and it doesn't seem like groveling or desperation. It seems like pride and anger. He wants you back, and he will keep coming after you until he gets what he wants."

"Well, he won't now. Whatever you've threatened him with, it worried him. He'll stay away."

"I hope so," Gabriel said, and started the car.

CHAPTER THIRTY-SEVEN

We didn't visit the Conway family. Though Ciara's body had been found, I still couldn't visit them in good conscience. I also knew what it meant to lose a loved one. When my dad died, I realized for the first time the cruelty of funeral customs that expect the family to meet and greet people mere hours after a death. Yes, I know, it's supposed to provide support. But I hadn't wanted support. I'd wanted to curl up in my bed and grieve. Gabriel didn't understand but agreed to wait until after Ciara's funeral.

Instead, we visited two friends and a teacher whom I'd found in my online research. That was all we could fit into an afternoon, and we were lucky to find many potential sources at home and willing to speak to us.

All we heard were variations on a story. Ciara was a good girl. Ciara was a troubled girl. Good but troubled — that was her epitaph. We asked if she'd expressed concerns about anyone following her, stalking her, contacting her. Nope. She was there, struggling through life. And then she wasn't.

By the time we finished the interviews, it was past seven. Gabriel was driving me home when he noticed the time and said, "I should have got you dinner."

Gabriel might not seem to take much interest in feeding himself, but God forbid I missed a meal. I was curled up in the passenger seat, half drowsing to the strains of Handel. I bit back a yawn. "I'd invite you over, but the only thing I have is dry cereal and bread. And I think the bread is sprouting a lovely shade of periwinkle."

"I'll take you out, then."

"That wasn't a hint."

"I know, but . . ." He pulled out his wallet and thumbed through the wad of bills from James. "It was a profitable day."

I laughed and shook my head. He glanced over, as if making sure I was really okay with him fleecing my former fiancé. I was. James fell for it and could afford it.

"Dinner it is, then," he said. "I believe we're past the point of pulling off the highway, so you'll have to settle for the diner."

"The food's good. The service is iffy, but

340

that new girl isn't on tonight, so it should be fine."

By the time we got there, the dinner crowd had cleared out and the place was more than half empty. That may explain why we seemed to provide the main source of entertainment. Ida, Veronica, and the other elders sat there, beaming and whispering until I felt like the wallflower who showed up for prom with the star quarterback.

"Next time?" I whispered. "You're getting dry cereal and toast. I'll scrape off the mold."

He glanced around. "It does inhibit conversation, doesn't it?"

"Mmm."

Patrick stopped by the table, slinging his laptop bag over his shoulder.

"Calling it a night?" I said.

"I am." He leaned over and lowered his voice. "Keep talking to me. Smile. Nod. Look happy."

"Why?"

"The old folks think I've done something right for a change. I see no point in disillusioning them. Just look like you're pleased to see me. You, too, Gabriel."

"What do we get for it?" I asked.

"My gratitude, which is valuable beyond

reckoning."

I snorted. Gabriel smiled and sipped his coffee.

Patrick turned to him. "How are you doing, Gabriel?"

"Very well, thank you."

"*Very* well?" An enigmatic smile. "I'm glad to hear it." He straightened. "All right, kids. Enjoy your meal and ignore the old folks." He started to leave, then turned. "Did I hear that the body of Ms. Conway disappeared in transit the other day?"

"It did," I said.

He pursed his lips. "Won't that impede the investigation?"

Gabriel shrugged. "It'll mean no autopsy, but there's still a coroner's report and crime scene analysis. They have what they require to proceed."

"Ah, right. Interesting." He seemed to look at the elders as he hefted his bag again. "Interesting."

He smiled over his shoulder and left.

Gabriel followed me home after dinner. That was understandable, given that he'd parked out front. Except he didn't stop at his car when we got there.

"I want to show you something," he said. "A personal project that will improve your

342

research skills."

"Do I get paid for it?" I asked as I followed him up the steps.

"Did you catch the *personal* part? I'm assisting you with something I believe you'll be interested in, and you'll receive the benefit of my experience in lieu of cash."

"I'd rather have the cash."

When we entered the apartment, TC went nuts, as if he hadn't seen me in days. I gave him a pat then bumped him off the kitchen table and set up my laptop.

"Okay, so what are we doing?" I asked.

"A public records search."

"You really know how to show a girl a fun night, don't you?"

He lowered himself into the other chair. "Records searches are one of the most necessary skills for a researcher. Also, one of the most tedious. Which is why I'm passing my knowledge on to you."

"Oh, joy." I opened a browser window and hit a bookmarked site. It brought up the online search for the Cook County records.

"Ah," Gabriel said. "Doing prep work, I see. Unfortunately, for tonight's purposes, that's the wrong county." Gabriel punched in the search terms and bookmarked another site for me. "We're going to pull up property records for the house where you found Ciara Conway's body." He glanced over. "That interests you, does it not?"

It did. After seeing those omen friezes and hearing Rose's story, I wanted to know more about the woman who owned the house.

"It isn't a simple matter of entering an address," he said.

"So I noticed when I looked at the Cook County site," I said. "Township, subdivision, lot number . . . They need a ton of information. And even then their records only go back to 1985. For transactions before that, you need to go to the office and dig through files."

"Which is a glorious way to spend a day. As you'll eventually discover."

"Don't you guys hire law clerks for that?"

"I have you. Fortunately, the records for this county go back further, probably because there are relatively few of them. I'll show you another time how to obtain property specifics. For now, here they are."

He passed me his cell, with the details on a text note. I entered them and got "property not found."

"You've made a mistake," Gabriel said.

"Naturally."

I let him double-check my input. It was correct. He entered information for Rose's house, which he'd brought for comparison. When it also came up blank, he fixed the screen with a cold stare.

"Intimidation only works on living things," I said. "Let me see what I can find."

The answer was on the records-search site, under FAQ. Records for Cainsville had not been digitized. They were available at the town records office, inside the library, and could be accessed by appointment only, with a minimum of forty-eight hours' notice.

"Seriously?" I said.

"Let's see what we can find by other means," Gabriel said. "Names of previous owners should be accessible elsewhere."

Eventually he found the full name of the last owner. Using that, he uncovered the original one.

"Glenys Carew," he said.

"I've heard that name," I said. "I know there are Carews in Cainsville. A few of them, anyway. I think Veronica said it was an old family. Glenys sounds familiar, too. I'll take a wild stab and guess it's Welsh?"

Gabriel's fingers flew over the keyboard, surprisingly adept for someone whose fingers looked like they'd hit three keys at a time. "It is. As is Carew. You're right — there are a few Carews in town. Presumably not direct descendants, given that they allowed the house to change hands."

He passed me the laptop and I ran a few searches, chatting as I did. "If Glenys advertised her services as a fortune-teller, I don't see any historical record of it. It isn't exactly a common name. Ah, here's something. A wedding announcement for a granddaughter from the *Morning Star,* which is apparently one of the newspapers that merged to become the *Rockford Register Star,* and —"

I stopped and stared at the screen, rereading the announcement. It was for the wedding of the daughter of Arthur Carew, only son of Owen and Glenys Carew, all of Cainsville, Illinois. The daughter, Daere Jean Carew, was marrying the only son of another Cainsville family — John Laurence Bowen.

"Daere Bowen," I whispered, barely able to get the word out. "That's —"

"Pamela's mother," Gabriel said. "Your maternal grandmother."

Pamela's mother had babysat me during the murders. I'd known her as Grandma Jean, but my research had said her first name was actually Daere.

"So my mother's family is from Cainsville," I said. "Like yours. My grandmother left after she married, according to this announcement." It said the newlyweds planned to move to Chicago, where John was employed as a factory foreman. "Your mother left, too."

"Yes, she moved to Chicago when she was pregnant with me."

"How did you get Pamela's case?"

"I pursued it after someone brought it to my attention. Yes, that someone was from Cainsville. Ida, in fact. I was not, however, aware that Pamela had any connection to the town. It didn't come up in our discussions, and there was no reason to delve that far into her family past."

His fingers drummed the tabletop. Annoyed that he hadn't known. I was still trying to process it all. I had a connection to Cainsville. My mother's family came from here. I didn't know what to make of that, but I had a good idea where to start asking questions.

"Is there any sense speaking to Pamela?" I said. "I hate to, after I said I won't until she'll talk about the omens and the hounds."

"No, this estrangement is wearing her down. She calls daily to see if you've changed your mind. Any information she can give on your omens is worth holding out for. I will mention Cainsville at our next meeting."

"Do *you* think it means anything?" I asked. "Or is it just a case of townies looking out for townies?"

"I don't know." More finger drumming. Then he stopped himself. "We should learn more about Glenys Carew. Find out if there's anyone here who remembers her. Some of the elders might."

"Okay." I closed the laptop. "It's late."

"It is. You should get to bed. I'll stay."

There was no reason for Gabriel to stay. Did I argue, though? No, I did not. I got out fresh towels for him, said good night, and went to bed.

When I got into my room, I texted Ricky.

Heading to bed. Gabriel still here. Sleeping on my sofa bed. Again.

I waited for the reply, wondering how I would interpret a delay. Taking a while to respond because he was busy at the clubhouse? Or because he wasn't sure what to say about Gabriel staying over?

His reply came less than ten seconds later.

LOL. Must be comfortable.

I exhaled. He'd given no signs that he was jealous of my time with Gabriel, but I kept waiting for it. I'm not sure how many guys would be fine with their girlfriend's boss sleeping on her sofa. I sent a final text and went to bed.

SECURITY

Gabriel sat on the edge of the sofa bed and looked around the moonlit apartment. The window shade was an inch short on all sides, and he could have blamed his sleeplessness on the light streaming through, but that wasn't the problem.

He opened the blind. Next door was a two-story house, the roofline below the window. There were no larger buildings on this side, no way for anyone to peer into Olivia's apartment. Or so she'd say. He had only to look at the tree between the apartment and the next house to see an easy vantage point for anyone.

TC hopped up onto the sill and peered out into the night with him, their reflections mirrored on the glass. Gabriel closed the blind. Then he turned to Olivia's door. Silent now. He'd heard the tap-tap of texting earlier.

He checked the locks and security system.

He'd expected to feel at ease when the alarms were installed. Yet he could still sense a threat out there, and the only thing that helped was prowling the damned apartment. What had Morgan called him? Olivia's pit bull. He bristled at the implication, but that was exactly what he felt like, checking and rechecking the locks.

A dead body outfitted to look like her would seem as overt a threat as one could imagine. But for a threat to be effective, there had to be an "if" attached to it. *If you do X, then Y will happen.* No "if" had been given. That was not how the game was played.

Was the X somehow implicit? *If you continue investigating your parents' case, you'll end up like this girl.* But when the body appeared in Olivia's car, Chandler was already in jail. When the head was left in her bed, she had already walked away from Gabriel and the investigation.

Was it the opposite, then? Keep digging *or* you'll die? If so, the message was far too obtuse.

He needed to speak to Chandler, damn him. He'd been digging for dirt on the man, but it was hard to find blackmail material that would rattle someone already facing multiple murder charges. Until then, Gabriel had no answers. No clear certainty even that Olivia was under a direct threat. Yet a gnawing anxiety said she was and that he needed to do something about it. Which was almost as bad. Why did *he* need to do something about it?

Caring about her did not explain this obsessive need to look out for her. She could manage that surprisingly well. When she did call him during an emergency, it was only because she needed legal advice.

Olivia was smart. She was capable. She had a gun and the will to use it. So what kept him running to her aid? Making excuses to spend the night and then spending it prowling her damned apartment? He had no idea. And that, perhaps, unsettled him more than anything.

One more check of the windows and then the door lock. He paused there, fingers on the handle.

Check outside.

He growled softly at the urge. Yet he didn't resist it. Once the anxiety settled, he'd be able to sleep. He was halfway out the door when he felt something brush his legs and looked down to see TC. The cat didn't seem to be making a run for it — he was simply accompanying him.

"Stay here," he murmured.

He managed to avoid the ridiculous temptation to add, "Watch over her." TC wasn't a guard dog, and he certainly hadn't protected her from the last intruder. *Because he hadn't been there. Because he'd been taken.* Someone had known the cat would have alerted Olivia to an intrusion, and so TC had been removed and shut in the Carew house where the killer was storing the body.

On the front stoop, Gabriel looked around. Checking for that sixth sense that told him a threat was near. "Sixth sense" wasn't the right term. That implied a preternatural power. This was an innate ability to survey a situation and note a threat where others saw none. Such as knowing when Seanna had needed a fix and didn't have drugs or the money to buy them, so he should stay away until she scored. Or when she brought home a man, that sense told him which ones wouldn't care if he was in the next room, which would kick his ass onto the street . . . and which might try to crawl into his bed.

The older he got, the more crucial the skill had become. By the time he was eight, he could no longer count on meals from Seanna. She'd deemed him old enough to fend for himself so she could save some precious drug money. When you need to steal everything from food to clothing to school supplies, the threats multiply a hundredfold. It's not just the police or the people you're stealing from. It's older kids, who'll notice the bills in your pocket and try to swipe them. It's teachers, who'll notice if you're exhausted and dirty and call children's services. It's your own mother, who'll notice you have new shoes and demand some of whatever you stole, and lock you out on the street if you don't pay your share of the nonexistent rent for a hole she gets free for banging the landlord.

When Seanna left, the dangers had multiplied again. That's when the games began. Life itself became a game, a con, a swindle. Not just against marks, but against everyone — from teachers to landlords to any person with the power to lock him up, either in jail or in a group home. He'd lived like a shark then, always moving, stop and perish.

So, out here at night, on this empty street, he kept prowling, assessing, trying to pinpoint the source of danger. But there was none. Just a deep sense of unease.

As he walked, he counted gargoyles. Most times, he didn't even look up to see them, just knew where they hid and mentally ticked them off. It helped settle his anxiety, as it had when he was young. A child's game, perhaps the only one he'd ever known. When he'd come here, to Cainsville with Rose, he was able to be just another boy. It wasn't like school, where kids knew where he lived, how he lived, who his mother was, and even if they didn't, they seemed to sense it on him, their own instincts for threat kicking in as they steered clear. In Cainsville, Gabriel could play in the same park as other children and count the same gargoyles.

He got to six before he sensed he wasn't alone and noticed Veronica half a block away. Insomnia, he presumed. Instinctively, he turned to head back, staying out of her path so he wouldn't startle her.

"Gabriel?" she called.

He could pretend not to hear. He wasn't in the mood for conversation. He rarely was, though he'd make the effort in Cainsville.

"Is something wrong?" she asked as she approached.

He felt the urge to say, "I don't know. Is there?" but stifled it. He was just feeling out of sorts. No need to inflict it on her.

"I'm staying with Olivia," he said. "We worked late."

Veronica smiled, a beaming smile that crinkled her eyes. She reached out and

355

squeezed his arm. "I'm glad to see it, Gabriel. So glad."

He knew what she presumed, no matter how quick he'd been to add the "working late" part. All the elders presumed it. He'd seen that in their faces at the diner. An unattached young man and woman, spending so much time together. They made the natural presumption. Which did not apply to Gabriel. He was already putting himself out enough with this relationship. Taking enough of a chance.

He murmured a demurral. It didn't matter. Veronica had made up her mind, and his denials were merely sweet and charming. Old-fashioned chivalry.

He tried to leave after that, but it was clear Veronica wanted to chat. He couldn't be rude to her. However, if she insisted on instigating a conversation, there was no reason he couldn't choose the topic.

"You've lived here all your life, correct?" Gabriel said.

It was a formality. All the elders had. They were as much a fixture of Cainsville as the gargoyles.

When Veronica nodded, he said, "Do you remember Glenys Carew?"

Her lips pursed, as if deep in thought. It was too deep a purse, too great an effort to pretend she needed to consider the question. When she said, "No, I don't believe I do," it was the answer he expected. Also, a lie. The fact of the lie didn't bother him. Everyone lied. The important question was why, and that was always more difficult to answer.

"How about Daere Bowen?" he said.

"Daere." She corrected his pronunciation to *Day-ree*. "Yes, I remember Daere."

"Did you know she was Pamela Larsen's mother?"

Veronica said nothing. She watched him, with a look he could feel in the pit of his gut. The look didn't promise threat. Yet it was a warning nonetheless, and when he met her gaze, he felt a tug, as if she was pulling the question from his mind. His anxiety ebbed. *There's nothing wrong. Go back to bed. Watch over Olivia. This isn't important.*

"Yes, it is."

When he heard himself say the words aloud, he stiffened, waiting for her to give him a look of confusion, of question. She blinked, then nodded, a smile playing at her lips, almost as if . . . pleased. She looked pleased.

"Olivia's going to want answers," he said.

"Yes, I suppose she will."

That look vanished, but she continued watching him. Waiting. For him to ask the questions? He knew it would do no good. They needed more information first.

"Is she in danger here?" he asked.

Veronica looked surprised. "Danger?"

"Yes, is Olivia in danger? Here. In Cainsville."

"No. Never." Her tone was firm, fierce even. "Neither of you are."

"It's Olivia I'm concerned about."

"I know."

"I won't allow anything to happen to her."

She smiled. Warm. Pleased again. He felt as if he'd given something away, revealed too much. The anxiety buzzed in the pit of his stomach, and he wanted to pull back the words.

"Go inside, Gabriel," she said. "Get some rest."

He nodded, more curtly than he'd intended, and escaped.

As he stepped into the apartment, he heard a meow and an "Oh!" and found Olivia in the middle of the room, her hair falling in a halo of soft curls, eyes wide with sleepy confusion. She wore only an over-sized shirt, feet bare, long legs bare. He jerked his gaze back to her face.

"Alarm," she said, and lunged for it.

He made it first, entering the code before it went off.

"I thought you'd changed your mind and gone home," she said. "I was just going to throw the bolt. Is everything okay?"

"I stepped out for some air. Did I wake you?"

She shook her head. "Something . . ."

He tensed. "You heard something?"

She waved off his concern. "No, no. You're okay, then?"

"I am."

"I'm sure that sofa isn't very comfortable. That might be why you aren't sleeping. If you'd like to leave . . ."

He searched her face for a sign that she wanted him gone. He knew he wouldn't find one. Even when she was annoyed with him, she never seemed to really want him gone. Still, he looked. He probably always would, watching for that signal that he wasn't wanted, and if he sensed that, he'd be out the door before she could say goodbye.

"I'm fine on the sofa," he said.

A smile, sleepy but genuine. Happy that he was staying.

"Go on," he said, waving toward her room.

Another smile as she retreated. "Good

night, Gabriel. Sleep well."

"I will."

Chapter Thirty-Eight

I served Gabriel breakfast the next day — Larry cooked it; I just served. Once Gabriel left, I stepped outside to call Ricky.

"What time do you start work tomorrow?" he asked.

"Ten. Gabriel has a morning appointment and doesn't need me there until then."

"Perfect. I have class at ten. How about an overnight trip to Wisconsin? We have a cabin up there. Monday nights are quiet, and the forecast is clear."

"Sounds good. Are we riding up?"

"I figured you might want the car for this one. It's almost two hours from Cainsville. A bit long for a bike if you're not used to it. I imagine you were a little sore after the other day."

"A little. But I don't think it was the bike."

He laughed.

"Either way, I'm not complaining," I said.

"Are you sure? I could slow down." He

361

paused. "The bike, at least. I'm not sure about the rest."

"I'm not even sure about the bike. You're pretty damned unstoppable either way."

"Mmm, maybe."

"Bring the bike."

I'll admit that I'd wondered if the excitement of that first bike ride had been more about the fact that I hadn't had sex in over a month. It wasn't. The rush was still there, in every way, and we made it about twenty miles before pulling off on another empty road for another lust-fueled pit stop. After that, I changed out of my skirt and into my jeans and Ricky made me wear a helmet — he'd brought an extra this time — and we headed onto the highway for the rest of the trip.

Ricky had warned that the cabin was rustic. It was also a bone-jarring five miles down a dirt road that tapered to a trail no car could breach. While our destination wasn't anything like the so-called cottages I'd visited growing up — million-dollar lakefront homes — it was surprisingly nice. A thousand or so square feet of log cabin with a massive deck. The deck did not overlook a lake, but there was a stream burbling past. And trees — lots and lots of trees — with no other dwellings in sight.

"Wow," I said, leaning on the railing, looking out into the endless green.

Ricky came up behind me. "It's okay?"

He wore the same expression he'd had after we first had sex, that uncertainty and doubt, his eyes anxious, hair still mussed from the helmet. It made him look deliciously vulnerable, and I pulled him over.

"Why wouldn't it be okay?" I asked.

"No lake," he said. "No swimming or boating. Definitely no jet-skiing."

"Not really my thing." I leaned back against the railing. "I like this. Completely quiet. Completely private."

A hint of a grin. "It is private. No need to worry about the neighbors."

"Not just that," I said. "It feels like . . ." I looked around and felt the calm of the forest slide over me. "Beyond peaceful. I'm pretty damned sure I can't get a cell or Internet signal. No need to check my phone. No need to feel like there's something else I should be doing. A complete break from everything and everybody."

"Except me."

"You don't count. You are the most low-maintenance guy I've ever dated, and this is the least demanding relationship."

"I do make demands."

"Sex would only be a demand if I didn't want the same, which is never a problem."

"I've noticed that." He slid his hands under my ass, shifting closer. "I'm glad you're okay with coming here." He looked out into the forest, and something glittered in his eyes, a hunger, a yearning. "I love this place. When I was a kid, my dad had to mark our weekends here on the calendar so I'd stop bugging him about when we were going. I still bugged, because it was never often enough. I'd spend hours out there, tramping through the woods. It was like Disney World for me."

"No place like it on earth?"

"Exactly. Even now, I come up here when I need a study break, and half the time I'm out there instead, walking around. It's like . . ." He struggled for the words. "Like recalibrating. After some time here, I'm ready to deal with all the shit in the regular world."

"I can understand that."

He nudged me back onto the railing, hands still cushioning my ass. "I've never brought anyone here before. Not a friend, not a girl. It's like . . . you have a place you love and then you bring someone, and they notice all the flaws and I feel like *I'm* being judged, too, for liking it. With you, I don't need to be anything. To do anything. I can just say 'this is me' and you seem happy with that."

"I'm *very* happy with that."

He looked me in the eyes, and that uncertainty flickered again, as if he wasn't sure I could be telling the truth. I pulled him into a kiss, but he resisted, leaning into my ear instead and whispering, "It's the same for me. I'm very, very happy."

I plucked at his shirt. "And there's no way I can make you any happier?"

"There's always a way."

"Good." I pushed his shirt up over his chest. "Then let's get you naked. 'Cause that always makes *me* happy."

He laughed, the sound echoing through the forest.

We'd come in at midnight, after hours of sitting around a campfire, drinking and talking. Lots of talking, one of the two things it seemed we never tired of. The other followed. By one, we were sated and asleep.

When I woke, refreshed and wide awake, it felt as if it must be morning. It wasn't even 2 A.M.

I tried to get back to sleep, but something pulled me from the bed, tugging me to the window. Finally, I gave in and slid from under Ricky's arm.

I didn't need to open the curtain. Moonlight already streamed through the crack. It was a waning moon, maybe three-quarters, so bright it was like headlights flooding the room.

A branch scraped the glass, the leaves plastered against it. I reached up and put my fingers against them, the cool glass sending a chill down my arm. As I looked out, I could imagine that chill against my skin, like riding on the bike, the bite and the burn of the wind. I shivered and pressed my whole hand to the window. It was open an inch, and when I moved closer, the breeze tickled over my naked body. I could smell our campfire, and I imagined I heard our voices and Ricky's laugh, and I shivered again, smiling.

I glanced over my shoulder at Ricky, sprawled over the bed, and drank in the sight of him, marveling at my luck in being here. I'd been telling the truth when I'd said how comfortable it was being with him. There was no jumping to get his attention. No struggle to make him smile. No treading warily, gauging his mood, tensed for the next betrayal.

I wanted to stay here. Tell the rest of the world to go to hell and leave me in this forest, alone with Ricky, at least for a little while.

Right now, though . . .

I turned back to the window. Right now I didn't want to be here at all. Not in this cabin, that is. I heard the sigh of the wind and the creak of trees, and smelled crisp fire and pungent cedar, and I wanted to be out there. To walk. To run. To see . . . whatever there was to see, because I felt as if I was missing something in here, as warm and comfortable as it was.

"You, too?"

I jumped as Ricky's hands slid around my waist.

"Sorry. Didn't mean to startle you," he said.

I went to turn around in his arms, but he only tightened them around me. I tugged open the curtains, and moonlight poured into the room. Ricky pressed up against me, warming my back as the cool breeze chilled my chest.

He lowered his head to nuzzle my neck. We stood there, him pressed warm against me as we gazed out into the forest.

"I was up doing this a little while ago," he said. "Woke thinking it was morning, and it turned out I'd only been asleep for ten minutes. It's that kind of night."

"It is."

We stood there, my fingers pressed to the glass, his hand caressing my hip, neither of us speaking for at least five minutes. Then I said, "I want to go out."

"Let's get dressed and go."

"I guess the dressing part isn't optional?"

A chuckle. "I would like to say it is completely optional, but while the bugs aren't bad, the underbrush is thick and the ground is rough. Jeans and sneakers are a must. As for the rest . . . I'm inclined to go with 'totally optional.' "

"Good."

CHAPTER THIRTY-NINE

"This way," Ricky said as we tromped down the steps to the forest's edge. "There's something I want to show you. No, wait. We'll do that later. First, there's something over here."

I bit back a laugh. He sounded like a boy showing off his special spots to a new friend. He shot a grin over, as if he knew that and didn't care, wasn't worried what I'd think. He grabbed my hand, fingers entwining with mine.

"I know the way," he said. "Even in the dark. I used to come out here sometimes, at night. Just . . . those nights. Like tonight. When it seems as if . . ." He tugged me along into the woods. "I'd wake up, and I couldn't sleep. I'd go out and spend the whole night out here, looking."

"Looking for what?"

He shrugged. "I don't know."

"What did your dad think of that?"

"Sometimes he'd be up, too. I'd come out, and he'd be on the porch. He'd stay there, but I'd get the feeling he didn't want to, you know? That he'd rather be out here, but . . . he made himself stay on the porch. He'd let me come out, though, which is one of the reasons I loved this place. He could be damned protective in the city. But here? It was like nothing here could hurt me. He'd still call out, now and then, and I had to shout back, but otherwise I had the run of the place. Even at three in the morning. City rules didn't apply."

Our first stop was a waterfall. A tiny one, the stream dropping over a boulder, but at night the moon caught it just right and the water sparkled. That wasn't the only thing that sparkled, either. When I looked over at Ricky, crouched on the other side of the stream, his eyes danced, and gold flecks in his irises glittered in the moonlight, and I thought for a moment that I'd seen that before, the light catching his eyes a certain way. I didn't pursue it; I just watched him.

He bent and waggled his fingers under the falling water.

"Cold?" I asked.

He flicked some my way. The droplets flew onto my bare skin.

"Mmm, yes," I said. "Definitely cold."

I scooped up a handful of icy water and splashed it on my face, letting it drip down my chest. That glint in Ricky's eyes turned to a much more familiar one.

"You are fucking gorgeous," he said.

"Even dripping wet?"

"Especially dripping wet."

I reached both hands into the waterfall and splashed water on my face and chest. It didn't matter if it was ice-cold and the night wasn't much warmer. It felt amazing, that burn and bite like wind on a motorcycle, my skin blazing hot beneath the droplets. When I looked at my hands, the moonlight made the water sparkle.

Ricky stared. Then he rose and started toward me. His sneaker clomped into the water as he stepped in the stream.

"Watch out," I said. "You'll get a soaker."

"Don't care."

I backed up. "You should. You'll catch a cold."

"Old wives' tale."

"Are you sure?"

His other sneaker came down in the middle of the stream. "Don't care if it's not."

I stepped back, and when I did, that glitter in his eyes grew brighter.

"You like that," I said.

"Like what?"

I moved back more. His eyes glowed now, and his breath quickened.

"Mmm, yes," I said. "You do."

"Come here."

"I don't think you want me to."

He moved forward. "Oh, yes, I do."

"No . . . I think you'd rather work for it."

"Work?"

"We're out here to enjoy the night, aren't we?"

A predatory edge in his smile set my pulse racing. "That's what I'm trying to do."

"And you will." I moved into the forest. "After we take a walk."

"Pretty sure I don't want to walk anymore."

"Then you'll have to convince me you have something better in mind. But first . . ." I ducked around a tree. "You have to catch me."

His grin then was nearly blinding as he lunged at me. I whipped around and tore into the forest.

The woods were too thick here for actual running, so it was more hide-and-seek, which would have worked so much better if Ricky hadn't moved through the forest like a damned guerrilla sniper. After he nearly caught me a third time, I checked to make sure he hadn't put on moccasins and night-vision goggles.

"How the hell can you see me?" I said as we circled a huge oak.

"You're right there."

"Hiding. Behind a *tree."*

"Not very well."

He lunged. I zipped around the tree.

"This game would be much more fun if you weren't so freaking good at it," I said as I stayed out of reach.

"Oh, I still think it's plenty fun."

He lunged again, and I took off, dodging trees and jumping logs. I looked for clearer ground, where I'd have an advantage. Ahead, moonlight streamed through a break in the tree cover. I ran for it. Then I glimpsed a shadow . . . in front of me. I stopped short. A flash of blond hair told me the shadow was Ricky before he disappeared behind a tree.

"How the hell do you do that?" I muttered.

He only chuckled.

"You have the home turf advantage," I said, turning toward the source of that chuckle. "You know the shortcuts. I'm probably running in circles."

"Maybe." His voice came from behind me

now and I wheeled, catching a flash of bare chest before he backed off, attack averted.

He went silent then. I pivoted slowly, trying to catch a crackle of dead leaves or snap of a twig. But all I heard was the sigh of the wind and rustle of leaves. I knew he was there, though, circling me, watching for an opening, and as soon as he had it, if I didn't notice in time to escape . . .

Heat shot through me. Of course, the obvious answer would be to not escape. Let him catch me. Get what I wanted. But the point of the game was that building anticipation, which was damned sweet.

As I turned, searching, I swore I could sense him circling, catch the glitter of his eyes through the trees, hear his breathing, coming faster now, the slight catch of it as he . . .

I wheeled to see him right behind me, midpounce. He snagged my belt loop and yanked me back, his free hand going around my waist, blazing hot against my cold skin, raising goose bumps as he pulled me to him.

I broke free and danced away. He chuckled, the sound reverberating through me, heat rising in its wake.

"Close," he said.

"But not close enough."

I ran. I headed straight for the clearing,

hoping it would be bigger than it looked and give me time to run on open ground. I was dashing into it when Ricky called, "No! Don't!"

I skidded to a stop. He ran up behind me, halting a few feet away.

"Sorry," he said. "Just don't . . . Don't go in there, okay?"

I was about to tease that he was stacking the deck, keeping me from open ground, but genuine worry shone from his eyes.

I glanced into the clearing.

"Unfair advantage," he said. "You're faster than I am on open ground."

Though he said it with a smile, there was a tightness in his voice. When I stepped toward the glade, he tensed, staying where he was but rocking on the balls of his feet, as if he wanted to grab me back. I peered in to see a circle of white mushrooms, glowing in the moonlight.

"That's a fairy ring," I said.

When I looked over at him, he flushed. "Um, yeah . . . Can we just . . . ? There's something over here I wanted to show you." He pointed in the other direction. When I looked back at the circle, he sighed. "Yeah, I'm superstitious. It's my grandmother's fault, and I know it's stupid, but something gets in your head like that —"

"And it's hard to shake, even if you know better."

"Yep." He walked over to me, his hands snaking around my waist. "She used to tell me stories about people getting trapped in fairy circles."

"They walk into a party that never ends, and they can't escape."

"You know your folklore."

"I do."

His lips brushed mine. "So here's the part where you get to mock me for being superstitious."

I put my arms around him. "Never."

"Just tease me about it, then."

I kissed him. "Never."

He returned the kiss, tentative at first, as if still worried he'd embarrassed himself, but when I didn't pull back, that heat from earlier licked, reigniting. I could smell the faint smoke and fire and feel the damp darkness like fog, creeping up, cool and brisk, as the heat of his body blazed through me.

I pulled back and looked up at him, his eyes glittering again with those golden sparks, his blond hair falling forward, brushing my face, his breath smelling faintly of . . . forest. I know it was a trick of perception, but that's what I smelled, all the rich scents of the forest, bathing my face in warm breath as he leaned in to kiss me again and —

I slid out of his grip and danced backward.

"You're not going to get far now," he warned.

"No?"

He stepped toward me. "No."

"Are you sure?"

"Absolutely."

I dodged. He grabbed my arm, but I wrenched away. When I started to run, he caught me, his hand on my elbow, fingers wrapping around my arm. He yanked me to him in a rough kiss, pulling me against him so tight I had no chance of slipping away.

"Give up?" he said, breaking the kiss.

"Mmm . . ." I gave a tentative wiggle.

A sexy, low chuckle. "Not a chance."

I laced my hands behind his head, pulling him down in a kiss so hard and deep he gasped, relaxing against me, all his energy going into that kiss as his grip relaxed, too. I propelled myself backward, trying to break free. His arms only tightened.

"Nope," he said, still kissing me.

I kissed him again, fingers entwined in his hair. Then I moved one hand lower, tickling down his side and squeezing between us to flick open the button on his jeans.

"That won't work, either," he said as his

hands moved to my ass and he pushed me against a tree.

"Pinning me now?" I asked.

"Just getting prepared . . ." He hissed as my hand slid into his jeans, wrapping around him. "For that."

"I thought you didn't get distracted."

"Mmm."

I stroked him until his eyes slitted, those gold flecks glowing. I tightened my grip, and he swore under his breath. I leaned in to kiss him, his hands squeezing my ass as he pushed me against the tree and I stroked him.

"You might not . . . want to keep . . . doing that," he panted between kisses. "That chasing . . ."

"Shortened your fuse?"

He managed a laugh, entwined with a groan. "Yeah."

"Don't worry. I know exactly how far —"

His breathing hitched.

"That far," I said, and let go, throwing my weight to the side . . . and getting absolutely nowhere as his arm shot out to stop me. "Damn," I said.

He chuckled, the sound ragged now, his eyes barely opening. "You really think I'm going to let you go *now*?" He pushed me against the tree, kissing me, lifting me up to straddle him.

"What if I dodged in that direction?" I said, nodding toward the fairy-circle clearing.

"Thought you weren't going to tease me about it."

"Not teasing. Using every trick at my disposal."

"Ah. Well, that one" — he hitched me higher on his hips — "is not going to work now. Focus, remember? When I want something . . ." He turned, putting my back toward the clearing. ". . . nothing gets in my way."

He kissed me and took three steps, bringing us into the clearing. Then he lowered me down, on my back, in the middle of it, and I felt the fairy circle being crushed under my back.

"That's gotta be bad luck," I said as he shoved my jeans down my hips.

"Yep. I'm trapped now." He grabbed my hips. "And that's fine by me."

He pushed into me, so hard I reared up, gasping. He did, too, his eyes opening wide. I gripped the ground, the damp earth under my fingers, and caught a scent on the air. Horses. I smelled horses. My fingers dug into the ground and I could feel it vibrating, the shocks rippling through me as Ricky thrust.

Then he stopped suddenly. Arched there, his eyes wider now.

"Fuck, no," he said. "No, no, no."

He held himself still, face screwed up, fighting climax as he panted.

"Hold on," he said. "Fuck. Sorry. Just hold on."

The ground kept shaking, the smell of horses stronger now, and his eyes opened as if he'd caught a whiff. I took his hands and pressed them against the ground. "Do you feel that?"

He stretched out his hands, braced on them, eyes widening. "Fuck, yes." He shivered, pushing deeper into me, hands pressed to the ground. "No, no, no," he whispered. "Fuck, no. Not yet —"

I wriggled. His eyes snapped open.

"No, I'm okay. Don't —"

"I want to see it." I pressed his hand to the ground again, mine on his, the vibrations rocking through us, and I had no idea what I was talking about, but I said it again: "I want to see it."

I pulled away from him, rolled over, and ran from the clearing.

CHAPTER FORTY

Our earlier chase had been a playful game of hide-and-seek. This was a hunt. I tore through the forest, vines snagging my legs, branches whipping my arms, rocks biting into my soles, Ricky one step behind, his breath coming so hard I had to look back to be sure it was him, half expecting to find a hound on my heels instead. As for why I was running, or where I was running, I'm not sure I could have even articulated it. I felt . . . drunk isn't the right word. But something like it. High on adrenaline, the hormone pounding through me, drowning out rational thought, telling me I wanted to see it, wanted to see it . . .

Wanted to see what?

Oh, I knew. I could say I didn't, but deep down I did. The ground vibrated under my feet. The smell of horses wafted over on the breeze. And then I heard it: the baying of hounds. Everything I'd smelled and heard in that hallway at the charity dinner, but this time there was no urge to run away. I couldn't imagine why I'd ever wanted to run away. Tonight I felt that and I heard it and I smelled it, and I ran toward it.

Then I saw it. The flicker of movement in the forest, the ground pounding so hard now I stumbled. Ricky caught me around the waist, keeping me upright. I looked into the forest and I saw fire, licking flames in the distance, and I heard the pounding of hooves and the panting of hounds. Ricky's hands closed around my waist and he tried to turn me around, but I wouldn't look away, kept straining to see. He pushed against me, hard and urgent, and said something, but his voice was too thick for me to pick up the words. I dropped to my knees, on all fours, Ricky dropping behind me.

I saw fire and shadows. Then I saw riders. Riders and hounds, and Ricky thrust into me, and after that I didn't care what I saw, didn't care at all.

What happened next? I wasn't even sure. Oh, I remembered the first part just fine. Sex. Amazing, unforgettable sex. Then collapsing on the ground, Ricky shuddering and panting, "Shit, holy shit," as he caught his breath, his arms around me, so warm it was like falling into that fire, the fire I could still smell on the breeze. And then . . . well, nothing. I could say I drifted off, but I don't even remember hitting the ground.

The next thing I knew, I was alone in the forest, sitting naked on the ground, blinking into the darkness.

"Ricky?"

"Right here. Sorry." He appeared through the trees, something gathered in his arms. "I thought I could make it back before you woke up."

He took our jeans and stretched them over me, then paused and looked down at his work.

"Not much of a blanket," he said.

I laughed softly. "I appreciate the effort. Very sweet." I reached for his hand and tugged him down.

He stretched out beside me, pulling me against him, which was warmer than any blanket. As I snuggled in, he said, "That, um, that was . . ."

"Intense?"

"Hell, yeah." He exhaled. "Intense." He was silent for a moment. "Was it . . . ? I mean, that wasn't quite . . . Is everything okay?"

In his eyes, I saw the real questions. *Was it*

too intense? Did I frighten you? Did I hurt you?

I put my arms around his neck and kissed him, answering that way. After a moment he relaxed, the kiss deepening, his hands on my ass as he pulled me closer.

"Is everything okay with *you*?" I asked as we broke for breath.

"Hell, yeah. I just wasn't sure if it was too much —"

I cut him off with a kiss. "For the record, I will always let you know if it's too much. I'm pretty sure I was the initiator there, and yes, I was following your lead, but I wouldn't do that just to make you happy. I'm not that selfless."

He smiled. "Okay. Thanks."

A few moments curled up together, light kisses, postponing the inevitable trip back to the cabin. Then he said, "In the forest . . . Did you see . . . ?"

"I saw something."

"Riders?"

I nodded.

"There's a stable nearby," he said. "I suppose that's what it was, but . . ."

"But . . . ?"

He looked at me. "You promised not to mock, right?"

"Absolutely. And I meant it."

He reclined with his arm still around me.

I twisted and rested on his chest, my chin propped up.

"It was riders from the stable," he said. "A midnight hunt. Logically, I know that. But when I was a kid, sometimes I'd hear the horses and the hounds, and I'd tell myself it was *the* Hunt."

"*The* Hunt?"

"I mentioned that my nana used to tell me stories. She's Irish, and she grew up with all that. I liked it, so she'd pass it on. Stories of fairy traps and enchantments. And the Wild Hunt." He lifted his head. "Have you heard of it?"

I was glad for the darkness, hiding my expression. "I have. Phantom riders and hounds that hunt the living and send them to the afterlife. If you see the Wild Hunt, it's a death omen."

"Nana said you aren't *supposed* to see them, but only because, if you do, they might be after you. They hunt evil. Spectral vigilantes. I like that version better."

"Nice. You'll have to tell me more of her stories."

"Better yet, you could meet her." He shifted, getting comfortable. "She's off on some hiking tour in Peru for the next few weeks, but when she gets back, if you'd like to meet her . . ."

"I would."

His arm tightened around me. "Good."

"They're your dad's parents, I presume?"

"His mom. His father isn't in the picture. Never was. He sent plenty of money, but there was no contact. That's one reason my dad insisted on keeping me, and made sure my mother stayed in touch."

"Wanting something better for you."

"Yeah." He shifted again and made a face, reaching under him.

"Yes, the ground is cold and rocky."

"That's not it. I'm lying on . . ." He pulled out the boar's tusk. "Um, okay . . ."

"Actually, that's mine. It must have fallen out of my jeans. Did I mention I wouldn't tease you about your superstitions? I have my own. It's a good luck charm."

"Huh." He turned it over in his hands. "I'd remember if I'd seen it before, but it looks familiar. A tooth of some kind?"

"Boar tusk — the tip of one."

"Really? And the writing? What does it mean?"

"I have no idea. I had someone take a look, and she could only decipher enough to figure out it's a protective amulet."

He peered at the etched letters. "It's old, whatever it is. Very cool. Especially this." He ran his thumb over the entwined moon and sun. Then he touched the words under it. "You have no idea what this says?"

"Nope."

"Huh. Well, as hard as I try not to be superstitious, I think you're right. It's good luck. You should keep it close."

"I am." I stuffed it into my jeans. "And I suppose I should put these back on so I don't lose it, which probably means we should head back to the cabin. It is a little nippy out here."

"We'll head back, and I'll get the fireplace roaring."

Ricky was having a dream. A bad one. I woke when he kung-fu-chopped me in the neck.

I scrambled up, ready to fight whatever monster had attacked in the night, only to find Ricky tossing and turning, moaning softly. Sweat plastered his hair and soaked the pillow. I tugged the covers off, in case he was just overheated.

He mumbled something I couldn't make out. He kept mumbling it, over and over. I rubbed his sweat-drenched back.

"Ricky?"

More mumbling. Then he shot up so fast he startled me.

"I know," he said, grabbing for me. "I

know it."

His eyes were wild, those golden flecks I'd seen earlier glowing. He held my arm tight, gaze fixed on mine, sweat dripping from his face.

"I know it, Liv."

"Okay." I loosened his iron grip on my arm.

"Sorry, sorry." He let go. "I know it."

"All right," I said. "What do you know?"

"The tusk. The writing. I know what it says. What it means."

"Okay. What?"

His mouth opened. Panic flooded his eyes. "No," he whispered. "No, no, no. I know. I know."

"Ricky . . ." I shifted to kneel beside him. "You were having a bad dream."

He shook his head, sweat-soaked hair lashing as I gripped his shoulder. "No. I remembered. It's important. It's *so* important."

I leaned in. "You're still half asleep. It's okay. It was just —"

"No! You need to know."

He pushed me away. It wasn't a hard shove, but it caught me off guard and I fell back.

"Fuck!" His eyes rounded as he grabbed my arms, steadying me. "Sorry. Fuck, I'm sorry. I'm so sorry."

388

"I'm fine." I reached out, ran my hand through his wet hair, and leaned over to brush my lips across his cheek. "You're having a bad dream."

He nodded and took deep, shuddering breaths. His arms went around me, pulling me against him, and I fell into them. He held me tight, still shaking, as I rubbed his back.

"I'm sorry," he whispered. "Fuck. I'm so sorry."

"Stop." I nuzzled his neck, kissing him. "It was a nightmare."

His head shook against my shoulder. "Not a nightmare. Well, yes, kind of. But more like a dream. I knew what the writing on the tusk meant, and I had to tell you. It was so important to tell you, and . . ." He took deep breaths. "And it was just a dream."

"Uh-huh."

"Fuck." He pulled back, looking abashed. "It seemed so real. I had to tell you, but part of me didn't want to, like I'd lose you if I told you, but you needed to know, and . . ."

Sharp breaths now, and I could feel him shivering as the dream passed and the sweat dried, leaving him cold and confused. I pushed him back on the bed and crawled in beside him, tugging the covers over us.

"Stay with me," he said.

"It was only a dream," I whispered as I curled up against him.

"I know. Just . . . stay with me."

"I will."

CHAPTER FORTY-ONE

Despite the events of the night before, I had little trouble waking up at the crack of dawn. I'll credit Ricky with that. His methods of waking me were much nicer than any alarm clock. The fact that he felt guilty over disturbing my sleep last night only made him that much more determined to ease my waking.

There wasn't much to pack — you can't fit a lot in saddlebags. Then homeward bound. Ricky dropped me at my apartment and zoomed off to make his morning class.

I showered and changed and fed TC, who was peeved and ignoring me. Then I took off to the city.

"Good morning," I said, handing Lydia a tea as I walked in. I heard voices in the meeting room and lowered mine. "Still in his appointment?"

"No, he had to cancel it. A more urgent one came up. You didn't get his message, I take it?"

Shit. I'd checked for messages over break-fast, when I had cell service, but only had e-mail, which I'd ignored. Ricky'd had a call from his dad. Some problem with a member of the gang. Nothing urgent, just asking him to phone later. Now that I could catch the voices from the meeting room, I knew who was in there with Gabriel.

"Olivia?"

Gabriel opened the meeting room door. Don Gallagher stood behind him. Another man sat across the room.

Gabriel walked out. "You didn't get my message?"

"No, sorry. I didn't check e-mail this morning."

I felt Don's gaze on me. Thinking that his son had also been out of touch last night? Shit.

"I could use you in here." Gabriel glanced at Don. "Is that all right? Olivia's getting a crash course in law, and this seems a good case for her. She's signed a confidentiality waiver, of course."

Should I be involved in a case regarding Ricky's gang? I hesitated. Don noticed. Shit.

As Gabriel asked Lydia to bring coffee for the clients, I quickly texted Ricky.

At office. Your dad's here.

The answer came back in seconds. *Yeah, I know. Didn't want to warn you. Better if you were honestly surprised.*

Except I missed Gabriel's message. So your dad knows I was out of contact last night. Like you.

Fuck. I'll fix this tonight. Sorry.

I signed off as we settled into the room. I thought no one had noticed me texting, but I looked up to see Don watching me.

"How are you doing, Olivia?" Don asked.

"Fine. Apologies for the disruption. I'm not used to having a job where I need to check e-mail."

He nodded. It was a pleasant nod, just as the inquiry had been pleasant. Civil and warm. No hint of suspicion, but I felt like a mouse squirming under a tiger's gaze. I suspect a lot of people feel like that around Don Gallagher. There's no mistaking he's Ricky's father — same blond hair, same dark eyes, same chiseled features, softer in Don. Those looks were the only softer part about him, though. Ricky could find his edge when it suited him; with Don, that edge never went away. It didn't matter if Don looked as if he belonged at the country club, with his clean-shaven good looks, golf shirt, and pressed trousers. You saw the set of his jaw and the glint in his eye and the

393

biceps straining the sleeves of that shirt and you knew this was a guy you did not want to piss off. Shit.

Gabriel brought me up to speed. The other guy in the room was Chad Sullivan, who naturally went by Sully. He was a big bruiser with a ponytail, beard, and tats. A stereotypical biker, which was actually the minority in the Saints.

The case was a personal matter. Except in a gang it seems that nothing is ever truly personal.

Sully's ex was after him for unpaid child support. Don was pissed about it. I could see it in his face, hear it in his tone. You have kids; you pay for them. No exceptions. When Don learned of Sully's debts, he'd paid them, with Sully owing him the money. Which would have been fine, except it came too late, Don having only found out about the problem last night, when Sully got arrested for assaulting his ex.

Whether Sully had assaulted his ex or not was a matter of debate. He swore he hadn't. Don was still pissed. Sully had let the child support slide to the point where it seemed she retaliated, and in doing so, he'd violated club rules, which said all legal matters had to be brought to Don's attention immediately.

Don and Sully left just before noon. Gabriel took a call before we could speak. When he came out of his office, I could tell something had happened. He waved me inside.

"The police put a rush on the DNA," he said. "The press is breathing down their necks. When a young woman turns up dead and mutilated, the assumption is 'serial killer,' even if that's rarely the case."

"Is there a problem with the DNA?" I asked.

"It's not a match for her mother."

"What?"

Gabriel motioned for me to sit. "They tested against the mother. That saves any unexpected family surprises."

"In case Dad's not the father. You can't lie about maternity, though."

"Yes. But it seems Ciara Conway isn't biologically related to her mother."

"Could it be . . . ?" I shook my head. "Okay, I was going to suggest she was adopted and the family was hiding it, like with me, but obviously not if they asked for the DNA." Even as I said it, my heart thudded. I guess I wasn't completely over that shock yet.

"Olivia?"

"I'm fine. Sorry." I forced a smile. "Back

to the subject at hand . . ."

"There's no hurry. Take a —" He cleared his throat. "I meant that if you want to . . ." He seemed to search for words.

"Take a minute?"

I'd given him crap a few weeks ago for that particular turn of phrase, one used when a client was upset. He meant it to sound sympathetic, but I always picked up that note of impatience bordering on contempt. *Really, this is an inconvenient time for all this emotional nonsense. If you must, get it over with quickly, please.*

This time I suspect he really was showing empathy. But it was like watching a teenage boy hold a baby, making a genuine effort while clearly as uncomfortable as hell.

"I'm fine," I said. "So the dead body isn't Mrs. Conway's biological daughter. Does that mean the corpse isn't Ciara? Or has there been a lab mix-up?"

Gabriel visibly exhaled, much happier to get back on the relatively safe ground of discussing dead people. "In reality, such mistakes are exceedingly rare. I also don't see how the body could have been someone other than Ciara Conway. While death photos are difficult to ID — given the difference in pallor and muscle tone — there seemed no doubt this was Ms. Conway."

"But if she isn't the child of her parents, what does that mean? Switched at birth? Does that even happen outside of soap operas?"

"That is what you're going to find out. I suspect the likelihood isn't any greater than that of a lab error or misidentification, which means we'll be looking at three equally dubious possibilities." He tapped his pen, frowning, his gaze distant.

"Whatever the answer, I think someone knew," I said.

"Hmmm?"

"Someone advised them to get that DNA test, when it seemed a complete waste of time and money. But it wasn't. We need to find out who advised them. I bet he — or she — knows what's going on here."

Gabriel nodded. "I'll try to make an appointment to speak to the Conways tomorrow. Are you free?"

"Until three again."

"Good. I'll set it up."

Switched at birth. There's actually a Wikipedia page for that, which was damned handy, but also a little disconcerting.

After my diner shift, I'd set about doing the research. As I expected, though, the idea was primarily used as a plot device. In fact, that's what most of the entry covered — all the ways it had been used in fiction and film. The list of actual documented cases was short. Of course, one could argue that only the cases that are discovered are documented, but it would still be exceedingly rare. Modern hospitals have measures in place — like wristbands — to prevent mix-ups.

As I zipped down the Wiki entry to the sources, a line caught my eye, under "see also" links to related entries. A link for changelings. When I read that, I heard Rose's voice.

You have no idea what a fairy circle is, do you? Which is shocking for a changeling child.

Changeling. A fairy child left in the place of a human one, to be raised by the unknowing parents. It applied to me metaphorically — my adoptive parents having raised me not knowing my true heritage.

I looked at the photo of Ciara. Another thing we had in common? A chill skittered over my skin.

I ran a Facebook search on Ciara Conway's family. Her mother and brother had pages. I clicked her mother's link for photos and skimmed until I found a family shot of all four Conways, taken a year ago. I enlarged the photo and stared at the screen.

Ciara Conway was not her parents' child.

Everyone knows genetics does wonky things. A family of blue-eyed blonds can have a green-eyed, red-headed throwback to some previous generation. But the resemblance will still be there, in deeper ways — the shape of the face, the eyes, the cheekbones. That's what was missing between me and my adoptive parents.

It was also missing between Ciara and the Conways.

Yes, there were similarities in the coloring. She was dark-haired. So was her father. But Ciara's hair was as dark as Gabriel's. Her coloring superficially resembled his and Rose's. Black Irish: black hair, pale skin, blue eyes. While she didn't closely resemble either of them, she could have passed for a Walsh better than for a member of her actual family.

No. I was jumping to conclusions. That damned Wiki entry had seized my imagination and made off with it.

I would show Gabriel the pictures, and he'd point out facial similarities, along with the general impossibility of my theory. The DNA confusion must be a lab error or misidentification of the body. Both were more likely than "switched at birth."

I was forwarding my conclusions to Gabriel when I got an e-mail from him. It was his usual terse missive, more like an elongated text message.

Heard from police contact. Conways advised by anonymous call. So-called psychic. Male. No name. Said Ciara alive. Urged to have DNA tested. Call traced to pay phone. Can still meet with Conways but see little point. Will talk tomorrow.

Anonymous call? From a supposed psychic? I wasn't even sure where to go with that. I finished my e-mail to Gabriel, hit Send, shut down my computer, and went to bed.

CHAPTER FORTY-TWO

I was still drifting off to sleep when my cell phone rang. Ricky's number illuminated on the screen.

"Hey," I said as I answered.

There was a pause. One so long I repeated the greeting before Ricky said, "Hey. Are you . . . ? You've gone to bed, right?"

"Yes, but I'm not asleep yet." I pulled myself upright, smile vanishing as I heard his tone, cautious and strained. "It didn't go well with your dad?"

"I just . . . I need to see you. Can I come by?"

"Of course. Where are you?"

Another long pause. "Outside."

"You're here?"

"Yeah. I came straight here, hoping you were still awake, but then I saw your light was off and got your good night text and . . ."

"Come on up."

I was barely at the door before Ricky rapped, just once, almost hesitant, as if I might have fallen asleep. When I opened it and saw him, I thought, *It's over. Don's told him to break it off. The club comes first.*

His gaze lifted to mine. A bruise was rising on his jaw, purple and red, and his lip was split, smears of blood on his chin where he'd wiped it off.

"Oh," I said. I reached to touch his face, but he caught my hand.

"I'm fine," he said, and came inside, shutting the door behind him. "I'm fine now."

His lips came to mine, and I held back, thinking of his cut, trying to be gentle, but he pulled me to him, his kiss hard and hungry, the faint taste of blood on my tongue.

I laced my arms around his neck, fingers in his hair as he swung me back against the wall, hands pushing up my nightshirt, fingers hooking in my panties. Then he paused, breaking the kiss, panting slightly as he whispered, "I need you."

"Yes," I said.

Afterward, we were on the floor, half in the front hall, half in the kitchen. Ricky lay on top of me, catching his breath. He glanced up as something snagged his attention.

"Hey, TC," he said.

I craned my head back to see the cat, sitting there, staring at him.

"Probably not the best way to make his acquaintance," Ricky said.

"It's not you. I swear, the first night Gabriel stayed over, TC sat on the couch and stared at him all night. He's assessing the situation. Determining how likely you are to steal his food and his blanket."

"I'll leave him to his bed and find my own." He started to rise. "Your room's through there?"

"It is." I pushed up on my elbows.

"Uh-uh. I got you out of bed. Least I can do is get you back there." He scooped me up.

"Mmm, impressive," I said.

He laughed, and I reveled in the sound, the look in his eyes, relaxed and centered now. He carried me to the bed and set me on it while he stood at the side.

"You okay with me staying tonight?" he said.

"I'd be more concerned if you finished your booty call and scrammed."

"It wasn't a booty call."

"I know," I said, reaching for him. "I was

teasing. Come to bed. Talk to me."

He stripped off his shirt and socks and slid into bed.

"You told your dad about us," I said.

"Yeah."

"And . . ." I touched the purpling bruise on his jaw. "He wasn't happy."

"Yeah." A pause, then his eyes widened as he made the connection. "No. He didn't —" He shook his head. "Definitely not. He's never laid a finger on me. That was . . ."

He took a deep breath and propped himself on his side, facing me. "We had some shit to do earlier. Territory issue. New guys. Not bikers — just punks with bikes who fancy themselves a club. They want territory, and they've decided, since we're the smallest club, they'll take ours. We've been trying to stomp them without causing serious trouble. Dad doesn't like trouble. It's bad for business. Anyway, we went to have a conversation, and the asshole in charge decided to come at me instead. He figured he had ammunition. That picture of us in the *Post*."

"Ah."

"Yeah. So he's trash-talking you, and usually I'm good at ignoring idiots. But he stepped over the line, and I went off on him. Hence . . ." He pointed at his jaw and lip.

"Bet he's feeling worse."

I smiled when I said it, expecting he'd joke back, but his eyes clouded. "Yeah. I . . . really went off on him. I'm not like that. I can fight, obviously. I have to. But my dad and I don't get into it the way the other guys do. Part of that's how we are, but part of it's a choice, too. Let the guys get down and dirty while we stay above that. We stay in charge. Never lose control. I lost it tonight."

I must have looked worried, because he hurried on. "In some ways, it probably helped. The guys respect my dad even if he doesn't mix it up. The old-timers have *seen* him mix it up, before he took over. Me, though? I've never done that, and I think some of them figure maybe I can't. The college boy. Smart, but . . ." Another shrug. "A little soft. So, yeah, they were impressed. My dad, though . . ."

"Is not impressed."

"Yeah. And considering what set me off? We didn't need to have our conversation after that. I should have told him about us. Finding out that way?" He shook his head.

"He's angry."

"Hurt, more like. Confused. It's always been just the two of us. Now here's this major change in my life that he knows noth-

405

ing about, and if it was just some girl from school, he could figure I was working up to an introduction. With you? No such excuse. He knows why I kept it from him, too — because I thought he wouldn't like it. And he doesn't. He really, really doesn't." Ricky rubbed his mouth and paused before saying, "It's worse than I expected. He told me to end it. Not as my father. As the president of my club. He's . . . he's never done that before."

The look in Ricky's eyes told me Don wasn't the only one hurt and confused here.

"Okay," I said carefully. "So that means you have to end it, right?"

He shook his head. "He took that back. I think he was testing me. Seeing how serious I am about you. When I argued, he retreated, but . . ." He looked over at me. "My dad and I don't fight. We disagree, sure, but even that's rare. We've never had the usual parent–kid issues. This was an issue."

"Because of Gabriel."

Ricky nodded. "I know how bad this will sound, so bear with me. In a club, women aren't exactly equal citizens, as you've figured out. They can't be members. Even wives are kept out of club business. You're supposed to treat women well, and there's some serious old-school chivalry there, but that leads to a certain mind-set. Your woman is your . . ."

"Property?"

He winced. "I wouldn't use that word, but it's the gist. One thing you don't do is go after another guy's girl. Ever."

"I'm not Gabriel's girl."

"To my dad, you are. It doesn't matter if you're not sleeping with him. He brought you in. You're with him. Therefore you are off-limits."

"In case Gabriel ever decides he does want to sleep with me?"

Another wince. "In *my* world, you can be friends with a girl and not go there. Not for my dad, though. Either you are there or you're heading there."

"Otherwise, what's the point?"

"I know that makes him sound like a Neanderthal. He's not. When my mom got pregnant, he never expected her to drop out of med school and marry him. He offered to get married, of course, but he didn't expect a yes. He was just happy she was willing to go through with the pregnancy. He never asked for anything else from her. Never tried to deny her rights, either. A lot of the guys didn't get that, and he took some lumps for it. He lost a few members when he took over, because Mr. Mom wasn't their idea of a club president." He stopped and flushed. "I didn't mean to rant."

"You didn't. I understand, and as long as *you* don't consider me your property —"

He laughed. "I know how far I'd get with that. Booted out the door. With my ass kicked the whole way. No, I'm not my father. But as a club member, I have to follow his rules. After you came by that first time, and I knew I wanted to see you again, I made sure I wasn't overstepping. I talked to Gabriel."

"And said what? *Hey, are you planning to hit that?*"

He gave me a look. "Not in so many words, but yeah. That's not sexist, either. If you met a guy through a woman you respected, wouldn't you check to see if she was interested in him before making a move?"

"Point taken. So what exactly did you say?"

He shrugged. "I asked if you guys were together, and when he said no, I asked if he was heading that way. He said absolutely not. You're a client, and that's grounds for disbarment. So I asked if that would change when you weren't a client. He gave me that cold stare and said it was a professional relationship. End of conversation. Or so I thought."

"So you thought?"

Ricky rolled onto his stomach and propped up on his forearms. "Gabriel's . . . different."

"Really?"

"No shit, huh." He chuckled. "But he's different in a whole lotta ways. Our last lawyer used to come to the club, hang out with the girls, go home with the hangers-on. It was a perk of the job. Gabriel? Hell, no. My dad suggested it once, and he got a very frosty *no thank you.* No girls. No drugs. Give him a drink, and he takes a few sips to be polite. Totally straight edge. He's driven and he's ambitious, and until he gets where he wants to be, nothing's getting in his way, including romantic entanglements. That means he's single-minded as hell. So when I ask about you, it takes a day or so for him to realize *why* I'm asking. He pops by the clubhouse on business. When I ask how you're doing, he pounces. He strongly advises against asking you out. We're both clients, and that would be problematic. Also, you're going through serious changes in your life and you don't need the disruption. I should steer clear."

"Bastard," I muttered.

Ricky seemed surprised by the venom in my voice. "Yeah, I'm sure you don't appreciate that, but on the other hand it means I *may* have overstepped after all. It gives ammunition to my dad's argument."

"No, it doesn't."

Ricky rubbed my bare hip. "Yeah, it kinda does. If Gabriel was that adamant about me not dating you, it could mean he really is —"

"He isn't." I told him about Gabriel's deal with James. When I finished, his mouth opened. Then it shut, and he shook his head.

"I'd say I'm stunned, but it's more like mildly surprised. Gabriel saw the chance to make a little extra on the side, and since it didn't hurt your case, it wasn't against your interests. On a professional level."

"Which is all that matters with Gabriel. The point is that your dad has zero reason to think you were overstepping. Gabriel was only guarding someone else's 'property.' If Gabriel still complains, it's only because us dating could add a mild complication to his business interests, which come first."

Ricky nodded slowly, digesting that. "That helps. On all levels."

"Good. Because I understand that the club comes first for *you,* and I won't interfere with that. But if we can make this work . . ."

"I'll make it work," he said and pulled me on top of him.

Chapter Forty-Three

When my phone rang, I surfaced from sleep, confused and groggy, thinking I heard a funeral toll, that slow dong that signifies a death. I leapt up, sleep falling away, Ricky stirring beside me. Then I heard the familiar tone of my phone. I checked it. Private caller.

I answered.

"E-Eden?" It was a woman, her voice pitched so high she sounded like a child. "Is th-this Eden Larsen?"

I tensed. Ricky touched my arm, telling me he could hear the caller.

"Where did you get this number?" I said.

"I-Is this Eden Larsen? Please. It's important."

"I don't go by that name, and if you're using it, you're not someone I want to speak to, especially at three in the —"

"Wait! Please, please, wait. He told me to ask for Eden Larsen. Get to this phone. Call this number. Ask for Eden. That's all I know." Her words tumbled out on a wave of panic.

"I'm hanging up now," I said carefully.

"No! Please, please, please." Her voice broke in a sob. "I only get this one call. It was programmed in. If you hang up, I can't phone back."

"Programmed in?"

"To the phone. I can't use any other number. I tried. I only get this one number and this one call. I have to speak to you and give you the message."

"Who are you?" I asked.

"Macy. My name is Macy. You don't know me. I don't know you. I was at a party with some friends. I left with this guy, and he brought me here and . . . and . . ." Her voice broke again.

"Okay, slow down. You said there's a message?"

"Yes. It's that you need to come find me." She paused. "You understand, right? You know what this is all about? Because I don't understand any of it." She hiccuped as she sped through the words. "Tell me this makes some kind of sense. That you know why he'd do this, and you'll come help me."

"Give me the whole message," I said, speaking slowly to calm her down.

413

"Call Eden Larsen. Tell her to come to this address. If she comes, I will let you go. I have information she needs, but she has to prove she's worthy of it. She must find you and she must save you. Then I will tell her the truth about her parents and her birthright. And if she does not come, I will —" Her voice cracked and she had to start again. "I will kill you."

"Where are you?"

She rattled off the GPS coordinates left for her. "So you'll come?"

"He *sent* you to that phone, correct? Meaning he isn't there right now. So how are you in danger? You can run for help."

"There's nowhere to run. I don't know where I am. There are all these abandoned buildings, and a cemetery. He's watching, too. He'll shoot me if I run." She paused. "You don't believe me. Oh God, you don't believe me."

She continued babbling. How cold am I if I admit I was ignoring her words and gauging her voice and her tone, trying to decide how genuine her plight was? Yet Ricky could hear, and he wasn't saying, *Come on! We need to go help her!* When I glanced over, I could tell he was assessing, too.

I made Macy go over her story again, in more detail. She'd been at a party. She'd left with a man. She didn't know who he was — it was a big party — only that he was alone and good-looking, and he'd singled her out for attention. They had a few drinks, and she was sure he must have slipped something in hers because otherwise she'd never just leave with him, especially without telling her friends.

He'd driven out of the city. She wasn't sure which way. They'd been talking and the next thing she knew they were in the countryside. He'd taken her to what looked like an army base, with lots of buildings. Then he'd gotten out and said he had to go inside and talk to someone.

After he'd left, she realized all the buildings were dark. When she'd taken a closer look at one, she'd seen boarded-up windows and doors. She'd just started to panic when a cell phone rang. It wasn't hers. She couldn't find hers. That's when she'd begun panicking for real. The phone kept ringing. She'd found it under the seat and answered. It was him.

He told her that she needed to follow his instructions and make a very important call. He gave her the directions and told her what would happen if she didn't do as he said. She started to scream. He hung up.

She'd tried to call 911, call anyone, but

the phone was blocked. Hers was gone. The car keys were gone. She'd made a break for it. When she ran past the building she was supposed to enter, he shot at her, the bullet hitting the ground at her feet.

"It's — it's horrible in here," she whispered. "He left me a flashlight, but it barely does anything, and it's dark and empty and there's writing on the walls. Writing everywhere. Crazy stuff. I hear noises. I think it's only rats." A high-pitched laugh. "*Only* rats. I can't believe I said that. I hate rats. Bats, too, and they're everywhere, flying out when I walk into a room and —"

"Where are you now?"

"Inside. With the phone. He said if he sees me leave, he'll shoot me. I can only go when you find me. You will come, right?"

"Which building are you in?"

She told me, then continued, "He said something else, too. He said to remember Ciara. I don't know what that means. I asked him, and he wouldn't tell me, and —"

The line went dead.

I speed-dialed Gabriel. When the line connected, I hung up. What was he going to do? This wasn't a legal matter. I'd be dragging him into this. Forcing him to make decisions that weren't his responsibility to make.

I glanced over. Ricky hadn't said a word.

"We are awake, right?" he said.

"I think so."

"Hard to tell after that call." He paused. "Do you know what she was talking about?"

I hesitated. There was so much he didn't know. Most of which I couldn't share.

"Some of it," I said. "The name she mentioned. Ciara. She's the girl whose body I found while rescuing TC. Her death may have something to do with me or my parents. Gabriel's been helping me look into that."

"Do you want to call him?"

Yes. "This isn't a legal issue."

"Do you really think he'd tell you to handle it yourself?"

No. He'd come.

I shook my head. "I've dragged him into enough trouble. Did she sound as if she believed she was in danger?"

"Yes. The fact that it makes no sense actually supports it being real — she'd dream up a better fake story. But even if she is in danger, it's almost certainly a trap, so . . ."

He trailed off, but I knew what he was thinking. Would I risk my life for a stranger? No. Whatever brand of heroism that requires, I don't have it.

I looked down at the GPS coordinates Macy had given me. Macy. She wasn't some anonymous victim. Even if she was, I don't think I could have ignored her.

"We can go check it out," Ricky said. "You've got your gun, and you've got me. I don't think whoever's doing this is expecting either."

"You don't have to —"

"You think I'd let you handle this while I go back to sleep?"

"We'll take my car," I said. "I want to explain more on the way."

CHAPTER FORTY-FOUR

While Ricky drove, I navigated and told him about Ciara, which wasn't easy, piecing the hole-ridden cloth into a plausible story. I told him about the body in the car, but I skipped the "head in the bed." That's where it seemed to cross the line to a potential legal issue for Gabriel, given that I'd had photographic proof and we didn't report it.

When I finished, Ricky just kept driving, despite me telling him to make a left. He got turned around and back on course before speaking.

"So someone put this girl's body in your car, wearing your clothes, dressed *as* you."

"And then, while I was inside waiting for Gabriel, the killer took away all the evidence. Which sounds completely crazy, so you can't blame him for thinking I was imagining things."

Ricky glanced over. "I'm sure Gabriel knew you weren't. I'm sure he told you to keep it quiet. I completely agree, and I'd expect him to do the same as *my* lawyer. I'll buy whatever story you sell me, Liv."

"I —"

"I know there's more to it. There are things about my life I can't share, either, because they could put you in jeopardy. I have secrets; you have secrets. I'm here for anything you want to tell me, but I'll never push. Fair enough?"

I nodded. "Thank you."

"So clearly that corpse was a warning. Clearly Gabriel is concerned, which explains him getting you that security system. But if you were in serious danger, something would have happened by now. Instead, it's *do as I say or this Macy girl ends up like Ciara.* Meaning he needs something from you. Something you can't give if you're dead."

"Presumably." I looked out the window. "Any idea where we are?"

"You're the one with the GPS."

"Yes, but I haven't seen a landmark for almost ten minutes."

We were in the countryside. That much was obvious. On a dark, empty secondary highway. About a half hour outside Chicago, if I'd calculated the distance properly.

"There's a town ahead," Ricky said. "Big one, judging by that glow."

I checked my phone GPS. "Looks like we're going to turn off before we reach it. Take the next right. We're getting close."

Two more turns and we were there. Wherever "there" was. We passed a laneway leading into a golf course. It wasn't one I recognized. I'm not much of a golfer, but James is, and this didn't look like a course we would have played. It was meant for locals who wanted to knock a few balls around a half-dozen times a year. At three in the morning, it was pitch-black.

The GPS led us past it to a laneway with gates. Huge gates, adorned with Keep Out and Private Property and Trespassers Will Be Prosecuted. Also, massive padlocks.

"Let me out here," I said.

Ricky did. I went up and checked the gates. Chains looped them shut, but the locks were unfastened. I peered through. The lane led to a group of dark buildings surrounded by empty fields. Hell of a place to drive into. Anyone watching would see us coming for a quarter mile.

I jangled the chains, then called back to Ricky, louder than necessary, "Seems to be locked tight."

He could see damn well that the chains weren't secured, but he said, "Think the call was a prank?"

"Maybe." I made a show of squinting through the gates again. "Let's drive around."

I climbed back into the car.

"It's too open," I said as he backed onto the road. "But if Macy's captor is listening, which I presume he is, I didn't want him to think we were taking off."

"You're pretty good at this stuff."

"It's in my genes," I said. "And I have Gabriel for a teacher."

"No shit, huh?"

As Macy had said, a cemetery bordered the property. Cemetery on one side, golf course on the other. Both dark and silent and empty. Two routes to choose from.

We parked at the golf course, looped around, and walked in through the cemetery. We'd dressed dark. Ricky wore a light T-shirt but had zipped his leather jacket over it. Remembering our game in the cabin woods, I let him take the lead. He walked silently, as if knowing where to step to avoid cracking twigs and crunching stones. As we moved, I could practically feel the low strum of energy vibrating from him, that dark and delicious mix of tension and adrenaline. When he'd glance back to check on me, his eyes glittered, as they had in the woods.

We reached the cemetery. It was a modern

one, no weathered headstones and moss-laden mausoleums. Just row after row of death. We cut our way through as if the gravestones were merely obstacles. If there was anything frightening about a cemetery at night, it was lost on me. Always had been.

A strip of woods separated the cemetery and the abandoned buildings. Ricky stopped at the edge. He glanced back to make sure I had my gun out. He nodded, took something from his jacket, and palmed it. When I leaned in to see what it was, he opened his fist to show a metal cylinder. He pressed a button. A knife shot out.

"Switchblade," I said. "Nice. I could use one of those."

"That's not enough?" he whispered, pointing at my gun.

"It does the job, if the job is to kill. I need a backup that's not always so lethal."

"You could try getting yourself into fewer situations where you need a weapon."

"I suspect that's not happening anytime soon."

A short laugh and he nodded as we carried on.

CHAPTER FORTY-FIVE

We reached the middle of the strip of forest, which was so thin we could see the fields on either side. When I heard an almost soundless *whoosh-whoosh,* I looked up to see an owl passing overhead. It was huge, like the ones I'd seen in Cainsville a month ago, a pair that had ripped apart a raven. I found myself looking for a second one. I knew this couldn't be the same owl, and I was sure they hunted alone. Yet when I looked, I saw another in a tree just ahead. The first lighted in the same one, and they sat there, watching us silently.

Oddly, seeing them seemed to calm me. Their unblinking gazes said to be alert and be safe. Stay watchful.

It took a moment for Ricky to notice them. When he did, he stopped.

"Now that's creepy," he said.

"Is it?"

He shivered. "Um, yeah."

I guess we didn't agree on everything. As we continued, he kept sneaking glances up at the owls, as if expecting them to dive-bomb us. It was cute, really. He'd just walked through a graveyard at night, accompanying me into a potential death trap, but what freaked him out was a pair of owls.

As we passed, they watched us go. Then they took off, flying overhead in the same direction we were heading.

"Hey, they're leading the way," I said as I pointed.

"To our deaths probably," Ricky muttered. "They carry off children in the night, you know."

"Then I guess it's a good thing we aren't children. Where'd you hear that?"

"I used to read all that stuff when I was a kid. Every now and then it just pops up."

"For me it's omens. Someone stuffed them in my head, and they crop up at the most inconvenient times."

"Yeah? Nothing about owls, then?"

"Only if it's daytime. Although if you hear an owl hoot between houses, it means someone has lost her virginity. I think we're okay there, too. And if a pregnant woman hears an owl, her child will be blessed. Again, we should be fine. At least, I hope so."

"They didn't hoot."

"Excellent."

He grinned back at me, and I returned the smile. I hadn't planned to mention the omens, but as soon as the topic came up, I'd jumped on it, as if eager to unburden myself. When I'd confessed my mental library of superstitions to James, he'd thought it was adorable, in that slightly condescending way that made me wish I'd never opened my mouth. Ricky only said, "So I guess you won't think my stories are so weird, huh?"

"I won't."

He returned to cutting the trail. He definitely must have better night vision than me, because he brought us out behind a building, where we could safely exit under cover of shadow.

We were behind a brick structure maybe half the size of the Gallaghers' cabin. Tiny for a residence, but that's what it looked like, one of at least a dozen squatting along a narrow road. Sterile brick boxes with barred windows and heavy doors. Cells more than homes. When I touched a brick, I shuddered.

"Can we agree this place is creepy?" Ricky whispered.

I nodded and pulled my hand back. "Macy

said it wasn't an army base, but that's what it looks like."

"Could be. We're heading to the biggest building, right?"

"Yep. In the middle."

He surveyed the landscape. Beyond the pillbox houses we could make out buildings a couple of stories tall. We stuck to shadows and silence as we made our way toward them.

I made notes of my surroundings, trying to arrange everything into a mental map. There'd been only one road leading in, but there were more here, laid out in a grid pattern. Like an army base or other "prepackaged" community. What else needed to be isolated like this? A prison? A commune? It seemed too open for the former and too industrial for the latter.

We were passing the last of the houselike buildings when I caught sight of words carved into the foundation. I touched Ricky's arm to stop him as I bent to read. Someone had painstakingly etched a sentence into the concrete blocks.

There is no freedom from the prison of the mind.

I looked around at the tiny houses with no glass in the barred windows. With doors that could be locked from the outside.

I fought chills as I rose. We continued on, me following in Ricky's tracks as we skirted a two-story building, circling until we could see around the front.

There was a car in the middle of the main road. The interior light was on, the passenger door open. Across the street stood a building that looked like a high school. A long three-story rectangle, saved from architectural obscurity by a tower rising an extra twenty feet over the main doors. On top of the tower was a cross with a broken arm. To the left, an empty flagpole groaned in the wind. There was a balcony on the front tower, half the railing missing.

Over the main doors, I could make out a sign, with letters big enough to read in the moonlight. Part of the first word was obscured, but I could see the rest. State Hospital.

"Hospital?" Ricky whispered. "Way out here? With cabins for patients?"

"It's a mental hospital."

"An asylum?"

I gazed around. Those locked box cabins wouldn't exactly meet modern standards for mental care, but they weren't cages, either. I took in the architecture. Early twentieth century. The rise of modern psychiatry, if I remembered my college classes. Not anyplace I'd want to stay but past the era of treating patients like animals.

"An early psychiatric institution," I whispered. "Not Bedlam, but not up to today's code."

An experiment, it seemed, in a more humane way to treat the mentally ill. Still locking them up and keeping them away from normal folks, but giving them some sense of a community. Yet I remembered those words carved in stone, and a chill ran through me, as it hadn't in the cemetery. That was death. Final and unavoidable. This . . . ?

There is no freedom from the prison of the mind.

I shook it off. Knowing the function of the compound helped, if only to keep my brain from whirring to solve the puzzle. Ricky motioned he was going to slip from the shelter of the building and take a look down the road. I stayed where I was and watched him as he crept along the wall. He moved three careful steps from it, staying in its shadow as he peered down the lane.

He scanned the collection of buildings. Then he gestured for me to wait as he set out, flush with the wall then crossing the gap to the next building with a few fluid steps, never pausing to check where he put his feet down, as if knowing they'd land silently. When he did pause, his gaze swept the road, his head moving slowly, deliberately.

He looks like he's hunting.

Desire and fascination mingled unbidden as I watched him. Wind blustered past, and his blond hair whipped against his face, but he didn't even seem to notice, just kept looking along the buildings. Then he returned to me.

"Someone's down there," he said. "Watching for us."

"Third building across the road, right? I noticed a faint light."

He shook his head. "Too obvious. That's a decoy. Same as the building beside this one where the door's cracked open. Both are staged. He's in the one to the right of it. Second story. Left front corner room."

"What's the giveaway?"

"I drew him out, standing in the road like that. He knows you're not alone now, which should put him on notice. If the girl's over there" — he pointed at the three-story building — "he can't get to her without us seeing. You can go look for her while I keep an eye on him."

"Thank you."

Keeping an eye on our mystery man

didn't mean staying where we were. There was no need, now that he'd spotted Ricky. So we darted to the car, using that for cover, before dashing to the three-story building across the road.

The open front door was plastered with more No Trespassing and Private Property signs, along with warnings that the building was in unsafe condition and trespassing could result in serious injury or death. Judging by the number of jimmy marks in the frame, the warnings hadn't stopped urban explorers intent on taking a look.

The door opened into a reception room. It seemed tiny, given the size of the building. I guess they hadn't expected many visitors. A counter extended across the room, with mail cubbies behind it. Bits of crumbled concrete and blown-in leaves littered the floor. My footsteps crunched across the debris as we walked.

I took out my phone, for both the flashlight and the directions I'd jotted down from Macy's instructions.

"I need to go that way," I said, pointing. There were doorways at either end of the reception area, the doors long gone.

"And I'll go that way." Ricky pointed opposite. "Upstairs, where I have a better vantage point. Can you stand watch while I do that? I'll text when I'm in place."

I nodded.

"Be careful in here," he whispered. "Just because I know where the girl's kidnapper is doesn't mean he's alone."

"I know."

It took Ricky a few minutes to get upstairs. Then he texted to say he could still see the guy, and I set out.

CHAPTER FORTY-SIX

The open doorway led to a hall. The exit I wanted was on my left, with its door hanging by the top hinge. I walked through it into another hall, this one so short I wondered why they bothered making it a hall at all. It was really more of an entranceway, leading into a cavernous room. I stepped inside.

Huge windows let in enough moonlight for me to look around. The room took up two stories, with rows of pipes hanging from the ceiling. *Were* they pipes? Or had they once held lighting? I couldn't tell from down here. As for what the room had been used for, there was little doubt of that. There were still a few metal bed frames, bolted to the floor.

As I moved through the ward, movement flickered above. Rotting rafters showed through chunks of missing ceiling. A black shape took form on one of the suspended pipes. I lifted my flashlight to see a perched raven watching me.

"Ewch i ffwrdd, bran," I muttered.

The raven lifted its wings, ruffling its feathers as if offended. Then it settled back into silent watching. At another flash of motion, I noticed a hole in the roof. Moonlight streamed through it. Then the moon vanished as an owl glided past.

Ravens and owls. That's no coincidence. They're here for a reason.

Watching me.

I kept going with one eye on the raven. It didn't move. I passed through the left doorway at the end of the ward and came out into . . .

A bathroom.

Not a restroom, but an actual room of baths. Four deep tubs, built right into the floor of the narrow room. For hydrotherapy, I presumed. Writing covered the walls. Not the "AJ was here!"–style graffiti I'd seen elsewhere, but lines like "a clean body is not a clean mind" and "out, damned spot" and "water cannot wash away the sins of the soul."

A squeak sounded from the farthest tub. When I walked over, I could see it was filled with water. Bits of paper floated on top.

No, not paper. Petals. Red poppy petals.

I looked back at the doorway, but there was no sign of the raven or the owls. Just me, alone in this room, seeing poppies. I forced myself forward. Filthy water reached almost to the brim. The petals floated on it.

With the gun in my right hand, I reached out my left and touched the water. As I scooped petals, my fingers brushed something under the surface. I stumbled back, but fingers grabbed my wrist. A shape shot up from the filthy water. The bloated corpse of a dark-haired woman. Her mouth opened, a horrible, twisted, swollen mouth, skin sloughing off, teeth hanging loose.

"Your fault," she said. "All yours."

I wrenched away and my hand came free, her skin still clinging to it, as if I'd yanked the bloated flesh from her bones. I fell back, hitting the floor, a scream clogged in my throat, looking up to see —

I was alone in an empty room.

I stuffed my gun in my pocket, and without thinking I pulled out something else. The boar's tusk. I gripped it tight and pushed to my feet and looked into the tub. It was empty. I reached down to see if the sides were wet. As I did, I realized I was still clutching something in my left hand. I opened it and a trio of damp poppy petals fell into the dry tub. I stared at them. Then

I picked them up, fingers rubbing the petals to reassure myself they were real. I put them into my pocket and continued on.

The next room was a lavatory, with a row of toilets along one wall. Only low walls divided them, and if there had ever been doors, I couldn't see any remnants of them.

I checked each stall as I moved through the room. Only when I reached the last did I notice writing on the opposite wall. Three words. Written in foot-high block letters.

I DON'T UNDERSTAND.

I swallowed and rubbed my arms. I tried to pull my gaze away, but it kept returning to those words, somehow more haunting than any that had come before.

I DON'T UNDERSTAND.

I didn't understand. Not any of it. Not the ravens, not the owls, not the hallucinations and the poppies, not even what the hell I was doing here, walking through an abandoned psychiatric hospital, clutching a gun and a boar's tusk. Part of me wanted to just stop and scream, "I don't understand!" and demand that the universe reply. That it give me answers. It wouldn't. Those were up to me.

As I pulled my gaze from the words, a shadow darted past the next doorway. I dashed to it just in time to see a figure run into yet another room in this labyrinth of decay.

I raced in to find the next room empty, with no sign of what it had been used for. According to the directions, the door to Macy was on my left. The figure had darted through the door to my right. I went right. I told myself I chose that because it might have *been* Macy, but I knew it wasn't. Someone else was here.

I jogged through that doorway and through another, following the dark figure. Then I stopped short. I was in an empty room with only one entrance. The door slapped shut behind me.

I swung my gun on the figure standing by the now-closed door. It was the guy I'd caught trying to break into Ricky's apartment.

"Oh." He looked at the gun, a faint smile on his lips. "Does that mean you'd like to leave?" He opened the door. "By all means. Go rescue the girl. We don't really need to talk."

I stayed where I was, my gun trained on him.

He laughed. "That's what I thought. Poor Macy. You aren't here for her at all, are you? You're here to find out why Ciara Conway died. Why her body turned up in your car.

Why I would use Macy to lure you in. Those answers are far, far more important than Macy herself, aren't they?"

"If I shoot, will you get to the point faster?"

"Hmm, no, sadly. It will be mildly inconvenient, but it won't hurt me. I think you know that."

"How would I?"

"How indeed. Aren't you wondering how I got past your lover?"

I stiffened, my gaze swinging to the door.

"Oh, he's fine. In fact, go ahead and text him to make sure. I wouldn't suggest mentioning I'm here. If he comes to your rescue, I'll have to leave. Better if he just keeps watching that building."

I texted Ricky. He replied: *All clear.*

"See?" the man said. "He can take care of himself. All his kind can."

He knew Ricky was a biker, then. How much else did he know about him? Even the thought made me anxious.

"You needn't worry about the boy," he said. "I know better than to hurt him. His family would retaliate, and they are more than I care to tackle."

"They are."

"Do you even know who I'm talking about?"

"The Saints. Ricky's gang."

He smiled. "Ah, yes. The bikers. Definitely not enemies one wishes to make." He looked around. "What do you think of this place? Does it look familiar?"

"Actually, yes, I remember staying here . . . despite the fact it's probably been closed since before I was born." I glowered at him. "I don't know what you're playing at —"

"Memory," he said. "I'm playing at memory, Eden Olivia. Prodding and pushing. You may have never stayed here, but you have relatives who did. Sad cases, really. The perils of mixing blood that was never meant to be mixed. There is so much that can go wrong. Just ask your parents. Or Seanna Walsh. Or Ciara Conway."

"What are you talking about?"

"I can't tell you. Too many ramifications. But I can poke at your memory. Inherited memory. If I prod enough, you will question, and if you question, you will find the answers and you will see exactly where you stand. On quicksand. Two sides offer you ropes. The two halves to your whole. Mortal enemies. Both want you. Both promise safe ground to stand on. Both lie."

Frustration welled in my gut, and I thought of those words in the bathroom. I DON'T UNDERSTAND. Goddamn it, I didn't

439

understand, and I was so sick of these teases, of these hints, of all this weird *shit* that meant something and didn't mean something, and I just wanted —

"To go back to your old life?" he said, as if I'd spoken the words aloud.

"What are you?" I asked. "I want answers, or —"

"Or you'll what, Eden Olivia? Shoot me? Walk away? Neither does you any good. As for what I am, that's a very personal question. I'll give you a name instead. You may call me Tristan."

My cell phone buzzed. I glanced down at the screen.

"Mr. Walsh, I presume?" Tristan asked.

It was. As the call went to voice mail, Tristan came closer. I lifted my gun.

He smiled. "I think we've already established that won't do any good."

"I'll take my chances."

"Go ahead." He put his hand over the barrel of the gun, palm blocking the end. "Fire at will, Eden Olivia."

Before I could decide whether to do it, he snatched the phone from my hand and danced backward, hitting Play on the voice mail as he did.

"I see you called a couple of hours ago," Gabriel's voice said. "But I'm certain my phone didn't ring. Is there a problem? Call me."

Tristan tapped the screen and started to text.

"Hey!"

I lunged. He dodged and kept typing until I managed to grab the phone. Too late. The message had been sent.

Need help. Please come. Followed by an address, then, *Don't call. Too dangerous. Just come. Please.*

I started to text him.

"You know that won't help. What will you say? *Sorry, but a madman who lured me to an abandoned hospital sent that. I really don't need help.*"

I hesitated.

Tristan continued. "Even if you could explain it, he'd come anyway, just in case. The cry for help has been sent. He must answer. It's his job."

"If you mean he's being paid to protect me —"

"Paid? No. I chose my words poorly. It's his duty. One he executes with pleasure. He's formed quite an attachment to you, as has young Mr. Gallagher. And you to them. Three pawns in a very old game. Do you like being a pawn, Eden Olivia?"

I said nothing.

"Of course you don't. You are Mallt-y-Nos. You rule over pawns; you are not one of them."

"I am *what*?"

"Special," he said. "Isn't that what every little mortal wants to be? Oh so very special. Except it's not nearly as wonderful as they think, because when you are special, you inspire avarice and fear. Everyone wants to control you. Use you. If they cannot, they will kill you, because if you are not theirs, you are dangerous. Right now, they circle, watching and waiting. You've seen the ravens. The owls and the hounds. Watching. Evaluating. Do you want to know why?"

"Yes."

"Then start asking questions, Eden Olivia. I've been sending some to you."

"You've been sending me *body parts*. You killed an innocent —"

"I did not kill Ciara Conway. I merely took advantage of her death to . . ." He smiled. "Stir the waters. Wake you up. Wake them up. You say Ciara Conway is innocent, and you are correct. Yet there is someone who was even more wronged in this: the girl waiting for you here. She's connected to Ciara and has suffered through that connection. Those responsible for her suffering surround you in Cainsville. Find the connection. Ask the questions. See what it has to do with you."

He turned and headed for the door.

"Hold on," I said. "I —"

"You'd best go find Miss Macy. I may have" — he grinned, all teeth — "moved her. I wouldn't suggest you leave until you find her. That would be very unfortunate for the poor girl. This place doesn't see many visitors."

He walked out. I ran after him, but when I got to the door, he'd vanished, just as he had that night at Ricky's apartment. I knew now that it hadn't been a trick of light and shadow.

As I retraced my steps, I called Ricky.

"He got past you," I said.

"Shit."

"Not your fault. It was some kind of trick. He's gone now, though, I think."

"Are you okay?"

"I'm fine. We just had a conversation. A very weird conversation. I'll get the girl and —"

I veered into the room where Macy said she'd be. It was empty.

"Damn it," I muttered. "She's not here. He said he moved her. Great."

"Hold on. I'll be right there."

CHAPTER FORTY-SEVEN

After I gave Ricky directions, I searched the room. It didn't take much. The place was about fifteen feet square, with one exit, no windows, and no debris large enough to hide anyone. The walls were covered in graffiti, but it was only the usual "I was here" markers.

As I paced, I tried to call Gabriel to let him know what was going on, but I got a "customer unavailable" recording. I texted a very basic *Everything's fine now. Call when you can.*

"Hey," Ricky said softly behind me.

I silenced my phone.

"You okay?" he asked.

I nodded. "I just want to find her and get out of here."

He gave my hand a squeeze. I relaxed against his shoulder — a brief moment of rest before I looked around.

"It's hide-and-go-seek now," I said.

444

"Are you sure it's not a wild-goose chase?"

"No, but he suggested he's put her someplace where she can't escape. Meaning she'll be there until someone else finds her. Which isn't likely to happen soon enough."

"Shit." He exhaled. "We don't have much choice, then."

"I think that's the point. Oh, and Gabriel's on the way." I explained what had happened.

"Well, that's not a bad thing," Ricky said. "Three of us can cover more ground."

We searched the main building methodically, starting at one end and moving through every room, checking any items big enough to hide someone. We were nearly at the end of the first floor when I stepped into what seemed to be a closet. I was about to leave when I noticed rungs, beginning six feet from the floor and extending into the darkness.

I was gaping up when Ricky joined me.

"Huh," he said, shining a light up. "Looks like the bottom rungs are missing. Not exactly an easy climb."

My gaze stayed fixed on those rungs.

"Your gut says she's up there."

"No, I . . ." I swallowed the denial. "We should take a look."

445

"Let me give you a boost."

He lifted me to the bottom rung, telling me to test it first. It seemed solid enough, so I pulled myself up and checked each rung as I climbed. Ricky swung up below me, which took some serious upper-body strength, but he managed it with only a few grunts. At the top was a hatch. With some effort, I heaved it open and lifted my flashlight through to —

Something creaked in the room above. My flashlight beam landed on a chair, rocking. It stopped as soon as the light hit it. I lifted the light higher and saw that the "rocking chair" had thick leather restraint straps across the base and the back, and two smaller ones on the arms.

That was the only thing in the tiny room. A rocking restraint chair.

"Liv?" Ricky whispered below me.

I continued up. Once I was standing in the room, I instinctively moved away from the chair, but I kept my gaze on it. That's when I noticed the writing on the ceiling.

We are imprisoned by the truth we dare not see.

We are imprisoned by the questions we dare not ask.

At another movement, my gaze moved down. A dark-haired woman in a straitjacket sat in the chair, strapped down, her eyes covered in bloody bandages. She rocked forward violently, gripping the wooden arms. Her mouth opened, but she made only a garbled croak, like a raven's caw. Flecks of blood flew from her mouth, and when she opened it, all I could see was a bloody, cavernous hole with no tongue. She kept making that noise, that terrible noise, and I was stumbling back —

Ricky caught me. He'd scrambled up and grabbed me from behind, and as soon as he touched me, the woman vanished.

Ricky held me for a moment. The warmth of his chest and his arms tight around me felt so damned good, the beating of his heart, solid and steady.

"Sorry," I said. "The chair was rocking. Gave me a start."

"Opening that hatch probably set it going. Change of air pressure."

"Which doesn't make *that* any less creepy." I pointed at the words on the ceiling.

He squinted up. I shone my light. The words were plain as could be, but he kept his gaze searching.

"I, uh, I thought I saw something up there." I rubbed my eyes. "Clearly this place is getting to me."

"I don't blame you. Spooky as hell." He gestured at the chair. "*That* gives me the creeps, for sure."

We headed out. The room led into a long hall lined with doors, all closed. I called for Macy. I'd been doing that since we'd started searching, and there'd been no answer. There wasn't now, either, but Ricky stood in the middle of the hall, listening and looking. His gaze traveled one way and then the other. Then, without a word, he started for the door at the end.

He eased the door open, switchblade in hand, me at his shoulder. After a quick look inside, he walked through.

It was a room with a half-dozen cribs. I stood in the doorway thinking, *There are babies in mental hospitals?* Then I realized the cribs weren't for children.

Like regular cribs, they were made of wood, with an elevated bed and spindles. Except these ones were adult sized, with lids that could be fastened using thick leather straps. Cribs to restrain patients. To hold them there, lying on their backs, unable to move —

A bump sounded, and I jumped, remembering the woman in the rocker. But Ricky heard this one and moved toward the noise, his switchblade in one hand, cell phone flashlight in the other. Another bump. Then the sound of muffled cries. I hurried forward to see a dark-haired woman in the last box.

I stopped short. I'd seen two hallucinations of dark-haired women already, but Ricky quickly unfastened the straps and pulled off the lid, and it was indeed a woman inside. She was a couple of years younger than me, blindfolded and gagged.

"Hold still," Ricky said. "I'm going to cut off —"

She went wild, thrashing and screaming behind her gag.

"Not the right thing to say?" he whispered to me.

I spoke louder, to be heard over her panicked struggles. "Macy? It's me. It's . . . Eden. You're okay. This guy is with me. He's going to take off your gag and blindfold. Just lie still."

She stopped moving and lay there, tense, sounding as if she was panting behind the gag. Ricky cut off her blindfold first, and when it fell away, he leaned over her.

"You okay?" he asked.

She stared up at him. Gaping, in fact. Yes, Ricky's face wasn't a bad first sight after a near-death experience. He didn't seem to notice, just cut off her gag. Then he went to work unfastening her hands and feet.

"I'm Rick," he said when he finished. "She prefers Olivia."

Macy took a moment to drag her gaze away from Ricky. When she saw me, she blinked.

"Olivia . . . ? Eden . . . ?" Her eyes rounded. "You're . . ."

She scrambled out of the crib, tipping it over in her haste. I dove after her and she gasped, like I was wielding a hatchet. Ricky grabbed me back as if *she* was wielding one.

"What the hell are you doing?" Ricky said to her.

"That's — She's — I saw her in the paper. She's —"

"Her name is Olivia," Ricky snarled in a tone I'd never heard him use. "And she just saved your fucking life, so you will show some respect."

"I-I need to leave."

"No, you need to answer some questions. If you don't, I'll lock you back in that damned box until you're feeling chatty."

One could argue this was not the kindest way to deal with a traumatized kidnap victim. But apparently Ricky wasn't in the mood to be charming.

My cell phone blipped with an unread message.

"Looks like I missed Gabriel's call," I said

as I took it out. "He pulled in five minutes ago. We'll go down and meet him."

"No," Macy said, shrinking into the corner as she stared at Ricky, her gaze far less admiring now. "I'm not going anywhere with you two. I know who she is."

"You know who my parents are," I said. "You know nothing about *me.*"

"Except that she saved your fucking life." Ricky glanced my way. "Tell Gabriel how to find us, and he can convince her to talk. I'd really rather not have to stuff her back in that box."

I called. Gabriel was trying to figure out which building to enter. I got him in the right one and on the path as I explained the situation. The basics, at least. I wasn't giving more with Macy right there.

I also made sure to tell him *I* hadn't sent that urgent message, either, which I suppose didn't need to be done right away, but I hated him thinking I'd dragged him out of bed for what hadn't turned out to be a dangerous situation. Apparently, though, our definitions of dangerous differed. In his books, being led through a condemned building by a crazy man still qualified.

One part of the story I left out? The part where I hadn't come here alone. As Gabriel got closer, Ricky motioned for me to mute the phone.

"Want me to take off?" he whispered. "Explain it later?"

I shook my head. "I'll go warn him."

As I relayed instructions to get Gabriel to the ladder, I walked to the room with the ladder and crouched at the hatch. A moment later, the top of his head appeared below.

He looked up.

"Found it," I said.

I grinned down at him. As calm as I'd tried to stay during this whole ordeal, there'd been a feeling that something was missing, something as essential as the gun nestled in my pocket. Seeing Gabriel, that knot untwisted.

"Are you all right?" he asked.

"Better now that you're here. Thanks."

His head tilted to the side, and he frowned, as if unsure he'd heard right.

"I tried to leave you out of this," I said. "That's why I hung up the first time. I didn't want to bother you when it wasn't a legal issue. I'm sorry that guy got my phone and texted you. But I'm glad you're here."

Another frown and searching look, as if he'd moved from suspecting he'd misheard to suspecting I'd been dosed.

I shook my head. "Just come up."

452

He gave the bottom rung a tug. "It's not going to hold me. Is there another route?"

"There must be, but it's a huge place. If you want to just stay down there, I can resolve this and —"

"No, I'll try." He gave the rung another test pull. "Please note, I'm not a gymnast."

"In other words, you'd appreciate it if I averted my gaze while you awkwardly try to haul yourself up?"

He rolled his eyes, but I did turn away. God forbid Gabriel should be seen doing something that might require actual effort. I suspected that was more of a concern than whether the rungs would hold his weight.

A few not-quite-stifled grunts as he got himself onto the ladder.

"How did *you* manage it?" he said. "That bottom rung was almost over my head."

"I, uh, had help. Ricky's here."

He stopped, standing on the ladder, his head still a few feet below the opening. "Ricky?"

"Gallagher."

He gave me a cool look. "I highly doubt we have any other mutual acquaintances who go by that moniker. The implied question was: what is Ricky doing here?"

"He was with me when I got the call."

"With you? Where?"

"Really?" I wanted to say, *It was two in the morning. Do I need to spell it out?* But Gabriel kept looking up at me with genuine confusion.

"I was at home. Asleep."

It still seemed to take a moment for him to make the mental leap. When he did, his eyes emptied, and that ice-cold stare blasted through me, and I felt like I'd just done something terrible. Something unforgivable.

I'd woken him in the middle of the night and dragged him out here, into a dangerous situation, expecting his help, and now he finds out I'm screwing around with another man? That was crazy on all counts — I hadn't woken him or dragged him or expected anything, and *we* weren't sleeping together or even moving in that direction. He was only annoyed that I hadn't told him about the relationship earlier. If I interpreted more, it was because I felt more.

That's why I hadn't told Gabriel I was seeing Ricky. Because of what it felt like, no matter how groundless that was. To feel guilty because a guy I wasn't dating found out I was involved with someone? That went beyond an overblown sense of fidelity and tripped straight into ludicrous.

After what felt like ten minutes of silence, he said, "I see." Another five seconds, then,

"I wasn't aware you were seeing one another."

"It's recent," I said. "We hadn't gotten to the stage of telling anyone. Ricky told Don last night."

"Which I suppose explains Don's message asking me to phone him in the morning. You are both my clients, Olivia. I already warned you that any relationship —"

"I'm not your client anymore."

"You are my employee. Which is worse."

"Can we discuss this later?" I said. "That girl's freaked out, and I really need to talk to her before she bolts."

He looked at me. Then he glanced down, as if considering retreat.

"Do you want to go?" I said. "I know this wasn't how you intended to spend your night, and I'm sorry you got dragged into it. Ricky and I can handle this."

His gaze moved up to mine. "Would you like me to leave?"

"No. As I said, I'm glad you're here. But I understand if you decide you don't need to be. I'm sure you have better things to do."

That cool stare. "It's four thirty in the morning, Olivia. What else would I have to do?"

"Sleep. Which is infinitely better than

crawling through an abandoned psych hospital."

I forced a smile. He didn't buy it, only watching me, assessing. Then he grunted, "Move," and waved me back so he could finish his climb. By the time he hauled himself through the hatch, I was staring up at the messages on the ceiling, above the restraint chair.

Before I could look away, Gabriel said, "What do you see?"

I told him and then added, "You don't see anything, right?"

"I don't."

"Neither did Ricky. There were other things, too. Visions, hallucinations . . ."

"You'll tell me later?"

"I will."

"And you didn't tell Ricky about any of it?"

"No. I wouldn't have brought him into this at all, but he overheard the phone call, so I couldn't exactly slip out and handle it myself."

"Which I would hope you'd never consider doing alone. Whether it's a legal matter or not, you should call me, Olivia. I would think you'd know that by now."

"I wanted to. I just . . . I didn't want to overstep. Anyway, I had to tell him about finding Ciara in the car. He knows there's more, but he's not pushing for answers." I looked up at Gabriel. "I've never had the feeling I can't trust him."

Gabriel hesitated, then said almost reluctantly, "You can."

"I won't tell him anything I don't have to. For his own sake. The rest is between you and me."

The ice thawed in his eyes. He nodded and waved me to the door. When I turned, he put his fingers lightly to my back, shepherding me along, as if *he* was the one who knew where we were going.

CHAPTER FORTY-EIGHT

On the walk to the room, I told Gabriel that Macy knew who I was and seemed to think I was going to axe-murder her.

He snorted. "Twit."

"That's Ricky's opinion, too, though he'd make it 'ungrateful twit.' He snapped at her, and now she's scared of us both. We should have handled it better, considering what she's been through."

"She should have considered what you've both been through, coming after her here. Ricky is correct. She's an ungrateful twit. I'm surprised you didn't stuff her back in the box."

"Ricky threatened to."

"Hmm, well, sadly, that would be considered forcible confinement, so I'd have to advise against it."

I felt a little sorry for Macy. She really deserved nicer rescuers. More sympathetic ones, at least.

"Well, it's not boding well for polite conversation," I said. "Which I need to have with her. That Tristan guy suggested she's not a random victim. She has answers even if she doesn't realize it. Maybe you can play good cop."

He turned his cool gaze on me.

"Or not." I rapped on the door and called, "It's us," then walked in.

Ricky was standing there, waiting. Macy was huddled against the wall. When she saw Gabriel, she pressed against it, her eyes rounding.

"Wh-who's that?" she asked.

"Our lawyer," I said.

She tried to glare at me, though it was about as intimidating as a kitten's snarl. "That's not funny."

"Because it isn't a joke." Gabriel turned to Ricky. "Have you done anything to her?"

"Besides rescuing her ass?"

"It's not an unreasonable question, considering you've obviously been involved in an altercation."

Ricky touched his split lip. "Right. Separate incident."

"It's been a long and interesting night," I said.

Gabriel turned to Macy. "You will agree, then, that they have done nothing to you?

459

And that your unfounded fear is simply a by-product of your captivity?"

She stared at him as if he were speaking Greek. "I-I want to go home."

"We will escort you out."

Ricky started to protest, but Gabriel said, "We don't want to detain the young woman against her will," in a tone that warned that, too, would be forcible confinement.

Ricky nodded.

Gabriel waved her to the door. "Macy, is it?"

"Y-yes." She skirted wide around him.

"And that would be Ms. . . . ?"

She didn't answer.

Once we'd descended the ladder, he continued, "I have not yet telephoned the police. I'm presuming you'd like that done now? I would offer to drive you to the station, but I suspect you would prefer a police escort."

"I can't call the police. My — my brother. There's a warrant out for him, and if I report this to the police and they come to our house . . ."

"Yes, I can see how that could be problematic."

Gabriel could have pointed out that the police didn't need to come to her house. But she wasn't paying him for legal advice.

And calling in the police *would* be problematic. For us.

"You should report it," he said. "However, you have no legal obligation to do so. Be aware, though, that the chances of being believed if you report it later decrease significantly."

She nodded. As soon as Gabriel walked outside, Macy bolted past him. I lunged forward. Gabriel's arm shot out, practically smacking me in the face as he stopped me and stepped into Ricky's path.

"She's getting —" Ricky began.

"I know. And as your lawyer, I would suggest you do not pursue her. Even if you manage to catch her, you'd need to hold her, which is a felony."

"But we haven't questioned her," I said. "We don't know where to find her. All we have is a first name and —"

Gabriel handed me a plastic rectangle. It was Macy's driver's license.

"How the hell — ?" I began. "That's why you so kindly helped her down the ladder. I should have known you were up to something."

"Yes, you should have," he said, taking no offense.

"You knew she was going to run."

"We made her nervous. I have no idea why."

I snorted and shone my flashlight on Macy's card and squinted at the photo. "Does she look familiar to you?"

"Yes, she bears a striking resemblance to the young woman who just fled."

Ricky laughed.

I glared at both of them. "I couldn't see her very well inside. Besides the lack of light, she was filthy and disheveled. This photo, though . . ." I looked again and shook my head. "Never mind. I'll figure it out later. So now what?"

"Now we get *ourselves* looking *less* filthy and disheveled," Ricky said. "Whose place is closer? Gabriel?"

Gabriel hesitated. Last month, during another long night, he'd been about to stop at his apartment. Then I suggested I wouldn't mind using his bathroom and suddenly his place was no longer on our route.

I was sure he *had* an apartment. A very nice one, given that he'd had no qualms about taking me as far as the building. I now suspected it was a matter of privacy. That was his home. Private and off-limits.

"Your place is closer," I said to Ricky.

Gabriel acknowledged my save with a nod of thanks.

"I'm parked over there," Gabriel said. "I presume you're elsewhere?"

"At the golf course," I said. "Can you give us a lift?"

He waved us to his car.

"Well, I guess we didn't hide it as well as we thought," I said, standing beside my car, looking down at the slashed tire.

"Got a spare?" Ricky asked. "I can change it."

"So can I. Unfortunately, I noticed last week that the tire isn't in the trunk. It must be at my parents' house."

"No problem. A couple of our garages have twenty-four-hour service. I'll get one to fix it." He looked at Gabriel, still in his Jag, window down. "That okay? You can give us a lift?"

"Of course."

We decided to wash up at Ricky's and then discuss the situation over breakfast. "I've got class at nine," Ricky said as we headed down the hall to his apartment. "You two?"

"I don't have any appointments," Gabriel said. "But yes, I should be at the office by nine. Olivia can join me."

"Thanks," I said.

He nodded, missing the sarcasm.

"Liv?" Ricky said as he unlocked his door. "You take the shower first. I'll —" He stopped. "Hey."

I glanced past Ricky to see Don rising from the couch, blinking, as if he'd been dozing there.

"I came over after you took off," Don said. "I tried calling, but you weren't . . ." He noticed me. "Oh, Olivia. I didn't see you — Gabriel?" He rubbed his eyes and double-checked, then frowned. "You're covered in . . ."

"Dust. And cobwebs. It's a long story." I turned to Ricky. "Gabriel and I will go for breakfast at the diner up the road. We'll hold a seat if you can make it, but it's fine if you can't. Just give me two minutes in the bathroom first."

"I'll also need —" Gabriel began.

"You look fine. We cleared the cobwebs for you." I nodded at Don and managed what I hoped was a friendly smile. "Sorry about all this. We'll be gone in two minutes."

"You don't have to —" Ricky began.

I caught his gaze and he nodded, mouthing, "Thanks," then saying, "I'll catch up. Go ahead and order."

CHAPTER FORTY-NINE

Gabriel and I didn't get five steps out of the apartment before he started.

"They argued last night, I presume? After Ricky told him about you?"

I nodded.

"And Ricky took off? Didn't answer Don's calls?"

"I guess so. He was pretty shaken up." I turned onto the sidewalk. "He'll work it out."

"I've known the Gallaghers for almost four years, Olivia. I have never seen them argue. They simply don't."

"I'm not trying to cause problems."

"But you obviously are."

I stiffened. "Yes, *obviously,* because I chased poor innocent Ricky down and seduced him."

"I am well aware of who did the chasing. For whatever reason, he wanted you, and —"

"For whatever reason?"

A pause. I didn't look up, but I swore I could sense him searching for a path out of the quagmire.

"I meant that he found you attractive, for whatever —"

He managed to stop himself. I still scowled at him.

"The point I'm making is that he pursued you," Gabriel said. "I realize that. But he's made a mistake. You both have. It may seem unfair to put the onus on you for recognizing that, but he's young —"

"He's twenty-two, not twelve. There's no mistake here. We're involved in a perfectly functional relationship —"

"Functional?" His brows arched. "That sounds romantic."

"I'm putting it in language you'll understand, because if I did make it sound romantic, you'd mock me. I know your opinion on the subject."

"If you think you're in love, you're suffering the emotional fallout from your breakup with James. I can understand that you'd be looking for that sort of thing again —"

"Umm, no. I'm not looking for that."

He looked relieved. "Good. Then you will have no problem breaking it off —"

"I mean I'm not wildly and blindly infatuated, not that I don't care about him. I know you're concerned, but Ricky doesn't discuss club business with me and I wouldn't discuss your legal business with him. You can keep me off any Saints cases, if that helps."

Gabriel grabbed the diner door and held it for me. "That's not the problem."

"Then what is?"

He didn't reply until we were seated at the table. He opened his mouth, and the server appeared, coffeepot in hand.

"She'll have some," Gabriel said.

I smiled and exchanged pleasantries with the server as she filled our mugs while Gabriel looked increasingly impatient at the entire ten seconds the process took.

"It's the commingling of professional and personal relationships that makes both Don and me uncomfortable," Gabriel said after she left. "The Saints are my primary clients, Olivia, and many of my other clients come through them directly or through my association with them. I cannot afford to muddy these waters."

"Then fire me."

He pulled back. "Is that what you want?"

"No. If I did, I'd quit. The issue is not that you or Don see an actual problem. You see the *potential* for problems. But this isn't about either of you. If you're going to threaten me with dismissal, get it over with."

"I'm not the one who mentioned it."

"Because I beat you to it."

The server approached with her order pad. Gabriel waved her off. I gave her a five-minute sign.

He shifted forward. "You say it's not serious, but you're willing to risk a good job for him. A lucrative job that you enjoy. You'll give that up for a man you have no future with. You realize that, don't you? Ricky isn't James. You won't get that life from him."

"I don't want another James. That's the point."

"I don't understand."

"You're comfortable with who you are, right?"

A slight frown, confused. "Of course."

"I've spent my life feeling like a cuckoo raised by robins. I grew up pretending to fit into my mother's world, and the whole time I felt suffocated. Then I went to Cainsville, and everything changed. I met people who know who I am and don't give a shit. Who don't expect me to be anything other than what I am. For me, that's huge. Being with Ricky is part of that. I have my own life. I have my own secrets. He doesn't care. He takes what I can give, and he's happy with it, and I'm happy with him. He's exactly what I need right now."

Gabriel sat there, saying nothing. I could tell myself he was processing, but in his eyes I saw anxiety and discomfort, as if he'd spent the entire monologue wishing I'd just shut up.

Damn it. I'd only wanted him to understand. It was so hard to figure out where the boundaries lay. Mostly because he set them, quietly and secretly, in places I could never quite discern. Interfering with my personal relationships? That was fine. Listening to me talk about how I felt? Hell, no. Keep that shit to yourself. Please.

"I'm sorry," I said after thirty more seconds of silence. "I only wanted to explain —"

"No, that's fine." His gaze traveled to the door as if measuring the distance to the escape hatch. He shifted. Adjusted his cuffs. Glanced around again. "All right. I think you're making a mistake, and I fear it will be a problem, but if it's what you want . . ." He seemed to choke on the words before saying, "I won't interfere."

"If it does become a problem — a real one — tell me," I said. "I want to keep my job, and I don't want to make trouble for you."

He nodded and waved the server over. As he was ordering, I got a text from Ricky, saying he was on his way and Don was coming with him. They'd worked it out. As I put down my phone, I was thinking of what had happened tonight and my cuckoo analogy, the two rubbing together until . . . *click.*

"Can I see Macy's license?" I said as I typed in a search on my phone's browser.

Gabriel passed it over. I took another look at it, then zoomed in on a photo on my screen. I passed both over.

"See a resemblance?"

"Yes, but if you're saying they're the same person —"

"Obviously not. There's at least twenty years between them. But could this woman — Mrs. Conway — be Macy's mother?" I didn't wait for an answer, instead flipping to Ciara's photo. "More than it could be *her* mother?"

"You think they were . . ." He hesitated. "Switched?"

"The guy who took Macy told me she was connected to Ciara. That she was 'more wronged' than Ciara by that connection. That what happened to them is connected to Cainsville. And to me. Somehow, it's all connected to me."

"We'll look into it. What else —"

He looked up as a hand squeezed my shoulder, and Ricky said, "Hey."

I pushed back the chair beside mine. He took it. I smiled at Don. I won't say he exactly beamed back, but his smile seemed genuine enough.

As we ate, I could feel Don's gaze on me, especially whenever Ricky and I were talking or teasing. He was taking the measure of our relationship, but even more, he was taking my measure. Would I treat Ricky well? Was I good enough for him? If the answer to either was no . . . well, then I suspected I'd see the real leader of the Saints.

CHAPTER FIFTY

When we walked into the office, Lydia stared at us. It took me a moment to realize why. I'd become so accustomed to having Gabriel around at any hour that I'd forgotten how it looked if his car stayed outside my apartment all night or we walked into the office, already deep in conversation, at seven thirty in the morning.

"Hey," I said with a wry smile. "I'm causing trouble early today. I got a flat tire, and Gabriel had to give me a ride —"

Gabriel cut me off with an impatient wave toward his office and a look that asked *Why the hell are you telling her that?*

I rolled my eyes for Lydia and followed him into his office. He closed the door behind me.

"We need to talk about Cainsville," he said. "I was thinking that the other day, when you discovered the history of that house. First, Chandler said there was a connection. And now this Tristan fellow says the same. Ciara Conway and your mother are both linked to the town. I don't see a connection between Ms. Conway and your parents' alleged crimes, but . . ."

"It does seem overly coincidental. All roads lead to Cainsville, yet I somehow refuse to follow them." I pulled over the extra chair. "I think that's what those messages meant tonight. *We are imprisoned by the truth we dare not see. We are imprisoned by the questions we dare not ask.* For weeks now, I've been seeing visions of corpses without eyes, and I keep presuming it's some ritualistic thing connected to my parents' crimes. But I think it's another type of omen. A message I refuse to see. Now I'm hallucinating a woman without a tongue. Which means even when I admit that I do see, I won't go to Cainsville and ask questions about the connections."

Gabriel leaned back in his chair, fingers drumming the desk, and there was a moment where I thought I'd lost him, as if he'd gotten bored with my speech and was mentally compiling the day's to-do list. But after a few seconds he said, "You aren't the only one who's seen those roads and refuses to follow them. As for why . . ."

More drumming before he pulled his

hand away, forcibly stopping himself and looking up, expression resolute, as if having decided to share something difficult. I braced myself.

"There are gargoyles in Cainsville," he said.

"Um, yes. I've noticed."

"There's a game children play . . ."

"The May Day contest. I've heard of it."

From the wary look he gave me, you would have thought I'd just announced having uncovered a dark secret through very underhanded means.

"Some of them are . . . hidden," he said finally.

"I know. There are those you can't see at first, but I found one — on the bank — that I can't see at all during the day. It's not there. Veronica called it a night gargoyle."

"There are others. Ones you can only see from certain angles. Or if the moon or the sun strikes it. There's one that appears in rain. One in fog. One only under the winter solstice moon. There's no rational explanation for that. There just isn't."

"I know. But I tell myself there is — there must be. I don't question. I . . . I don't want to."

"Exactly. That is the contradiction that I cannot wrap my head around. I have no hesitation seeking answers. I make my living doing that. Except when it comes to Cainsville." He straightened. "I was a boy when I learned about the hidden gargoyles. I went to Rose for answers. She told me it was magic. I was angry. It felt as if she was treating me like a child. So I wanted to ask others. But I couldn't. The more I thought about it, the more I simply wanted to accept it."

"Maybe if we talk to Rose again? You're not a kid anymore. If we ask her — *seriously* ask her —"

"When it comes to Cainsville, she refuses to question or to answer. She has a good life there. The town is safe and welcoming, and it's as if . . ." He seemed unable to find the right words. "I remember when I was eleven or so, I was talking to . . . I can't remember exactly. I always want to say it was Patrick, but it couldn't have been — he's not old enough. Perhaps a brother or relative? I'd spoken to this man before. He even gave me a hint on the last hidden gargoyle. We were talking that day, and Seanna caught us. She didn't usually come to Cainsville — Rose would pick me up in the city. This time, Seanna brought me in a friend's car and stayed to visit. I'm guessing she needed money. She must have gotten it from Rose and wanted to leave quickly to buy her fix. When she found me with this man, she was furious. Dragged me away. She asked me if I'd ever spoken to him before. I lied and said no. She said I was never to talk to him. I asked why not, and she hit me."

I must have winced, because he said, "That was unusual. She'd cuff me when I was younger, but by that age I was big enough that she'd likely started to worry I might hit back. So when she struck me, I knew it was serious. She made me swear never to speak to him again. I asked Rose, later, why Seanna was so upset. She said she didn't know, but she told me I *could* speak to him. In fact, if he talked to me, I should never refuse to answer. I was to be polite and respectful to all the adults in Cainsville. And not ask questions. Above all, don't ask questions."

"So you still don't," I said. "I don't, either. That means something. It has to." I paused. "Chandler was the first to mention a Cainsville connection. Do you remember what Patrick said about mind control? That it was beyond the realm of science but prevalent in folklore and magic."

"If you're saying that we're magically blocked from asking questions . . ."

He trailed off. I knew he wanted to finish the sentence with *that's preposterous.* So did I. But neither of us did.

"Let's call it preternatural," I said. "If you say magic, I think of Disney witches and fairies and pixie dust, and my brain won't go there. But I see omens, and that's definitely not natural. Same with giant hounds and the Wild Hunt and hallucinations and visions and second sight."

Gabriel shook his head. "But to say that I'm being prevented from asking questions by powers beyond my control feels like an excuse."

"Now you know why I kept denying I could see omens. It feels like hearing voices and thinking, 'I don't have schizophrenia; I can speak to the dead.' There's something preternatural happening, and we know it. So let's make a list of everything we want answers on, especially connected to Cainsville. We'll put it in writing so we can't shove it under the rug."

As I pulled over a legal pad and pen, he pushed back from the desk and shook his head. "I don't think that's necessary. We certainly will look into this, but there's hardly any need for a list. We have things to do —"

"So urgent that we don't have ten minutes

for this?"

He checked his watch.

"You don't have any appointments, Gabriel. You already said that."

"Yes, but I have work —"

"You came in early. It's barely eight." I looked at him. "Fine. Go on. I'll make this list and —"

"You don't need to —" He paused. "This is it. This is exactly it. There's no good reason for me to stop you from making that list. So why am I arguing?"

"It's magic."

He glowered at me then rolled his shoulders, scowling as he did, as if he could frighten the compulsion away. That's what it felt like: something compelling us not to ask questions.

"Write it," he said.

Ten minutes later, Gabriel got a call. A client in trouble. Urgent "I'm sitting in the precinct awaiting interrogation" trouble. He left. I stayed behind to investigate any link between Macy and Ciara, and spent two hours delving into Macy's life and Ciara's life, trying to fit the two together in a puzzle that wouldn't quite work.

Macy *could* have been the Conways' daughter, in both her coloring and her features. As for Macy's family, that was harder to trace. No family pics on Facebook for them. I did get an older sister, though. When I pulled up the photo, it could have been Ciara in ten years . . . except she was only four years older. Prematurely hard and old. I'd seen that same look in the photos of Seanna Walsh. Macy's sister was an addict.

With help from Lydia, I tracked down the brother, too — or his record, at least. At twenty-seven, he already had almost a dozen arrests for drugs, assault, and petty larceny. Macy, though? She was clean. A nursing school student with no arrest record.

I thought of Ciara. Of her home in the suburbs. Of her parents, so confused over the path their daughter had stumbled on, how far she'd fallen, how little they'd been able to help. There's a genetic component to addiction. I knew that from my volunteer work at a women's shelter. Gabriel obviously knew it, too — I had only to glance across his office and see the expensive bottles on his fireplace mantel, unopened gifts coated in a fine layer of dust.

I looked at the photos and the evidence of addiction. Circumstantial evidence. It wasn't enough.

The girls had been born nine days apart. But at different hospitals. So how could they have been swapped? At the doctor's office? You take your newborn in and put her down and — whoops — pick up the wrong one? Wouldn't you know what your child was wearing? By nine days, wouldn't you know what she *looked* like?

Crimbils.

The word sprang to mind, unbidden, and scratched there, at the front of consciousness. When I started to ignore it, my gaze moved to that list on Gabriel's desk.

Tristan said I had some kind of hereditary memory. That was what kept prompting me with words and visions. With answers. Yet I pushed them aside.

I looked up *crimbils.* I wasn't sure of the spelling, but I figured it was Welsh, so I added that to the search and ran through a few possibilities before I hit the one I knew was right.

Crimbils. The Welsh word for changelings. As in the usual folklore, fairies would put their own child in the cradle of a human baby, to be foster raised. Through magic, the child would initially resemble the missing infant, but over time would revert to his or her own appearance, so it would seem that the child's looks were just changing naturally.

Clearly, either Ciara or Macy was a fairy

child who'd been secreted into a human family. Which would make perfect sense . . . if you lived in the Middle Ages and believed in fairies.

I kept digging, but it soon became apparent there was only one way to prove my switched-at-birth theory: get Macy's DNA.

CHAPTER FIFTY-ONE

As promised, the Gallaghers' auto shops had my car fixed and waiting for me by noon. An hour later, I was headed back to Cainsville for my diner shift.

Patrick arrived around four, and the moment he walked through the door I was at his table, filling the mug. When Larry made banana nut muffins for the evening crowd, I brought Patrick one straight from the oven. Yes, I was not subtle about courting his favor. But Patrick doesn't need subtle. He practically purred under the attention.

The elders noticed, and they were not nearly so pleased. Some game was in play, and they were stuck on the sidelines.

At eight, as Patrick was preparing to leave, I sidled over to his table and pulled out a chair, leaning in to speak to him privately, while making sure everyone else saw me speaking to him privately.

"I need to talk to you," I whispered.

A satisfied smile. "I thought you might. Why don't I come back and walk you home after your shift?"

"Thank you."

As I moved away, I felt Ida's gaze on me. She sat with Walter and two of the other elders I knew less well — Minnie and Roger. When I headed for the kitchen, she waved me over, ostensibly for pie.

"How are things, Olivia?" she asked. "We really haven't had time to chat lately. You've been so busy."

"I have."

"Anything interesting?" Walter asked.

"Not really." I refilled their teapot with fresh hot water. "I met a girl with a connection to Ciara Conway that I'm trying to puzzle out. Someone mentioned she might have lived in Cainsville. Macy Shaw?"

"Doesn't sound familiar," Walter mused. "We may have had a family by that surname, but it's been years."

"Many years," said Ida.

The others nodded.

"I'll keep digging, then," I said.

"You'll let us know if you find anything?" Ida asked.

"Of course."

At eleven, Patrick was waiting outside the diner.

"I presume this chat will take longer than the five-minute walk to your apartment?" he said as I joined him.

"It will."

We headed for the park.

"The elders aren't happy with me," I said. "Seems I was paying a little too much attention to you."

He smiled. "Their old egos are so fragile."

"And you do love to see them dented."

The smile grew. "Perhaps."

"Then I've done you a favor, haven't I?"

"You have." He slanted a look my way as he held the gate open. "For credit, I presume. Which you intend to call on now."

"I do."

Normally, people don't like to think you're only being nice to them because you want something. Patrick didn't seem to mind at all. Quite the contrary — from the look on his face, he was pleased with me. I understood the game and played it fairly.

"How old are you?" I asked as we sat on the bench.

His dark eyes gleamed. "How old do you want me to be?"

"Gabriel remembers you when he came back before college. You were older than

484

him then."

"Then presumably I still am."

"Presumably. He told me a story today," I said. "When he was young, a man in Cainsville used to speak to him. He'd give him hints about the hidden gargoyles. One day, Gabriel's mother — Seanna — caught him talking to this man, and she was furious. Made Gabriel swear never to speak to him again."

"How rude."

"It is, isn't it? The man didn't try to lure him off with candy or any such thing. They just talked. Gabriel never understood why Seanna was so angry."

"I don't blame him."

"Here's the thing. When Gabriel remembers the man, he seems to think it was you, though he knows it couldn't be. Clearly you're not old enough."

"Clearly."

"But in his memory, he associates the man with you. Do you know why?"

Patrick shrugged. "Memory is a mystery we cannot hope to solve. I grew up in Cainsville. I have family here."

"Then would you know why his mother told him not to speak to this man?"

"She must have had some reason for disliking him."

"Because Seanna herself was from Cainsville originally."

"So I've heard."

"And you don't know what she'd have against this man, who was obviously not you."

Patrick looked at me, and I waited for him to say he had no idea. Instead, he smiled. "Perhaps he gave her a gift she did not want. It happens, between men and women."

I went quiet for a moment. Then I said, "If I ask you what's going on in Cainsville, will you tell me?"

Again, there was an easy answer: play dumb. *What's going on? Do you mean local news? Events?* But that was one game Patrick didn't play. He said only, "No."

"Can I earn the answers?"

"By currying favor with me? No. I like my life here, Olivia. It's very comfortable. You need to find your own answers. Or get close enough to them that I can help."

"*Will* you help?"

"If it's in my best interests. Currying favor goes both ways."

"Let's change the subject, then. Mind control."

"Ah."

"We discussed it right before Gabriel and

I solved the mystery of my parents' last crimes. You've never asked if that solution had anything to do with mind control. Because you know it did, don't you?"

"Or I'm simply not interested in knowing. As a possibility, mind control is intriguing. In reality? I have no interest in making people do anything they don't want to. Far too much effort." He paused. "Unless it could compel them to buy my books . . ."

"Compel. That's an interesting word."

"Is it?"

"You said I need to find my own answers. But what if I was somehow being compelled *not* to ask the questions? Mentally influenced to avoid even posing those questions?"

"Brainwashed, you mean? Compelled to accept the unbelievable based on faith alone?" He peered at me. "You aren't going to church, are you?"

I gave him a look.

"Religion exists to instill false security and blind faith," he continued. "Yet it is imperfect. To accept the message, you must hear the message. You must 'drink the Kool-Aid,' so to speak. But how would that work on a practical level? Disseminate something in the air or water to keep people from asking questions about Cainsville? That's science.

Otherwise, if there is a message — or charm or compulsion — it would need to be delivered in person, repeatedly, to be maintained. Completely impractical."

"So you're saying it couldn't happen."

That maddening curve of his lips. I was clearly frustrated, and that amused him. What did he see when he looked at me? A child. I was sure of that. Like the Huntsman. Like Tristan.

They were one thing and we were another, and to them we were children. Adorable and entertaining toddlers, fumbling in the dark. Like Macy, when she'd gotten angry at the hospital. I bared my teeth and I hissed and I flashed my claws, and Patrick saw not a wildcat but a kitten. Adorable in her infinitely tiny fury.

"For the purposes of transmission, consider it a disease," he said. "A condition. How does it pass from source to recipient?"

I shifted, not wanting to play his game but not wanting to walk away, either. "Methods of transmission . . . Air. Water. Direct contact. Consuming infected material."

"None of the above."

"Heredity?" I said. "Passed through the genes?"

"That would be a convenient method for an isolated little town."

I opened my mouth to argue that I wasn't from Cainsville. Neither was Gabriel. Except both of our families came from here.

He pushed to his feet. "And there ends tonight's conversation. When you have more, ask me more. Until then, have a pleasant night, Olivia."

He started to walk away.

"You lied about the hound," I called after him.

He turned, brows arching, and a memory twitched, telling me —

I inhaled. I knew what it was telling me. And I pushed it aside. For now.

"The hound. I asked you about big black hounds, and you said the only folklore you knew of was the Black Shuck. You forgot Cŵn Annwn."

He tensed. I saw a flicker and . . . nothing. I *saw* nothing. But I *sensed* a reaction.

"The hounds of the Otherworld," I said. "That's what it means, literally. But not necessarily what it *is*, right? Cŵn Annwn is the Wild Hunt. The hounds are only part of it. Like the horses. The real Cŵn Annwn are the hunters."

Patrick's gaze bored into me, and again that look tweaked my memory. Again I knew why and ignored it for now.

"I met one," I said. "A Huntsman, I think

they're called. He gave me this." I opened my hand to show the boar's tusk. "I don't suppose there's any chance you can decipher what it says?"

After a long moment of silence, Patrick said, "I suppose this has to do with the boy."

"Boy?"

"Young Mr. Gallagher."

I fought to hide my confusion. "No. I was at dinner with James. The Huntsman lured me into the back hall."

"James? Ah, yes, the former fiancé." The grim intensity fell from Patrick's face, the old amusement bouncing back. "So many men hovering about you, Liv. It's hard to keep them straight. Not that there's anything wrong with that. Variety is the spice of life, they say. As for that" — he pointed to the tusk — "it's a pretty bauble. Keep it with you, for now. Just don't get too attached to it. Or to Mr. Gallagher."

He turned to go.

"What does Ricky have to do with this?" I said, walking after him.

Again, he turned. "Nothing. Everything. It depends on the perspective. From his? Nothing, I'm sure. He knows nothing."

"Like me," I said, remembering Tristan's words. "Like Gabriel. We're pawns."

"Only if you allow yourselves to be," he

said, and walked into the night.

I had the next day off at the diner, which meant a full day working for Gabriel. I was expected in by nine. Before I left, I got an e-mail from Howard asking me to call.

He had two items of business.

"Your mother is coming home," he said.

"Great. Have her call me when she gets settled."

"She'd like you to pick her up at the airport."

"No."

Silence. Apparently not the response he'd expected. "Your mother is looking forward to seeing you, Olivia, and you should make an effort to mend fences —"

"I didn't break any fences. This isn't me being petty, Howard. She doesn't want me to meet her. She wants a chauffeur."

"She could well afford to hire a car. She'd like you to pick her up. And she'd like you to stay at the house."

"Until she finds a live-in housekeeper and chauffeur? Again, no."

"If she wished that, I could hire them before she returns. What she wants is a reunion with her daughter. She'd like you to come home."

Come home. There'd been a time when I

longed for that. Now I couldn't imagine it.

"If she wants me to meet her at the airport, she needs to call me. Herself. What else is there?"

"I have a package for you. From James. He doesn't know your address, so he's asked me to send it along."

I stifled a sigh. Probably clothing I'd left at his place. At least he was accepting that it was over.

"Send it to Gabriel Walsh's office," I said.

A pause. "You're still involved with Mr. Walsh?"

"I was never *involved* with Mr. Walsh. He's representing Pamela. I'll be at his office today. You can have someone run the parcel over."

"Your mother will not be pleased when she hears of this continuing association."

"I'll be at his office for most of the day, and I'd appreciate receiving that package. Thank you for your time, Howard."

CHAPTER FIFTY-TWO

I arrived at the office by eight thirty, with my drive-thru beverage tray. The boss was leaning over Lydia's desk, palms on the top, his shadow engulfing her as she typed. For most people, this would be as discomforting as having a panther poised on the rock overhead as you cooked lunch. Lydia just typed away, talking as she did.

When I came in, Gabriel looked up and waved me to his office. I left Lydia's tea behind and followed.

As Gabriel took his coffee, I studied his posture and expression, both relaxed. I'm sure he'd been up late working, but there was no sign of it, no hint of that haggardness from a week ago. I was glad to see it. With Gabriel, a good mood was like finding a rare sunny patch by the window.

"I have a few things to do this morning," he said. "But you can use my office. We'll pay Macy a visit after lunch. First, though, how did it go with Patrick?"

"My plan to get him talking worked. As for how useful it was . . . that's debatable. He won't answer direct questions, so —"

A tap at the door. Lydia poked her head in. "Sorry to interrupt. I have a package from Olivia's family lawyer. It's apparently important."

"Not really," I said. "It's from James. Something I left at his place, I'm guessing."

She lifted the parcel. "It doesn't seem like clothing."

It was a flat, legal-sized envelope about an inch thick.

"Legal documents?" I said. "What's he doing? Suing me for breach of contract because I ended the engagement?"

"That law was abolished in the thirties," Gabriel said.

"I was kidding." I took the envelope and thanked Lydia, and she retreated. Gabriel watched as I stuffed the envelope in my bag.

"You aren't going to open that?" he said.

"It's been a good day so far. I'd rather not ruin it before nine."

He settled back into his chair but kept glancing toward my bag.

I sighed. "It's going to bug you until I open it, isn't it?"

"It *does* look like a legal document. Do

494

you share any property or goods in common?"

"Nope. I even gave the ring back."

"Have you borrowed anything from him? Money perhaps?"

"If I didn't take a handout from my mother, I sure as hell wouldn't take it from my ex."

His gaze slid to my bag again, as if magnetized. I sighed again, reached down, and opened it. Only as I was pulling out the papers did he say, "If you'd rather not . . ." because he knew it was too late. I tugged out two file folders and opened the thinner one.

"What the hell?" I muttered.

Gabriel moved behind me to read over my shoulder.

"I don't know how he got this," I said. "But I don't think he should have it."

Gabriel bent and flipped through. "No, it's a matter of public record. Charges laid against members of the Satan's Saints since Don Gallagher took over in the late nineties."

"And let me guess where *you* took over as counsel of record . . ." I ran my finger down the pages. The first two were a mix of sentences, acquittals, and a dozen plea bargains. Then the mix changed to charges dropped, acquittals, and two plea bargains. "Right about there," I said, pointing.

He smiled, pleased. "Yes, that would be it. I regret the plea bargains, but sometimes acquittal is too much to hope for." The smile faded as he lifted the pages. "As for why Morgan is giving you this . . ." He flipped to the first page. "Ah."

"James thought he'd provide a little background information on Ricky. Except it's not on Ricky. It's on the Saints."

"Because there's nothing he could dig up on Ricky other than his association with the club. He's never been charged with an offense. He's had a couple of traffic violations, but I was able to successfully argue that they were based purely on the fact that he was driving a Harley and wearing a club patch. Ricky knows the value of a clean record."

"So what's in this other . . ." I flipped open the thicker file and saw the cover sheet. "Oh."

Gabriel didn't even seem to bend down to read it. "Yes, that would be mine. It appears Morgan had a little more luck there."

I closed the folder and handed it up to him. "Shred it. And if you want to retaliate with the McNeil business you mentioned, go ahead."

That same pleased smile he'd given when

I complimented his defense record.

"Did you think I'd read it?" I said.

"Perhaps, but I didn't expect you to suggest retaliation." He pulled his chair over and sat with the folder on his lap. "I want to ignore him. He's making that increasingly difficult, though."

"Sorry."

Gabriel opened the file. "As for this . . ." He skimmed the top sheet. "True." He set it on the desk and checked the next. "Not true." He started a second pile and checked the third. "Not entirely true — there is a basis in fact, but the primary accusation is wrong."

He began another pile, in between the two. He continued through the stack. When he finished, the three piles were about equal. He leaned back in his chair.

"There. Go ahead. Take a look."

I shook my head. "Will Evans tried the same thing."

"And as long as you associate with me, there will be someone who thinks it's his duty to tell you exactly how horrible I am. Whoever Morgan hired to investigate me was certainly thorough. Every charge I've ever heard is here. I will rest easier if we get this over with. Clear away the rumors. Render the ammunition useless."

I looked at him, pulled over the first pile, and began reading.

What did I find in those piles? Nothing worse than I'd heard. Nothing worse than I suspected. I knew Gabriel had a juvenile record for pickpocketing. I also suspected he'd continued picking pockets, along with other methods of theft, through his teen years, to support himself. He just got better at hiding it.

There were accusations of assault. Some true; most not. Again, what I'd expect. I'd seen Gabriel use his fists, but he was more comfortable intimidating with his size, as he'd done with James. There was an accusation of murder. He scoffed at that.

"Killing a business rival?" he said. "It suggests I *need* to eliminate an opponent to defeat him."

"Terribly insulting," I said.

"It is." He paused. "Also, untrue."

A large chunk of the file concerned his activities during college. How he paid for his degree. The rumors were that he'd dealt drugs or run an illegal gambling ring.

"I'm going with gambling," I said. I checked the piles. "Ooh, I win. Wait. Book-making and usury, too? So you ran the gambling ring, took bets, and lent money?"

"You know I hate hiring help."

I laughed. The drug dealing accusations were in the "lies and damn lies" pile. As I expected.

The biggest part of the file dealt with Gabriel's business activities. Accusations of blackmail, extortion, bribery, intimidation . . . The list went on. The only one that he denied was judicial bribery. As for the rest . . .

"If I did those things as often as they claim, I'd never have time to actually practice law."

"That's why you hired me."

A faint smile. "Perhaps." He waved at the guilty-as-charged pile. "I've done them all. Just not nearly in the quantity suggested."

That left traffic violations — guilty — and a paternity suit. The latter was in the "damn lies" pile.

"It was a setup," he said. "I was defending one of two men charged with a series of bank robberies. They'd turned on each other. The opposing lawyer sent a young woman to seduce me in hopes of getting my files."

"Ah. Honey trap. Let me guess. She couldn't get the files, so the other lawyer tried blackmail instead, claiming you'd gotten the girl pregnant."

He glanced at me.

"Ouch," I said. "I think I just got frostbite from that look."

"I am hardly foolish enough to fall for seduction in the first place."

"Hey, I never said you fell for anything. It's a freebie. No reason not to take advantage."

"Not unless I have a shred of dignity. I'm not that desperate, Olivia."

"And again, I didn't say that. But okay, so you didn't sleep with her, and she still claimed paternity. I'm guessing it didn't get far."

"It did not. It was merely an attempt to embarrass me professionally. I spoke to my opponent — the one who sent the girl — and suggested it would be very embarrassing if I persuaded his wife to have the baby's DNA tested against his. He convinced the young woman to withdraw the suit."

"I'm amused by the fact you were more offended by *that* accusation than the murder one."

"I'm not disallowing the possibility that I *could* commit murder, under extreme circumstances. But falling into a honey trap? Unknowingly fathering a child? Absolutely not."

"Noted. That's it, then. All your sins laid

bare." I leaned back. "I can reciprocate if you like. I stole a Dr Pepper when I was twelve."

His brows shot up in mock horror.

"It was an accident," I said. "I was distracted and thought I'd paid. I still felt bad."

He shook his head. "I suppose you smoked a cigarette once, too."

"Twice. I had a wild youth, but I've overcome it. The only things I've done recently are lying to witnesses, trespassing, breaking and entering, and shooting people. All in the last six weeks, roughly coinciding with when I met you."

"A coincidence."

"Indeed."

He reached for his now-cold coffee. He was still calm, at ease, the wall down, blue eyes as warm as they'd been earlier. James's stunt hadn't changed his mood. If anything, he seemed happier to have cleared the air.

Lydia buzzed, and Gabriel wrinkled his nose, not exactly resenting the intrusion but not appreciating it, either.

"That would be my ten o'clock appointment," he said.

"Do you want me to move into the — ?"

"Stay. Keep working on Cainsville. I'll check in when I'm done."

CHAPTER FIFTY-THREE

Last night before bed, I'd jotted down notes from my chat with Patrick. Now I wrote them out, adding questions as I went.

The first question: *What is he?*

It was hard to even acknowledge the need to ask that. What was Patrick? A young writer who lived in Cainsville and made the diner his office. Yet I knew that wasn't the whole truth. I was also damned sure I couldn't find my answers by plugging search terms into a browser.

I thought Patrick *was* the man Gabriel had spoken to as a child. More significantly, I thought I knew why he'd sought out Gabriel, and why that had upset Seanna. To confirm my suspicion, I'd need to confront him. Once I had ammunition.

If Patrick was the man Gabriel had spoken to twenty years ago, then he could not be human. And so the questions circled in on themselves, threatening to tangle me in impossibilities. I had to pluck out this single thread and follow it to the end.

I knew Patrick's pen name. Patricia Rees. Yes, he used a woman's name, not surprising considering he wrote paranormal romances. Given what I suspected about him, his chosen genre was all kinds of ironic. I'm sure he was well aware of that. Even his pseudonymous surname came with a nudge and a wink. It's Welsh, derived from *ris,* meaning "ardor."

Patrick told me he'd published six books. That was not entirely true. Patricia Rees was credited with six in paranormal romance — and another four in gothic romance before that.

Gabriel remembered Patrick being a young man when Gabriel returned to Cainsville before college. I had assumed he was misremembering. Seeing Patrick's publication history, I knew he was at least as old as Gabriel thought. Yet that still meant he could not have been the man Gabriel remembered speaking to as a boy. It was noon before I had my answer.

Patrice Rhys. Novelist in the seventies. Author of a dozen bestselling novels of "gothic horror." Patrick Rice. Novelist in the fifties. Author of twenty novels — noir thrillers "with a gothic touch." The connec-

503

tion came through a master's thesis written five years ago — one of the many pieces of flotsam and jetsam that wash up on the Internet. The student had been writing on the evolution of gothic romance and had compared the works of Patrick, Patrice, and Patricia. She'd found enough thematic and stylistic similarities to decide that Patrice and Patricia had been heavily influenced by Patrick, down to using a variation on his name for their pseudonyms.

Or they could be the same person.

I found a photograph of Patrick Rice from the fifties in an archived interview. Otherwise, Rice was something of a recluse, as were Patrice and Patricia, none of them touring or giving interviews. But for Patrick, there was that one photo. And I had only to look at it to know, beyond a doubt, that Patrick Rice was Patrick from Cainsville.

I was printing the photograph when Gabriel swung into the office with "Lunch?"

I handed him the picture. "Meet Patrick Rice. Noir author from the fifties."

Gabriel's brows lifted in a flash of surprise before his expression settled into a pensive frown.

"Yes, I know," I said. "We could argue it's his grandfather or some relative who looks exactly like him — and shares his first name and occupation."

As Gabriel studied the photo, I could see that compulsion sliding in, insidious and overwhelming, manifesting in the undeniable urge to say, *It's a coincidence.*

"That's him," he said finally. "I don't understand how, but that is undeniably Patrick. You found it on the Internet?"

I nodded.

"Then it could have been planted or —" He stopped so abruptly his teeth clicked shut. "I'm sorry. Yes, that's him."

"And I *have* checked the source. It's from the archives of a Chicago magazine. I found a secondary reference, too, in a biographical sketch that references the article. Patrick has become much more careful about interviews, but in the fifties no one would have guessed that one day we could locate that photo from the comfort of our homes."

"It's still risky, though. Living in the same place, staying the same age. We're mistaken. We must be —" Another emphatic stop. "Why can I not stop doing that?"

"Part of it is simple logic. We're reasonably intelligent, educated people. If we saw a man biting a woman's neck in an alley, we'd presume kinky sex, not vampirism."

"Please don't tell me you think vampirism is the explanation here."

I shuddered. "God, I hope not."

"We *do* see Patrick during the day," Gabriel said.

"Bram Stoker's Dracula went out in the daytime."

"You aren't helping."

"Sorry." I wanted to tell him what I suspected, but I couldn't bring myself to, not until I had more. "The specific answer isn't as important as the general one, which is that Patrick isn't human. That something is going on in Cainsville, and we're caught up in it, and Macy Shaw seems to be caught up in it, too. So we need to talk to her."

"Give me two minutes."

CHAPTER FIFTY-FOUR

Macy Shaw lived in Bridgeport. In Chicago's distant past, the Irish ruled the neighborhood. It's a lot more diverse now, but you can still see its roots, including unmarked pubs that you'd best not enter unless you know a regular.

Bridgeport is working-class. There are signs of gentrification, but that's common everywhere people see cheap property and think they can change the landscape to better suit their tastes. Bridgeport is a strong enough community to hold out, and I'm glad to see it. The city is for everyone.

There are, however, areas where . . . well, a little gentrification wouldn't be a bad thing, if it meant architectural preservation. Pockets where the beautiful old homes and buildings are in sore need of a little support — financial and structural. Macy's street was marked by neglect. While the residents couldn't afford the massive renovations needed to return their homes to their former glory, you got the feeling most wouldn't see the point anyway. The long grass and weeds in the yards hid some, but not all, of the trash littered there. People sat on dilapidated front porches, eyes narrowing as we went by, more like junkyard dogs than proud home owners.

We passed one house with three men on the porch. All had the build of retired construction workers: wide shoulders, brawny biceps, and potbellies. None was over thirty, though. The porch was the most decrepit one on the street, so run-down that it made me nervous to see one guy leaning against the railing.

As we passed, Gabriel murmured, "Move to my other side, please."

His gaze was fixed on the road ahead, with no sign that he'd even seen the men, but he said again, "Olivia? My other side. Please."

By the time I figured out what he meant, the three were on their feet, coming off the porch, and I wasn't about to scurry behind Gabriel then. He still tried to move in front of me, but I put out my arm to stop him.

He took off his shades and fixed his gaze on them, his eyes chilling further with every step they took.

"Humor me," I whispered.

"I would prefer —"

"I know."

"You want something here?" one of the men said.

Gabriel moved so close I could feel him against my back. The guy stopped. His gaze traveled up. He was only my height, meaning he had to look a long way up to meet Gabriel's eyes, and when he did, he stopped walking. His two confederates flanked him, but neither moved another inch.

The lead guy looked back at me. "You want something here?" he repeated.

"Not from you." I turned to the one with the smallest potbelly. "Tommy Shaw?"

The guy froze.

"Jane Walker," I said. "Bail bonds —"

Tommy bolted. One of his friends lunged forward, fists up. Gabriel hit him with a right hook that knocked him off his feet. The other friend stopped midjump. He looked at Gabriel. He looked at his buddy on the ground. He ran.

"Take him instead," I said to Gabriel, waving at the guy on the ground, his nose streaming blood. "I'm sure someone wants him."

The guy scrambled up and tore off.

"Sorry about that," I said to Gabriel. "I thought they'd all run."

He adjusted his right sleeve. "It was a reasonable gamble with an acceptable outcome. Far better than having to take on all three. I wasn't looking forward to removing my jacket. It's a new shirt." He motioned for me to resume walking. "Thank you for recognizing Ms. Shaw's brother. That certainly made things easier."

"It also means that we don't need to worry about meeting up with him at the house."

That house was three doors down. We knocked at the front door. When Macy answered, Gabriel had the screen door open and blocked the inside door. She did try to shut it on him, but halfheartedly, stopping when Gabriel held up her driver's license.

"You dropped this the other night," he said. "May we talk?"

She glanced around.

"Your brother took off," I said. "But you might not want the neighbors to see you chatting to us on the front step."

"Right. Um, come in." She backed up. "My parents are out . . ."

"Excellent." Gabriel pushed open the door. "We'll keep this short."

She escorted us into the living room and cleared away beer bottles and a pizza box before we sat on the sofa.

"Sorry," she said. "My brother. He never picks up after himself."

Judging by the condition of the room, no one did. Her cheeks reddened when I surveyed the overflowing ashtrays and clutter. I stopped looking and lowered myself to the sofa.

"I'm sorry I took off the other night," she said as she gathered an armful of clothing.

"It was a traumatic experience," Gabriel said.

She nodded. "I tried to look Miss, um, Jones up, but I couldn't get any contact information. Otherwise, I'd have called you."

"Let me properly introduce myself, then. Gabriel Walsh." He held out his card. "For next time."

She took it with some reluctance.

"And this, as you know, is Ms. Jones," he said.

"Olivia. Please. I'm so sorry for what happened the other night. We're still trying to figure out exactly what *did* happen. You know who my parents are. Unfortunately, the crazies seem to be coming out of the woodwork. I'm still not sure what message that man wanted to convey, but he seems to have been a, uh, fan of theirs."

She looked appalled. "Fan? Of —"

"It happens," Gabriel cut in. "There are some seriously disturbed individuals out there, which is why I came to assist Ms. Jones, along with her . . ." He seemed to struggle for the word. "Friend," he said finally. "It's a very difficult and dangerous time for Ms. Jones."

"I can imagine." Macy tried for sympathy, but it was a struggle. At least she wasn't cowering in the corner, waiting for me to pull a knife.

Gabriel continued, "I'm glad she was able to come to your aid, despite the potential risk to her own life."

"Yes. Thank you." Her gaze flitted my way and was even able to make eye contact before zooming back to Gabriel.

"We're trying to determine why this man chose you, what connection you might have to Ciara Conway, what connection Ms. Conway has to Ms. Jones, and so on."

I smiled wryly. "A lot of questions."

"While we're hoping this man chose you at random, if he did not, we are concerned for your safety."

Now we both got a genuine thank-you.

Gabriel settled in. "Having had time to reflect, do you remember anything more about the man who took you? Did anyone at the party get a picture of him? Do you recall having seen him another time — before or since? Any detail you can give, however small, will help."

To her credit, Macy tried her best. She wasn't actively blocking us. We just made her uncomfortable — the serial killers' daughter and her hulking lawyer.

She hadn't seen the man since, nor could she recall having met him before. While she'd checked Facebook to see if anyone from the party had posted his photo, she hadn't asked around to see if anyone knew him. She would do that now if we wanted. We did. Beyond that, she could only provide additional details about his appearance, but since I'd seen the man myself, that wasn't very helpful.

While Gabriel questioned her, I kept feeling my gaze being tugged up to the bookshelf. There wasn't much there — just Macy's school texts, various biology and anatomy and nursing tomes. Fascinating stuff, I'm sure. Especially the one on thanatochemistry, whatever the hell that was.

As our queries wound down, Gabriel excused himself to use the washroom. Gathering DNA, actually. While he was gone, I asked about Ciara Conway. She'd looked up the name online but found nothing. When Gabriel came back in, I showed her Ciara's photo.

"Have you ever seen this young woman?" I asked.

"Sure, that's my —" She stopped and lifted the photo. "I was going to say it's my sister, Jackie, when she was younger, but it's not . . ." She trailed off, staring at the photo. Then her eyes widened. "Is this Ciara Conway?"

"You know her, then?"

"No. I mean, yes, only from the papers. A high school friend sent me the article, thinking it might be a relative because the girl looked so much like Jackie. But when I was searching online for the name my kidnapper said, I was using Kira with a *K*. I thought Ciara with a *C* was a soft *C*, like Sierra." Her gaze dipped. "I'm so embarrassed."

"It isn't a common name," Gabriel said.

She looked at the photo again. "She *does* look like my sister. My mom, too. Other than that?" She shrugged. "We seem to be about the same age. Maybe we were switched at birth." She laughed, joking, but there was a note of wistfulness there.

"If it was fifty years ago, I'd be wondering myself," I said.

"Anyone who looks like me in her family?" She said it lightly, but that note of something like hope remained. "I don't suppose she was born at St. Joe's?"

"Northwestern."

That laugh again. "I was only kidding. That doesn't happen these days. I remember when I was a kid, though, I'd see it in movies or read it in books, and I'd have dreams where it had happened to me. I'm sure every kid does that. Your family doesn't understand you. The grass is always greener. So on and so forth."

Anyone could see Macy didn't belong here — the well-dressed girl sitting primly on the edge of the chair, like a relative visiting from the suburbs, waiting until she's put in her time and can flee.

Except Macy couldn't flee. Unless she wanted to start life with a substantial debt, she had to tough it out here until she graduated. No matter how trapped I'd felt in my old life, I could have survived in that world. Macy was suffocating. And if we were right, and she was the real Ciara Conway, then I understood what Tristan had meant. Macy had indeed been more wronged than Ciara.

CHAPTER FIFTY-FIVE

It was a bit of a hike back to the car. Gabriel always parks the Jag someplace relatively safe and walks. One could argue — and I have — that it would be easier to catch a cab, but he doesn't take cabs. I suspect he hates the idea of putting someone else in charge. Which makes me even happier when he hands over the keys, as he did that day. True, he needed to work, which he could do better from the passenger seat, but letting me take the wheel while he immersed himself in e-mail was a vote of trust I doubt he gives to anyone else.

That afternoon, he had enough messages to keep him busy until I pulled into the lane beside his office. Even then, I was almost out of the car before I realized he was still in his seat, cell phone in hand, his gaze distant.

"Everything okay?" I asked.

He started. "Yes. Of course." He climbed

from the car. "Pamela called."

"She's still not offering to answer my questions, I'm presuming."

"No, but she's becoming increasingly frantic at not seeing you. I'm wondering if we ought to take advantage of that. She's the best place to get our answers." He paused. "Or the second-best."

"Second-best?"

He took the keys and headed toward the front door. "In the last message, she asked if you've been to see Todd yet. While she was initially eager for you to see him, it seems she's changed her mind."

"Because whatever she knows, he'll know, and she suspects he'll part with it more easily. Would she be right? I mean, I know you've never met him . . ."

"Given what I know of the case, he would be more likely to talk, particularly if the request came from you."

He ushered me past Lydia, a raised finger saying he'd be back to speak to her. Once we were in his office, he closed the door.

"You may not wish to hear this, but I believe, in the current context, it's important. Pamela has said, after you were lost in the adoption system, they hired private investigators to search for you. She stopped paying when it seemed apparent there was nothing to find. Todd did not. He didn't tell her, because he didn't wish to upset her, but I know from his lawyer that he never stopped looking for you."

When I didn't answer, his gaze bored into me.

"As I suspected, it's not something you wished to know."

"No, you're right. It helps to understand the situation if we're going to do an end run around Pamela. Anytime you can get me in to see him, I'll go. I'm guessing Lydia hasn't managed it yet?"

"No. It should be a simple matter of paperwork, but she is having inordinate trouble cutting through it. Calls aren't returned. Paperwork goes missing . . ."

"Do you think that's intentional?"

"I'm trying not to draw that conclusion, because it smacks of paranoia. I've asked Lydia to pursue the matter more aggressively, using the network of contacts from her CIA days. I don't like to impose on that, but this appears to require it, and she's happy to do so."

"Thanks. To both of you."

It was six thirty when Gabriel popped his head into the meeting room where I was working. Lydia was long gone and I'd lost track of time.

"Sorry," I said, grabbing my laptop. "You want to lock up."

"I was going to ask if you had dinner plans. There are things we could discuss."

Things we could discuss. Not a specific case. Not even things we *should* discuss. In other words, he was asking if I wanted to join him for dinner. God forbid he should just say that.

"Sure," I said. "Give me five minutes."

Gabriel took me to the restaurant that was quickly becoming "our place." We sat in a quiet corner and shared a good meal and wine and conversation, and when dessert ended, I had to struggle not to find some excuse for lingering. Gabriel seemed to want to, too, and when the server started eyeing us and the late-dinner line at the door, I said, "We should probably give up our table." Gabriel shot a cold stare across the restaurant, and I'm sure he would have said, "Screw them" — in some far less vulgar language — but I insisted.

When we got outside, he said, "Would you like to come to my apartment?" He cleared his throat. "I mean for a drink. Clients give me bottles, and my building isn't far. I'll drive you back to your car after. Or home, if need be."

"Depending on how much I drink?" I smiled. "I'm sure I'll be fine, but yes, if it's nearby, and it's not an inconvenience . . ."

"It's not."

CHAPTER FIFTY-SIX

I was going to Gabriel's apartment. He'd offered so casually that I wondered if I'd been mistaken about his reluctance to have guests. Still, I played it cool, making general conversation, with no comments on the neighborhood or even the building. I certainly could have commented on both.

When Gabriel first took me to his office, I'd expected a modern skyscraper suite in a high-rent neighborhood. Wrong for his office; dead-on for his residence. He lived in the near-north district of Chicago, just over the Loop. It was an impressive building, and I craned to look up at the top floors as I imagined the amazing view. I was so engrossed in my surroundings that I didn't notice Gabriel had gone quiet. He parked without a word, got out of the Jag, and led me to the elevator in continued silence.

He'd spent most of the trip here talking, that slightly animated chatter that came after his standard half glass of wine. And I could say that had worn off and he'd retreated into a more typical thoughtful silence. But it didn't feel that way.

As we waited for the elevator, I could feel anxiety strumming off him as his fingers drummed his leg. My gut dropped, any lingering buzz from the wine evaporating.

Gabriel didn't want to bring me here. He'd had an impulse, and now it had passed, and he desperately wanted to rescind the invitation.

"Is this all right?" I asked.

He glanced over. "Hmm?"

"We can grab a drink someplace else." I forced a smile. "You look like you're wondering if the cleaning lady came by today. I know what that's like. You get busy, and I swear the clutter starts reproducing itself. We can go someplace else . . ."

I was giving him an escape route. *Yes, actually, the place is a mess. Let's go down the street instead.* But he stared as if I was speaking Swahili. Finally, he seemed to process enough to understand.

"No, of course not," he said, ushering me into the elevator. "The apartment's fine."

He pressed a button. As the doors closed, I leaned over to see which floor he'd selected.

"Fifty-five? Damn. That's got to have an amazing view. North or south?"

"South."

"So it overlooks the river, then? Sweet."

"Yes, it's . . ."

He seemed to lose his train of thought, as if the effort of making mundane conversation was too much.

"Fifty-five is a lucky number," I said. "Multiples of eleven are always good."

Not exactly scintillating conversation, but he didn't even acknowledge that I'd spoken. My gut was churning now, the queasiness laced with growing anger. He'd invited me here. I hadn't asked. I hadn't hinted. I'd *never* hinted.

"You're right," he blurted finally, hitting the garage button. "It's a mess. I'd forgotten that. Let's go somewhere else."

I hit the next-floor button. He looked over as the elevator stopped abruptly.

I stepped off and turned, holding the door. "Go on up, Gabriel. I can find my way out."

"Of course not. We'll —"

"Cut the crap. You don't want me here. Maybe it's just me; maybe it's everyone. It doesn't matter. I was fine with that. What I'm not fine with? Being invited over and then made to feel as welcome as Typhoid Mary."

"That's not —"

"It is. Good night, Gabriel."

I released the elevator door. He stood there. Just stood there and let the doors start to close. Only then did he make a move to grab them. Too late. Intentionally too late. They shut, and I went in search of the stairwell.

Gabriel made no attempt to find me. He could have. It would have been a simple matter of taking the elevator back down and cutting me off at the stairwell. I had eighteen flights to descend. It took a while.

When I reached the bottom and saw no sign of him, I started to text Ricky. Telling him I couldn't stop by as we'd planned. I stopped before I sent the message. That wasn't fair or honest. So I called. He answered on the second ring.

"You're still up?" I asked.

A pause, then a chuckle. "It's nine o'clock."

"Right." It certainly felt later. "Is it still okay if I come over? Or are you busy?"

"Even if I was busy, it would be absolutely okay if you came over. I was just getting a head start on my readings."

"I'll be there in about an hour. I need to grab a taxi first and get my car from the office."

"Taxi? Can't Gabriel drive you . . . ?" He trailed off. "What'd he do now?"

I managed a laugh. "Not even going to suggest *I* might have done something?"

"Nope. But I won't pry. Where are you?"

"Just north of the Loop. I'll be there —"

"Give me an address and twenty minutes."

I did.

I lay under Ricky, the night-chilled earth against my back, the heat of his bare chest against mine, both of us catching our breath. We'd gone for a ride outside the city and, as usual, ended up like this, in some quiet spot that I only vaguely remembered him pulling into.

"Damn, that never gets old," he said.

"I hope not."

I shifted under him, my fingers tickling down his back. Goose bumps rose in their wake as he shivered, eyes half closed, smile playing on his lips.

"Thank you for the distraction," I said.

His eyes opened. "*That* wasn't the distraction. I had something special in mind."

"Oh, that's plenty special."

"Something a little more unusual, then."

He eased off me and flipped me onto him instead as he settled onto his back. "I thought I'd teach you how to ride."

"Shit. Am I doing it wrong?"

A laugh. "No, you are absolutely not doing it wrong, and you know that's not what I mean. My bike. I'm going to teach you how to drive it."

"I'm pretty sure there's got to be a rule against letting your girlfriend drive."

"Yeah. Which is bullshit, and I'm ignoring it. At least between us."

"So I can learn to ride it. Just not tell anyone."

"Yeah. Sorry."

"Don't apologize. You don't agree with the philosophy, so I am fine with it. In public, I will stay on the bitch seat, keep my gaze downcast, and follow behind at five paces."

"Right. I can't even get you to follow behind when we're scouting an abandoned psych hospital."

"That's because I had the gun. Unless you can throw your switchblade, it's not going to stop someone coming at us."

"So I guess you don't want this?" He reached for his discarded jeans and tugged something from the back pocket.

"Ooh." I took the knife. It was about three

inches long, black and stainless steel.

"Want?" he said.

"Want very much."

He pushed a button on top. An LED light turned on. "I'd get shit for adding that to mine, but I figured you could use it for those treks through moonlit alleys. Or for stabbing someone in the dark."

"It's perfect." I kissed him. "Thank you."

"Thank *you,* for making gift-giving very easy for me. I'm much better at choosing weapons than candy and flowers."

I flicked the blade out. "Sex, a switchblade, and motorcycle lessons. You really are making sure my night ends on a high note."

"I am. Now, let's get dressed and get you riding."

FORTRESS

Gabriel stared out across the night city, lights glinting off the river as a barge made its way toward the harbor. He'd bought the condo for this view. There were taller buildings, but none in his line of sight, and he could stand in front of the floor-to-ceiling window and imagine he was alone in the silence and the darkness. Alone and safe.

In college, a fellow student's father owned a condo three floors up in this building. They came by once, and Gabriel had stood in front of that window and thought, "This is what I want." A goal. One he'd realized sooner than expected, pouncing on a foreclosure in the real estate crash. So he got his condo and he got his view, and any other night he'd have stood here sipping a cup of Rose's tea and feeling very pleased with himself.

Tonight, he saw that glass barrier clearly, his reflection in it, standing here, the empty apartment behind him.

He'd started thinking about bringing Olivia here a few weeks ago, when they'd taken a skyscraper escalator and Olivia had practically pressed her nose against the glass to enjoy the view, clearly captivated. He'd imagined what she'd think of the one from his apartment. Not that he'd had any intention of showing it to her. No one came in his apartment. No one.

Olivia had said something about it being the cleaning lady's day off. In law school, his classmates said the first thing they'd do with a decent paycheck was hire a housekeeping service. Gabriel hadn't. He never would. He was accustomed to looking after himself. More important, he could not abide the thought of a stranger in his apartment every week. Service people were bad enough.

But as the weeks went by, he kept noticing Olivia admiring a view or standing near a window, and he'd started wanting to bring her here. He hadn't intended for that day to be tonight. He could blame the wine, but really, he'd been happy for the excuse. It would have been the perfect end to a very good day.

The day hadn't started so well, with the arrival of James's package. Yet what could have ruined it did exactly the opposite. He'd watched Olivia push the file aside, utterly uninterested. That's when he decided to take a step he would once have considered as implausible as asking someone up to his apartment. He'd sorted those piles and waited for a reaction that never came. She didn't care. He'd given her enough to ruin him, and she'd only processed the information and set it aside.

That was the point at which he realized he could invite her up to his apartment. On the drive, he'd imagined what it would be like. He'd pictured her at the window, drink in hand, then curled up on his sofa, talking with him into the night, forgetting that she'd had plans to see Ricky. She hadn't admitted she did, but he'd noticed her surreptitiously texting. Telling Ricky she wouldn't make it right after work. Then that she wouldn't make it for dinner. That she might not make it at all.

That had pleased him more than it should. Not for the obvious reasons. He was very good at distancing himself from *those* feelings, and having resolved to do so with Olivia, he dispelled any stray thoughts with the reminder that he'd lose her if he went there. So he wouldn't.

As for her relationship with Ricky . . . it

felt like a betrayal. It wasn't, of course. But he'd spent so much time with Olivia, they'd shared so much, that the thought that she'd been involved with Ricky, and he'd never realized it, had been . . . unsettling.

At least Ricky had no problem with Gabriel's relationship with Olivia. Gabriel could be insulted that Ricky didn't see him as a threat, but Ricky was right — if Olivia wanted to be with someone else, she would be.

He liked Ricky. He trusted him to treat Olivia well. He trusted him to make her happy. Which made the whole situation very uncomfortable.

But tonight, it had been fine. Olivia had been coming back to his apartment, and then . . .

And then.

Again, he could blame the wine. It wore off, and he'd lost his nerve. Again, that was more excuse than truth. As they'd neared his apartment, he'd realized how big a chance he was taking. How he could ruin what they had. And for what? She'd been fine with not visiting his place.

If he couldn't leave well enough alone, why hadn't he just gone through with it?

He walked into the bathroom and looked around, seeing nothing that would pique

Olivia's curiosity. Everything a guest could need was within sight: towels, soap, even extra toilet paper. She wouldn't have snooped. Even if she did . . . He opened the bathroom linen closet and saw towels and backup supplies. Nothing out of the ordinary — unless she pulled out the extra towels and looked behind them. And then . . .

Coke. Stacks of it.

Not cocaine, of course. Just cans of soda. If she did see that, she'd only tease that he must have found a really good sale or that it was his emergency caffeine for late nights.

And the rest?

If she went into his kitchen and dug into the cupboards, she'd find stacks of other canned goods, mostly beef stew. She'd joke that he should stop shopping at Costco, or that he must really like Coke and canned stew.

The truth? He could live happily if he never drank another Coke or ate another bowl of canned stew. Living on the streets, those had been his staples. Coke was cheap energy. Beef stew was protein and vitamins.

He could say that he kept caseloads of both as a reminder of how far he'd come. That was bullshit.

He had other stashes, too. Money, for one.

A hundred thousand dollars in cash, secreted in various locations throughout the apartment. Other valuables as well, just in case. Then there were weapons. Guns, knives, a baseball bat . . . Olivia's gun had come from here. He wouldn't miss it. He never carried a weapon. He just had them. In case.

In case of what?

The apocalypse? Nuclear war? Biological attack?

At least those would make some measure of sense. His reasons had no basis in rational thought. He had these things because some deep-rooted, impossible-to-uproot part of his psyche required them, like a child with a security blanket.

He'd spent years on the streets. Years when he'd guzzle Coke and eat cold stew from a can. While other street kids dreamed of hot meals and warm beds, his fantasies were simple. He wanted enough to eat. In a cruel twist of irony, his body decided it needed its tremendous growth spurt at a time when he could least afford it. There'd been months when hunger seemed to be the driving force in his life.

Money solved the food problem, obviously, and it could also provide that more elusive of creature comforts: shelter. He could usually scrape together enough to rent a place in the worst of winter, but he spent the summers wherever he could find a safe haven. He had to save for college. That was the only way out of the situation. His golden ticket. With a degree, he could have a legitimate, steady source of income, not spend his life looking over his shoulder for the law, like most Walshes. To get to college, though, meant going through high school, which meant conning his way in with a false address and then showing up every day in decent clothing, with decent supplies, so teachers wouldn't question his home situation. It also meant squirreling away money for college. So there was never enough for food, and he'd dreamed of a day when there would be.

As for the weapons, that was another problem altogether. Before those growth spurts made him an unpalatable target, he'd woken too often to a knife at his throat. He'd stolen a blade of his own only to have it turned against him. After that, he settled for hiding the bulk of his money and keeping only a few small bills on him. Then he started growing, and they mostly left him alone. Mostly. No matter how big he was, he couldn't fight three armed punks who really wanted the twenty bucks in his wallet.

There were other dangers in the world, too, ones his size offered no defense against. There'd been a girl. His first. Just a street kid. She traded sex for protection. Nowadays, he'd never take advantage of a woman that way, but at seventeen, if a girl was offering it . . . yes, he'd taken it. Right up until the night he woke with a knife poised a lot lower than his throat, as her real boyfriend helped her steal a thousand dollars of his college savings — and all of his pride.

It was a mistake he never made again. Sex was an instinct, like hunger or thirst, one to be dealt with but controlled, so it would never again pose a threat to the pursuit of his goals. Keep his eyes on the future. Don't get distracted. Slow down to admire the scenery and the world will overtake you. Or devour you.

So he had the Coke and the stew and the money and the weapons. And it all added up to one thing: fear. It didn't matter how old he was or how big he'd grown or how successful he'd become. He was safely up here, above the city, behind locks and a security system, and there were still nights when he bolted awake, heart pounding so hard he could barely breathe. The only thing that helped was knowing everything he needed was here, everything he hadn't had half a lifetime ago.

Olivia admired him for overcoming his past. He could see it in her face when the subject arose. It had taken him to a level in her estimation that "Gabriel Walsh, attorney-at-law" could never reach. He'd come from the streets and had a million-dollar condo before the age of thirty. That spoke to her of strength. Of victory.

And this? The Coke and the stew and the money and the weapons? They told a very different story. They said that Gabriel Walsh hadn't sailed out of that life unscathed. The frightened and hungry kid who'd lived on the streets wasn't gone. He was hiding up here, with his security blankets.

There was no reason for Olivia to know that. What he presented to her wasn't a false front. She was happy with the ninety percent of him that she saw, and that's what he wanted. Olivia to be happy.

Except, right now, Olivia was not happy. He should have gone after her. That was the proper procedure. He'd behaved poorly, and she was hurt. She'd stormed off. He should have followed. Except he couldn't. She'd left him. He would not follow. He knew well what a psychiatrist would say about that, tracing it back to Seanna's abandonment.

He didn't care. It was what it was.

He could rectify that now. Send a text. *I'm sorry. I behaved badly.*

Please come back.

Gabriel made a noise in his throat and turned on his heel, shoe squeaking on the polished floor.

He would not say that last part, of course. He would never say that. But it was what he wanted — for Olivia to read his apology and understand how hard it was to make it, and even if she was lying beside Ricky, for her to leave his bed and come back. To give him another chance.

Which was pathetic. Weak and pathetic and desperate. He'd made a mistake, a relatively small one. By tomorrow, he wouldn't even need to apologize.

But he should.

When his cell phone rang, he jumped, then cursed himself for startling like a spooked cat. It rang again, and the surprise and the annoyance fell away as he thought, *It's her.* Olivia. Calling to tell him what a jerk he was. He didn't care. She was calling.

He hit the button so fast that it wasn't until he'd already pressed it that he actually saw the name: James Morgan.

He almost hung up as the line connected. He would have, if it couldn't be seen as a sign of cowardice. He almost swore, too. That wasn't quite as great a faux pas, but it was a personal line he preferred not to cross. The world liked to paint him as a thug. His size, his choice of clients, his moral ambiguity — it all added up to that conclusion. Gabriel Walsh was an ill-bred, uncouth thug. He would not give them the satisfaction of hearing him speak like one. He would watch his word choice and his diction, and not be what they expected.

So he didn't curse when the line connected.

"Olivia isn't here," he snapped in greeting.

A pause. Then, "I should hope not. It's ten at night. Whatever mistakes she's making, that's not going to be one of them."

Any other time, the insult would have rolled off. Morgan was an idiot. He didn't know Olivia. Didn't understand her. Mocking Gabriel was the desperate, weak ploy of a desperate, weak man. But now Gabriel had fucked up and Olivia had walked out, and this asshole sneered at the very suggestion she might have stayed.

"What do you want?" Gabriel managed to say.

"I have copies."

"Copies?"

"Of the file I sent Olivia. I just learned that it was routed to your office, which explains why I haven't heard from her. You think that by shoving it through the shredder you can stop her from finding out about you."

Gabriel laughed. The sound was sharp as a blade, and Morgan should have taken the hint.

"I'm glad you find this funny," Morgan said.

"Oh, I don't find it funny at all. You're so certain you know what happened, because you're so certain you know Olivia. If she'd read that file, she'd have come running back and thrown herself into your arms, begging for forgiveness and protection. Is that how your fantasies run, Morgan?"

Silence.

"I'm sure they do, which only proves you are a bigger fool than I imagined. Olivia read the file, and I would suggest that you are lucky she didn't pay you a visit. It would not have gone well."

"Bullshit."

"I can ask her to confirm receipt tomorrow if you like."

"What did you say to her? No, wait — I don't need to ask. You said it was lies. All lies. Poor Gabriel Walsh, unfairly perse-cuted."

"Yes, that's exactly what I said, because she knows I would never stoop to something as distasteful as blackmail or intimidation. It would be like accepting money to protect my client."

Silence as Morgan thought this through. Gabriel resisted the urge to call him an idiot again. He wasn't really. He couldn't be, hav-ing achieved his level of success. But Mor-gan had a technical mind, which served him well in his chosen field. Beyond that he was, functionally, an idiot.

"If you wish to speak to Olivia on this matter, I will ask her to call you," Gabriel said. "After that conversation, you will make no further attempts to contact her. Your obsession is becoming wearisome. Cut your losses. Walk away."

"Or what? Or you'll blackmail me with that McNeil business? Go ahead and try. You made a mistake tipping your hand, Walsh. I will not back off until I have Olivia. Let me offer the same advice. Cut your losses. Walk away."

Morgan hung up. Gabriel stood there, staring at the phone, all the emotions of the evening bubbling up, the rage and the confusion and the hurt seething together into a perfect storm, with a perfect target.

Gabriel grabbed his keys from the hall and stalked out.

CHAPTER FIFTY-SEVEN

I wanted a motorcycle. Preferably a Harley, though I would settle for something smaller, as long as the reduced size didn't mean a reduction in engine power.

First a gun, then a switchblade, now a motorcycle. Next thing you knew, I'd be making appointments for tats and piercings.

When I told Ricky that, as we lay in a patch of forest, naked and sleepy, he said, "I'd be up for the ink. Get one together. Something meaningful."

I was taken aback at first. When I thought of couples getting joint tattoos, what came to mind were those unfortunate "Candy Forever" ones that in five years would have the guy telling new girlfriends it referred to his love for Tootsie Pops. That wasn't what Ricky meant, though. He had tattoos. Four, each marking something he wanted to remember, and that's what he was suggesting.

Would I do that? This relationship marked a stage in my life that was significant. A person who was significant. A time I would not regret.

"I'd go for that," I said.

He opened one eye, looking surprised. "Yeah?"

"Yeah."

He pulled me on top of him. "Well, give it some thought. I'll bring it up again in a few days, after the buzz of the riding lesson wears off."

"I still want a bike."

"I know. We can talk about that, too," he said, and pulled me down in a kiss.

After we finished, Ricky muttered a sleepy "Gonna close my eyes for a sec," and zonked out.

I touched the tattoo on his shoulder blade. It was the Saints patch, to commemorate the day he'd become a full member. It wasn't exactly a screaming symbol of defiance, but it was there, and it said this was his life, his choice, one he wouldn't be able to shuck by throwing out his jacket, selling his bike, and moving to the suburbs. I liked that — the attitude, the commitment, the single-mindedness, to be able to say at twenty that you'd known exactly what you wanted from life.

I was tracing my fingers over the tattoo and, yes, maybe hoping he'd stir. As peaceful as this patch of forest was, it was getting chilly.

"He won't wake," a voice said.

I scrambled up to see the Huntsman from the charity dinner. He was standing less than five feet away, smiling indulgently. I measured the distance to my gun, while glancing at Ricky.

"As I said, he won't wake."

My hand flew to Ricky's neck, frantically checking —

"Oh, he's fine," he said. "I would never harm him. I'm just allowing him to sleep while we talk. He needs his rest. You seem to enjoy each other quite vigorously."

I glowered at him.

"Merely an observation," he said. "And certainly not one I'm displeased to see. You make him happy. He makes you happy. One can ask for little more from another person than that." He paused. "Do you still have the boar's tusk?"

"Yes."

"Good. I have a feeling you'll need it. I hear you've had an encounter. With a third party."

"Tristan."

"Yes. He's warning you about us, and about those in Cainsville. Yet the accusation he levels against us could be directed at himself. He wants something from you. Everyone does. Except him." He nodded at Ricky. "You can sense that, which is why you feel so comfortable around him. He only wants to be with you. The same cannot be said for anyone else in your life right now."

I thought of Gabriel.

The man's lips compressed. "Gabriel Walsh is damaged, Olivia. You know that, and you feel an urge to fix him. That's natural, all things considered. But you can't save him. The damage is done, and if you want to know where the blame for that lies, look at Cainsville."

When I said nothing, he tilted his head. "You don't ask what I mean. You know. Or you suspect. You haven't reached all the conclusions, but you are on the path."

"Am I on the *right* path?"

"Yes, but it's a long road, and no one in Cainsville will help you. Safety through ignorance. That has always been their religion. They hide and they lie and they deceive. We do not. You know what I am, and I do not deny it. I offer you answers. You need only to ask."

"And the cost?"

"Consideration. I would earn the right to show you what we offer."

"What else?"

A flicker of surprise, as if he had expected me to buy the goods as offered. "Nothing more. Except that, naturally, if we are wooing you, you cannot continue to align yourself with them. You leave Cainsville. You renounce your association with Gabriel Walsh. You divorce yourself from their influence so you may fairly consider our offer."

"You do realize I have no fucking idea what you're talking about, right? You act like I'm a high school quarterback being wooed by two NFL teams, and I should know exactly what I am and what I'm worth and why the hell you both want me. I don't."

"That is what I'm offering. Answers."

"While I appreciate the shortcut, I think I'll take the long road. It looks a lot less treacherous."

He only smiled. "As I expected. You can't blame me for trying, though. Enjoy the trip. I'll give some free advice, then. There are two things you'd best keep close, for protection: the boar's tusk and the boy there. They'll look after you. You can't trust anything or anyone else. You know that."

His gaze met mine, and I knew what he

meant. Who he meant. Gabriel. Would he push me away again? Lie to me? Betray me? Ricky wouldn't. Trusting Gabriel was like pitching camp on a fault line; Ricky was solid ground.

"Exactly," the man said.

I glared.

"Would you prefer I didn't admit I know what you're thinking? Don't worry. It's too draining to maintain for long. But I'll use what tools I have to understand the situation. You can't blame me for that. I'll bid you good night, then." After two steps, he glanced back to see me settling on the ground beside Ricky. "How's your back, Olivia? I'll presume it doesn't give you any trouble?"

"My back? It's fine."

"Good." He turned to walk away, then glanced at me again. "You're welcome," he said, and vanished into the forest.

SHARK TANK

The Morgan residence was patrolled by a security guard. At what level of wealth did one require a home security guard? Actually, Gabriel knew the answer to that, having dug deep into Morgan's finances while looking for ammunition to use against him.

Morgan was rich. A juvenile term. At Gabriel's age, he should be more specific with his terminology. But he'd been young when he set his sights on his future goals, and that was the wording he used, at least to himself.

He could not achieve "rich" — it was for those who came from money, though it allowed for the occasional entrepreneur. Gabriel's goal was "successful." Wealthy and very successful.

Morgan's wealth came from both family money and his business, and it far exceeded anything Gabriel could hope for. It did not, however, warrant a roving security guard.

One problem with the rich was that they lacked basic survival skills. Morgan considered himself a shark, devouring anything that got in his way, but he was a shark in a tank, relying on others to keep him safe. The rich bought their fancy locks and security systems and, it seemed, even security guards. Yet it was like wearing a breastplate into battle — it still took only one good stroke to lop off your head.

And so it was here. The guard was useless. Stationed a hundred feet away from the house, at the gate. Patrolling the grounds every twenty minutes. Once Gabriel determined the schedule, he waited until the guard returned to his post and then scaled the back fence. Two minutes later, he was knocking on the front door.

Morgan answered. He stopped short, and his gaze shot to the guard post.

Gabriel waved at the manicured spruce behind him. "While I'm loath to criticize gardening choices, may I suggest that's a very poor place for a shrub?"

Morgan cursed under his breath as he realized that the tree blocked Gabriel from the guard's view. Then Morgan's hand slid up the wall.

"You can certainly summon the guard," Gabriel said. "I'll understand if you'd like him to be privy to our conversation. While my size is no fault of my own, some men find it intimidating."

Morgan's lips tightened, and his hand moved away from the intercom. Such a fool. There was nothing wrong with being a shark in a tank — Gabriel supposed it was a fine and comfortable life — but one should have the good sense to see the glass walls and realize one's limitations.

"May I come in?" Gabriel asked.

Morgan nodded and moved back. As Gabriel entered, he heard a noise on the steps and looked up to see an older woman eyeing him with suspicion. It didn't matter how fine his manners or impeccable his dress, when women like this saw him, they backed up clutching their purses. Which was not an unwarranted reaction, all things considered. Ten years ago, he'd have salivated walking into a house like this, mentally running through all the most likely hiding places for valuables and mapping out the most efficient route for snatching them. He didn't miss those days, but admittedly there were still times when he looked at a woman's necklace or a man's watch and his brain threw out a dollar figure — not the cost but how much he could fence it for.

"It's Olivia's lawyer," Morgan called up to

her. "On business."

"At this hour?"

"It's barely eleven. Everything's fine, Mom. Go back to bed."

She retreated, but slowly, still eyeing Gabriel, her expression less fear than warning now. Gabriel turned his back on her.

"May we speak in another room?" he asked Morgan.

Morgan waved him into a parlor or some such room designed for sitting, which neither of them did. They walked to the middle and faced each other.

"If you're here to intimidate me . . ." Morgan began.

"In your own home? With your mother and your security guard at hand? That would seem unwise."

Gabriel kept his voice soft, free of emphasis, but Morgan still tensed at the mention of his mother and his guard.

"I would like you to stop contacting Olivia," Gabriel said.

"I'm sure you would. The answer, as I said, is no."

"Let me rephrase, then. I insist you stop contacting her or I will obtain a restraining order, which I will publicize."

"If you do, I'll tell my side of the story, and it will be clear who is the victim here. I will also send a copy of that file to every reporter in my contact list."

Gabriel took out his phone. "In that case, I'll e-mail you my list of journalist contacts. Please send copies to all of them. Some would be very put out if they were excluded."

Morgan studied him, squint-eyed. He probably thought it made him seem tougher, but he only looked as if his contact lens had slipped.

"Don't bluff, Walsh," he said. "I'll call you on it."

"Go ahead. What you'll discover is that most reporters have heard every allegation in that file. While I'm sure most suspect there are kernels of truth, rooting them out has proven too much trouble. It is established fact that I have been persecuted and maligned by false accusations since I passed the bar exam. Unless you have a video of me bludgeoning prostitutes to death — and expert witnesses to guarantee the veracity of the recording — no one's going to touch it. But I'm sure you know that. So let's discuss your backup plan."

"Backup plan?"

Gabriel lowered himself onto the sofa. "Don't play coy with me. If you are an expert at this game, as you claimed, then you know exactly what I'm talking about. The file is the decoy; as was my threat about McNeil. Naturally, you have more, as do I."

Morgan's squint deepened. "You're saying that if I send out the file, you'll retaliate with some other blackmail."

"Certainly not. I gave you permission to send the file. The difficulty comes if you refuse to leave Olivia alone. Then I will be forced to reveal what other intelligence I've gathered on you."

"I will not leave Olivia —"

Gabriel sprang to his feet and had Morgan against the wall before the man could blink. He pinned him there, feet barely touching the ground, his shirtfront gathered in Gabriel's fist, pressing into his windpipe.

"You will leave her alone. If you harm her, in any way, you will wish to God for blackmail, because you can recover from that."

"Is that a death threat?"

"I would never be so unimaginative."

Gabriel dropped Morgan but stayed where he was, effectively keeping him pinned there, unable to move more than an inch.

"You tell me you love her, but this isn't love," Gabriel said. "It's anger and it's wounded pride. Your history is open to anyone with a laptop, Morgan. You had another woman you planned to marry, but she was dull and insipid. Olivia is neither. You dumped the old girlfriend. You pursued Olivia. You won Olivia. Now you've lost her. And that looks bad."

"You think this is about politics? Her biological parents —"

"— are convicted serial killers. Now about to undergo an appeal, which may set them free. And you stuck by Olivia the whole time. You believed in her. Except . . . she wasn't grateful. Now she's run off with a biker. A *biker.* How humiliating. You should walk away. But you can't. You want her to grovel. You want her to pay."

"I would never —"

"No? Look me in the eye and tell me this is about love."

Morgan's jaw worked, and Gabriel eased back to watch him squirm. He noticed the movement a split second too late. His own fault, really, the smug satisfaction that he'd intimidated Morgan into impotence. Then the blow to his jaw that sent him reeling.

Gabriel recovered and slammed his fist into Morgan's gut. He caught Morgan's expression when he saw the blow coming. Shock, as if he couldn't believe Gabriel would pull such an ungentlemanly move. Again proving the man was an idiot. On the streets, there's no place for fairness. You put your opponent down fast, by any means possible.

Morgan crumpled to the floor, doubled over, his eyes bulging as he gasped for breath.

"You might want to see a doctor about that," Gabriel said. "I believe Olivia was telling me just the other day that Harry Houdini died from an untreated blow to the stomach."

He walked into the hall. As he did, he heard the pounding of Mrs. Morgan's footsteps on the stairs.

Gabriel looked up at her. "May I suggest you teach your son not to strike a man significantly larger than him. It rarely ends well."

She started shrieking threats. Creative threats, actually, making Gabriel suspect she would have been a far more worthy adversary than her son. He continued to the door as she hurried down to tend to her wounded boy.

Gabriel pulled open the door — and nearly yanked the security guard in with it. Behind the guard were two uniformed police officers.

"Gabriel Walsh, you're under arrest for trespass, breaking and entering, issuing threats . . ."

CHAPTER FIFTY-EIGHT

After the Huntsman left, I fell asleep. I'm sure there was something preternatural in that — there was no way I'd drift off with everything pinging through my head.

When my phone rang, Ricky woke first, and by the time I surfaced, he'd already pulled my cell from my discarded slacks.

He swore and turned the phone toward me. It was James. The call went to voice mail.

"What time is it?" I asked.

"Two in the morning. Has he been doing this?"

"No. It's because . . . he sent a package this morning."

His look of concern sharpened to alarm, and I laughed softly.

"It wasn't a bomb or a dead rat," I said. "Just a file on Gabriel. Rumors and allegations. There was one on you, too. He didn't dig up anything more than a couple of dismissed traffic violations, but I should have mentioned it. I planned to, and then last night . . ."

"You had trouble with Gabriel, followed by motorcycle rides, which aren't conducive to conversation. We *should* talk, though. If James is —"

The phone rang again. Still James.

"Okay," Ricky said. "Three ways to handle this. One, you answer, though I'd rather you didn't, because it seems to only give him an excuse to keep calling. Two, you turn the phone off. Three, I answer."

"Go for it."

His eyes glinted. "Seriously?"

"I was hoping for a mature breakup, but he's not letting me have it."

Ricky answered. There was a pause, as James presumably processed the fact that a man was answering my phone at this hour. Then Ricky said, "It's Rick Gallagher. We haven't met."

A murmur on the other end of the line.

"It's the middle of the night. Can I pass on a message?"

Another murmur.

"If it's important, I'll wake her, but she's been working double shifts. I'd like to let her sleep."

He could have insinuated some other

557

reason why I was exhausted, but he was taking the high road. Which was more than I could say for the guy calling me at 2 A.M.

Ricky listened for another minute, and I could see confusion and then surprise in his eyes. "Sure. I'll tell her. Oh, but I'm going to ask you not to call her in the middle of the night anymore, okay?"

I heard James start to respond, but Ricky cut him off. "Also, I heard you sent her some information on me yesterday. If you're interested in getting to know me better, just ask. In fact, if you'd like to get together for coffee, I could stop by your office tomorrow —"

Ricky stopped. He looked at me. "He hung up."

"And you were being so polite."

"I was." He handed me the phone. "He called about Gabriel." Ricky reached for our clothing and tossed me my slacks as he sorted through it. "It seems your boss paid your ex a visit tonight, in response to that package. He's been arrested."

I had my shirt half on. I stopped. "Gabriel?"

"Yeah. James made it sound like Gabriel tore over there, broke in, and beat the shit out of him, which I know isn't the real story. Whatever happened, though, Gabriel's in jail. I'm going to go bail him out."

"I'll do it."

"Bailing guys out is actually one of my jobs for the club. But you're welcome to come along. Unless you're so pissed off that you'd like to see him stew in a cell overnight."

"Mmm, tempting. But no. I'll come. I should learn how to do this for clients."

I don't think this particular station was accustomed to seeing bikers. Considering the median property value of the area it serviced, that's probably a given. I was the one the desk clerk recognized first. Ricky introduced himself and told the clerk why we were there, and suddenly I swear every officer in the place found an excuse to come up front as we waited.

It was like the setup to a joke: the gang leader's son and the serial killers' daughter walk into a police station and . . . Well, hilarious shenanigans ensue, I'm sure.

The reality, I fear, was not nearly as entertaining. Ricky and I waited, talking in low voices, causing two officers to creep ever closer until they overheard Ricky discussing a marketing project. One walked away in disgust. The other hovered, as if convinced it was really code for some nefarious scheme.

Finally, someone came to process our bail request. In Chicago, you pay the police, not a bondsman. Bail had been set at under two thousand dollars, which is why Gabriel hadn't called anyone to spring him — he'd be able to cover it himself with a call to the bank in the morning. The police knew that, so they were holding him in the drunk tank rather than shipping him to the Cook County jail. They *could* have let him stop at an ATM on the way, but this was Gabriel Walsh. The cops weren't doing him any favors.

The desk sergeant was a middle-aged woman who seemed to know exactly who we were and, quite frankly, didn't give a damn. We were being polite, so she was polite back.

According to her, James hadn't called the police. His mother — Maura — had. Maura claimed Gabriel had broken in, drunk, and proceeded to beat the crap out of James, while issuing death and blackmail threats. When the police actually arrived, they'd discovered a few flaws in Maura's story. One, no sign of break-in. Two, Gabriel was obviously sober. Three, no matter what they might think of him, they knew he wasn't going to suddenly go raging bull on anyone.

That wasn't his rep.

The charges were simple assault and trespass, which were both misdemeanors. Serious enough, though, when you were an attorney. Yes, according to the desk sergeant, James had been taken to the hospital for possible internal injuries, but Gabriel would never have gut-punched him without provocation. James was being something I never would have thought possible. He was being an asshole.

Ricky and I were left in a room while the officer went to get Gabriel. When that door opened, I started forward, but Ricky stopped me. As Gabriel saw us, humiliation flickered over his face. It vanished in a blink, helped by the fact that I *didn't* rush to him. We played it cool, as if this sort of thing happened all the time. The officer who'd escorted Gabriel gruffly told us to see ourselves out and then retreated.

Once the door closed, Ricky said, "Aren't I supposed to be on that side of the room, and you over here?"

Gabriel only grunted, then seemed to realize Ricky was trying to lighten the mood and said, "I hope it never is reversed. I trust you know better than to *get* on this side. I'm presuming the police notified you, because I certainly didn't ask them to call."

"You should have," I said. "And no, it was James, actually."

"Liv was going to come bail you out," Ricky said. "But I'm the one with the experience. So now that that's done, I'm going to guess you're okay handling car retrieval? I should grab some sleep before morning classes."

He gave me a sidelong look, in case I was thinking of reminding him he didn't have any morning classes. He was trying to make an awkward situation easier by extricating himself. I glanced at Gabriel. He looked like hell — exhausted and disheveled, with a bruise on his jaw and blood spatter on his shirt. There was a vaguely disoriented look in his eyes, too, as if he'd lost his footing and still hadn't found it. I wasn't letting him go anywhere on his own.

"I'll go with Gabriel to fetch his car," I said, passing Ricky my helmet. "Thank you."

"Call me?"

I nodded. He made it halfway out the door before Gabriel seemed to snap out of it.

"Thank you," he said to Ricky. "I won't forget this."

Ricky grinned. "That would be the idea. And I'd hope I don't need to say it, but I'll keep this between us. I'm sure you'll get it

562

resolved."

I waited until he was gone, then handed Gabriel a hairbrush and tissue I'd dug out of my bag. I gave him my makeup compact, too, for the mirror.

"Since I'm guessing there's no back way out . . ." I said.

"Right. Thanks."

"If you pat some powder on your jaw, it'll make the bruise less noticeable."

He did. Yes, no one except the cops would see him. But to Gabriel, it still mattered. He cleaned up and brushed his hair, and by the time he looked presentable, he seemed a little more himself, reoriented, the usual chill back in his eyes, the steel in his jaw and spine. When we turned to go, that resolve softened again as he glanced over at me.

"Thank you," he said. "For coming. I know I don't deserve —" He cut himself short and pulled up straight again. "We'll talk later."

Gabriel's car was where he'd left it — a half mile from James's place. We took a cab and picked it up. I suggested Gabriel drop me off at the office, where I could hang out with a coffee while he went home and cleaned up.

"There's coffee at my place," he said.

I tensed. "That wasn't a hint."

"I know. I'm offering. I would be fine with it."

I looked across the car at him. "No, you wouldn't, and I'd like you to stop pretending otherwise. Your place is your place. I get that. You aren't inviting everyone else over and telling *me* I'm not welcome, so I'm not offended."

"You *are* welcome."

"Can we drop this, please? Last night was not fun. I feel like I overreacted, and that's embarrassing, but I don't understand why you'd invite me —" I stopped and shook my head. "And *that's* not dropping the subject. If you don't want to leave me at the office, then join me for a coffee. I know a few spots we can hang out and watch the sunrise."

It was almost comical to watch him process why anyone would *want* to watch a sunrise.

"We could do that," he said at last.

"All right, then. You find me coffee, and I'll show you a scenic parking spot."

CHAPTER FIFTY-NINE

I had a few sunrise spots — places Dad had found where he could drive and enjoy some peace without leaving the city. This one was on a bluff. As we drove up, Gabriel peered around the darkness.

"Yes, I know," I said. "It looks like a make-out point."

"I was thinking more a convenient location for the exchange of illegal goods."

"I'm sure it's both at the right time of night, but at this hour it's always empty. My dad used to bring me up here for hot chocolate before my early morning skating practices."

"Figure skating?"

"Don't give me that look."

"I wasn't —"

"Yes, you were. You are trying and failing to picture me in a tutu on ice. With good reason. It was my mother's idea. Some mornings, if Dad and I got to talking up here, he'd conveniently lose track of time and I'd miss my lesson. When my mother finally realized I wasn't getting better at skating — shockingly — she let me quit. Then I got to take up rowing, which was a compromise. It wasn't quite as feminine as she'd like, but it was a suitably upper-class pursuit. What I really wanted to do was horseback riding."

"I didn't think one could get much more upper-class than that."

"Exactly my point. But she said she had a friend whose child died after being thrown from a horse. Years later, I found out she'd just watched *Gone with the Wind* too many times."

"So you never went riding?"

"Not until I was old enough to do it on my own, and by then I was driving. Horses don't have quite the same . . ."

"Horsepower?"

I laughed. "Exactly."

He ratcheted back his seat, getting comfortable. I waited until he was settled, then said, "I'm going to have to ask, you know. About tonight."

He grunted, stared out the windshield, and sipped his coffee.

"If you don't tell me, James will."

Another sip of his coffee before he put the

566

cup into the holder. "I made a mistake." A pause. "I made several tonight. I'm not quite sure how that happened. They seemed to . . ."

"Snowball? Yeah. Mistakes are like that. So he called you after I left?"

Gabriel glanced at me as if surprised.

"I know you didn't just randomly go over there and confront him. He must have called."

"He did. We had words."

"I bet you did."

"The call was relatively civil, but it became clear that no matter what I said, he was not going to stop trying to contact you. I decided a personal visit was in order."

"So you snuck past the gate."

"I wouldn't say snuck . . ."

"You found an alternate entrance. You rang the bell, presumably, since the breaking and entering charge was dropped. You then intimidated James into not calling for help."

"I wouldn't say —"

"You made him feel that calling for help would be cowardly."

"I'm beginning to think I don't need to tell you this story after all."

"I'm saving time. You confront him. You 'have words.' He makes the boneheaded move of hitting you in the jaw, so you gut-punched him —"

"Gut-punch is a strong —"

My look silenced him. "Do I have the basics right?"

"You do."

"Good. Anything else I should know?"

He considered, then said, "I am more concerned about him than before. No matter what I do — threats, blackmail, intimidation, or even civilized requests — the situation seems to deteriorate. I will admit that I'm not quite certain how to proceed. I could act on my blackmail threats . . ."

"The McNeil business?"

"No, that was merely a decoy. Morgan plugged the hole while I focused my attention elsewhere."

"Is he really that dirty?"

"He's a successful businessman. He has vulnerabilities. Mostly business problems that were resolved with a bribe to the proper parties. That's common enough. It would, however, damage his political chances."

I sighed and slid down in my seat. "If you'd told me he'd pull this crap a month ago, I'd have said you were delusional. The big question now is how this will affect you."

"I'll resolve it easily enough. It's simply an embarrassing footnote to my career."

When silence fell, I said, "To completely change the subject, I talked to that Huntsman tonight. The one who gave me the tusk."

I told him what happened. Well, most of it. I didn't explain exactly where I'd been or what I'd been doing when I met him. I also didn't tell Gabriel what the Huntsman had said about him.

"It sounds crazy, right?" I said.

"It does."

"What if it is? If I'm being set up with some crazy-assed scheme? Oh, look, I'm a special snowflake, and dark supernatural forces are fighting over me. Maybe I'm just unbalanced enough these days to actually fall for it."

"While I wouldn't eliminate the possibility it's an elaborate scheme for some criminal purpose, that does seem unlikely. And you aren't unbalanced. At least, not enough to fall for such a story."

"Thanks," I said.

We exchanged a smile and then lapsed into silence, watching the sunrise.

We were about to leave when James phoned.

"I'm going to answer," I said. "Otherwise, he'll keep calling." I picked up with a warm "Hey, there," which earned me a full five

569

seconds of silence.

Then James said, "I take it you haven't spoken to Richard."

"Ricky? Sure. Thanks for letting me know about Gabriel. He'd have been in that cell until morning if you hadn't called."

More silence. Then, "I'm guessing that's sarcasm."

"Irony, actually, but close enough. I am glad I got the heads-up to bail him out, though I'm not nearly so impressed that you put him in there in the first place."

"That *I* put him in there? The man put *me* in the hospital."

"A punch to the stomach for a right hook to the jaw. You reap what you sow. I hope you're okay, but I'm not going to pretend it isn't your fault."

Another five seconds of silence. "What has happened to you, Liv? Is this his influence?"

"Yes. Completely, because I was such a sweet little doormat before."

"I'm concerned about you, Liv."

"You don't need to be. Now —"

"There are people out there who are very worried about Gabriel Walsh and his influence on you."

I gripped the phone. "Who?"

"It's not important. I'm calling because I regret what happened, and I want to make amends. I'd like to drop the charges."

"I would appreciate that."

"Good. Then you'll join me for dinner?"

"Um, no. It's over, James, and as much as I regret how that happened —"

"Do you want those charges dropped, Olivia?"

It was a few moments before I could reply. "That sounds like extortion."

Gabriel's head whipped my way, his eyes narrowing.

"Of course not," James said. "I'm just saying —"

"That you'll drop the charges if I go to dinner with you."

"No," Gabriel said. "Absolutely not."

"Is that — ?" James began.

"Of course it is," I snapped. "You called at two in the morning to tell me he was in jail. Do you think I'm just going to bail him out and take off? If this is about getting me away from Gabriel, it was a dumb-ass move, wasn't it? The more you threaten him, the closer I'll stick to watch out for him."

"And the same for threatening you," Gabriel rumbled. "Tell him I *don't* want the charges dropped."

"James? I'm sure you caught that."

No answer, but I swore I could hear him seething.

Gabriel continued, "Tell him that dropping the charges suggests they had merit, and that he was coerced into withdrawing them. I will get them dismissed instead. The only question is whether he wishes to go public with them."

"Hell, yes, I'm going public," James said as I put the phone on speaker.

"Excellent. I will save you the trouble and place the calls myself."

"So you can lie to the press?"

"No, so I can tell the truth. About the harassment my client and employee is receiving at the hands of her ex, and how my attempt at a private discussion, following a documented late-night call from him, resulted in a physical altercation. I regret what occurred, but I would strongly suggest that the other party seek counseling, as he presents an obvious danger to others, most alarmingly the ex-fiancée who is struggling to rebuild her life after the tragic revelations of the past two months." He paused. "How does that sound?"

"If you —"

"If you run with your story, they will contact me for a quote, and that is the one I will give. Now, it's late. Or early, as the case may be. Good day, Mr. Morgan."

I hung up.

CHAPTER SIXTY

I went in to work with Gabriel. I didn't have an official shift, but I'd sent out some feelers, building those victim profiles for my parents' case, and I hoped one of them might have paid off in the form of a possible interview. Calls would come to Lydia. I didn't even get a chance to ask her about them. As soon as we walked in, she stood, motioning that she needed to speak to me. Gabriel continued on to his office.

Once the door closed behind him, Lydia picked up an envelope off her desk. "This came for you."

It was a letter-sized white envelope. On the front, it read OLIVIA TAYLOR-JONES in careful block letters. As soon as I saw those letters, I went still. I saw that handwriting, and I flashed to a Christmas gift label. My name on it, in the same printed letters. TO EDEN. LOVE DADDY.

"Todd," I whispered.

My gaze shot to the return address on the back, which confirmed it. Lydia caught my elbow, and I realized it was shaking. She nodded toward the meeting room door. I let her usher me inside. I made my way blindly to the table, dropped the letter on it, and sat there staring at it.

"I could call Gabriel in, if you'd like," she said. When I shook my head vehemently, she said, "That's what I thought. Not exactly Mr. Empathy. He means well . . ." She trailed off, then checked that the door was closed before sitting beside me.

"Todd's probably telling me why he won't see me," I said, indicating the envelope. "He doesn't think it's wise. Or he just doesn't want to, after all these years."

I thought of what Gabriel had said, that Todd had kept looking for me long after Pamela had given up. Now that I'd turned up, had he realized he wasn't going to get that fantasy reunion with his little girl? That I *wasn't* his little girl anymore, but a grown woman, a stranger?

I remembered going to a state fair with my adoptive dad when I was eight. It was magical — all bright lights and whirling rides and delicious treats. I'd returned at eighteen and wished I hadn't — the lights had been garish, the rides dilapidated, the treats seeming to guarantee food poisoning. Memories forever tainted. Is that what Todd feared?

"That might not be why he's writing," Lydia said.

I nodded and dropped the envelope, unopened, into my bag. "I'll read it later."

"If you want to talk about it . . ."

I smiled wanly. "Thanks. I might take you up on that. Not a lot . . ." I trailed off. *Not a lot of people I can talk to about it these days.* That sounded sad. Pathetic, even. The truth was that I'd never had a lot of people I could unload on. I was the shoulder to cry on. I'd never needed that myself, because I'd always had it, with my dad. Then he was gone, and . . .

And no one was there to replace him, and maybe I was looking for that in Todd. Which was the worst possible thing I could do. Not because he was a convicted serial killer, but because it wasn't fair to Todd. Expecting him to take the role of my beloved dad would be like him expecting me to take that of his two-year-old daughter.

"I'll let you know what it says tomorrow," I said. "If he doesn't want to see me, you can stop trying."

"If you want to talk before that . . ."

I smiled at her, more genuine now.

"Thanks."

With the arrival of that letter, my enthusiasm for work soured. There were no calls on my leads, and I wasn't sure I'd have set up an interview even if I could. I finished what I could do, and at eleven I was rapping on Gabriel's office door.

"Come in," he called.

He was at his desk, surrounded by papers.

"I'm taking off."

He looked up, as if startled, and checked his watch.

"I wasn't scheduled to work today," I said. "If you need me to do something, I'm happy to stay another hour or so, but otherwise I wouldn't mind getting home and grabbing a nap before my diner shift."

"Yes, of course."

I turned to leave.

"Olivia?"

When I looked back, he waved me in. I closed the door and he said, "Have you given any more thought to quitting the diner?"

"I didn't know I was supposed to be considering it."

"I'd like you to. Yes, you don't want to depend on me for your income, but your trust fund comes due in a few months. Your expenses are low. I suspect that, in a crunch, you would be fine until then." When I didn't answer, he said, "You also mentioned applying for your private investigator license."

I made a face. "I was just talking. I'll get it if this works out, but I'm not in any rush. The real issue is those few months until my trust fund. I'd rather keep my job at the diner. It's not interfering, is it?"

He hesitated.

"You don't want me working at the diner," I said. "Why?"

"Because it puts you at their mercy and under their watch."

"The elders, you mean."

"Yes. I know they don't pay your wages, but I've seen the way Larry treats them. If they wished you gone, he'd do it. Of course, that would leave you no worse off than if you quit, but . . . The balance of power makes me uneasy."

I wasn't eager to quit the diner. It felt like saying two months as a server was as much "real-person life" as this former socialite could bear.

"I'll think about it," I said. "Do you want me to check in later — ?"

His phone rang, Lydia patching in a call. He glanced at it.

"Take that," I said. "Just call me later if —"

"Hold on."

He answered. It was a short call. His end was just "Yes" and "No" and "Are you certain?" and "Please send the results to my office."

"That was the laboratory," he said.

"With the results already?"

"I put a rush on them."

Which would have cost extra. Another time, I'd have joked about him docking it from my wages, but now that seemed un-charitable.

"Your theory was correct," he said. "Macy and Ciara were, indeed, switched at birth."

CHAPTER SIXTY-ONE

Using hairs from Macy's brush and from one in her parents' room, the lab confirmed that the familial match was reversed. Macy was the Conways' daughter. Ciara was the Shaws'. As for how that happened, it did no good to speculate. We had the information. Now I had to figure out how to act on it.

I went home to think. And to nap, though I got little sleep. I tossed and turned until I gave up and went to my laptop and started punching in terms.

It took nearly two hours of searching before I found it. Not a connection. Not a direct one, anyway. But another case, pulled from the archives of a Chicago newspaper. In the late sixties, a family claimed their young son was a changeling. The boy was "severely troubled," according to his grandmother. The child told intricate stories of "another world," a fairy realm, ergo he must be a changeling.

People had been sensible enough to dismiss the idea as amusingly primitive. The boy's grandmother was a first-generation Irish immigrant. Clearly, she'd brought some of that old-world nonsense over with her. After all, she was the one who made the claims by taking the child to the local priest. The priest had refused to help, so she'd found another, and somehow — to the parents' shock and dismay — the story leaked to the paper, where it seemed to have been included merely for entertainment. Or to show how much more progressive Americans were, dismissing old-world nonsense and superstition.

So what caught my attention in this tale? The grandmother claimed that her real grandson had been switched with a fairy child from Cainsville. Her daughter-in-law had family there, and the parents visited often. That, she said, was where it happened. And her proof? Well, she had none. Only that there was "something wrong with that town." Something she felt every time she visited. The town took far too great an interest in her grandson and his problems, and the old folks there went out of their way to convince her that the boy was fine, and that if she loved him and raised him well, he would grow into a strong and capable young man.

Of course, all of that was dismissed, with the columnist waxing poetic about the tight bonds and loving care that a small town bestows on its own. How much different was life in the bustling, impersonal city? How much better might troubled children like this one be if they were instead raised in the pastoral perfection of the countryside?

I read that article and I saw that my blossoming theory, however mad it seemed, might actually be right. I just needed to prove it.

When Macy called me shortly before my diner shift, I swear there was a moment, after she introduced herself, where I was unable to find my voice, certain that . . . I don't know. That the universe had prodded her to call me, knowing I had information that could change her life? It was merely coincidence, of course, given that I'd handed her my card only twenty-four hours earlier and asked her to call if she remembered anything.

"The man who took me said something else," she said. "Something weird. One of those things that you think you've heard wrong, but then you can't figure out what else it could have been."

"What's that?"

"He asked if I'd had any tests done."

"Tests?"

"That's what I thought. I figured . . ." A pause, and when her voice came back, it was lowered, as if sharing a secret. "I don't sleep around, Ms. Jones. I really don't, and I don't want you to get the wrong impression when I say this."

"Okay."

"I thought he meant STD tests. I thought —" She swallowed. "I thought he was taking me somewhere for sex, and I was okay with that, which is why I think I must have been drugged."

"It did seem like it when I met you."

"It did?" An exhale of relief. "Good. So I thought he was asking if I'd been tested recently. I said I hadn't . . . been with anyone in a while. He laughed and said that wasn't what he meant. And then he asked if we'd had other tests, me and my parents, and I was so embarrassed about the STD thing that I figured I was hearing wrong and said no. He said we should." Macy paused. "Do you know what he meant?"

Yes. And I can't tell you. Not until I've figured it all out, and even then I don't know if I will. If I can. Despite what a difference it could make to your life.

582

"No, I don't know," I said. "Did he say anything else about it?"

"That was it. I should have asked, but it didn't seem important."

"It probably wasn't. But if I find out what he meant, I'll let you know."

"Please."

At the diner, I got a text from Ricky saying he needed to talk as soon as I got a moment. I called him back between orders.

"You know how I mentioned my dad was taking off to Florida for a few days?" Ricky said.

"Miami, on business."

"He just told me he has other obligations, and I need to take his place."

"Huh."

"Yeah, *huh*. Any other time, I'd be thrilled at the chance to prove myself. But this is because I promised him our relationship wasn't going to interfere with my club duties . . ."

"He's testing you."

"Right."

"Go," I said.

"I'd rather not. This shit with James . . . I feel like I should be here, in case you need me."

I hesitated, thinking of what the Huntsman had said about keeping Ricky close. I dismissed it. The man wanted something from me and would say whatever was needed to make me run to him for protection and answers.

"I'll be fine," I said. "Go."

During my shift, I passed a note to Patrick, asking him to meet me after work. He agreed with a smug smile.

He was waiting in the park for me.

"Changelings," I said as I walked over.

He blinked, then recovered as he smiled and said, "Good evening to you, too."

"Tell me about changelings."

"Mmm." He waved for me to join him on the bench. "That's a very old piece of folklore, used to explain children who weren't quite right. A mentally challenged child. A mentally ill child. A wild and uncontrollable child. No parent wants to believe they've created such a thing. So according to the folklore —"

"I know the folklore. I want to know how it works in Cainsville."

He paused, then said slowly, "How it works?"

"How you do it. Why you do it. You and the other elders."

It took him a moment to find the proper

look of confusion and shock, and even when he did, he took no great pains to make it genuine, the expression underneath one of pleasure and pride. Like a parent secretly delighted that their child is clever enough to have deduced there is no Santa Claus.

"I have no idea what you're —"

"Robert Sheehan," I said, naming the boy from the newspaper. "Ciara Conway. Macy Shaw."

"Conway . . . That's the girl whose body you found, isn't it?"

"Not really. Ciara Conway is alive. Macy Shaw is the one who died. The real Macy Shaw, that is. They were switched at birth. Changelings of a sort."

"That's quite a tale. I've heard of such mix-ups —"

"The elders got rid of Ciara's body — the switched Ciara, that is. I don't know how. As for why — that's obvious. They were worried the truth would be discovered. They just weren't savvy enough to realize the techs had already taken DNA samples. Someone advised the Conways to have their DNA tested. Ostensibly to be sure the dead girl was Ciara. Now they know she isn't their daughter. I know who is — a young woman who was kidnapped and used to lure me to an abandoned mental hospital. She was taken by a man named Tristan. Well, not a man, I'm sure. No more than you are."

"I don't know —"

"What are you? *Bòcan?* Bogart? Some kind of hobgoblin? That's my guess. Mischievous. Dangerous if you get on his bad side. Helpful if you stay on his good, and if you understand the rules. Tit for tat. Fair trade."

He opened his mouth, but before he got a word out, I said, "Patrick Rice. Patricia Rees. Patrice Rhys. I can show you the photograph of Patrick Rice. Just for kicks, of course, because I don't expect you to confirm any of this. What I want from you is another answer. A trade-off. You don't confirm this, but you do confirm that. Tit for tat."

A pause. Then, "Perhaps. If I can." He met my gaze. "You understand that, I hope, Olivia. There are things I cannot do. Things I cannot tell you."

"Whatever. For now, I have a hypothetical about the changelings, to help me figure out what's going on, why a girl died and why I'm being targeted in relation to that death."

"By this Tristan? If you tell me more about him, I might be able to help."

"Gabriel and I will handle him. For now, hypothetically, if babies *were* being

586

switched, babies that are connected to a small town populated by fairies —"

"Tylwyth Teg. Hypothetically."

"What? The word 'fairies' offends you?"

"Hypothetically. Fae if you must."

"Fine. So these babies get switched. Why?"

He seemed to consider this, and I was bracing for him to refuse to answer when he said, "Take a look at the families involved. What do you see?"

"Well, the children don't resemble the parents —"

"Look deeper, Olivia. There is a very marked difference in the families."

"They come from different sides of the track, so to speak. One is upper-middle-class. The other is lower. The income level —"

"Deeper."

I considered. "The Conways are solid citizens. Well educated, no trouble with the law, and so on. The Shaws are none of the above. Criminal records. Addictions. A family with deep-rooted problems."

"Hmm."

"And the point is? So you took —"

"*I* did nothing."

"Hypothetically."

"Hypothetically or not, I did nothing."

"Fine. So *someone* takes a girl from a

good family and switches her —"

"Reverse the situation."

"Someone takes a girl from a troubled family and —" I looked up sharply. "And gives her a better chance."

"Perhaps."

"Why would — ?" I stopped myself. "Because she's the one who matters. The girl born to the Shaws, who grew up as Ciara Conway."

To collect my thoughts, I got up and walked to the fence. I absently rubbed one of the chimeras, and when I did, I imagined the shrieks of children, delighted shrieks, and even if I don't have a maternal bone in my body, I felt what a parent must feel, that burst of pleasure and of pride and of something else — the instinct to keep their children happy, to keep them safe, to mow down every obstacle in their path to do it.

When I looked out again, I saw something on the grass, glowing in the moonlight. A ring of mushrooms.

A fairy ring.

I opened the gate.

"Olivia?" Patrick called.

I ignored him and walked to the ring and knelt beside it. Mushrooms, perfectly arranged in a circle. No, not quite perfectly — there were a few stray ones in the middle.

Small ones, lost in the grass. Protected within the circle.

I reached to touch one . . . and the ring vanished. Gone in a blink, because it had never been there. It was a vision, a nudge in the direction I already knew was correct.

Patrick stood outside the gate, watching me.

"They're your children," I said. "Fae children. They're Tylwyth Teg."

"Not Tylwyth —"

"Partly," I said. "You built this place. Cainsville is yours. Yet not quite. Not at first. There were other settlers. Humans. You needed that to be accepted as a community. But the danger of allowing others into your sanctuary is that they outnumber you. When a native population is in danger of being engulfed by the newcomers, their best choice for survival is co-breeding."

Patrick moved aside to let me back into the park. I sat on the bench. He stayed where he was, facing me.

"Depending on the subtype, the descendants inherit both gifts and curses," I said. "Sometimes more one than the other. A hobgoblin, for example, might bestow on his children a knack for mischief and trouble, one that could serve them well in life . . . or see them serving a life sentence in prison. Every now and then, when things get too badly out of hand, action must be taken to safeguard the children. Take one from a troubled family and give her a better chance in life. Switch her into a family untainted by the blood but with ties to Cainsville, a family that the Tylwyth Teg can be certain will give their descendant the best possible chance at life." I looked up at Patrick. "Is that a reasonable theory? Hypothetically speaking?"

"Adjacent to reasonable," he said. "Hypothetically speaking. Was that your question, then?"

"No. The question is more specific and more personal." I rose and took a step toward him. "What are you to Gabriel?"

His lips twitched, and in that familiar ghost of a smile I saw my answer. I'd always seen my answer. But I asked the question again, and he said, "I believe the solution to that mystery lies in your hypothetical, Olivia."

"The Walsh family is descended from your kind. Well, Tylwyth Teg, that is. And it's more complicated than a single ancestor from a single type. The Walshes are gifted. The Walshes are royally fucked up. Some one or the other. Some both. That's not the result of a single hobgoblin screwing a Walsh girl two hundred years ago. It's more complicated than that. And with Gabriel, it's much more complicated, because the screwing happened relatively recently. About thirty years ago, I'd guess."

As I looked for a reaction, I realized how eerily still he was. People are rarely still. They blink or they shift or they twitch or they tap. Patrick stood perfectly motionless. No sign to tell me that I was on the right path. But no denial, either. He just waited.

"When I mentioned the man that Seanna wanted Gabriel to stay away from, you said, 'Perhaps he gave her a gift she didn't want. It happens, between men and women.' That was my hint, wasn't it? Or maybe you were just amusing yourself, presuming I was too clueless to get it."

"I would never underestimate you, Olivia."

"But you won't tell me anything, either. You fear the others."

Did I hope that would spur him to talk, like a child proving he isn't afraid of the bullies? If so, I needed to remind myself that he wasn't human. I couldn't expect him to act like one.

He shrugged. "I fear the loss of a comfortable life. But I do believe there are exceptions to rules, times when rules ought to be broken. It would be better for all if you understood more. Safer. For you, in particular."

"No, for *Gabriel* in particular, because you're the one who gave Seanna that so-called gift. You gave her a son."

He said nothing.

"I'm right, aren't I?" I said.

"Is that your question?"

Yes, it was, and he didn't even need to answer. I could see it in his reaction — or his lack of one.

"How old was she?" I said.

"Old enough."

"So you impregnated a drug-addled —"

"Seanna's problems came later. At the time, she was a promising young woman."

"Until she was, what, eighteen and saddled with a baby?"

He eased back. "Yes, I seduced her. For my own amusement. The outcome was not intended, but it's the risk you take. And there were signs."

"Signs?"

"Yes, signs. Portents, your area of expertise. And I'll say no more on the matter or I really will get myself in trouble. I seduced Seanna. She became pregnant. While charms were enough for her to forget exactly who the father was, she clearly retained enough awareness to not want Gabriel associating with me." He got to his feet. "And with that, I should take my leave —"

"Like you took your leave of Gabriel?"

He looked at me.

"You abandoned him," I said. "You watched him grow up. You had to know what happened later, when she died and he was alone. And you did nothing."

"What would you have me do, Olivia? Find him a better family? That's what they wanted. The other elders. I refused. He needed to stay with his mother."

"The drug addict who neglected him. Who made his life such a hell that when she disappeared, he never even thought she might be dead. How bad does a mother need to be for her fifteen-year-old to presume she'd abandon him?"

"So you think I should have let them switch him?" His brows lifted. "We are monsters for what we did to the Conways' child, giving her to a troubled family to make way for our own, but if it was Gabriel who'd have gotten a better life . . . ?"

"I only meant that you should have done *something*. You were responsible for him, Patrick. For creating him. For creating the situation. And when it all went to hell, you turned your back —"

"Do you know how they temper steel,

Olivia?"

"I don't care —"

"The application of controlled heat. As strong as the metal will withstand. That produces the most resilient steel. Too much and it will break. It must be tough, yet slightly malleable. Adaptable to the greatest number of situations. That's Gabriel. He's been tested and tempered and —"

"And he is a person!" I roared, unable to hold back any longer. "He is not a sword. Not a tool. I don't care what the hell you had in mind for him. You screwed him over, and now you tell me you were tempering —"

The sound of footsteps cut me short. They came from the walkway to my apartment, as a figure ran down the path. It was too dark to see more than a shape, but there was no question who it was. Gabriel didn't slow until he'd emerged into the moonlight and saw who I was with.

"Sorry," I called. "Everything's fine."

He glanced at Patrick, then at me again. "I'll wait . . ." He motioned back toward the path.

I nodded, and he retreated between the buildings, far enough for privacy but not letting me out of his sight, either.

I started walking away. I had what I'd

come for. The rest was just anger, futile rage.

Before I could open the gate, Patrick caught my arm.

"Look at him, Olivia," he whispered.

I did, in spite of myself, glancing at Gabriel, backed into the shadows now but still visible, the set of his shoulders and his jaw, the glitter of his pale eyes, fixed on us, watching for trouble.

"You know what kind of man he is," Patrick said, his voice low. "You know what he's capable of. His intelligence. His strength. His resourcefulness. That is the result of the choices I made. Would you really have him any other way?"

"Yes." I met Patrick's gaze. "I would have him happy."

He didn't miss a beat. "Maybe that part is up to you."

"No, I don't think it is."

I pulled away and walked to Gabriel.

CHAPTER SIXTY-TWO

"Hey," I said as I drew close to Gabriel, fixing on my best everything-is-just-fine smile. "I didn't expect to see you tonight. Visiting Rose?"

He shook his head. "Waiting for you. Ricky called. He told me about the Miami trip. He was concerned, leaving you alone, with everything that's happened. I thought it best if I came over and spent the night."

"He didn't need —"

"He wasn't asking me to. He simply mentioned that he wouldn't be around, and you might need the extra . . ."

"Protection?"

"I was avoiding that particular term. Support. Attention. Given what's happening with James." He motioned for me to accompany him back down the path.

"I wouldn't have been alone. I have my cat. And a security system, a gun, and a switchblade."

"Switchblade?"

"Ricky carries one. I liked it."

He shook his head, then said, "Are you telling me to go home or simply pointing out that you're capable of taking care of yourself?"

"Door number two." I glanced over at him. "I'm glad you came, though. The cat's not a very good conversationalist."

We walked a few more steps, then he said, "Given the shouting, I take it Patrick didn't confess to the switching of Macy and Ciara."

"He didn't, but he confirmed it in every other possible way. We were right about Cainsville. What it is. What he is. What happened with the girls. I know why it happened, too. I'm not ready to go inside yet. Can we walk while I tell you?"

"Certainly."

We passed the apartment and continued down Rowan as I told Gabriel why Ciara and Macy had been switched. I did not tell him that Patrick was his father. Not now. Maybe not ever. What good would it do to know that the whole time he'd been fighting for survival, his father had watched and done nothing?

I did, however, tell him that the Walshes

were one of "the" families — the unwitting recipients of fae blood. After I said that, we walked half a block in silence.

"So which part don't you believe?" I said. "That Cainsville is a refuge for fairies? That they've been interbreeding with the human population? Or that your family is part of the breeding stock?" I paused. "And having just heard myself say those three sentences, I should be glad you aren't suggesting we take a ride to the psych hospital. If we do, though, can you at least find me a place that's still open? That last one was a bit primitive for long-term residency."

A few more steps in silence.

"Gabriel?"

"Oh, are you finished? I didn't want to get in the way of your backpedaling. And don't give me that look or I will return it in kind. I thought we were past the point of laughing this off. Also past the point of interpreting my thoughtful silence as disbelief."

"Sorry."

"I was processing the information. I believe all of it. How could I not? I come from a family with strange gifts. Second sight is the most obvious, but we have other abilities, less obviously supernatural but clearly above normal. Inherent . . . aptitudes for certain iniquitous talents."

"Like deception? Lying? Betray —"

"I was going to say sleight of hand."

"Ah." We turned a corner, and I continued. "So the girl raised as Ciara Conway was a modern-day changeling. Switched at birth to give her a better life."

"Although, given her recent addiction, it didn't matter. What's bred in the bone . . ."

I glanced over and saw the tightness in his face, his gaze fixed ahead while he continued. "As for the murder of Ciara Conway and what it means to you, that part is still a mystery."

"Is it?" I stopped walking. "Yes. There has to be a motive beyond publicly exposing the switch, which has failed anyway. Who killed her? I don't care what Tristan says, he was involved. As for what it means to me? A way to reveal the secrets of Cainsville that might make me turn tail and run? I don't know. I need to find more answers."

"And you expect to find them here?"

He waved, and I looked over to see where I'd stopped. In front of the Carew house. Gabriel peered at me.

"Ah, not an intentional choice of destination, then," he said. "Following the signs."

"I wasn't —"

"Of course you were. You just didn't realize it. Come along. We have a house to break into."

Again, there was no need to break in. The rear door was still unlocked.

"Lead on," Gabriel said as we stood in the kitchen.

"I don't know where —"

"You followed your instincts here. Keep following them."

I gazed around the kitchen. The windows were still shuttered, shrouding the room in darkness. I took out my switchblade and flipped on the LED.

"Your new knife has a light?" he said.

"Ricky thought it might come in handy," I said. "I don't know where he got that idea."

Gabriel chuckled. I looked at him, poised there, scanning the room, his body tense but his face relaxed, eyes glittering with the same thing I felt, adrenaline coursing through me, enjoying the adventure far more than I should. Gabriel glanced over, a smile playing on his lips, and for a split second the room faded and I was standing —

"Olivia?"

I snapped back to the kitchen and looked around, getting my bearings.

"Follow your gut," he said.

I nodded and headed into the dining room. As I passed through it and into the living room, my gaze tripped along the friezes at the top, the magpies and the crows. I shone my light up at them. "That's an answer, isn't it?"

"To which question?"

"One about me. About the Carews and the Bowens. They have fae blood. I have it."

He tilted his head as if to say, *Was that really in question?* I suppose I had already drawn that conclusion. I just hadn't articulated it.

When we reached the top of the stairs, I didn't pause to figure out where to go. Into the room with the triskelion owl inlay. The room where I'd seen the vision of the *bean nighe.*

I opened the blinds. Once again moonlight shone through all three shards of stained glass to light the owls.

"The last time I stepped into that circle, I saw a vision. Let's see if I can do it again."

I had to pass Gabriel, and when I did, he gave my hand a squeeze, so subtle I could almost believe our hands merely brushed. I offered a wan smile. Then I stepped into the circle and the room disappeared.

I woke on a balcony. It took me a moment

to realize that, my senses coming to life in slow succession. Smell first, the rich scent of night and fire and, on the breeze, forest and hounds and horses. Sensation next, that breeze caressing my face, tugging at me. Then sound, the breeze whispering for me to come out and play. Come out and hunt. Finally sight, seeing the distant forest across a seemingly endless meadow.

I felt metal beneath my hands and looked down to see them gripping a railing that shimmered in the moonlight, bright gold inlaid with silver. When I blinked, the silver and gold seemed to ripple and I could make out moving images within. It was the most amazing thing, and I wanted to look closer, but my body wouldn't move. Instead, I felt the pull of that forest and leaned over the railing, my hair blowing in the breeze as I strained to see . . .

"Matilda?"

I turned. Or, not me, just as it hadn't been me straining over the balcony. *I* had wanted a closer look at the railing. Whoever's body I inhabited did not. Now she turned to the open balcony doors. A figure stood in the darkness and her heart leapt. She laughed softly, as if to herself.

Will that never change? We'll be married tomorrow, and I still feel this way every time I see him. The sun rises when he arrives and sets when he goes.

Except, sometimes, as warm and bright as that sun is, I long for night.

"Matilda?"

The man was still in shadow, but it did little to hide him. His skin glowed golden. His hair, too, shimmered with an unearthly light.

"Come in," he said. "It's cold, and it's dark."

"I'm going out. One last hunt." She smiled and hoped it carried enough charm to fend off —

His lips curved in a frown. There was no anger in it. Just concern and, maybe, disappointment.

"You know you can't. It's our wedding day."

"Not yet. We still have —"

"The clock has struck twelve. It's the day. You agreed —"

"One last time. Before we're wed. I won't be long. It just . . ." She looked out at the forest. "It calls to me."

"It will always call to you. Here calls to you. There calls to you. I call to you. He calls to you."

She glanced back. "Arawn is a friend. Mine and yours. Nothing more. Never more. I've never been unfaithful, not in word or deed, not in heart or head."

"There's more than heart and head, Matilda." He stepped forward, and I swore I could feel the warmth of him, more delicious than any fire. "You had to choose. I realize that's not fair. It's choosing between two halves of your soul. But that is what had to be. *Mallt-y-Dydd. Mallt-y-Nos.* That is your choice. Your fate. If you believe you chose wrong . . ."

"Never."

She stepped into his arms, and as they wrapped around her, heat enveloped me, his lips coming to hers as his kiss consumed her, burned away every shred of doubt.

This is the right choice. It has always been the right choice.

His hands moved down to her waist, heat burning like wildfire in their wake.

"Let me make you my wife," he said. "Now."

"The ceremony —"

"No one will know."

She wanted that, as she'd wanted nothing else in her life. Lust and desire and need. And love. She wanted to be with him for now and forever, and nothing else —

A hound bayed. She turned to follow the sound. She looked out and saw nothing, but she knew they were there, in the darkness. The hounds and the riders. The Cŵn Annwn. Calling her back for one last ride. One last hunt. One last goodbye.

"Tonight," she said as she pulled away. "I will be yours tonight. As soon as I return."

He tried to grab her, but she was already out of reach. She ran. She heard him behind her, running after her, begging her not to do this.

"You made a vow," he shouted, his voice growing dimmer as she raced through the castle. "The day has come. You cannot break your vow. If you do —"

The baying of hounds and the stomping of steeds drowned him out. She ran into the courtyard. They were there. The riders. The hounds. And Arawn. He smiled and reached down to take her hand, pulling her effortlessly onto the back of his mount.

She held him tight, arms and legs wrapped around him. He reached back, his hand on her thigh, but she pushed it off.

That is not the choice I'm making. I just want this last night, this last hunt.

As we rode, a boom sounded over the thunder of the hooves. Matilda turned to look back at the castle, and she instinctively shaded her eyes, knowing it would shine blindingly bright. Her castle. The palace of the Tylwyth Teg, where she would dance on her wedding night and —

There was no glowing castle. Only darkness, lit by a single spot of light. A single sunbeam.

She scrambled off the horse, falling behind its hooves, one striking her in the thigh. Arawn cried out, circling back, but she was already on her feet, running.

The castle was gone. No sign of it. Only that ray of light. Still she ran, somehow faster than the horses, hot on her heels. Arawn called for her, told her it was gone, forever gone, and that was the choice she had made, the right choice, and she would never regret it.

No! I made my choice. Gwynn. The Tylwyth Teg. It was just one last hunt, before our wedding night. One last night, before endless day.

But now it was night, all around her, closing in, and she didn't feel the pull of it, the seduction of it. It was dark, and it was cold. Yet one ray remained. One last ray. One way to touch him.

To say I was wrong. I was young. I was foolish.

"Matilda! No!"

She ran into the beam and braced for the light and the warmth, imagining the feel of it against her skin —

Fire. Flame scorched through her, white-hot agony. She screamed and fell to her knees and —

CHAPTER SIXTY-THREE

I crumpled to the ground, hard ground, so unbelievably cool against my burning skin that I stretched out, plastering my cheek and hands to it.

Hands pulled me up, and when I lifted my gaze and saw a face, I thought it was him, the golden-haired man, and I let out a cry, relief convulsing through me. It wasn't too late. I hadn't lost everything.

Then the fever cleared for a second, and I saw pale blue eyes and black hair, and I sobbed louder then, the relief like a tidal wave, seeing Gabriel, knowing I was back and everything would be fine.

He said something, his words garbled. I blinked hard to clear my head, but the pain and the relief seemed to engulf me, and I couldn't fight my way free. Cool tears slid down my burning cheeks, and I reached up to wipe them away.

"Sorry," I said. "It's the vision. Just hold on."

He spoke again, his voice sharp with confusion and concern, and I struggled to fix on him, but part of my brain stayed lost in that vision, still disconnected. The room was blurred and tinged with red. I could see Gabriel's face over mine, but it wouldn't come into focus and his words were still garbled, unintelligible.

"I don't understand you," I said. "I —"

Heat roared through me, like being thrust back into that fiery ray of sunlight, and I convulsed, gasping. His cool hand went to my forehead. An exclamation that might have been a curse, but the word meant nothing to me. His arm slid around my shoulders. He said something. I struggled to focus, but even keeping my eyes open was too much effort. The room dipped and flared red.

He said the word again. I heard syllables then, but still nothing that made any sense. His arm gripped me, his fingers digging into my shoulder.

"— a!" His voice came clear. "Olivia!"

I passed out.

I surfaced into a nightmare world. I was a child, being stolen from my home, carried through the dark streets by a stranger. I'd been asleep when he took me and now I woke, in his arms, feeling the rush of cold night air against my skin, hearing the pound of his footsteps, smelling the stink of sweat and fear.

My limbs shot out, punching and jabbing and kicking as I struggled to be free. The man said something unintelligible. His face hovered above me. Yet it was no face. Just a pale blur. When I swung, he caught me by the wrist.

A pounding, like someone kicking a door. A white door. It swung open. A monstrous face leaned out, mouth opening, sharp teeth flashing, coming for me.

I screamed. Another rush of air as we tumbled through the doorway, the man still holding me tight against my struggles.

A woman's voice now, the words meaningless. I caught sight of the man's featureless face again and swung my fist up. It connected with a *thwack.* The man grunted but still didn't let go, carrying me upstairs now, into a yawning pit of darkness lit only by a distant wavering orange light.

Fire. He was taking me into the fire. My skin already burned, and he was going to throw me into —

Another light. Blinding. White. The shock

of it stopped the pounding in my head for a split second, and I heard a voice, and words now.

"Ice! We need ice!"

The arms lowered me to the floor. I thrashed there, moaning, fire scouring through me, so hot it burned away the nightmare, and I caught sight of a purple towel hanging on a rack. I'd seen that towel before. Admired the color.

Where had I seen it? Where was I?

A gurgling sound. Then a roar. Water rushing into a tub.

Whose bathroom?

I struggled to hold on to the questions. My brain kept dropping them as I writhed on the floor, moaning, my mind and body ablaze. A dark shape blocked the searing light, and I blinked up to see —

Gabriel. I saw Gabriel.

I tried to say something, but words wouldn't come. He scooped me up. Then he lowered me into a tub of cold water. I yelped and flailed. He held me down, and the world threatened to tip into nightmare again, being held in a tub of cold water, drowned in —

"Olivia? Can you hear me?"

He knelt beside the tub, face above mine, hands on my shoulders, holding me in the tub but not pushing me under.

"You have a fever," he said. "You're burning up. You were delirious."

"Where . . . ?" The answer came with a click as I saw the towels again. "Rose."

"She's downstairs calling the doctor and getting ice."

"Ice." I shivered at the thought of it. "Please. Yes. So . . ." My throat seemed to seize, parched. "So hot."

"I know."

His hand brushed sweat-soaked hair from my face. Then he dipped his hand into the water and did it again, the chill so refreshing I sighed.

"Better?"

I nodded.

He leaned over the tub. "You'll be all right."

He looked down at me, and all I could see were his eyes, those gorgeous blue eyes, sharp with worry, and I swore I could feel their coolness wash over me. I wanted to lose myself in those eyes, just —

"Ice." Rose strode in, appearing over Gabriel. She looked down at me in the tub. "She's still dressed."

"Of course," Gabriel said.

A strained half smile as she shook her head then bent with the bowl of ice. "Is she lucid?" she asked.

Gabriel nodded as he grabbed the ice and dumped it in. I let out a gasp as the ice hit the water — and me.

"I was asking so I could warn her before doing that," Rose said. "Can you hear me, Olivia?"

I nodded.

"I've called the doctor. She'll be here soon. You should go to the hospital, but Gabriel said —"

"N-no hospital," I said, teeth chattering. "Please."

"I know. Gabriel said you don't like them, but if this fever doesn't drop —"

I didn't hear the rest. The room was tilting, the bright light flickering. My eyelids flagged as I struggled to focus, and then . . . Dark.

I surfaced to lucidity a few times. Dr. Webster was there once, while I was still in the tub. She said yes, the fever was dropping. Then I woke again as Rose was stripping me out of my wet clothing and Gabriel was pacing outside the closed door, complaining that it was taking so long, that the doctor said I needed to be in bed, Rose snapping that some idiot put me in a tub while dressed and my clothes were practically glued on now.

Then I woke in bed, Gabriel trying to get me to drink, which he really should have done *after* I was fully awake, because I was still fevered and thought I was being poisoned, which meant he ended up wearing the water before I drifted off again.

When I woke next, it was to Gabriel and Rose arguing — I was dehydrated and if they couldn't get fluids into me, I had to go to the hospital. I roused myself enough then to drink a whole glass of water. Then I zonked out, dimly aware of the glass falling from my hand, hearing it shatter as it hit the hardwood —

Darkness.

No matter how deeply my body slept, my fevered brain stayed wide awake, pelting me with nightmares.

I was back in the Tylwyth Teg castle, as Matilda, smiling when the golden-haired man appeared in the doorway. He kissed me, that incredible storybook kiss, desire and lust and love and need, and I clung to him, never wanting it to end. But then I heard the hounds and the horses, and I pulled from his arms and turned to look out —

At a cityscape. I was high above the city, the night bejeweled with lights. Gabriel's apartment. I gripped the balcony, and when I looked down, I saw my own hands and heard the distant rev of a motorcycle engine.

I turned. Gabriel stood in the open patio doorway, his huge frame filling the space, looking awkward and uncomfortable.

"You don't want me here," I said.

"It's not that simple."

"It should be."

I stepped toward Gabriel. He backed up fast, as if I might do something crazy, like touch him. Below, the rev of the engine called to me.

I strode to the apartment door. Gabriel made no move to stop me. I pulled it open.

"Don't leave."

I caught the words as I walked out, his voice low, as if he hoped I wouldn't hear them. I glanced back. The apartment door was open and empty, only darkness and silence beyond. I ran back, heart pounding as I raced over the threshold into —

Into a morgue. A single light illuminated a table. A corpse lay on it. My corpse. Someone was working on it, a slight figure in hospital scrubs and a face mask.

"You're supposed to be standing watch," the figure said. It was a woman's voice. Vaguely familiar but too muffled by the mask to be identifiable.

"I am," said a man.

I turned to see Tristan sitting on a counter, his legs dangling. He looked amused.

"If anyone catches me here . . ." the woman began.

"They won't. Now finish."

At first I thought it was an autopsy, but after a moment I realized she was embalming my corpse, naked on the table. There was a book on a cart. A text. *Thanatochemistry.* Where had I seen that before?

I remembered where I'd seen the book, and as soon as I did, the woman pulled down her mask.

Macy Shaw.

She turned to Tristan. "If you want the head, you have to do that yourself."

He sighed and lifted a bone saw. The floor vanished under my feet, sucking me down and spitting me out —

I was lying on the mortuary table. I tried to leap up, but I couldn't move. Fire rushed through my veins. Fire and poison, and I gasped, but it made no sound. I saw Tristan approaching, the light above the table glinting off the saw blade, and I tried to scream —

He kissed me. I was standing on a balcony again, feeling arms wrapped around me, but it wasn't the same kiss as in the vision. It was one I knew, one that sparked feelings of grief and nostalgia and anger.

"James," I whispered as I pushed away.

An engine sounded below. Not the rev of a motorcycle. The purr of a high-performance car. I twisted out of James's arms. I was at his mother's house, on the tiny balcony overlooking the driveway. Gabriel was below, standing beside his Jag. It was daytime and he had his shades on. He tugged them off and cast an impatient look up at me.

"Olivia," he called. "We need to go."

"I'll be right —" I began, but James yanked me back.

"He's dangerous," he said.

I sighed. "Yes, I know. I got the file and your message. It doesn't matter. I —"

"No, Liv. You don't understand. Walsh has a plan. An agenda. He's going to use you, and he's going to hurt you. He's a psychopath. You know that, don't you? Will Evans tried to warn you."

"Will Evans helped cover up the murder of his own son. He lied about Gabriel to cover —"

"Evans didn't kill anyone. He got caught up in —" James shook his head. "It doesn't matter. You need to believe me. I've been warned about Walsh, what he'll do to you."

"By who?"

"Men who know what they're talking about. Men who can give us what we want, you and me, the kind of life we want."

I tugged from his grip. "Are they Cŵn Annwn or Tylwyth Teg?"

"What?" His face screwed up.

"They're lying. That's what they do. Tell lies and sell dreams. You need —"

"Olivia?"

I glanced over the balcony. Gabriel tapped his watch.

"We have work to do," he called.

"Coming," I called back.

I started for the door. James grabbed my arm. I yanked, but he yanked back, pulling me off my feet. I hit the wall, the wind knocked out of me, and I struggled to my feet, staring at him.

"What the hell are you doing?" I said.

"Protecting you," he said, advancing.

He caught my arm as it swung to ward him off. He dragged me to the balcony railing, and then there was no railing and I was standing on a ledge outside Gabriel's apartment, fifty-five stories above the street. Below, I could just barely make out the Jag, under a streetlight, and Gabriel beside it, his arms waving.

"Olivia!" His shout reached me. "No!"

James gave me a tremendous shove, and I went over the edge.

CHAPTER SIXTY-FOUR

I jolted upright in bed, shouting, "No!"

Beside me, I heard a gasp as Gabriel leapt from his chair, eyes wide, fists raised.

We stared at each other for a second, both yanked from sleep.

I recovered first and laughed softly. "Well, I'm glad I was out of punching range when I woke you this time." I'd made the mistake of waking him once, when he'd slept on my couch.

He rubbed his face and fell back into the chair. "Did you cry out?" he said.

"Hmm, I think so. Bad dreams."

"What about?"

I stifled a yawn as I stretched. "I was arguing with James about you, something about what he said yesterday, and . . ." I shook my head. "That's all I remember."

"How do you feel?"

"Like a train ran me over, followed by a steamroller and then a herd of wild horses."

I shifted to get comfortable and winced as every muscle screamed in a wave that threatened to knock me back onto the bed again. Gabriel rose and pushed pillows behind my back to keep me upright. He reached for a water pitcher on the bed-stand, saying the doctor wanted me drinking as much as I could.

I resisted the urge to joke about his nursing skills. If I did, he'd be back in that chair in a second, and I wanted to hold on to this a little longer, these few moments where he wasn't quite fully awake. I watched him pouring the water, hair tumbling forward, face smooth, gaze open. That's when I noticed the gouges under his dark stubble.

"Ouch. Did I do that?" I reached out, fingers stopping an inch from his cheek. *Look, don't touch.*

He pulled a face. "Just a scratch. You were delirious." He handed me the glass of water. "Drink up."

Rose appeared in the doorway. When she saw us, she started to retreat. I would have let her, but Gabriel turned as if sensing someone there. He paused and it seemed as if he was going to pretend he hadn't noticed her, but then he cleared his throat and called, "Rose?"

She returned.

"I was going to ask Olivia what she remembers from her vision at the house," he said. "You should be here for that."

"I'll make tea and toast," she said. "Get some food in you."

I wanted to tell her yes, go on, give us a few more minutes alone, but my eyelids were flagging, lethargy pulling me under. "We'd better do this now, before I fall asleep again. I don't want to forget it."

I told them about the vision. When I finished, Rose left, saying she'd check her books.

"I'll see what I can find online," Gabriel said to me when she was gone.

"I can do —" I couldn't stifle a yawn, then tried again. "I can do that."

"Normally, I would be quite happy to let you," he said. "Right now, the best thing you can do is sleep."

"We need to talk about the rest first. About Cainsville. Rose has to know." I glanced over. "If she doesn't already."

Gabriel's expression betrayed him then, a tightening of his lips, and I knew this was the part he'd been dreading. Not telling Rose about Cainsville, but finding out how much she already knew. How much she'd kept from him.

"I can do that," I said. "Why don't you go get some rest —"

"I'm fine."

"Clothing, then." I glanced down at the satin chemise wrapped around me. "While this is lovely, I really should . . ." Another yawn.

"Take a minute," Gabriel said, tugging the pillow out from under me so I slid down onto the bed.

I struggled to smile. "Thought you weren't allowed to say that."

"Only when I don't mean it. Close your eyes."

"Just for a moment," I said, my lids dropping as if obeying a summons.

I fell asleep.

I awoke to find myself staring into a pair of eyes. Yellow eyes.

"TC?" I croaked, lifting my head from the pillow.

He blinked in response.

"I brought him over," Gabriel said from the chair. "I was picking up your clothing, and he seemed concerned about you. I thought he might help you feel better."

I looked at TC, sitting rigid and unblinking on the other pillow.

"Did you hear that?" I said. "I'm sick.

You're supposed to curl up with me. Cuddle. Purr."

He lifted a paw and started to clean it. Then he hopped down and strolled from the room, tail high.

"Ingrate," I called after him. I rolled over to look at Gabriel. "Is Rose downstairs? I really should talk to her."

"I already did."

"Oh." I paused. "How did it go?"

He tensed. "Fine."

Another pause, longer, then I pushed the words out. "Are you okay?"

I'd hesitated before asking, because this was one of those boundaries. *Don't ask him how he's feeling. It presumes that he would have an emotional reaction, and, moreover, that he'd deign to share it with me.*

So why did I ask? Because every time we drew closer, I had to press my fingers against those boundaries and see if they were still there. See if I'd made any progress.

I got as far as "Are you —" before the wall slammed down. His shoulders stiffened. His gaze cooled. Any hint of emotion emptied from his face.

"Yes, of course," he said, words clipped.

I slumped back on the pillows.

There'd been a time when I'd imagined how many women over the years must have thought they'd be the one to break through Gabriel's wall, and I'd decided I would never be so foolish.

Respect his boundaries. Don't test them. Accept this relationship for what it is, because hoping for more is like hoping for that damned cat to race in here, cuddle up, and start purring.

I was closing my eyes when the door clicked, and my gut dropped, and I hated it for dropping, hated myself for reacting to him walking out.

The faint creak of chair springs made me jump. I rolled over to see Gabriel there again. The door was closed.

"I don't think she knew exactly what Cainsville was," he said, his voice low. "I may be deluding myself in that. I think . . ." He cocked his head as if searching for phrasing. "I believe she understood at some level but never articulated it."

"Which is why she was always joking about fairies and hobgoblins and wards."

He nodded. "She wants to talk to us about your vision. I'll bring you breakfast, and we'll talk."

"No, I'll come down," I said. I peeled back the covers and a wave of dizziness made my gorge rise.

Gabriel pulled up the covers. "Dr. Webster said the fever will drain you for a few days. Either you stay in bed or you go to the hospital —"

I tugged the sheets to my chin.

A brief smile. "I thought so. I'll bring Rose and food."

CHAPTER SIXTY-FIVE

"This Tristan called you Mallt-y-Nos," Rose said as we settled in. "You dreamed that you were a young woman named Matilda —"

"No, she wasn't me. I was inside her."

"All right. Mallt-y-Nos is, not surprisingly, a figure in Welsh folklore. Otherwise known as Matilda of the Night, or Matilda the Crone."

"Crone, huh? That's flattering."

"Perhaps you'd prefer the other translations? Night Curse. Night Fiend. Night Hag."

"And the story with Matilda is . . . ?"

"She's associated with the Wild Hunt, again not surprisingly. She's the only woman who rides with them. In some stories, she leads them. The Hunt rides in pursuit of the recently dead, and if she captures a soul, it goes to the Otherworld. If she fails, it has a chance to pass to heaven."

"So the Otherworld is hell?"

"That's a late interpretation. Post-Christian, obviously. In the early stories, the Otherworld is merely the afterlife, undifferentiated, as in many pagan religions. In those older tales, I would presume Matilda just captures them and sends them on their way."

"Like the grim reaper on horseback. In those versions, then, the Hunt chases spirits, not the living."

"Sometimes. Other times, they hunt those not yet dead, those who may deserve death. Matilda sets the hounds on them, and they rip the victim limb from limb, and she seizes the soul."

"Lovely. So my vision has nothing to do with the story, then. Except for the hunt aspect."

"No, that part, I believe, relates back to Matilda's origin legend. One version says she was a beautiful noblewoman who loved to hunt. She declared that if there was no hunting in heaven, she did not wish to go there."

"And so, on her death, she was doomed to hunt forever."

Rose smiled. "You're good at this."

"Legends. So predictable. That's not quite what I saw . . ."

"The other story is that Matilda was due to wed, and her husband disapproved of her hunting, so she promised never to go again after they were married. But she snuck out. He caught her and doomed her —"

"To ride forever," I finished.

"And, yes, again, not what you saw but rather a variation on it. In your vision, you — or Matilda — were to wed a fae king or prince." She paused. "Did you hear his name?"

"I . . . don't think so." Some faint memory twitched. *Had* I heard names? Other than Matilda? I couldn't remember.

"All right," Rose said. "So Matilda was to wed this man, but she could not resist the call of the Wild Hunt, despite a vow never to join it again. In making that impulsive decision, the fae realm was closed to Matilda forever. Given what you've said of Cainsville and what's happened to you, that has its parallels here."

"Two sides wooing me. I must choose one. Despite the fact that I have no goddamned idea why they want *me.*"

"Mallt-y-Nos," she said. "Mallt-y-Dydd. Matilda of the Night. Matilda of the Day. Those are your options."

"When you put it like that . . . it *still* doesn't make a damn bit of sense."

"I know," she said. "I'll keep looking. Though I don't know how much more I'll find that will be useful. Folklore is a way of explaining the inexplicable. It's humans guessing at the mysteries of the unknown. If there's a true story, it's not going to be in my books."

I glanced over at Gabriel. He'd been silent during the discussion. Now his brows arched as if to say, *Don't ask me. I'm as confused as you are.*

"Okay, so back to the real world," I said. "I need to — Shit! Work. My shift starts at —"

"I've called in sick for you," Gabriel said.

"Thanks." I paused. "I'm sure *you* have work to do, though."

He fixed me with a cool look. "If I wanted to leave, I would. If you want me to leave, I should hope you would tell me to go. I do not feel obligated to stay. Nor do I require false niceties if you'd prefer I didn't."

"Nothing's ever simple with you, is it?"

"I don't see how it could be simpler. If I want —"

"Enough," Rose cut in. "Don't dissect the question, Gabriel. Just answer it."

A pause. Then, "It's Saturday. I do not need to work. However, my laptop is in the car, and I was going to retrieve it to do some work, but I drifted off." He rose. "I'll go get that, if it will make you feel less like you are imposing on my time."

"It would."

"He's right," Rose said as we heard Gabriel's footsteps going down the stairs. "He didn't stay because he felt obligated. If Gabriel does something, it's because he wants to."

"I know."

"Do you also know what he would have done if anyone else had passed out at his feet? Called an ambulance. Oh, he'd stay until it came, but only because he might be sued for negligence otherwise. Then he'd be gone. He carried you back here. Running the entire way, I'm sure. You feel like you aren't making progress —"

"Before he comes back, we need to talk about something."

I pushed myself from the bed and joined her at the window. Gabriel was talking to Grace.

"Patrick is Gabriel's father," I said.

Her mouth opened, and I braced for the expected responses. *Was I crazy? How could that be possible?*

"Did Patrick say that?"

"He didn't admit it outright, but he didn't

deny it, and I get the feeling that's as much as he can do. As much as he's allowed to do."

She lowered herself to the bed, her fair skin paling. "Did you tell him?"

"Gabriel? God, no." I glanced out the window again. Gabriel seemed to be talking to some guy getting out of a van. "Patrick screwed around with Seanna and fucked up her life. Then he fucked off on Gabriel. Abandoned him. He saw what was happening. Hell, all the elders apparently knew, because they wanted to do their changeling trick with Gabriel, but Patrick wouldn't let them. He left Gabriel in that situation, with no support. And do you know why? To toughen him up. That's what he said." I realized how harsh my voice had gotten and stepped from the window. "No, I'd never tell him."

A long silence, as Rose stared at the wall, her expression blank but her eyes moving, as if seeing something there. Footsteps sounded on the stairs. Rose stood quickly, maybe worrying he'd overheard, but his steps kept coming at his normal pace, steady and deliberate.

A single rap on the almost-closed door.

"Come in."

He pushed it open and stepped through,

holding . . . daisies. He was clutching a bouquet of daisies with sprigs of small purple flowers. The stems were short, his hand dwarfing them, and he held them awkwardly, as if they were something he'd found on the road and didn't quite know what to do with.

"Yours," he said, thrusting the bouquet at me as Rose stepped out. "Ricky."

"Ricky?"

"He called your cell this morning. I answered and told him you weren't feeling well. Mild food poisoning. That seemed the simplest way to explain the situation in a way that wouldn't bring him on the next plane."

I took my flowers to the bed. "He'd know better than to hop a plane unless I was in critical condition, but yes, that'll keep him from worrying. Thanks."

The card with the flowers said only, "Check your e-mail when you're up to it." He'd left a longer message there:

Hope you're feeling better. I told you I'm not good at flowers, but these reminded me of the ones at the cabin. I just hope they aren't actually weeds. If they are . . . um, sorry. Either way, I'll make it up to you with an actual trip to the cabin when I get back. Call me, but only when you feel better. I mean that, too. Rest up. All is fine here. Talk soon.

I fired off a *Love the daisies. Call in an hour?* and then laid my phone aside and said, "Okay, so where are we on everything?"

CHAPTER SIXTY-SIX

"Macy called me yesterday, and . . ."

"And?" Gabriel prodded when I didn't continue.

I gave my head a sharp shake. "Sorry, just . . . there was something about Macy from my dreams, when I had the fever. Not surprisingly, considering she's on my mind as much as the rest of it."

"What did you dream?"

A short laugh. "Believe me, mine are not prophetic. I'll leave that to Rose. I don't even remember what it was. Probably some mixed-up nonsense like the rest of it. Did I mention I dreamed that James threw me off your balcony?"

"I don't have a balcony."

"Whew."

"I wouldn't say that's without meaning. Your subconscious is acknowledging the threat that James poses and —"

"And did I say Macy called? I think she

suspects something's up with her and Ciara. Maybe it's a gut feeling. Anyway, we need to discuss how we're going to handle that. We can't show up on her doorstep and announce . . ." A memory niggling at me again.

"I will refrain from telling you to take a minute," Gabriel said. "But I think you should. There's something there."

"I know," I muttered. "Follow the signs. Macy. Something about visiting her — *Thanatochemistry*. That book was on Macy's shelf, with her nursing texts." I did a quick search on my phone. "Thanatochemistry is mortuary science. I dreamed that Macy was going to embalm me, and Tristan was going to cut off my head."

"Your subconscious was linking the textbook to Ciara's embalming."

"But I'm sure they don't teach that in nursing school. Macy's records indicate she went straight from high school to college. Maybe she'd been interested in mortuary science? If so, I might find it online."

"I can't imagine you'd add that to a dating profile."

I sputtered. "I was referring to social media. Facebook, Twitter, and so on."

A slight curl of his lip. "Ah."

"Yes. I'm going to bet you don't have a Facebook page."

"My practice does, which Lydia maintains. We have Facebook and possibly MySpace."

"MySpace? It's 2012, Gabriel."

"Perhaps not MySpace. That's the one I recall from my college days."

"Never had a page then, either, did you?"

"Certainly not. It's a waste of time, *and* it's dangerous. I've only ever been on Facebook when gathering information to influence potential sources."

"*Influence.* I like that. So much nicer than *blackmail.* Back to the point, though. The actual purpose of Facebook is not to provide sources of potential *influence,* but to socialize. To talk to friends and to share things like hobbies and interests in hopes of finding new friends."

His look said he couldn't imagine the point. Whether he meant hobbies or friends, I don't know. Probably both.

"People talk about their interests online. Let's see if Macy ever mentioned dead people." I picked up my laptop. "Later, I'll set up a Twitter feed for the firm. Don't worry — I'll run it, too. Advertising tweets like: *Gabriel Walsh, Attorney-at-Law. Finding the Saint in Satan's Saints.* Or helpful tips like: *Note to clients, quicklime is a preservative, not a corrosive.*"

He gave me a look.

"We'll work on it," I said.

"Work on *that*." He pointed at the laptop.

I'd gone through Macy's online presences before now, but briefly, as a way to get to know her before our meeting. I didn't find "embalming" in her list of Facebook interests or photos of amazing pre-funeral reconstruction work on her Pinterest account.

What I did find was more subtle. A tag on a friend's wall post from last Halloween. The friend had been dressing up as a zombie and tagged Macy, saying she should get Macy to help with the makeup because of "all that time she spent with dead people." Another friend asked what she meant, and the thread went on to joke about Macy hanging out at a local funeral home. Then Macy herself jumped in to snap that she hadn't been "hanging out." The conversation ended there.

I hadn't actually thought Macy did embalm Ciara, as I'd seen in my dream. If I had, I wouldn't have been joking with Gabriel about Facebook and Twitter. But now . . .

"That would mean she's not an innocent bystander," I said as I showed Gabriel the thread. "She didn't meet Tristan at a party. She may have actually killed Ciara. For what? To get her family back? Tristan tells Macy that she should be living Ciara's life, and she decides to . . . I can't fathom that. I just can't."

"As legal grounds for defense, it's so flimsy I wouldn't even attempt it. Diminished capacity would be the only way to play it. Drugs, alcohol, mental illness." He took my laptop. "Now, before we speculate any further, the comment mentions a funeral home on Lawrence Avenue. We'll start there."

There were three funeral parlors on Lawrence. I called the first. Someone picked up on the second ring.

"Walker Funeral Home," a man said. "Kendrick Walker speaking. How may I assist you?"

His voice was pleasant, sounding older than I'd expect from someone named Kendrick. Once I explained that I was checking a reference on Macy Shaw, though, his tone changed, becoming younger and brighter, as if throwing off his professional voice once he realized I wasn't a grieving relative.

"Oh, sure, Macy and I went to school together. Well, high school, and only for a couple of years before my parents moved."

"Did she volunteer or work there?"

"In senior year. She wanted to become a mortician, so she worked here for two summers, but . . . Well, trust me, it's not an easy career choice. Especially for a girl. Eventually the pressure got to her. She went into nursing. She kept working here for almost a year after she started college. She told people it was just for the money, but I think she was still considering."

"May I ask you for a reference? Or should that go through someone else?"

"Probably my dad. I'd just tell you she was great. If you talk to her, tell her Kendrick said hi. It's been a while."

"I'll do that. And on another note . . . This is a little awkward, but as long as I have you on the phone . . ."

"What's up?"

"I have an uncle in palliative care, and the funeral home we always used has closed down. I know that's the last thing on my aunt's mind, but . . . the end is close. Is there any chance I could come over and have a chat with someone? See your establishment?"

"When?"

"As soon as possible. It really is . . . close to the end."

"I completely understand." His tone changed, reverting to the soothing one. "We

640

can make an appointment for tomorrow, or tonight after seven — there's a viewing right now."

"Seven would be great."

CHAPTER SIXTY-SEVEN

Gabriel fell asleep before we hit the outskirts of Cainsville. This would have been much more troubling if he'd been the one behind the wheel.

That left me with a sleeping passenger and a long stretch of road to play with. A boring, straight stretch. The scenery wasn't much, either. Farmer's fields on my left, the river to my right. The river would have been lovely, if I could have actually seen it — it was at the bottom of a gully. So a boring road and boring scenery, but the car made up for it, so smooth it was like riding on glass. The June sun was just beginning to dip, the car interior cool, the leather seats comfortable, the music . . .

Well, the music needed a shake-up. It was Chopin's Funeral March, which was appropriate, given our destination, but really not a driving tune. I flipped through his library, looking for a Mendelssohn piece I'd heard earlier. I finally found it, and the information scrolled across the display. It was the Overture to *A Midsummer Night's Dream.*

As I heard Rose's voice, quoting from the fairy play, I looked back at the road. There, in the distance, was a hound. Standing on the road.

I hit my brakes, but as soon as I did, metal crunched and the car swerved. The side air bag whacked into me as the car sheered off the road.

It went over the gully, careening down, then hitting something and flipping and —

The front air bag slammed me in the face. I didn't pass out, but it was as if I mentally left for a few seconds, shock shutting down thought until the car stopped . . . and I was hanging upside down.

I clawed at the seat belt, desperate to get free. Then I managed to stop myself. Nothing was burning. Slow down. Assess.

It took a second for me to even remember what had been happening before the crash. All I could see were the air bags, deflating around me.

I was in Gabriel's car.

Gabriel.

I twisted, calling his name. He was there, slumped onto the roof.

"Gabriel?"

No answer.

I reached over and nudged his shoulder. "Gabriel!"

Still nothing. That's when I scrambled to get free again, caution be damned. I got halfway out of my belt before I found the release. I hit it and fell, knocking my head hard on the roof.

I twisted and writhed, hearing my shirt rip as it caught. My skin ripped, too, warm blood welling up on my arm. I ignored it and got myself right side up, crouched there between the seat and the roof.

I could reach Gabriel, but he was doubled forward. I couldn't see his face. I couldn't get to his neck or wrist to check for a pulse. The solid wall of his shirt blocked me.

I backed out through the driver's window. It was shattered, the remaining safety glass crumbling when I went through. As I pushed myself out, I could see the driver's door was bashed in. We'd been hit. That's why the side air bag deployed. Someone had hit us. Pushed the car over the embankment.

I craned to look up the gully. It was only about a thirty-foot drop but nearly perpendicular. The top was clear. No sign of another vehicle. No sign of a passerby who'd witnessed the accident. There'd been no one else on the damned road. So where had the other car been — ? A billboard. There were several along this stretch.

Had someone been lying in wait?

Was I really trying to figure that out while Gabriel lay in a car wreck?

His window had smashed, too, on the roll down the gully. I swiped out the remaining glass and shoved my head and shoulders through. Gabriel's head hung down, but I could see his face from this angle. There was a moment there when I don't think he was breathing. Then it came, that faint rasp, and when I pressed my hand to his neck, his pulse was strong.

He'd laid his jacket in the back before we set off, and there were only a few drops of blood on his white shirt. I searched for the source. A wound on his head.

As much as I wanted to get him out of there, I knew better than to move him, in case there was spinal damage. It seemed as if he was only hunched awkwardly — his height not accommodating the crushed roof — but I wasn't taking any chances. I backed out. That's when I saw the smoke.

The engine was on fire, wisps of smoke snaking from under the hood. There are a half-dozen flammable things in an engine.

While they're well contained, they aren't meant to withstand a serious crash and a rollover landing. And the barrier between the engine and the passengers isn't good enough to hold off fire for long.

I ran to the front of the car and peered under the crumpled hood, praying I wouldn't see —

Flame. I saw flame.

I tore back to the passenger side, squeezed in, and undid Gabriel's seat belt. It wasn't jammed. Gabriel was, though — wedged in tight enough that he didn't even budge when the belt came loose. As I tugged at him, he groaned.

"Gabriel?" I said. "Gabriel!"

I shook him, but he slid out of consciousness again without even opening his eyes.

I could smell the smoke now and hear the whoosh of fire. No time to second-guess. I grabbed his shirt by one shoulder and heaved, my other hand bracing his head. I had to brace my legs, too, against the car, using every bit of leverage I could, until —

His head and shoulders swung free and he fell, nearly knocking me down with the dead-weight drop. I dragged him out of the car. Smoke billowed, making me cough, my eyes tearing up. I had Gabriel out on his back, my hands wrapped in his shirt, and thank God it was well made, because I'm sure I wouldn't have gotten him very far otherwise. As it was, the seams still ripped while I dragged him over the rocky ground.

Once he was out of the smoke, I went for my cell phone . . . and remembered it was in my purse. I dropped down beside Gabriel and patted his trouser pockets. No phone. It must be in his jacket.

I raced back to the car. Flames poured from the engine, but they hadn't yet broken through to the interior. I fell onto all fours and pushed in through the passenger window. The interior was filled with smoke, and I had to close my eyes, pull my shirt over my nose, and feel around blindly. I couldn't find my purse. I didn't try hard because I knew Gabriel's jacket was in the back. I located it after fumbling and groping. I backed out of the car, sputtering now, eyes streaming tears as I returned to Gabriel's side, where the air was clear, reached into his jacket and —

There was no goddamned cell phone.

I crouched on the ground, heaving breath, my lungs burning.

Get Gabriel somewhere safe and go for help. There was no other option. The car was on fire. I'd never find my phone in time.

I looked around for a place to drag Gabriel. The car had landed at the base of the cliff, twenty feet from the river. That limited my choices.

I grabbed Gabriel's shirt again and hauled him another ten feet before the fabric gave way. I tried putting my hands under his armpits, but I couldn't get any leverage. He was too big.

I looked back at the car. Fire still burned in the engine compartment. How much longer until it reached the gas tank? Even if it did, Gabriel was far enough away.

I tried rousing him again, but after dragging him twenty feet from a burning car, I had to acknowledge that he wasn't waking up. I hoped he was just out cold. Otherwise . . . I wasn't even thinking of "otherwise." I already knew the damage I could have caused, hauling him from that car.

I made sure he seemed okay, then started climbing the embankment.

CHAPTER SIXTY-EIGHT

I got about halfway up the cliff, grabbing whatever I could and hauling myself up the nearly perpendicular incline. Then there was nothing else to grab, and I scrabbled for a handhold, my fingers digging into dirt, nails breaking as I frantically pulled myself —

I lost my grip and fell backward, my ass hitting the ground hard enough to bring tears to my eyes. I scrambled up and looked around.

The gully was shallower farther down. I really should have looked before trying to scale the damned cliff.

I ran, pain jolting through my body with each stride. I was still exhausted from the fever, and climbing the cliff had me panting already.

I saw a path heading up the gully. Just another twenty feet. Ten —

There was blood on the cliff side. A patch of bright red, just ahead. My feet skidded to a halt as my brain processed the sight.

Not blood. Poppies. Growing on the cliff.

I whirled back toward Gabriel.

A dark shape rose from behind a bush.

I hit the ground. Even as I dropped, my brain said, *What the hell are you doing?* But I dropped anyway, and a bullet hit the cliff beside me, dirt exploding.

My gun. Where was — ?

In my purse. With my cell phone. And my switchblade.

God-fucking-damn it! I armed myself and then stuck it all in my purse like I was still a goddamn socialite.

I dove behind a boulder as the second shot fired. As I did, I thought of Gabriel. Unconscious. Defenseless. With a killer between us.

I dashed to the next boulder. Then the next. Drawing the shooter away from Gabriel.

Yet as I ran, no shots rang out. Instead, a voice called, "Stop."

It was a woman's voice. Macy's.

I darted to the next source of cover, a sofa, dumped over the cliff.

"Do you think I won't shoot you?" She fired a bullet into the sofa as I dropped behind it. "You're not going to make it to the road, Eden, and even if you did, do you have any idea how long it would take for someone to find you? I was behind that billboard for twenty minutes and yours was the first car I saw. I could have killed you, you know. We're both lucky that fancy car has side air bags."

"We're *both* lucky?" I croaked a laugh. "I could have sworn you were *trying* to kill me."

"No. I thought he'd be driving. The lawyer. It's his car."

She sounded put out, as if I'd deliberately thwarted her plans.

"I bet you're wondering how I intercepted you so fast," she continued.

Um, no. Last thing on my mind, really.

"I was at a motel off the next exit," she said. "Trying to figure out how to talk to you. How to make you listen to me. Then Kendrick called."

"And you decided the best way to talk to me was to run me off the road?"

"No, I realized we were past the point of talking. You'd figured everything out. It was time to cut a deal. Or kill you."

"I'd prefer a deal."

She laughed. "I'm sure you would."

I shifted behind the couch. As I did, I swore I smelled cat pee, as I had hiding behind the sofa at Will Evans's house, the odor triggering some hidden memory that started my gut twisting.

There weren't enough cover spots for me to dodge my way to safety. My best bet was to stall and hope Gabriel woke up. Which, given that he hadn't done so before now, seemed unlikely. Failing that, maybe if I talked long enough, I'd actually come up with a plan.

"You killed Ciara," I said.

"No." The denial came hot and fast. "I wanted to talk to her, but she kept screaming. The sedatives weren't working, and she wouldn't be quiet. I just wanted her to be quiet. I wasn't *trying* to choke her. It was her own fault."

"And then you embalmed her."

"It was his idea. Tristan's."

"He's the one who told you who you were."

"Yes. Tristan told me about my birthright. About Ciara. He took me to see her, that rich bitch, turning her back on a good life to tweak in a scummy apartment. She belonged with my family — she'd fit right in."

"And you belonged with hers. So Ciara dies, and Tristan has you embalm her and cut off her head —"

"No, *he* cut off her head. But only to protect me. To erase any evidence I left strangling her. Afterward, he realized he could use her head to get your attention."

Tristan had done his work here, weaving Macy a story that she could accept. Sprinkled with pixie dust to make it go down easier.

A shadow passed. I looked up to see a raven circling, leisurely, as if getting the lay of the land.

Are you here to help? To observe? To gloat?

The raven winged off toward the wreck, as if to check that out, too.

Not hindering. Not helping, either. There was no help here. No sudden brainstorm that would solve my predicament. Only the obvious plan — play along and watch for my opportunity to get that gun from her.

"You mentioned a deal?" I said.

"I want you to tell the police about the switch. That's what Tristan said you'd do. You'd investigate, and you'd realize what happened, and you'd tell the police. And then it wouldn't matter how Ciara died, because my real parents would have their real daughter and they'd be happy. *Her* real parents wouldn't care who killed her. They only care about themselves. Everything would be fixed."

Did she really think a murder investigation could be halted if no one cared about

653

the victim? That the Conways *wouldn't* care about the girl they'd raised?

"So you want me to forget what I know about Ciara's death and go to the authorities with the DNA results."

"Exactly."

I pretended to weigh the moral ramifications of this. Except there were no ramifications, because once I got to safety, there would be nothing to stop me from turning her in.

"All right," I said. "You walk away. I'll say I fell asleep at the wheel. I had a fever last night, which my doctor can verify. I drifted off and crashed the car. Then I'll turn over the DNA results."

"Do you really think I'd make it that easy?" Macy said. "You walk away scot-free?"

Why shouldn't I? I wanted to say. I haven't done anything. But I bit my tongue and said, "I've crashed a very expensive car. I'm battered and bruised. I might have seriously injured a guy who won't hesitate to sue me for every penny of my trust fund. That's not scot-free."

"You're right. You need to get rid of the lawyer."

"Exactly. I'll fire him."

"I mean kill him."

"What?" I prairie-dogged up for a split second before dropping behind the sofa again.

"Is that a problem?" she said.

"Is murdering someone a problem? Hell, yes. You know who my parents are, so maybe you think that makes it easy for me, but no, I'm not going to kill Gabriel. I'll deal with any fallout —"

"It's not an option," she said. "You're going to shoot him with this gun. I'm going to take a video of you doing it. If you double-cross me, I'll hand it over to the police. Refuse, and I will shoot both of you."

She wasn't as stupid as I'd thought. Just crazy. Another shadow passed, and I looked up to see an owl now, silently winging past to land in a distant treetop. Ravens and owls. Not so much an omen as a reminder of the puppet master pulling Macy's strings.

"Does Tristan know you're doing this?" I said. "I bet he doesn't. He wants me alive."

"Because you're *valuable*?" She spat the word. "Tristan is full of shit. I figured that out at that psych hospital, how he treated me there, like a prop in his play for an audience of one. *You.*"

"Do you know why he thinks I'm important?"

"Because you're rich. That's why everyone

is important. Your adoptive family has the kind of power and money that makes the Conways look lower-class. And you don't deserve it any more than Ciara did. You're the child of murdering freaks. You should have been locked up with them, before you grew up into a monster, too. But no, you got special treatment. A special family. They put me with the Shaws and put Ciara with the Conways. And you? They put you with the goddamn Taylor-Joneses."

Put me? Had I been placed with my family? A child of fae blood slipped into a human home, a better home? Just like Ciara?

Everyone wondered how I'd vanished into the system. How the child of serial killers ended up with the Taylor-Joneses. How the Larsens "lost" me in a so-called bureaucratic mix-up.

The owl rose from its tree, winging to a closer one. I watched it.

"Who put me with my family?" I asked.

"The same people who switched me," she said, with a snap in her voice, annoyed with me for being so dense.

"What people? Why?"

"If I knew who did it, I'd be going after them, wouldn't I? As for why, money obviously. It's always about money."

"So these people are switching babies for

profit. And that's all they are: people. Like Tristan. He's just a regular guy. Nothing more."

A pause. "You know who's behind this, don't you? Is it the government? Is that what you mean?"

Macy had no idea what she was really involved in. Why would she? She didn't have the blood. No one cared about her. Tristan was only using her as a means to his end. He certainly wasn't going to share their secrets.

"Enough of this," Macy said. "Time to make your choice."

"Fine. I'll kill Gabriel. But I'm not coming out of here while you're holding a gun on me."

She laughed. "Should I toss it to you?"

"No, just hold it up, in one hand, over your head. Then start walking to the wreck."

"Giving you the chance to jump me from behind?"

Damn, I really wished she was dumber. "Walk backward, then. Gun in the air."

The gun rose, where I could see it. I crept from behind the sofa, and we started for the car.

CHAPTER SIXTY-NINE

While I would have liked to get that gun from Macy before we reached Gabriel, her gaze never left me, and she made me stay ten feet away — too far to dash and catch her off guard. I kept hoping she'd trip as she walked backward. She didn't.

What I really needed was that damned owl or raven to swoop at her head. No such luck. If they were still around, they were observing only, as they had at the psych hospital, each watching the situation for their respective team.

Barring interference by the birds, I hoped Gabriel had woken and could suss out the situation and distract her while I got the gun. Again, no such luck. I could see him ahead, lying exactly where I'd left him. So it was all up to me.

"You're really going to kill him?" she said as she stopped ten feet behind Gabriel's head.

"Do I have a choice?"

"You can die with him."

"Not really an option."

She smiled. "I didn't think so. Now come over here, on that side of him, put your hands around his neck, and squeeze."

"Wh-what?"

Another smile as she shook her head. "You thought I was going to give you the gun? Not a chance. He'll die the way Ciara did. Strangulation. It's easier than you'd think."

Shit. Still not stupid.

When I didn't move, she said, "Trying to find a way out of this? There isn't one. You'll kill him or you'll die." She paused. "Or there is a third option."

"What?"

"God, you're quick to jump on that, aren't you? I guess you aren't your parents' daughter after all. Can't kill someone even to save your own life. Or does it depend on who the someone is? I bet you'd have killed me, if Tristan had given you this choice in that hospital. But him —" She motioned at Gabriel. "He's different. So here's option number three. You crawl back into that burning car. You die in there. He lives."

I looked over sharply at her. "Bullshit. You wouldn't let —"

"Why not? You dragged him out and went

back in for something and died. Tragic accident. Once you're dead, Gabriel Walsh won't care about Ciara and the case. Tristan will accept that it was an accident, and I'll get my DNA results another way."

"The moment I'm in that car, you'll shoot Gabriel."

"If he's dead of a gunshot, that's no accident."

"Then you'll drag him back into the car."

"With what? A crane? I can't make his death look like an accident, Eden, so he gets to live. That's the deal. The question is, will you take it?"

I looked at her. I looked at Gabriel. She was too far away for me to get a jump on her. I had no weapons. My gun was . . .

I looked at the smoke-filled car. The flames were in the front seat now, licking the fabric. If I could find my purse . . .

What exactly were the chances of that? Finding my purse and getting my gun before passing out from smoke inhalation? Not good. But the alternative? There wasn't one.

"I'll do it," I said.

She didn't answer, just looked at me as if I was a fool.

I walked to the car. Heat and smoke streamed out. I couldn't even see the door, just the dark shape of the black car, lost in the smoke. I dropped to all fours.

"Don't stall," Macy said. "If you give me any excuse, I have a backup plan. I'll shoot you both."

I crawled through the smoke, eyes closed as I breathed through my nose. My fingers touched the side of the car, and I let out a yelp, metal burning my fingertips.

"Keep going," Macy said. "If I can still see your shoes in ten seconds —"

A shot fired. I hit the ground, flat on my stomach.

Oh God, she'd shot Gabriel.

I jumped up into a crouch —

"Don't move or I fire again."

I froze there, brain stuck on the words. No, not the words. They were exactly what I'd expect. It was the voice that stopped me.

"Olivia? Are you all right?"

Gabriel's voice. Then his footfalls.

I staggered from the smoke to see him jogging toward the car with my gun trained on Macy, who was hunched on the ground, her hand pressed to her side, blood streaming through her fingers. Her gun hung from her other hand.

I wheeled on Gabriel. "Make her drop — !"

"Drop the gun," he said before I could finish.

She raised her head and looked from him to me, her eyes dull with shock.

"I said drop it." Gabriel took two steps toward her. "You're injured. Perhaps badly. You need an ambulance, and as soon as you put that gun down, I will call one."

She lifted the gun, slowly, training it on me. Gabriel fired. His shot hit her in the leg, and she fell back with a stifled scream.

"I won't kill you," he said. "No matter how much you might want that. I will simply continue to shoot you until you pass out and drop the gun."

She raised her head and stared at him, her eyes blazing, furious. She'd go to jail for killing Ciara, and that reunion with her real family would never happen. It was over, and all she wanted now was some final satisfaction. To die knowing we'd suffer, too, fighting to clear our names. If we wouldn't give her that . . .

"She's going to —" I didn't get the rest of the words out.

Macy swung the gun up. Gabriel fired. She did, too — gun trained upward, shot going through the bottom of her jaw. She was dead before she slumped to the ground.

Gabriel still ran over . . . to grab the gun

from her hand as it dropped to her side. Only then did he seem to realize the shot had been fatal, and he stood there, looking down at her. Then he lowered himself to one knee, reached into her pocket, took out her cell phone, and called the police.

"I think we've been here before," I said to Gabriel as he sat on the back bumper of the ambulance while a paramedic examined the gash on his head. "Except last time, I didn't total your car."

"It wasn't your fault," he said. "And it's well insured."

"I still feel bad."

A soft chuckle, pointing out, I suppose, that of everything that had happened this evening, his car ought to be the least of my concerns. I *was* more worried about him, but I knew better than to say that. I'd asked, of course, right after he'd called the police, and he'd brushed the question aside with a brusque "I'm fine."

Now he was struggling to sit with relative patience as the paramedic checked him over. I'd already had my examination — Gabriel had insisted I go first. I'd swallowed some smoke, bumped my head, sliced open my arm, and possibly cracked a rib in the crash, though I'd begun to notice the pain only after everything settled down.

Macy was dead. How did I feel about that? Relieved that Gabriel hadn't been the one to shoot her, because I didn't want him dealing with that, either legally or emotionally. As for how he'd gotten my gun, he'd apparently regained consciousness while I was hiding behind that couch. My purse — with the gun — hadn't been in the car at all, but had been thrown free from the wreck. He'd spotted it, retrieved the gun, and played possum until he got his chance.

Otherwise, what did I feel about Macy? Not much. She'd had a crappy life, but that didn't justify murder. Ciara hadn't done anything wrong. She'd been struggling with the biological destiny of having fae blood. Her death was a tragedy. Macy's was not.

Macy's death was, however, a problem, because, as I said, Gabriel and I had been here before, a month ago, police and paramedics called to the scene after someone tried to kill us. There's a limit to how often that can happen before the cops start to wonder what the hell you're up to. I think that limit is one.

Gabriel's basic advice was to keep my mouth shut. We'd both suffered head injuries. Given the crash and the aftermath, we could claim confusion and trauma, and say as little as possible.

The paramedic finished and proclaimed that Gabriel might be suffering from a mild concussion. He should get himself to the hospital, and he should be woken every hour tonight. I doubted I'd get him into a hospital, but I promised to look after him.

When the paramedic left, Gabriel stood. I would have sworn it wasn't possible for someone with skin so fair to turn pale, but he did. There was a tinge of green there, too.

"Take it easy," I said.

"I'm —"

"I didn't ask if you were okay. I know better than to do that more than once, and even then not to expect an honest answer. I'm just asking you to take it easy, because you look like you're going to throw up, and that will get you hauled to the hospital whether you like it or not."

He nodded and straightened, tugging on his shirt and adjusting it, as if it wasn't blood-spattered and filthy. Then he looked down at me. "I am a little queasy. And my head hurts. Also, there's a slight pain in my shoulder, but it didn't seem worth mentioning. None of that, however, will impede me."

I smiled. "Nothing ever does. Come on. Let's talk to the police and get out of here."

CHAPTER SEVENTY

The state police weren't all that interested in questioning our story, probably because they didn't know that we'd called the Chicago cops to a similar scene three weeks ago. To them, we were just the victims of a crazy woman.

They'd found Macy's truck — her brother's, actually — and the smashed front end proved that she'd pushed us into the gully. The coroner supported our story that while Gabriel had shot Macy in self-defense, the fatal bullet had come from her own weapon. All this would require an autopsy and further investigation, but Gabriel had identified himself as a defense lawyer, and they didn't seem concerned he was a flight risk. We were injured and confused and could provide full statements later.

The police were going to drive us back to Cainsville, but as we were about to leave, Rose drove up. So did a second vehicle. The

Clarks' Buick pulled over in front of Rose.

I asked Gabriel to go speak to his aunt while I talked to the Clarks.

"Olivia." Ida hurried over faster than a seventy-odd-year-old pair of legs ought to hurry. I'd seen signs of this before — little points of evidence that the elders weren't nearly as old as they appeared.

"What happened?" She looked genuinely concerned, as did Walter beside her. I wished they didn't.

"Macy Shaw drove us off the road and tried to kill us."

"Macy . . . ?"

"Don't pretend you don't know who that is," I said, lowering my voice as I subtly moved them away from the police. "She's the girl you took from the Conways and swapped out for Ciara. I know she doesn't concern you as much as Ciara did. Macy was human. A pawn. Then again, we're all pawns, whether we have fae blood or not. I know I am."

There are two ways of reacting to that: confused shock and alarmed shock. While the Tylwyth Teg of Cainsville were good at hiding responses, they still reacted, and it was definitely alarm, squelching any remaining doubts.

"What — ?" Walter began after a moment.

"Whatever are you talking about, Olivia? Have you hit your head?"

Ida waved him to silence, her bright eyes piercing mine. "It was Patrick, wasn't it? Patrick and his wild stories. He likes to cause trouble —"

"Of course. That's what hobgoblins do." I moved closer, towering over her. "You don't need to admit to anything, Ida. Just don't insult me by denying it. I ran the DNA. I know the girls were switched. I know why. I know why I can see omens, too. Why Rose has the second sight. I know how the Larsens managed to lose me in the system. Another form of changeling magic. Not a switch of children, but of parents, which is the point anyway. Like a bird sneaking its eggs into another nest, hoping to give its offspring a better chance at survival, which sounds very sweet, except they're just birds — they don't care about their chicks, only about their blood, their lineage. Sound familiar?"

"That is not true, Olivia. Every parent cares —"

"Like Patrick? How he cares about Gabriel?"

Surprise flashed across her face. I lowered my voice again and made sure Gabriel was still talking to his aunt. "I know who Gabriel's father is. I put the pieces together. Patrick didn't tell me anything, so don't blame him. *I'll* blame him, though, for what he did to Gabriel. Like I blame you for nearly getting us killed tonight, and for the dead girl who's being taken back to a morgue in Chicago, and for the dead girl I found in the Carew house — the one whose body you stole — robbing her parents even of the chance to bury her. I blame you for all of it."

"No amount of explanation will convince you we are blameless. We aren't. But you need to understand, even if you can't agree with what we've done." She laid her hand on my arm. "Give us a chance to explain."

I looked into her eyes, and I felt the tug of her words. Maybe it was influence or fae charm. Maybe it was just me. I loved Cainsville. I loved my place here, my home here. I wanted an explanation that could put things right.

"Olivia?"

Gabriel's voice made me jump. He took a step my way. Just a step. A question. Did I want him over here?

"He cares for you," Ida murmured. "As you care for him."

"Someone has to," I snapped back. "God knows you didn't."

Did I imagine it or did she flinch?

"We tried —" she began.

"You wanted to switch him. Patrick wouldn't allow it. That's not what I mean. There are other ways of looking after your young, Ida. Human ways. But I guess that's too much trouble. Pawn them off on someone else. Let them deal with the problems you inflicted, the problems your blood caused."

"We —"

"Save the excuses. If I need answers" — I pulled the boar's tusk from my purse and waggled it at her — "the Cŵn Annwn are more than willing to give them. That's where I should have gone in the first place. Maybe I could have prevented all this."

I walked away. She tried to call me back. Walter stepped into my path. That had Gabriel striding forward, clearing his throat in warning, and they backed off, settling instead for turning their pleas to him. We needed to talk. All of us. They would explain. This wasn't what it seemed.

Gabriel steered me to Rose's car. She stood outside the driver's door, and I could tell this scene made her uncomfortable. She wanted us to listen to the elders. But when we got into the car, she climbed in and drove us back to Cainsville without another word.

I stood on the sidewalk outside my apartment building. Rose had retreated into her house. Gabriel was beside me, saying nothing, just letting me look up at the building in the gathering darkness.

"I can't stay here," I said.

"I'm sure Rose —"

"Cainsville, I mean. I can't stay."

Silence. I looked over, expecting him to argue, to tell me I was being foolish.

"I would agree," he said. "For now."

"Until we figure this out, it's like living in enemy territory. Maybe that's being dramatic —"

"It's not. That's why I suggested you quit at the diner. You are accepting their protection and their hospitality, which puts you in their debt now that you realize it."

"I'll take a few days off at the diner. And away from here. I'll grab a hotel room while I sort this out."

"You can, if you insist, but I have a better idea."

CHAPTER SEVENTY-ONE

I stood at the wall-sized window in Gabriel's fifty-fifth-floor condo and fought the urge to press my nose against the glass. The night view was amazing. I swore I could see the entire city, lit up.

Gabriel poured drinks behind me. Two, judging by the tinkle of glasses. I suspected he might need one, and not because he could have died in a fiery crash tonight. That was, I think, easier than bringing me up here. But he'd survived both. So far.

He had suggested I stay at his place. He needed someone to check him in the night, and he'd already imposed on Rose with my fever last night. If I was willing to help him with that, he'd be happy to share his apartment for a few days.

I'm sure "happy" wasn't quite the right word, but even as my gut had seized up, everything in me saying, "Hell, no, I won't go through that again," I'd seen in his expression that he was genuinely offering. More than that, he wanted me there. Which didn't mean that I thought I'd actually make it through the door before he changed his mind. But as he'd waited for my answer, I realized it didn't matter if he went through with it or not. This was about him, not me. I couldn't make it about me. He wanted it. He was trying. That was enough.

So I'd agreed. I'd packed a bag while he went over to ask Rose if she'd keep TC for a few days. Gabriel drove my car so I could call Ricky, on the chance he'd hear about the crash and the shooting before I talked to him tomorrow. Then we'd arrived at Gabriel's condo, came up the elevator, through the door, and . . . I was here. Looking at this amazing view while Gabriel fixed me a drink.

When he went quiet behind me, that sinking feeling started again. He was having second thoughts. Trying to think of a way to get me out, as politely as possible. I took a deep breath and lifted my gaze. I could see his reflection in the glass. He was just standing there, holding the glasses, watching me.

"Earlier," he said as I turned. "At the crash site. You *did* know I was awake. That I had the gun."

"Hmm?"

I took my drink from him. Scotch. Hard stuff, but I'd earned it.

"When you agreed to crawl back into the car. You knew I'd get the jump on her."

It wasn't a statement but a question, even if he didn't phrase it that way.

"Mmm, not exactly. But I had a plan."

A lousy plan. One that almost certainly wouldn't have worked in my favor. But I didn't say that because I could tell it wasn't what he wanted to hear.

"Good," he said on a breath of relief, before taking a sip of his whiskey. Then he lowered the glass and caught my gaze. "Don't put yourself at risk for anyone, Olivia. Ever. It isn't worth it."

That's what he said, and while he meant it, what he was really saying was, "Don't put yourself at risk for me." I remembered when we'd faced Chandler's goons, and Gabriel had wanted me to get to safety. *Don't stay for me,* he'd said. *I wouldn't do it for you.*

I'd believed him. And I hadn't cared. Whether or not he'd have stayed, he'd put himself at risk for me many times since. Yet he didn't want me doing it for him.

I'd said to myself once that Gabriel preferred a life where he felt as little responsibility for others as possible. That was true. But even more true is the fact that he preferred a life where others felt no responsibility for *him.*

"Quid pro quo," Patrick had said when I first met him. *You scratch my back and I scratch yours.* Gabriel might have inherited that sense of fairness, of balance, but it went further with him. *You stay away from me, and I'll stay away from you. Do nothing for me, and I'll do nothing for you.* A clean slate was easier to balance than any accumulation of debts.

How do you have a personal relationship with someone who thinks that way? You just do. You accept it, and you understand it, and you don't take offense, because none is intended. You read actions and ignore words.

Gabriel said he wouldn't have stayed for me. But he did, and he didn't just stay, he came running whenever I needed him. Same as I'd do for him, and as long as we both pretended otherwise, he could accept that.

"There's still Tristan to worry about." I walked to the sofa and sat at one end. "He wanted me to know about the changeling switch and about Cainsville. Now that I do, there must be some response he's expecting. I'll have to deal with that."

"*We'll* deal with that," he said, sitting at

the opposite end.

I nodded and twisted, sitting sideways, knees pulled up, glass resting on them.

"I also had a call from the state attorney's office this evening," he said. "About your parents' case. Things are finally moving on that. They want to speak to us."

"Lots to do, then."

"Yes, lots to do. Lots to talk about."

"Should we start now?"

"In a few minutes," he said as he eased back onto the sofa. "No rush."

I smiled, curled up, sipped my drink, and relaxed. Plenty to do another day. For now, we had this, and it was enough.

After Gabriel went to bed, I lay on the sofa, lost in a warm fog of Scotch and happiness. I shouldn't be happy. I had a hundred reasons not to be happy, and maybe it was fifty percent Scotch and fifty percent ebbing adrenaline from the evening's events, but damn it, I was happy. And that's when I remembered Todd's letter. That's when I decided to read it. Yes, it would ruin this fuzzy-headed bliss, but this was the right time — when I was alone, feeling good and feeling safe and feeling a little tipsy. When whatever that letter brought might not hurt me as much.

I took it from my purse. Then, not wanting to turn on a light in case Gabriel saw it under his door, I walked to the window, sat with my back to it, and opened the letter by moonlight.

It was a single sheet, written in that familiar hand, a little blocky, a little oversized, as if by someone without much experience putting words on paper. Or perhaps by someone whose only experience writing to me had come at a time when I needed those big, blocky letters.

OLIVIA.

That's how it started. Not to Eden, but to Olivia. Not to a child, then, but to a woman. I relaxed a little and leaned back against the cool glass before continuing.

I'm sorry.

There's no way to start except with an apology, though I suspect it's not what you want to hear. You know I'm sorry. I'd be a monster if I wasn't. But I still need to say it. I'm sorry for so many things, and I won't list them here or this letter will go on so long that you'll crumple it and toss it aside. So I will say only that I am sorry.

I'd like to see you. I know you've been to see Pamela, and maybe you've gotten whatever you need from her. I have to presume that you don't want to see me. That you don't need to, and maybe it's easier, just facing one of us, and she is your mother, so I understand that. But I would like to see you. I would very much like to see you.

I've hesitated to write and say that because I know you're going through so much, and you don't need this on top of it, and if you've decided not to see me, that's your choice and I will respect it, but I know Pamela made her plea in the papers, and so there is the chance that you haven't come because you aren't sure I want to see you, so I have to speak up and say yes. Unreservedly yes. I want to see you.

I promise I will make this visit as easy on you as possible. It can be as short as you need it to be, and if it is not repeated, I'll understand that. I just want to see you.

I know I said I wouldn't list all the things I'm sorry for, but I need to say one, before I sign off. The one thing I am most sorry for.

I am sorry for leaving you. I told you

so many times that I never would, and then I did, and whether it was by choice or not doesn't matter. I made a promise and I broke it, and I am so, so sorry.

Love always,
Todd

Todd. Not "your father." Not Dad. Like the opening, so careful and so respectful. It didn't matter. I read that letter and I heard his voice and I didn't see "Todd" at the end. I saw the first words I'd ever learned to read, on a surprise gift he'd given me. *To Eden. Love always, Daddy.*

I folded the letter and started to cry.

ABOUT THE AUTHOR

Kelley Armstrong is the bestselling author of the Women of the Otherworld series, as well as the *New York Times* #1 bestselling young adult trilogy Darkest Powers, the Darkness Rising trilogy, the Age of Legends trilogy, and the Nadia Stafford crime series. She lives in rural Ontario with her family.

www.kelleyarmstrong.com